C000259183

READING & REBELLION

EDITED BY

kimberley REYNOLDS | jane ROSEN | michael ROSEN

Reading & Rebellion

AN ANTHOLOGY OF RADICAL WRITING FOR CHILDREN 1900–1960

Great Clarendon Street, Oxford, OX2 6DP,
United Kingdom

Oxford University Press is a department of the University of Oxford.
It furthers the University's objective of excellence in research, scholarship,
and education by publishing worldwide. Oxford is a registered trade mark of
Oxford University Press in the UK and in certain other countries

First Edition published in 2018

Impression: 1

Published in the United States of America by Oxford University Press
198 Madison Avenue, New York, NY 10016, United States of America

British Library Cataloguing in Publication Data
Data available

Library of Congress Control Number: 2017964281

ISBN 978-0-19-880618-9

Printed in Great Britain by
Bell & Bain Ltd., Glasgow

For Josh, Sophie, and George

KR

For my Red Rosa

JR

In memory of Harold and Connie Rosen, and for Emma, Elsie, and Emile

MR

CONTENTS

PART SEVEN Fighting Fascism

PART EIGHT Science and Social Transformation

PART NINE Sex for Beginners

PART TEN Visions of the Future

PREFACE

Stories from childhood sink deep into our lifelong imagination. Earliest memories from books, comics, and films are easily stirred, never erased. That's why stories have always been used to seek to mould the morals and politics of the young. In this remarkable collection of left-wing writing for twentieth-century children, political messages may or may not have been as immediately clear to young readers as they emerge to us reading them now.

Some of the extracts here are from writers on the Left that my parents gave me—that I may or may not have known had political meaning. As everything in a leftist household is political, these writings were just the natural furniture of our minds. I read all of Geoffrey Trease's historical novels, *Bows Against the Barons* best of all, but until reading this book, I knew nothing of his communism. I read Eleanor Farjeon poems, I had books illustrated by the socialist Walter Crane, many times over I read and re-read Jennie Lee's inspiring autobiography *Tomorrow is a New Day*, adapted for children. Erich Kästner's *Emil and the Detectives* was about a gang of urban children any child would yearn to join: did I know he was a leftist? Probably not, but his books were burned by the Nazis.

As ever, what lasts are the best stories, with characters walking off the page as crisply now as the day they were written. I had the whole set of E. Nesbit books that my mother had collected as a child: Nesbit the leftist writer was thoroughly approved by my left-wing grandmother. But her writing lives on because she understood children, their voices, their quarrels, their bad behaviour, and their thinking: they certainly have a finely tuned sense of natural justice. For class awareness, nothing is more excruciating than the Railway Children's misunderstood gifts to Albert Perks the station porter, who is affronted by their condescension.

Most of the writings here will come as a revelation, as they did to me, unfamiliar but redolent of a socialist milieu of hope and expectation that the sheer blindingly obvious virtues of the cause must win through with the next generation. The undeserving rich will get their comeuppance, the poor will get their fair share, workers will not be oppressed by greedy factory owners, and that tallies with every child's natural instinct for fairness.

At the same time, there was a whole other strand of writing for children: jingoistic histories of empire filled with derring-do battles with bone-in-the-nose natives. Those stories were not found in the homes of leftist families, but plentiful in libraries and oozing out of the comics we read. Enid Blyton not banned exactly but mocked: it was secret reading under the covers to follow the doings of those clean-hanky Famous Five, forever trouncing and handing over to the police unsavoury badly spoken oiks, ill-doers of darkly working-class and gypsy types. You don't have to look far through the secondhand bookshelves to find old children's books rancid with racism and snobbery.

But if you stand back and survey most of children's—and adult—literature and folk tales, one dominant thread runs through them since the beginning of time—and it is a story from the Left, not the Right. The poor are good, the rich bad. Who sides with the Sheriff of Nottingham against Robin Hood's Sherwood gang? That pattern holds good through all of Roald Dahl: Charlie Bucket is the nice poor boy, up against spoiled rich kids who bought their golden tickets. The runt, the underdog is always the hero, while the possessors are the villains in stories old and new. Baby Jesus had to be born in a stable, King Herod in the palace.

That is the prevailing strand even in capitalist Hollywood, and that instinctive red thread runs all through Walt Disney too: the little guy wins out against big money, big banks, big power. So as you read these leftist children's authors, remember there is nothing so exceptional about their themes. There is more social realism among true-to-life stories of political struggle and of strikes, with a deliberate consciousness-raising in the telling of history. The story of progress has always felt as inevitable as evolution for the Left, while the Right struggles to create its own mythology in palatable stories for children: where are the nursery Ayn Rand fairy tales or the child's Hayek storybook for the offspring of right-wing families? That would be a thin anthology.

Read these extracts for pleasure, read them for a taste of an era when these authors hoped they would breathe socialist values into a new generation and see how many stand the test of time.

Polly Toynbee

INTRODUCTION

This book combines personal memories and research to create a snapshot of the kind of books, periodicals, drama, and music that shaped the lives of British children growing up in radical, left-leaning, and progressive homes in the first part of the previous century. Some memoirs and histories of communism and the Left more broadly briefly refer to children's reading, but this is the first attempt to try to reconstruct both the publications—in many forms—and a sense of what it was like to read, sing, or perform them. To add colour to this image, we have tried to incorporate the voices of those who remember these texts from their own childhoods.[1] Who were these children? They came from across Britain, not least the devolved nations; Scotland in particular contributed substantially to producing reading matter and organizations for children growing up in families and communities that were seeking alternatives to the way British society was organized and its dependence on the inequities and vagaries of capitalism. But these materials were found and read by children, parents, and educators in most parts of the country and also from a range of backgrounds. Some came from the very poorest areas, where access to the necessities of life was often precarious, others from more comfortably off working-class communities, and some from solidly middle-class and even wealthy, titled families.[2] Leading figures in the work of engaging children in the debates around revisioning, reconfiguring, and rebuilding Britain in the light of what, for much of the time covered by this volume, was perceived as the great Soviet experiment, came from all these backgrounds.[3] This volume

1. For example, Thomas Linehan's *Communism in Britain 1920–39* includes a short discussion of the books and periodicals that resulted from the call by the Communist Party of Great Britain and communist parents for 'an alternative literature that spoke to radical ideals' (23). The titles mentioned, *The Red Corner Book*, *Martin's Annual*, and F. Le Gros and Ida Clark's *Adventures of the Little Pig and Other Stories*, are all represented in this volume, as are titles recalled by Raphael Samuel in *The Lost World of British Communism*.
2. Readers outside the UK may find the term 'middle class' refers to a rather different segment of the population than it does in, for example, the USA, where class is often more closely related to wealth. In Britain, class labels have at least as much to do with cultural capital as they do with financial status or, in Marixst terms, access to the means of production, so members of the middle class tend to be highly educated professionals, comparable to 'white-collar' workers in the USA. However, the British middle class is a broad band that is often divided into three groups: lower-middle class, middle class, and upper-middle class, and those in the lower-middle class might be designated 'blue-collar' workers in the USA, while members of the upper-middle class are generally close to or even part of the ruling elite.
3. Kimberley Reynolds's *Left Out: The Forgotten Tradition of Radical Publishing for Children in Britain, 1910–1949* provides more detailed information about readers and what they read.

brings together writers, illustrators, and young readers from across the class spectrum and captures a time when opportunities for the British working class were expanding. The 1944 Education Act saw many talented working-class children educated out of their class into the middle class in ways that have permanently enlivened and enriched British culture, though initially, at least, not everyone found the new class mobility easy or desirable.

There is little in the way of sales figures or demographic analysis of who bought or read left-wing publications; in any case, statistics about sales or trying to take evidence from reviews in the relevant papers and journals will not tell us how these books 'worked' or what their function was. The point is that they were part of a movement, part of activism. They passed between people as an informal left-wing children's lending library. Two of the editors of this anthology, Jane Rosen (b. 1963) and Michael Rosen (b. 1946), represent the young left-wing readers of their generations. We begin with their reflections on the role reading played in their left-wing childhoods; their personal insights, as well as those of other readers we have interviewed or who have written accounts of their reading experiences, give a sense of why and how far these works signified then—and now.

MICHAEL ROSEN REMEMBERS

When I was around nine years old, in 1955, one of my favourite books was A White Sail Gleams *by a Russian writer, Valentin Katayev.*[4] *If I ask myself, why was I reading this book, or how did an English child living in a flat over a shop in the London suburbs come to be reading this Russian book, then the answer at one level is simple: my parents were members of the Communist Party of Great Britain. What went with this affiliation was a good deal more than what is usually described as 'activism': demonstrations, meetings, lobbies, vigils, petitions, strikes, and the like. It was more than the writing and selling of newspapers, magazines, and pamphlets. The way many of us experienced the 'Party' when we were children was through culture: songs, poems, stories, and plays which were performed and distributed through books, camping holidays, bazaars, film shows, and the informal gatherings of friends and relatives.*

I gathered pretty early on in my life that there was an official culture put out by school, radio, film, and TV, and which my parents encouraged me to participate in fully. This involved books read to us in school, borrowed from the local library, listened to on the BBC Home Service's Children's Hour, *children's programmes on BBC Television*

4. Both the book and the film adaptation were popular among children and families on the Left. In *The Lost World of British Communism* (2006), Raphael Samuel, raised in a communist household, writes, 'I was brought up as a true believer. My first film—a show arranged by my mother in the village hall of Apsley Guise—was *Lone White Sail* [sic]' (2006 74).

(ITV didn't come along till I was ten) and family movies such as Treasure Island *or Saturday Morning 'flicks' for the ABC Minors. Out of sight and to one side of this was the Party culture.* A White Sail Gleams *came to me via a Communist Party bazaar held in a church hall in Wealdstone, a working-class enclave in the midst of the north-west London suburbs, along with other titles you'll find in this collection including N. Nosov's* Jolly Family *(1950) and Mikhail Ilin's* Black on White *(1932). If you turn to the 'prelims' of* A White Sail Gleams, *and almost all of the books that came from Russia, you find the name 'Progress Publishers, Moscow'. This tells us that people sitting in Moscow, authorized by the Soviet government, translated Russian books for children, which were then distributed through the communist movement, through 'sympathetic bookshops' like Collet's in London, and through Party members' sales at bazaars and fundraising events.*

My parents saw themselves as discerning, highly critical people. They both came from the East End of London, where their forbears had settled in the 1890s and early 1900s, having fled from Eastern Europe—Russia and what used to be called 'Russified Poland'. They were all Jews and had developed their socialist and Communist ideas out of the poverty, persecution, and aspirations of those times. The fact that they were still Communists some ten years or so after they had got themselves into teaching jobs and a comfortable flat in the suburbs points to a certain tenacity, a grip that these ideas had over them and which superseded their specific conditions of work and home life. In their case, though, membership of the Communist Party didn't last beyond 1957. They had joined in 1936, as seventeen year olds, and so my position as a 'son of Communists' only lasted till I was eleven. However, unlike some 'leavers', they carried on being activists and socialists, and each in their different ways tried to discover how to integrate ideas from their childhood, adolescence, student days, through middle age, and, in my father's case, into old age. (My mother died when she was fifty-six.) You could say that, though it was comparatively easy for them to leave the Party, the Party never left them. And one of the ways in which it stuck was through the kind of culture in this book. As teachers, they were always on the lookout for new books for their classes, and they were extremely—almost obsessively—involved parents. They made it very clear throughout my brother's and my childhoods and teenage years that they rated culture. In retrospect, I can see that their view was that it is through a broad range of culture, from the informal and trivial through to the high, classical forms, we get to understand what it means to be human, how we might overcome our sorrows, and how we might aim for a better world.

Because I am inside this worldview, it's not easy for me to imagine what it looks like from the outside. I do know, though, that contemporaries of mine at school, parents of friends, relations, and of course the press, radio, and TV looked on us as traitors, enemies, and spear-holders for the great enemy, the Soviet Union. People like my parents claimed legitimacy by, as they put it, being an integral part of the British labour movement, and felt entitled to hold onto their views about the world as informed by their experience of life as migrants, as ex-soldiers, or as civilian British citizens. The problem—and there's no getting away from it—was the Soviet Union. Though between 1940 and 1945 the UK and the USSR were allies in one of the world's bloodiest conflicts, and though there is no way of telling the story of those years—or indeed of the survival of the UK as an independent country—without describing the invasion of Germany from the east, by the mid-1950s, the situation between the two countries was as bad as it could be short of open warfare. The point of this state of affairs in relation to this book is that by the time I was reading A White Sail Gleams, *all ideas connected to Russia lay under a tidal wave of fear and loathing expressed towards the Soviet Union.*

Now that Soviet communism has come to an end and the Cold War phase in UK–Russian relations is over, it's a little easier to come to conclusions about Soviet and communist culture without becoming embroiled in the politics of, say, the Berlin airlift, the invasion of Czechoslovakia and Hungary, and the gulag. When assembling this volume we were constantly confronted by the question which lies at its heart: is it possible to look at the material in this book and consider its worth without seeing it necessarily through the prism of, for example, the persecution of Russian writers, Stalin's obsessive personal control over film-makers and composers, or, as some would argue, much worse in terms of human toll, the mass deaths in the Ukraine and the 'archipeligo' of prison camps?

I don't propose an easy answer to this, nor an apology for it. I am guessing, but it seems likely that many people reading this book enjoy the arts of Ancient Greece and Rome without attending too much to the fact that these societies were based on slavery. Many of us read the literature and admire the art and music of white Americans, Spaniards, Portuguese, and British from, say, 1600 to 1830 without constantly interrupting ourselves to reflect on the horror and significance of the transatlantic slave trade and plantation life. Often we assume that the best artists overcome the oppressive, exploitative, tyrannical, or totalitarian societies they find themselves in by documenting or responding to them in ways that seem to express something of the human condition. We can quite rightly debate whether this kind of art is 'consoling' or 'collaborative' or 'self-serving' or 'propagandist'. As a ten year old I was under the impression that the Russian, Chinese, Polish, Hungarian, Czechoslovakian, and Romanian governments were on the side of the people, working with the people (and the people working with their governments) to create a new, fairer, more just world, in which people would be treated as equals, and all would benefit from the wealth created by those societies. The books, films, and songs that were part of the life I led at this time were part of why I thought this. They were also part of why I thought that this kind of 'progress' or society was going to one day come to Britain and indeed one day the whole world would benefit from this idea. You'll see from the way I'm expressing this I didn't think that this future was particularly Soviet or 'Eastern Bloc'. The vision offered me was not that we would live life as equals under Soviet rule. The Soviet Union was pictured to us as a place where they were doing it already, and we would eventually come along and do it too. That's why, as a child, it was good to read Russian books. They had a head start on us. They had had nearly forty years of trying out words and pictures, music and film to see what was helping them arrive at this fair and just future, so of course we would be reading and watching and singing those. Russian arts represented all that was 'advanced' and 'progressive'.

In my case, the shock came when, in 1957, my family went to East Germany and then in the autumn, our parents came to my brother and me and said they were 'leaving the Party'. In the many years since this major event (in the family, not in the world as a whole!) I have pieced together exactly why my parents made this move. It wasn't because Kruschev related at the 1956 Party congress a long list of Stalin's crimes against the Russian people; it wasn't because Krushchev commanded the invasion of Hungary. It was because my parents had joined that faction of the CPGB which favoured what they called 'inner-party democracy', produced a report outlining what was meant by this, and then experienced the report being rejected by the Party's Central Committee. In other words, though they felt that their core beliefs in socialism and communism (of some kind) were intact, their belief that the British Communist Party and/or the Soviet Union could bring this about was shattered.

Again, in relation to this anthology, this meant that they didn't immediately throw out the books, films, writers, artists, and musicians represented here. They didn't comb through cast lists, contents lists, and the like and where Communists were represented instruct us or themselves to avoid the art in question. My copies of Black on White *and* A White Sail Gleams *were not thrown out. That's because they were situated in another tradition that cannot be simply or only confined to the words 'Communist', 'Russian', or 'Soviet'. As I said, I was aware of a culture above or beyond the books that came to us through Party bazaars and the like: a school/radio/TV/cinema culture. My parents were part of school culture, too. However, there was something neither purely Party nor purely 'above or beyond'. It was a general leftish children's culture expressed more informally than being directly attached to the Party. Most well known of these is the role taken up first in the USA but then later in the UK of musicians and collectors who worked with what we call 'folk music'. Songs originating with people who were more often than not neither Communists nor socialists were collected, sung, and adapted by people who were often Communists and socialists. New songs in the style of those collected songs were written and sung, too. This was a major part of what is sometimes called 'the second folk song revival'. As children being taken on camps that were by no means exclusively Communist or on demonstrations or at meetings that were likewise intended for all, we heard and learnt many of these songs. Some even found their way into the popular media and into the charts of the 1960s.*

Another strand represented here might be expressed as the writings of the 'progressive', or 'left-leaning', or 'libertarian', or 'bohemian', or plain old 'socialist' intelligentsia. Many such people brushed shoulders with Communists in the artistic movements and meetings from the First World War onwards. My grandmother, a poverty-stricken, disabled single mother to my father, somehow or another found her way to be a friend of none other than one of Modigliani's partners and models: Beatrix Hastings, poet, essayist, and socialist. You could make a case for arguing that contributing to my parents' move out of the Communist Party was their immersion in various artistic movements of the middle years of the twentieth century: the new poetry of Auden and Isherwood, the theatre workshop of Joan Littlewood, modern libertarian ideas about sex education, children's creativity, and the so-called 'progressive' movement in education as a whole. Some people who moved in these informal circles produced books for children and you'll find them in the following pages.

Someone like Geoffrey Trease (represented here) was for one short moment very close to the Soviet Union and even attended the famous Congress of 1934, at which the principles of socialist realism were laid down. Others, like Jennie Lee or Olive Dehn, came from different traditions: labour and anarchist. No matter how bitter and divided the left-wing movement was at the adult level, books, films, plays, and songs moved freely between the children of members of different parties, sects, and tendencies. What's more, as you might expect, members of these left groupings found 'progressive' tendencies in many books published by mainstream publishers. As a child, I'm not sure that I was able to make a firm distinction between the allegiances, memberships, and credentials of, say, E. Nesbit, Eleanor Farjeon, Geoffrey Trease, Amabel Williams-Ellis, Jennie Lee, Lancelot Hogben, the makers of the movie Hue and Cry, *and Alan Lomax, all of whom I was nudged into reading (or seeing), discovered and read with enjoyment myself, and talked about with my friends. The way it worked was that we had a strong sense in life as a whole that certain things, people, movements, organizations, artists were 'in', or OK, and others were not. As a very young child, I probably thought Marmite (which my mother gave me and which I loved) was in the Communist Party and lemon curd (which she didn't) was Tory.*

When it came to the arts, Picasso was in, Dali was out. Erich Kästner was in, Henry Treece (fascist tendencies) was out—though I hasten to add, I read him and neither of my parents banned him! Ewan MacColl was in, the White Heather Club was out. Joan Littlewood was in, Noel Coward was out, . . . and so on. In some ways, this book represents this tradition of 'inning' people, too. It is, then, a taste of how the children of left, left-leaning, libertarian, socialist, Communist, and anarchist parents and grandparents read, sang, went to the movies, and enjoyed culture over a period of some sixty years or so. It's a story that has never been told before. The collected extracts that make up this anthology can't tell the whole story, but they give some sense of how children's books and periodicals gave pleasure while providing the foundations of a worldview that for many has lasted a lifetime.

READING AND RADICALISM IN JANE ROSEN'S CHILDHOOD

In common with Michael Rosen—no relation, just a similar name and background—I had a radical upbringing. My grandfather had a dramatic escape from a troop train in Russia after being arrested for revolutionary activities; my grandmother had been taught at one of the Socialist Sunday Schools (SSS) described in the Introduction to Part One. Hers was in London, and her teacher was the Russian revolutionary Theodore Rothstein. She was the first generation of children for whom the working-class movement began to provide a supply of radical writing. My copy of The Red Corner Book for Children, *discussed in Part Three, was chosen by my aunt and mother. Much loved by them, it did the rounds of my cousins before eventually coming back to me, where it joined an eclectic collection of books amongst which were titles not usually found on the bookshelves of my contemporaries.*

Whilst collaborating on this anthology, I became interested in finding out about the reading experiences of others I know who grew up as children from radical backgrounds. In discussion with them, it became apparent that there were certain things common to all. There was consensus on the fact that there was exposure to books, books of every kind, and an encouragement to read those books, to discover the world in their pages, and to question what was read. Always to question, and never to take anything for granted. There were no restrictions on what was read; there might be discussions about what was in the book, but nothing was taboo. There was always a Soviet book or two around. One of the volunteers at the Library of the Society for Co-operation in Russian and Soviet Studies stated in conversation: 'I'm used to being surrounded by a library of Soviet books—I grew up with it' (personal conversation, October 2016). He also said that if he ever expressed an interest in anything a book would be found to fulfil that interest—usually from books already in the house. Another person remembered being told that she could not take a particular book out of her school library. Her parents went to complain, and succeeded in persuading the school to let her borrow it. It was a life of Jesus,[5] *thus proving, perhaps contrary to expectation, that no books were frowned upon or forbidden, though there were, of course, discussions about certain books and the ideology that they propagated.*

Radical books for children followed me into adulthood, expanding into an interest in radical education as well, including writings that appeared after the Russian Revolution and which would have been available to the second generation of my family. Children's literature underwent some changes after 1917. Some writers in Britain became more radical, and authors who had been more revolutionary—Alex Gossip and Tom Anderson, for example—were joined by younger writers such as Tom Wintringham (1898–1949),

5. Jo Manning in email to Jane Rosen, 22 December 2016. The reason that the book was denied to her in the first instance was because she was Jewish!

Charles Ashleigh (1892–19??), and for a short time, Geoffrey Trease (1909–98). Children in revolutionary writing no longer waited for the princess to bestow socialism on them, as in The Young Socialist (YS) *frequently mentioned in this collection; but went out, and paraphrasing Tom Anderson, took what was rightly theirs.*[6] *It was heady stuff.*

In 1918 Mark Starr wrote in one of the most radical juvenile publications of our period (The Revolution *is discussed in Part Two of this anthology*):

> *Readers of 'The Revolution' should never be mere book collectors. They should make earnest endeavour to truly mentally possess their books, and not to let them be only a stock of printed papers and boards. Again, it is not even the mental food you swallow, but that which you digest and assimilate which counts. (163)*

Starr, a former miner, was in many ways typical of the working-class autodidact that Jonathan Rose describes in The Intellectual Life of the British Working Classes *(2001). At the time of writing this article, he was a conscientious objector who, while imprisoned for refusing to fight, learned Esperanto, the constructed international auxiliary language that it was hoped would form a basis for international harmony and practical communication. It was favoured by the political organizations of the working class, and some of the articles in* YS *were written about and even in Esperanto. Not long after this piece appeared, Starr became a leading member of the Plebs League.*[7] *He emigrated to the USA, where he became the educational director of the International Ladies' Garment Workers' Union.*

Starr is making an important point about the necessity to digest what is being read. It was not enough for radical children to read; they were expected to discuss and assimilate what they had learned. I read these words as an adult and realized that this had been my experience of reading and being encouraged to read as a child. Essentially, this reading was an encouragement to think and to question all, including our parents' ideas. We were encouraged to think for ourselves and sometimes the rebellion was against the ideas of our parents. If we have a point to make, it is that these fabulous, radical, thoughtful, engaging works helped to produce children who were trained to question everything, and everything included the status quo.

KIMBERLEY REYNOLDS ON RECOVERING THE HISTORY OF RADICAL CHILDREN'S LITERATURE

Unlike Michael and Jane, I didn't grow up in a radical household and I was not born in Britain, though I have lived here most of my life. I came to these books

6. *Socialist Sunday Schools: A Review, and How to Open and Conduct a Proletarian School* (Glasgow: Proletarian School, 1918).
7. The Plebs League was formed by a group of students at Ruskin College, Oxford, a college for the working class. They were dissatisfied with the lack of Marxist political economy education on offer. They set up the Plebs League in November 1908, the Central Labour College in 1909, and agitated for the education of the worker in the interests of the worker.

as an academic specializing in children's literature, with an interest in left-wing politics. I was a university student in the USA at the height of student activism against the war in Vietnam, and I took three degrees at the University of Sussex, which at the time was known for its radical politics. For years I had been struck by the way children's books of the 1920s and 1940s in particular were dismissed in histories of the subject. Eventually, I was moved to investigate how accurate this perception was, and when I did, I discovered not just a large body of fascinating but forgotten work, but many individuals who vividly recalled reading the politically radical books that had been consigned to the back of the library stacks—if they were kept at all. What began as a small quest to learn about these neglected works grew into a book called *Left Out: The Forgotten Tradition of Radical Publishing for Children in Britain, 1910–1949* (2016), which begins the task of reconstructing and reconsidering the forgotten tradition of radical publishing for children in Britain during the previous century. That in turn gave birth to the idea for this anthology.

In their accounts of growing up as children of the Left, Michael and Jane are unusually alert to the lasting impression made on them by childhood reading. For the most part, the influence of children's books on culture is vastly underestimated. Even though there are now degrees and research centres dedicated to the study of children's literature, and children's books underpin such key culture industries as publishing, theatre, television, and film, there is a widespread tendency to dismiss them as something that is—or should be—left behind in the course of growing up. In fact, because it is one of the first ways in which we encounter stories and begin to explore other people, places, and ideas, children's literature can play an important part in shaping how we understand and think about the world. There is evidence, for instance, that the new ways of seeing and representing the world associated with modernism in early-twentieth-century arts and letters can be traced back to Lewis Carroll's Alice books (Dusinberre, 1987), while many well-known writers, from Graham Greene to Salman Rushdie, acknowledge the influence of childhood reading on their own writing (see Greenway, 2005; Reynolds, 2007). Francis Spufford's *The Child That Books Built* (2002) and Maria Tatar's *Enchanted Hunters: The Power of Stories in Childhood* (2009) both explore the lasting benefits of childhood reading, while Herbert Kohl's *Should We Burn Babar? Essays on Children's Literature and the Power of Stories* (2006) and Joseph Zornado's *Inventing Childhood: Culture, Ideology and the Story of Childhood* (2006) offer a more ambivalent interpretation of the ways in which children's literature shapes children.

Often the impact of childhood reading is unconscious and unpredictable, but the extracts assembled here are all examples of works that deliberately set out to influence young readers in some very specific ways, foremost of these being to inspire children and young people to think independently and to become socially and politically engaged. Although they weren't produced by an organized group of people or under the banner of any particular manifesto, these books constitute a recognizable—and continuing—strand of children's publishing that in this book we call 'radical children's literature'. I have written about this at length in *Left Out*, but in short, radical children's literature urges its readers to understand that the way the world is organized is not inevitable, and that even the youngest members of society can help to change it. To this end, radical writers use fiction, non-fiction, journalism, verse, graphic novels, picturebooks, and, indeed, any genre or format to raise concerns about injustice, inequality, or discrimination. They do this in a variety of ways, including by promoting equality and peace, discrediting stereotypes, and encouraging readers to become aware of the many challenges facing the health of the planet and the wellbeing of people in all parts of the world. To help achieve their goals, radical texts introduce new social visions, and work to give young readers the skills, ideas, and information they will need to bring about progressive

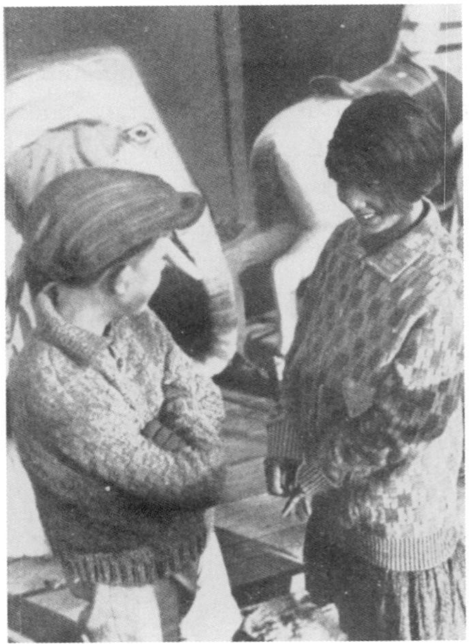

Cover and internal image from *Eddie and the Gipsy: A Story for Boys and Girls* by Alex Wedding (Martin Lawrence, 1935). *Eddie and the Gipsy*, first published in Germany, is typical of the kind of books read by children growing up in left-leaning households. The photographs by John Heartfield reflect the book's bold representation of friendship across races as Hitler was coming to power. The book is discussed in Part One.
Images supplied courtesy of the Bodleian Library, University of Oxford.

change. Most also feature many kinds of children, not just the white, middle-class, able-bodied, largely male children who have dominated mainstream juvenile publishing for most of its history. Perhaps most importantly, they assume children and young people are socially aware and interested in changing society.

This desire to promote social change sets radical writing apart from the mainstream of children's literature. In *Retelling Stories, Framing Culture* (1998), a study of the stories that have been told to children across generations, John Stephens and Robyn McCallum identify a set of interlocking ideas and values rooted in earlier centuries that broadly shape writing for children. Examples of these attributes include duty, loyalty, and obedience to parents and other forms of authority. Together these comprise what Stephens and McCallum call the 'Western metaethic', a mechanism for initiating young readers into culture in ways that tend to repress change and uphold the status quo. Although he didn't know the term 'Western metaethic', this phenomenon caught the attention of Geoffrey Trease in the 1930s, when he was a new young writer with left-leaning sympathies. He didn't have a term such as 'Western metaethic' to describe what he observed, but Trease was similarly struck by the way, almost without exception, the world shown in children's books was dominated by white, patriarchal, Christian, upper and middle-class values and a world view in which Britons were pre-eminent. Children's books, he maintained, were stuck in the past and the time had come to eradicate pernicious old ways of thinking. During an extended visit to the USSR in 1935, Trease wrote a lengthy letter titled 'Revolutionary Literature for the Young', which appeared in the journal *International Literature: Organ of the International Union of Revolutionary Writers*. The letter is both a diagnosis of what he regarded as the ills of children's literature and a call for writers to help overthrow the existing canon and replace it with an alternative body of progressive writing. In it he declares:

> This is what we have to do, then. To build up alongside the growing revolutionary literature of the adults a corresponding body of literature for the young.... We must create our own juvenile writers, who choose this genre seriously as their special craft, and make a study of the technique with which they can successfully approach the child. Our editors and publishers... must set their faces resolutely against anything which falls below a certain standard. And above all they must guard against the type of material which, while ideologically excellent, lacks the interest essential to the child's enjoyment.... (101)

Over the next few years, Trease worked tirelessly on this campaign. He produced children's books, wrote articles explaining the need for change, spoke at venues up and down the country to audiences of adults and children alike, and reviewed any publication for children with left-wing sympathies he could locate. This anthology is evidence of the range of individuals who shared in the work of reforming writing for children. That Trease disassociated himself from the Far Left, and almost all the radical children's literature from this period has been forgotten, does not mean that the campaign failed. As Trease explained when, late in life, he looked back on his decision to move to the mainstream of children's literature, he changed his tactics, but not his values. Instead of replacing the canon, he infiltrated mainstream publishing and changed it from inside.

> when my overtly left-wing attack barely dented the embattled defences... I changed my tactics. I wrote, for an anything-but-left publishing house, a story about the first East India Company, and managed to say all that I wished to say: that the English had originally gone to India not to spread the Gospel nor to build an empire, but simply to make fantastic profits. (1983, 154)

The campaign for an alternative canon may not have come about exactly as Trease planned, but by the time his last children's book was published in 1989, it was widely accepted that children's literature should show girls as the equals of boys and to feature without recourse to pernicious stereotypes people from all backgrounds, races, and ethnicities. Historical fiction now regularly centres on the lives of ordinary people, celebrates rebels, and emphasizes the follies of war rather than any heroic acts it might inspire. This was not all the work of one writer; these changes are part of the legacy of *all* those who set out to create radical children's literature. Together they succeeded in gradually reforming British children's literature in significant and lasting ways. The following pages give a sense of the variety, spirit, flavour, ambition—and fun—to be found in the radical texts of the first decades of the previous century.

PART ONE

STORIES FOR YOUNG SOCIALISTS

INTRODUCTION

In the interests of reforming society, socialists have always been interested in learning from and developing alternative methods of education. One of the most obvious areas that required improvement was the publications produced for children, often by youth organizations and societies. For instance, the late nineteenth century saw the development of the Socialist Sunday School (SSS) movement, which largely emerged from the ideas of Keir Hardie (1856–1915), a principal member of the Independent Labour Party (ILP) and editor of its newspaper, *The Labour Leader.* In the May 1893 issue, Hardie proposed the setting up of a Crusaders' movement for children under the age of sixteen. The success of this call led various supporters, including the leading Glasgow trade unionists and radical leaders Alex Gossip (1862–1952), Archie McArthur, Lizzie Glasier, and Tom Anderson (1863–1947), to set up the first SSSs. These, in combination with the Socialist Democratic Federation (SDF), the Cinderella Schools, organized by the readers of the *Clarion*, Britain's most successful socialist newspaper from 1891 to 1931, and the Christian Socialist Labour Church Schools, organized by John Trevor, were to form the basis of the national SSS.[1] Many of the writers who appear in this section and throughout this volume were supporters of the SSS movement, including Gossip, Anderson, Margaret McMillan, and F. J. Gould.

Fundamental to the organization of the movement was the involvement of children in all aspects of running the SSS classes. They served as minute takers and helped to organize the meetings. Fred Reid, a scholar during the Second World War noted,

> The adults expect that we will all grow up to take our places in the Labour Movement, as trade unionists and socialists. So it is important that we young people rehearse the serious business of the adult movement: attending meetings regularly, taking office if elected, acquiring the discipline of listening to a

1. Although Glasgow became the centre of the SSS movement, the first SSS was actually formed in Battersea, South West London, in 1892 by Mary Gray of the SDF. She was motivated by the poverty of the children around her to form a school for working-class children so that they could learn socialism, the reasons why they lived under such conditions, and why their parents were unemployed. Her first students consisted of her two daughters and one other boy. From this modest beginning the school prospered and continued well into the next century.

speaker, thinking over his message and asking intelligent questions of him or her afterwards.[2]

The classes themselves were run along the lines of traditional Sunday Schools, often beginning with singing, a recitation of the ten SSS precepts or a question and answer session echoing the Christian catechism, and a lesson either from the School superintendent or another visiting adult. The lesson could cover subjects such as economics, history, evolution, or ethics. Central to the teaching of the SSS were the ideas of internationalism, anti-militarism, and secularism.

Within the first ten years of their existence the SSS spread throughout Scotland, London, and Yorkshire, mostly concentrated in working-class and urban areas. By 1912 there were ninety-six schools organized into a National Council of British Socialist Sunday School Unions, and the total membership was recorded as 4,540 children, 1,788 adolescents, and 6,328 adults.[3]

In 1901, Archie McArthur launched *The Young Socialist* (*YS*), the journal of the SSS. Its first edition was four duplicated pages in length, printed by Twentieth Century Press, the publisher of the SDF. It echoed the movement's development as it expanded, eventually reaching twenty-four pages. The *YS* provided not only a periodical for the young people of the SSS, but also a forum for the adults for discussion of socialist education for children, including regular advice in its pages for lessons and other activities.[4] It also reflected discussion ongoing in the adult movement such as the divisions between those that proposed the 'religion of socialism'[5] and those who were more Marxist and revolutionary in their beliefs. These debates led to a split in the movement when Tom Anderson, who appears at several points in this volume, left to form his Proletarian Schools, which produced their own set of 'maxims', including the fifth, which stated 'Thou Shalt Teach Revolution'.[6]

Yet it was the First World War that was to really cause discord and threaten the SSS. This discord reflected the split in the reaction of the international working-class movement to the war. For example, in Britain, the Labour Party was praised for its commitment to the war effort; H. M. Hyndman, former leader of the SDF, supported British involvement; and the Communist Kropotkin was also pro war. Amongst the well-known opponents of the war were Jean Jaurés

2. Fred Reid, in *Socialist Sunday Schools in Retrospect* (1), available at http://www.fredreid.co.uk/ and accessed 21 March 2017.
3. All figures from Reid.
4. Both the National Council and individual schools provided pamphlets, reading lists, and syllabi to further assist the preparation of educational material. They also produced and distributed play scripts for theatrical performances.
5. These included figures such as John and Katharine Bruce Glasier of the ILP.
6. Jane Rosen, 'Thou Shalt Teach Revolution—Tom Anderson and his Contribution to the Education of the Children in Glasgow', in Ruth Ewan (ed.), *The Glasgow Schools* (2012).

of France, who was assassinated for his beliefs; Karl Liebknecht and Rosa Luxemburg in Germany; Lenin in Russia; Eugene V. Debs in the United States; and E. Malatesta, Rudolf Rocker, Sylvia Pankhurst, and Fenner Brockway in Britain.

In Britain's SSS this division led to dissension at the annual National Conferences. Those adult members who were aligned with the ILP tended to be anti-war and against conscription. The SSS in Lancashire generally followed Robert Blatchford and *The Clarion* in supporting the war. The fact that *The Young Socialist*, although representing all scholars of the movement whether they enlisted or were conscientious objectors, used its editorials and articles to propound the cause of peace and campaign against conscription did lead to constant criticism for bringing the adult political crisis into the children's journal. However, as the editors, Lizzie and Fred Glasier Foster, pointed out, this was simply the reflection of the resolution passed by the National Conference in 1915: 'That this Conference of British Socialist Sunday School Unions express the opinion that the only flag we recognise is the Red Flag, and our only war is against Capitalism.'

In his recollections of his time in the SSS, Fred Reid points out that this principled stand received support from those who campaigned against the war, and membership increased as a result. However, for various reasons this achievement was short-lived. Many of the new recruits were from either the left wing of the ILP or the newly formed CP, and in 1922 the latter formally disassociated itself from the SSS to concentrate on its own educational programme for working-class children, though individuals often continued to be involved.[7] Other reasons include the defeat of the General Strike in 1926, a blow from which the socialist movement never recovered, and of course, the crippling unemployment of the 1930s, which meant that working-class members, who were the main supporters of the movement, were often unable to provide financial support to the SSS or pay their subscriptions. Throughout the 1930s, the movement shrank, largely as a consequence of sticking to its anti-militarist beliefs even when faced with the threat and the reality of the rise of fascism. The result of this was a fall in the number of SSSs from 149 at the movement's height in 1918 to 34 in 1935.

It was a remarkable achievement that, despite this dissent within the movement, the SSS did generally succeed in uniting all tendencies of the socialism represented by its adult members and organizers in the education of socialist children. The weekly class was central to this, but the SSS also organized rambles,

7. Fred Reid, 'Socialist Sunday Schools in Britain, 1892–1939', *International Review of Social History* 11 (1966), 18–47.

camping trips, and festivals of dance, theatre, art, music, and crafts (see Part Six, 'Performing Leftness'). Though it never again reached the heights of its popularity of 1918, the movement survived into the late twentieth century; the last school, in Glasgow, naturally, closed in 1980.

Among organizers of SSS, discussions about the type of literature to be provided for children were many, and mainstream writers were not completely discarded. For example, the commonly regarded imperialist authors Rudyard Kipling and G. A. Henty were considered acceptable on some SSS syllabi, and along with other writers such as Alexandre Dumas featured on the recommended reading lists produced by 'Mr Wiseacre' in the 1930s. However, as the selections in this anthology show, original new work, often modelled on traditional forms such as parables, primers, fairy tales, and retellings of myths and historical anecdotes, was produced by writers such as F. J. Gould, whose work features in the following pages, and Katharine Bruce Glasier. Much of the prose from this early period is heavily didactic, and many authors interact directly with their audience. This interaction reflects the long tradition of education through catechism; much of the teaching in the SSS and the Proletarian Schools was in this form of question and answer, as was a great deal of early children's literature.

The use of traditional forms did not always sit easily with all constituencies on the Left, however. For example, one of the major controversies in the SSS was the idealistic fantasy writing in the *YS*. Contributors such as John Bruce Glasier and May Westoby, sometime editor of the *YS*, provided winsome fairy tales with evil giants representing capitalism and landlordism. When, at the age of nine, Andrew Rothstein, later a leading CP activist and son of the Russian revolutionary Theodore Rothstein, produced a factual article on a trip to Switzerland for the children's pages of *YS*, the editor asked him to talk about Swiss ice fairies![8] Instances such as this led some to suggest that the writing was not revolutionary enough, and indeed not representative enough of the working class. They had a point: many of the working-class children who appear in *YS* stories fulfil the same role as they do in mainstream publications, meaning that the ultimate prizes of socialism and equality are bestowed rather than won.[9] Alex Gossip's short retelling of the Midas legend and Eleanor Farjeon's (1881–1965) poem 'Greed', both reproduced in Part One, provide a corrective to this tendency.

8. It is interesting to note that this discussion about the role of fantasy in children's books was raised again in the Soviet Union, with Korney Chukovsky, amongst others, campaigning for the necessity of fantasy and nonsense in works for children.
9. See, for example, 'Lords and Comrades' by Margaret H. Barber (serialized in the *YS* between July and August 1920), where a princess bestows socialism on her country and agrees to be elected Supreme Comrade.

'Greed', as well as the other publications represented here, were produced after the Russian Revolution. The effects of this, and the influence of the left-wing publisher Martin Lawrence are discussed in more detail in Part Three. However, the new situation meant that more revolutionary texts for young readers were required, and there was an understanding that the working class, and particularly working-class children, should be their main protagonists. Sometimes these stories had to be imported, from Germany as in the cases of 'Eddie and the Gipsy', represented in the following pages, and 'Little Peter', discussed in Part Three. Martin Lawrence, however, also published British works, commissioning historical fiction from Geoffrey Trease, and the radical tales of Frederick Le Gros Clark (1892–1977) and Ida Clark (n.d.), both featured in Part One.

With the welfare state and the advent of the Cold War, such explicitly revolutionary writing tended to disappear. Radical writing for children became less confrontational in its class consciousness, although working-class children became more central to the action in the books, and more proactive in the solution to the fictional situation and the stories' denouement. Fielden Hughes's *Hue and Cry* (1956), the final extract in Part One, can be regarded as the culmination of the recognition by early socialist educators of the problematic nature of the representation of working-class characters in writing for children and young people.

‘KING MIDAS’

The Young Socialist, November 1902

Written by Alexander Gossip

Alex Gossip (1862–1952) was a leading trade unionist with a strong commitment to the education of socialist children. One of the most loved personalities of the Socialist movement, he was a life-long supporter of the Socialist Sunday School (SSS) movement, which had its beginning in Glasgow in 1896 through the efforts of Gossip’s friend, Keir Hardie. As mentioned in the Introduction to Part One, the SSS had a magazine, *The Young Socialist*, and Gossip was a stalwart contributor, both under his own name and the pen-name ‘Kalek’. On becoming the General Secretary of the National Amalgamated Furnishing Trades Association in 1902, he moved to London, where he founded at least two SSSs and supported several more. Gossip led Fulham School from its foundation. During this time he successfully countered attempts by the London County Council to stop the SSS meeting on their premises, and during the First World War, he attended the tribunals of the SSS’s conscientious objectors (COs) and organized the Fulham children in singing outside Wormwood Scrubs in support of the COs incarcerated there. He remained the honorary leader of the Fulham SSS until his death.

Most of Gossip’s contributions to the journal were reports of activities, so the piece included here is a rare example of fiction by him in print, though he was known for his storytelling at SSS events. The SSS movement was split on its attitude to revolution, but Gossip managed, whilst being a supporter of revolutionary means, to keep on good terms with everyone. This story encourages child readers to apply its lessons to their own lives and time, and goes further than most retellings of the Midas legend in showing the results of a whole society devoted to the love of gold. The last lines make it clear that Alex Gossip was firmly on the side of the revolutionaries in being prepared to overthrow the status quo.

The Young Socialist.

A MAGAZINE OF JUSTICE AND LOVE.

"The new world—its foundations to be justice; love to be the spirit of its inhabitants."

This Magazine is owned by the Glasgow Socialist Sunday-School Union, and carried on by it in the interest of the Socialist children of the country.
Vol. II., No. 11.] London, November, 1902. [Price One Halfpenny.

KING MIDAS.

By Alexander Gossip (London).

Dear Young Comrades,—Once upon a time (that is the way all good stories begin) there lived a king in a country several thousand miles away from our own dear land. He was very rich, and did not require to worry and annoy himself in the way that so many fathers and mothers that we know have to do sometimes about getting food and clothes for their children. He lived in a great big palace, for which he paid no rent. The walls inside were hung with all sorts of beautiful pictures, and the rooms were filled with the best of furniture, not at all like some of the trumpery articles which it almost breaks the heart of the cabinet-maker to have to make to-day. Some of you know that I am interested in furniture, and that is possibly why I am making a special note of this. Anyway, this king's palace was furnished with the very best of everything. He had also all sorts of nice clothes to wear, and did not require to get them patched when they began to get worn a bit, as plenty have to do, but he just threw them aside then and put on a new suit. All the best kinds of food that could be procured were at his disposal, and a number of men and women cooks were kept busy all day long preparing dainty dishes for him. I know two or three of the grown-ups who will be shaking their heads when they read about these dainty dishes, but we cannot help that just now, can we, children? A large, beautiful garden was attached to the palace, and all sorts of lovely flowers grew there, and it was a real pleasure just to get a tiny whiff of the delicious perfume that came from them. Last, but by no means least, the king had a young and very pretty daughter, who was very much in love with her father, and he loved her very much in return. The story does not say, but I expect they used to have nice, jolly romps together, just as we have sometimes at our picnics and at-homes.

The name of this king was Midas, and you would naturally think that he would be quite satisfied and contented with all these nice things that I have mentioned. Midas, however, was not, and having quarrelled with the gods one day they determined to punish him with his own weapons. He conceived the idea that he would like to be able to turn everything that he touched into gold, and one day this power was granted him, and he was to be able to exercise it the following morning.

When he awoke the next morning he very naturally wished to know if the promise of the gods had been kept, and in order to test it he touched the posts of his bed. Great was his delight when they immediately turned into solid gold. The story goes on to describe how King Midas, by touching the various articles in his room, changed them into the yellow metal, but not content with that he went out into the garden and did the same to his beautiful flowers.

Up to now he was delighted with his newly acquired gift, and he thought to himself what a glorious time he would have, and commenced to lay his plans for the future, as the grown-ups say. Feeling hungry, however, after all this work, he went indoors and sat down to breakfast, but what was his astonishment to find that whenever he touched the food it at once turned into gold also. King Midas was not prepared for this, and I daresay he looked rather foolish now. So much was he taken up, however, with his new power that he did not fully understand what it all meant and he decided to go out again to the garden. When there, his little daughter, catching sight of him, came running as usual to get her morning kiss. The king snatched her up in his arms, as was his custom, but to his horror and dismay she also turned into gold.

The awful results arising from his wicked greed dawned upon him at last, and he realised, in all its bitterness, what a fool he had been. So keenly did he feel the dreadful position that he had placed himself in, that the gods at last, taking pity on him, took back the fatal gift and restored to him once more his well-beloved child.

Isn't that a wonderful story, dear young comrades? But, of course, these things never really happened, and the story is told just to show how the love of gold carries with it its own punishment, and people who devote their whole time and energy to securing it, regardless of other things, find that in gaining it they, like poor King Midas, have lost everything worth having, and that, instead of bringing with it happiness, it invariably causes misery and suffering. The beautiful flowers in the king's garden lost their perfume the moment the hateful touch was felt, and in the same way to-day the lust for gold has robbed a large part of our once beautiful country of all its charms. The pursuit of it has made the lives of millions of men, women, and children almost unbearable, and the few only gain it at the expense of the many.

We Socialists want many of the nice things that King Midas had, but we cannot afford to pay the price that he did for his golden touch, though under Socialism this would not be necessary. The happy, joyous life has gone out of thousands upon thousands of our little boys and girls, and left in its place something hard and unlovely, just like the king's little daughter after her father's touch, all because a few men and women are not content with an abundance of good things, but must have more, regardless of the cost in misery and unhappiness to others and also to themselves, though, unlike King Midas, some of them have not yet realised that.

We, I hope, dear children are working for the day when our country will be full of beautiful, sweet-scented flowers, and the hearts of the grown-ups will be gladdened by the sight of happy, romping boys and girls; and if the King Midases of to-day do not learn their lesson themselves, you and I, dear comrades, will have to teach them.

'THE COAL CARGO'

from *Pages for Young Socialists*
The National Labour Press, 1913

Written by Frederick James Gould

F. J. Gould (1855–1938) was an indefatigable writer of stories for children based on his socialist humanist beliefs. This puts him at variance with a strong strand within the Labour Party of the twentieth century which arose out of Methodist and Anglican traditions as expressed by the phrase 'Christian Socialist'.

Gould was born in Brighton but grew up in London, the son of evangelical Anglicans. He spent some time as a choir boy and by 1877 was a head teacher of a church school. However, by the early 1880s he was an active 'secularist', while he pursued his teaching career under the auspices of the London School Board in London's East End. Being an avowed and public atheist in the early Victorian era carried with it the penalty of imprisonment.[1] Neither the British state nor the education system has ever been secularized, though by the time Gould was active in the secularist movement his behaviour was not illegal.

He stayed in teaching till 1896, and from that time until his death he devoted himself to politics (from 1904 to 1910 he was a Labour councillor in Leicester), writing books, leaflets, and stories, and giving talks all over Britain as well as tours of the USA and India.

Gould's stories for children are written in a didactic style, full of rhetorical questions which encouraged readers to ponder on what Gould perceived as injustices and contradictions. Like many of the teaching and writing methods of the Socialist Sunday Schools (discussed in detail in the Introduction to Part One), this method goes back at least to the parables of Jesus, includes the 'exempla' tales of medieval sermons. Nearer to home, the technique resembles what would have been his own parents' preaching.

1. Leading atheists such as Charles Southwell and George Holyoake were imprisoned for speaking and writing about atheism in 1842. Later, Charles Bradlaugh was incarcerated by the Sergeant-at-Arms at the Houses of Parliament in 1880, for insisting on his right to affirm rather than swear the religious oath. For an account of nineteenth-century atheism and its proponents, see David Berman's *A History of Atheism in Britain: From Hobbes to Russell* (1988).

THE COAL CARGO.

Cover, F. J. Gould's *Pages for Young Socialists*. The book is illustrated throughout by Walter Crane (1845–1915), who regularly gave his work to publications associated with the international socialist movement.

IN the summer of 1909 a ship named the "Deccan," carrying a cargo of coals and a crew of 27 men, sailed from Port Talbot, in South Wales, for South America. Captain Parnell was in command. Across the broad Atlantic the "Deccan" cut its way week after week—the captain watching the compass, the sea, and the stars; and the sailors busy in cleaning, altering the canvas to suit the wind, and taking their turns at the watch. And why all this labour? Because the furnaces and engines of some place in South America needed Welsh coal. To supply this useful fuel the men of the "Deccan" devoted their daily and nightly labour.

"I feel ill," said Captain Parnell one day when the ship was near Cape Horn. He was put ashore at Port Stanley, and thence was carried in another vessel to his home at Portmadoc, and there, in sight of the ever-moving sea, the sailor died.

Soon after the Captain had left the "Deccan" fire broke out on board; and the flames were quenched only after severe effort. Then a storm smote with mighty power upon the coal-ship; the mainmast fell; a hole was opened in the hull; water poured in, and the crew took to the boats. The men had snatched up a few biscuits and some tinned meat. Fifteen minutes later, the "Deccan" sank, and the crew were alone on a wild sea.

After hard rowing, they landed on a sandy beach on one of the islands of the Fire-Country—Tierra del Fuego. Rain came down in torrents; sleet blew in the men's faces, and all their shelter was a strip of sail-cloth. Biscuits and meat having been eaten, the sailors searched sand and rocks for moss and shell-fish.

One day, as they wandered in this dreary land, they saw a number of human skeletons lying on the earth, telling the tale of ship-wrecked folk who had died in this far-off corner of the earth.

Thirteen days after the coal-ship sank, a whaling vessel was sighted. Signals were put up. The whaler came to anchor. Soon the weary and hungry sailors were taken on board the saviour-ship, and, in January, 1910, they landed in the port of Liverpool.

And why all this battle with wind, wave, storm, hunger and sickness, and death? Because coal was wanted in South America.

Suppose you and I could travel over the globe to see what we could see, like Columbus or Magellan or Vasco da Gama; not in search of new lands, but in search of the works done by the labour of the common people. What a wonderful journey we should take! What marvellous scenes we should behold! Everywhere we should witness the sights of the magic of labour—the magic of human hands. Let me tell only a few words out of the vast Book of Labour.

We see the ploughed fields; the hedges and ditches; the planted trees in the orchards; the sheep tended by the shepherd, and prepared for the shearer; the swine in the styes; the corn on the farm lands; the barns; the out-houses; the thatched cottages; the mansions and manor-houses; the stone churches and grand cathedrals; the schools and colleges; the shops, and streets, and theatres, and rinks, and circuses, and gates, and archways, and roads, and bridges, and parks, and fences, and railroads and stations.

Wondrous magic of men's hands!

We see the steam-engines, the trains, the electric cars, the carts, the wagons, the trolleys, the carriages, the motors, the cycles, the flying-machines, the balloons; we see the tools, the spades, the hammers, the axes, the chisels, the knives, the brushes, the pulleys, the levers, the screws, the cranes, the dynamos; and we see (though I am not so glad to name some of these things) the swords, the rifles, the cannons, the bombs, the barrels of gunpowder, the packets of guncotton.

Wondrous magic of human hands!

We see the quarries, the mines, the felled timber in the forests, the plantations of tea, coffee, cocoa, etc., the tanneries, the weaving-sheds, the sugar refineries, the sawmills, the blast furnaces, the shoe factories, the cotton mills, the warehouses, the docks, the harbour, the embankments.

Wondrous magic of human hands!

We see the boats, the liners, the fishing-smacks, the warships, the buoys, the lighthouses, the marine cables, and the observatories on the hills, whence the learned astronomers gaze at planets and stars, and map the heavens for the use of the sailor on the boundless ocean.

Wondrous magic of human hands!

There are folk who take no share in this splendid labour. Some are poor and idle; some are rich and idle. But let us look at those who do the vast handwork of the wide, wide world. From these magic hands flow forth the works that enrich the Home of Man. And what gifts are poured into these wondrous hands in return? What do the day-labourers and weekly-wage earners of the United Kingdom—the Union Jack Islands—receive for their labour?

There are more than 40 million people in the Kingdom. Of these, about 15 million of girls, boys, women and men are wage-earners. If all their earnings are added up for the year 1904, and divided by the number of workers, so as to get the average, the average sum per worker would come to about £1 per week. Suppose we look at one trade alone—a trade which is one of the chief labours in the Kingdom—the weaving or textile trade; that is, the trade whose magic hands give us our cotton goods, woollen, worsted, linen, jute, silk, hosiery, and lace. In the year 1906, the average weekly earnings of a man was 28s., a woman 15s.

In the year 1906–7, about two million people in the Kingdom came to the door of the Poor Law, and asked for help in hunger, nakedness, or sickness; that is, two millions of the citizens in these beautiful islands—the land of Alfred and Milton and Tennyson—were at some time or other during the year in the position of beggars or paupers. You have yourself seen the crowds of unemployed in the streets. You know how men go to the labour exchanges and give in their names in the hope of getting work, and how often they ask in vain. You know how often the food of the workers is impure, and mixed with evil matters; it is adulterated. You know how the workers suffer at their work from poison, accident, and many terrors of mine, quarry, and storm. The sailors of the coal ship "Deccan" are a picture, or type, of the workers of the world.

Wondrous magic of human hands!

Yes, but some day these hands will gather richer fruit from the Tree of Labour which they have planted and tended since the first man used the first tool and lit the first fire.

'GREED THE GUY'

from *Tomfooleries*
The Daily Herald, 1920

'THE FIRST OF MAY'

from *Moonshine*
The London Publishing Company
and George, Allen and Unwin, 1921

Written by 'Tom Fool'

'Tom Fool' was a pseudonym used by Eleanor Farjeon (1881–1965) when writing poems for the *Daily Herald*, a left-wing newspaper founded in 1912 by a group of trade unionist and socialists, and Reynolds News, a left-leaning Sunday paper founded in 1850, which became linked to the Co-operative Party in 1929.[1] She also wrote as 'Merry Andrew' for *The New Leader*, a socialist newspaper that went through several names from the time of its founding by Keir Hardie as *The Miner* in 1887.

Farjeon is best known for her books of poems aimed specifically at children, such as *Nursery Rhymes of London Town* (1916), and her collection of short stories, *The Little Bookroom* (1955). Individual poems such as 'Cats Sleep Anywhere' have appeared many times in children's and school anthologies, and her poem 'A Morning Song' (1931) became the hugely popular hymn, 'Morning Has Broken', sung by most British children attending school assembly from the time of its first publication to this day. Perhaps due to her use of pseudonyms, it has never been much known that in the 1920s and 1930s Farjeon was one of

1. The Co-operative Party, founded in 1917, is the political arm of the much older British Co-operative Movement. Both party and movement are dedicated to the principle that industries, agriculture, and commercial businesses should be owned and managed by those who work in them and who also share the economic benefits of ownership.

the leading English poets writing from an explicitly socialist point of view. She received the Carnegie Medal and the Hans Christian Andersen Award for *The Little Bookroom*.

Farjeon's father, Benjamin Farjeon, was a prolific novelist, playwright, and journalist who had been raised as an Orthodox Jew but who broke away from his parents and emigrated to Australia and New Zealand before coming back to England and marrying Margaret Jefferson, Farjeon's mother. It was a literary background, with Eleanor Farjeon striking up friendships with such people as D. H. Lawrence, Edward Thomas, Walter de la Mare, and the American poet Robert Frost.

'Greed the Guy' turns on bringing together two images of popular culture: Greed (one of the Seven Deadly Sins) and the Guy, representing the Catholic conspirator Guy Fawkes, burnt on bonfires every year on November 5th in memory of the failed Gunpowder Plot of 1605. Similarly, 'The First of May' uses an image from popular culture. May 1st is when the traditional fertility festival May Day, which leads to the summer solstice, is celebrated, but in the late nineteenth century it was adopted as International Workers' Day or Labour/Labor Day by the working-class movement (see the discussion of this in the introduction to *The World's May Day* in Part Six). Though these poems appeared in national newspapers and books nominally for adults, by using moments in the calendar that most British children participated in with enthusiasm, Farjeon reached out to a cross-generational audience.

GREED THE GUY

"GUY! Guy! Guy!
Stick him in the eye!"
All down the road I hear 'em cry;
And many a Guy in all men's sight
Will burn in the bonfires this here night.
If I could choose and have my turn,
I'd choose Greed for my Guy to burn—
Greed, who steals the poor man's crust
And, sated, drops it in the dust;
Greed, who grabs the poor man's shirt
And, stifled, trails it in the dirt;
I would stuff the glutton's maw
With a feast of chaff and straw;
I would dress the creature's body
With some tramp's discarded shoddy.
Then the ugly, useless thing
To the bonfires I would bring,
And with all the crowd would cry:
"Stick him in the eye!
Guy! Guy! Guy!"

THE FIRST OF MAY

LOVELIEST month! that fills the ready nest,
And in the orchard sets the apple-flower,
And brings the crumpled beech-leaf to the crest
Of beauty, and in one immortal hour
Wakes the first nightingale—O heavenly May,
Moving among the meadows like a bride,
Not all men's children know how you to-day
With songs and blossoms fill the country-side.
If I who know and love you might entreat
One other bounty, I would bid you come
Down every crowded city's meanest street

And print its filth with flowers, and in each slum
Teach the shy nightingale to build and sing,
And in dark areas where pale children play
Give also them some cause to know the Spring
And tell each other, "It's the First of May."

'THE STORY OF THE ISLAND OF FISH'

from *Eddie and the Gipsy*
Martin Lawrence, 1935

Written by 'Alex Wedding' [pen name of Grete Weiskopf]. Translated by Charles Ashleigh. Illustrated by John Heartfield

Grete Weiskopf (1905–66) took her pen name, Alex Wedding, from a working-class suburb of Berlin which is where her book, first published as *Ede und Unku* in 1931, is set. The publisher was the Communist publishing house Malik-Verlag, founded by Wieland Herzfeld, brother of the well-known photo-montage artist John Heartfield, whose photographs illustrate the text. The translation by Charles Ashleigh was published by the left-wing publishing firm Martin Lawrence in 1935, two years after the Nazis came to power, and when Weiskopf, Heartfield, and Herzfeld were forced to leave Germany. All returned to East Germany after the end of the Second World War.

The book is set in working-class Berlin, and has as its background the economic depression and social unrest that marked the rise of the National Socialist Party. Eddie's father, a loyal worker who in the past has broken strikes and found ways for his employers to make more money, has been laid off. The book charts Eddie's efforts to earn money for his family, helped by his friend Max, the son of a Communist trade unionist who is on strike, and Unku, a Sinti child whom he helps and who in turn becomes his friend and ally.

The extract comes after Eddie's first meeting with Unku, and his realization that she is a gypsy. Eddie has gone to his friend Max's home, where he receives a lesson about the economics of unemployment from Max's father in the form of a story. This form of storytelling was in common usage by radicals to teach socialist economics. A variation on this practice is found in E. F. Stucley's *Pollycon* (1933), represented in Part Eight.

It should be noted that the people on whom Unku and her family are based and who feature in Heartfield's photographs were deported to Auschwitz in 1943, and of the eleven Sinti children mentioned, only one survived. In 2011, a street in Berlin was named after the book.

CHAPTER IV

THE STORY OF THE ISLAND OF FISH

EDDIE crossed the street and found himself before a great, grey, tenement house. He took his notebook out, and carefully read once more the Klabundes' address. This was the right number; this must be Max's place.

Eddie had never been in Max's home, for the Sperlings' flat was on the way to school, and, whenever Max walked home with Eddie, he had left him at his house door and gone on alone.

Also, Eddie did not know Max's parents, and he was very curious to see what Communists really looked like. Did they always talk in whispers, like thieves? Or people who had broken the law and were afraid of the police? Eddie was just a trifle scared, it must be confessed. He remembered that his father had always said that the Reds wanted to divide everything up. Suppose he had to go home without his coat! But no, it couldn't be as bad as all that!

As fast as he could, Eddie raced up the stairway. At last, after having spelt out all the names on the doors, he arrived—on the top floor—at the door of the Klabundes' flat. His heart was beating fast. First he got his breath back, and then rang the bell.

"Ah, that must be him!" he heard a female voice cry from the darkness of the hall, as the door was opened.

"Mrs. Klabunde? I am very glad to meet you," said Eddie politely, taking off his cap and making a little bow.

"The same to you!" replied Mrs. Klabunde, laughing good-naturedly and taking Eddie's cap and coat, which she hung up behind a curtain in the hall. Now he was able to get a good look at her. As a matter of fact, she didn't look unlike his mother, except that she was somewhat younger and wore her hair short. Eddie was pleasantly surprised.

"Just go into the living-room, Eddie," said Mrs. Klabunde. "We were all waiting for you. I'll be in, in a minute."

"Excuse me for coming so late," said Eddie, and opened the door of the kitchen living-room.

Father Klabunde was sitting in his shirt-sleeves, reading the paper. He rose and came towards Eddie and shook him heartily by the hand. "So this is what Eddie looks like! We've heard so much about you! But where's Max? Max, Eddie's here!"

Max came rushing out of the next room.

"Why, kid," he laughed, "your gold watch must be losing! The coffee will be cold. To-day's a regular feast-day for us because you're coming! Coffee—and I've been to get some doughnuts. We only have those for special occasions!"

"Sit down, Eddie, my boy," said the father.

"Thanks," said Eddie, and took a chair.

"Listen—you don't have to bow and scrape in front of my parents," explained Max and laughingly looked towards his father. "You can just talk naturally."

Somehow Eddie felt completely at home with Max's father, and his shyness disappeared.

Then a clatter of china was heard, and Max announced, "Here comes the coffee!"

Mrs. Klabunde came in, holding the tray with both hands, upon which the cups tinkled merrily. She stepped cautiously, so as not to spill the coffee from the tall pot.

"Now, my boy, try some of this first," she said, pouring out a cup of steaming coffee for Eddie.

"Why didn't you get here earlier?" asked Max who, by the way, seemed to lead the conversation here.

"Mr. Abendstund butted in to-day, just when we had settled down to dinner," explained Eddie. "And afterwards mother sent me off quickly to buy potatoes, so that father shouldn't whack me. And then I dawdled a bit in front of our door, thinking of something. Then I lost my way, too—"

"A whacking?" interrupted Max, with his mouth full of doughnut, and scratching thoughtfully behind his ear. "But what for? What happened?"

"It was all about Abendstund," said Eddie, looking angry for a moment.

"But who is this Abendstund? Tell us about it—complaining's no good," said Mrs. Klabunde.

"I've got no use for him!" began Eddie—and, as he remembered it all, he didn't know where to start with his story! "You see, he's a retired postal official, with a pension—and then he inherited quite a bit of money, and he always eats plenty and of the best. And my father's unemployed. And father and mother thought that maybe Abendstund could help some way. But, not a hope! All the old windbag talked about to-day, at our place, was cutting down expenses, and we ought to use margarine instead of butter, and so on, and then he kept on making his stupid jokes. But I didn't laugh at them. All the time I was thinking about father not having a job, and what we could do about it, and I told him that, too—"

"Some swine, this Abendstund!" commented Max, listening spellbound.

"And so then he said," continued Eddie resentfully, "that I was only a child, and should look on the bright side of things, and muck like that—and that I ought to pay more attention to my school work!"

"Well, a guy like that!—somebody ought to tell him what they think of him!" exclaimed Max angrily.

"Well, and then what?" asked Mr. Klabunde.

"Then," continued Eddie, "he pulled another of his lousy jokes, and told me I ought to laugh at it!"

"Well, and—?" asked Max, fidgeting excitedly on his chair.

"Then I let him have it! 'Mr. Abendstund,' I told him, straight out, 'I'm not an automatic machine that you put a bad joke into, and a laugh comes out!' "

"That's a swell answer!" cried Max, delighted, and he took an enormous bite out of his doughnut.

"Pretty strong!" said Klabunde. He wished to repress the laughter which shone in his eyes, but he couldn't quite. He didn't exactly applaud Eddie, but he didn't blame him, either.

"Still, it would be better, next time, if you could control yourself better, Eddie," said Klabunde, gently. "I understand exactly how you felt, but there are much worse things than Abendstund, believe me!"

"Yes, the machines, for instance," answered Eddie thoughtfully.

"What? Why, what have the machines done then?" inquired Klabunde, astonished.

"Eddie, you go so far back—you remind me of our teacher, Schmidt, who starts to talk about the Thirty Years' War, and goes right back to the earth-worms," Max interjected.

At any other time, Eddie would have jumped onto this interruption, but he was now engrossed in more serious matters.

"They sacked my father because they've got some new machinery now. These machines do father's work—that's clear, isn't it?"

"You're a regular street-corner speaker!" said Mrs. Klabunde, smiling. "Now eat and drink something, and let the others talk for a bit!"

"It's true—life isn't all beer and skittles," pondered Klabunde. "And factories aren't charitable institutions. But that isn't the fault of the machinery, my boy!"

"But it must be!" responded Eddie.

"No, it's not the fault of the machinery," repeated Klabunde. "But you don't understand that yet, Eddie."

"But Father told me—it must be so," said Eddie with conviction.

"If you're right, I'd be glad to change my mind," said Klabunde, earnestly. "It wouldn't be the first time I have learnt something from a youngster!"

"Yes—like turning somersaults, and jujitsu, from me!" confirmed Max proudly, and, to prove it, immediately stood up and turned a marvellous somersault!

"Are you joking?" asked Eddie. He simply couldn't believe that anyone's father would do such a thing.

"Yes, that's right," replied Klabunde for Max. "I can't prove it to you here—otherwise the plaster of the ceiling down below—Mrs. Miller's place—would drop into her stew-pot. But, out of doors, I can turn ten of 'em, one after the other, until you can't see me for dust! Isn't that true, Max?"

"You're certainly O.K.!" said Eddie, enraptured. "Maybe you'll race me some time, when we're out together?"

"That's a bet, young fellow!" agreed Klabunde. "But let's just settle this little matter of the machines. Now, listen, Eddie: the more work the machines do for people, the less work is there left over for people to do—isn't that so?"

"Sure!" cried both Eddie and Max together.

"Therefore things ought to be easier for the working-men," continued Klabunde. "Isn't that so, too?"

"Sure!" they shouted again.

"Good," said Klabunde. "Then the machines should be a benefit to the workers—but, instead of that, the better the machines become, the worse it gets for the worker. Something must be wrong there, mustn't it?"

Both Eddie and Max nodded vigorously.

"Well, what is wrong there?" asked Klabunde now, and tapped Eddie on the shoulder. "Where's the trouble—can you tell me?"

Eddie scratched his ear in perplexity. Then he looked inquiringly at Max. At school, Eddie and Max always used to help each other out; but now, even Max's wisdom appeared to be unequal to this problem.

"Now, I'll help you to think this out," said Klabunde, and laid his two hands, with fingers outstretched, upon the table. "Just suppose that you two, with eight of your pals, are on a sailing-ship."

"What are you grinning at?" said Max to Eddie, digging him in the ribs with his elbow.

"We'll have Rollmops Willy with us!" proposed Eddie. A chorus of laughter arose.

"It's not true—we're just supposing!" declared Max.

"Well, now, let's get on with it!" continued Klabunde. "On the ship there are Fritz and that hefty boy, Frank, and fat Ernie, and his friend, 'Boss-Eye,' and—if you want him—Rollmops Willy. And you two. And another three boys. Ten, altogether. Then, suddenly comes a storm—the sailing-boat is swept ashore and breaks up. And the ten of you find yourselves stranded on a desert island."

"Oh, boy, wouldn't that be smashing!" rejoiced Eddie, so excited that he jumped up and down in his chair. "Just like Robinson Crusoe on his island, with his cave, and the Indian Friday, and everything!"

"That's right!" agreed Father Klabunde. "And, just like Robinson Crusoe, too, you have to look for something to eat. Because there aren't any shops on the island, you know, where you can go and buy a pound of potatoes or a bottle of milk. Also, this island is barren—nothing grows on it, no trees or plants. So, if you don't want to starve, you have to catch fish, with your bare hands, of course!"

"But can that be done?" wondered Eddie.

"Yes, it can be," said Max. "But it's difficult. I've read about how it's done. You must catch them very, very carefully, in your hand, and you must wait—perhaps for hours—crouching by a rock. And even then they often escape you at the last moment!"

"But why don't we use a net or a line?" asked Eddie smartly.

"Yes, that's just what you will do!" replied Father Klabunde. He rose and, with his hands in his pockets, strode up and down the room, rather like some of Eddie's teachers. "You've managed to save a length of rope from the ship, and out of that you make yourselves a fishing-net."

"Oh, may I have it?" demanded Eddie eagerly. For a moment he really thought himself to be upon the island.

"Yes," said Klabunde. "That's just the trouble: each of you wants to own the net, so then starts a regular rough-house. The hefty lad, Frank, wins, and so gets the net."

"Yes, that's so," said Eddie. "Frank's a pretty strong chap."

"True, but that wouldn't be enough to enable him to keep the net for long, with all the rest against him. But, out of the fish he catches with his net—and he gets plenty, believe me!—he gives a couple to the fat Ernie and a couple to 'Boss-Eye.' Then those two strong, well-nourished rascals attack any one of you who attempts to catch a fish with your hands, as before. So that the seven of you get weaker and weaker with hunger, because there's nothing else to eat on the island."

"But there's plenty of fish—why can't Frank give us some of his?" asked Max wonderingly.

"That's just where you're wrong, young fellow! That's not his idea at all! What he does say is: If anyone wants to eat, he must work for it; whoever wants my fish, must catch them for me, and then I'll give him a couple of fins for himself! And so he lets first one of you, then another, put out the net; but Ernie and 'Boss-Eye' stand by to watch that all the fish you catch are delivered up.

"So Frank gets fatter and fatter—he loafs about all day in the sun, and lets the seven of you work for him. Of course, he can't eat all the fish you catch—but would he give the rest to you? Not on your life! He'd rather see the fish go rotten. Because, if your stomachs aren't empty, you wouldn't be begging him to let you use his net. And you certainly do beg him, I can tell you! You see, the lazy Frank is getting more and more fish, as time goes on, because, from day to day, you get more and more skilful at the job and catch more. So, of course, you hope he'll make your share—which is your wages—bigger. Aha, don't you wish you may get it! But all he does is to let out his net less often, and then you struggle still harder, each to get the use of the net. And so, just because you have become such good fishermen, you are hungrier than ever!"

"What a rotten trick!" cried Eddie indignantly, and Max signified his agreement.

"You bet it is!" chimed in Father Klabunde. "But why is it? Whose fault is it, that your bellies are empty while Frank's is full to bursting? Is it the fault of the net—or—?"

"Why, it's Frank's fault!" chorused Eddie and Max.

"Exactly!" exclaimed Klabunde. "It's not the fault of the net, but of the person who owns the net! And that's just the same with regard to machinery. If they sack your father, Eddie, for example, the machines aren't to blame, but the people to whom the machines belong!"

He was just going to continue, when Max broke in with:

"But what about it, Father, if we don't allow them to get away with it, on the island? I mean, supposing I have a scrap with Frank and beat him, and take the net away from him?"

"That's hopeless. First of all, he's a good deal stronger than you. And then, besides, Ernie and 'Boss-Eye' wouldn't let you get to him." And his father dismissed Max's idea with a smile.

"What a rotten mess!" cried Eddie feelingly. "But supposing all seven of us boys gang up on those three robbers at once—we'd soon settle them then! And then—and then—yes! the net would belong to all of us! That would be the only way out!"

"And now you've hit it!" applauded Mrs. Klabunde, her eyes shining with pleasure and eagerness.

"Yes! All stand together! That's right! That's the whole point, boys: all work together so that the worker will at last be able to live like a human being!" cried Father Klabunde, and sat down again. "Now, have you both understood it?"

"Sure!" cried the famous chorus, Eddie and Max.

"Well, then, don't forget it!" concluded Klabunde. "And mind you act accordingly!"

For a moment everything was quiet. They all sat leaning over the table. And it seemed to Eddie that now he also was one of the family.

"Yes, Mr. Klabunde, I shall always act accordingly," said Eddie solemnly. "But I'd like to ask one thing more." He gazed at Klabunde with wide-open, bright eyes. "How is it that there are workers, and then also other people who own the machines? Why weren't human beings more clever, right from the start, so as not to let this happen?"

"I'll explain that another time, Eddie, old man.

'HOW THE LITTLE PIG SPENT CHRISTMAS EVE' AND 'HOW THE LITTLE PIG GOT THE BETTER OF THE LANDLORD'

from *Adventures of the Little Pig and Other Stories*
Martin Lawrence, 1936

Written by F[rederick] Le Gros and Ida Clark.
Illustrator not identified.

The left-wing publishing firm Lawrence and Wishart produced two small books by this husband and wife team. Frederick Le Gros Clark (1892–1977) was a distinguished social scientist who specialized in the effects of undernourishment on children's development. These stories suggest that he was interested in feeding children's minds as well as their bodies.

The volumes are made up of tales that combine aspects of many traditional story types including fairy tales, fables, and picaresque incidents of the kind from which this extract is taken. The eponymous pig has a variety of adventures that allow him to demonstrate the value of work, education, generosity, and collective action and to expose the evils of greed, drink, and exploitation. The Clarks' stories were praised for their unobtrusive didacticism, and for avoiding the tendency for children's books to insult the intelligence of children.

In 1937, *The Adventures of the Little Pig* was featured as a 'supplementary' title, meaning that it was advertised alongside the main offer, to members of the Left Book Club (LBC). The LBC was the brainchild of the publisher Victor Gollancz. Between 1936 and 1948 it promoted books likely to appeal to left-sympathizing readers. At one point there were plans to have a Junior Left Book Club, and though this never transpired, the LBC included several children's books in its newsletter, catalogues, and promotional literature.

It has been suggested that *The Adventures of the Little Pig*, with its talking animals who work together to overthrow an exploitative farmer, may have sown a seed in George Orwell's mind for the work that became *Animal Farm* (1946).[1] Orwell (also writing for Gollancz in 1936–7) fulminated against the right-wing bias of boys' weekly magazines, and he would no doubt have noticed the resemblance of the volumes to comics: the books are soft-bound, highly illustrated, and measure 18.5 × 12.5 cm.

1. No doubt there were many influences: the illustrator Gertrude Elias claimed that the idea for *Animal Farm* came from an unpublished satirical cartoon she showed Orwell. See http://www.grahamstevenson.me.uk/index.php?option=com_content&view=article&id=1446:elias-gertrude&catid=5:e&Itemid=20

HOW THE LITTLE PIG SPENT CHRISTMAS EVE

Cover, Frederick Le Gros Clark and Ida Clark's *The Adventures of the Little Pig and Other Stories*. The illustrator is not credited.

FOR many months did that little pig work in his carpenter's shop; and so well did he work that after a time he had collected up a little pile of gold and silver coins. And when Christmas was near, a great desire grew in him to see his old mother again. So on Christmas Eve he wrapped up the money carefully in an old red handkerchief and hung it on the end of a stick; and with it he set out to tramp home.

His way lay through a deep black forest. It was lonely and it grew very cold, but he whistled to keep up his spirits and he kept a good watch out on every side. After a while it became clear that he had lost his path. This was very alarming. He stopped and gazed about him. The wind was blowing wildly through the tree-tops. And as he stood quietly trying to recollect, he heard nearby the sound of sobbing and sighing.

He crept up to a bush and looked over. There on the ground lay an old jackdaw dying; and about her stood her six children sobbing as though their hearts would break, while she gave them her last words of advice and her blessing. Then one of them saw the little pig just as he would have crept away. So he came round the bush and stood there with his hat in his hand.

The old jackdaw said, "Alas, there is one thing I wish. I wish I had saved a little money to afford a hearse and two black horses with feathers at the funeral."

The little pig was so sorry that he opened his red handkerchief and took out a gold coin and gave it to the old jackdaw. She could hardly believe her eyes. "Now I shall die happy," she said; and soon after she folded her wings and died. The young jackdaws put their wings in front of their eyes and wept bitterly.

When they felt better they said, "You are very kind to us. How can we repay you?"

"I am getting very hungry," said the little pig. "You can easily fly to the town. Couldn't you get me something to eat?"

"Of course!" they cried. They all flew away gaily and came back with a large mince pie in each beak. So the little pig sat down and enjoyed himself in the shelter of the bushes.

"Now," said the jackdaws, "we must go off to arrange about the funeral. But we will keep an eye on you while you are in the forest and see you come to no harm."

Left alone, the little pig tramped on. Far away he heard the bells of Christmas Eve ringing faintly and it cheered him up. It grew darker and darker and colder and colder. At last when it was almost pitch dark, he spied a fire gleaming among the trees and he made his way towards it. Three big men sat round the fire; and for a time the little pig hesitated. But the fire was so attractive that he had to come nearer and nearer.

Then one of them saw him. "Ha," he said, "here is a traveller. What have you in that red handkerchief, little pig?"

"Please, Sir," said the little pig, "only something to eat on the way." For he saw that they were three robbers and had big sticks and daggers.

"Come and sit by the fire and have something to eat," said one of the men who looked kind and friendly. The other two were dark-faced and ugly and gazed at the little pig's bundle till he felt nervous. But it was growing very cold, so there was nothing for it but to sit down.

After they had eaten, the kindly man said, "You'd better sleep by the fire or you'll be frozen to death. Here's a blanket." The little pig thanked him and took it and wrapped himself up with his red bundle of money carefully hidden under him. For the more he saw of them, the less he liked the two ugly robbers though they smiled at him. Over them stretched a big old holly-tree with masses of red berries gleaming in the firelight. It was very like Christmas.

Soon the friendly man also tucked himself up and went to sleep. And the little pig pretended to sleep too, though he really kept wide awake listening. The two bad robbers were whispering together and he heard one say at last, "Later on I shall get up and with my big stick I shall deal him a fine blow. I want to see what's inside that red handkerchief."

The other laughed. "Ah," he said—and he jerked his thumb at the good robber who lay sleeping peacefully—"this fellow doesn't like that. He thinks we ought only to steal from the rich to give to the poor."

"I'm sick of him," answered the first one. "I'll wallop him too and be rid of him."

You may be sure the little pig did not sleep after that. He lay wondering what to do and prepared to run at any minute. But the two robbers were in no hurry. They too lay down and went to sleep.

The little pig thought and thought. He knew that if he wandered away from the fire he might easily freeze to death. At last he thought of a plan. He decided to climb up the tree and hide there. So he crept out very quietly and made his blanket look as though he were still wrapped up in it. Then with the bundle between his teeth he climbed up the tree. It was very prickly but he knew that in the branches he would still feel the warmth of the fire.

There he waited. He took care not to get just above the fire in case he should go to sleep and fall into it and be roasted. An hour went by. Then he was suddenly startled by a voice next to him and looking round he saw that it was the youngest of the jackdaws whose name was Lily, though in reality she was as black as soot.

"What are you doing, little pig?" she said.

Quickly the little pig explained what had happened.

"Why," she said, "this is dreadful. I'll get all my brothers and sisters to come and help you. You stay here." And away she flew as quietly as she had come.

As she went, one of the robbers woke up and then the other stirred. The good man still slept soundly by the fire. One of the villains rose and took his stick and crept forward to the little pig's blanket. The other crept behind him and waited just below where the little pig sat in the branches of the tree.

Then the man with the stick raised it and brought it down with a wallop on the blanket; and so excited was the little pig that he dropped the bundle of money on the ground and it fell with a clatter of gold and silver just beside the second robber who was looking on. The man with the stick turned round with surprise. He saw the bundle. He thought the other man had stolen it first. "Ha, you wretch," he shouted, "you tried to get the money first, did you, and do me out of my share." Whereupon he raised his stick and rushed at the other robber and in a moment they were fighting like fun—hitting, biting, kicking, stabbing, scratching, howling, wrestling, swearing. My word, it *was* a scene. The kindly robber woke and sat up rubbing his eyes with amazement.

And in the middle of it along came all the jackdaws, and sat down on the tree. "What shall we do?" they cried. "What shall we do?"

The little pig thought of a fine plan. He whispered to them. And then all at once and all together they started to shout from the tree, "Run. Run. The police are coming. The police are coming. Run." At the same time they picked off great handfuls of the red holly-berries and hurled them down on the two robbers who were frightened out of their wits and thought they were being shot at from right and left. They took to their heels as if the devil were after them.

Down scrambled the little pig and he and the good robber chased them with sticks, beating them till they howled; and all the jackdaws flew after them beating them with their wings. Then they all came back to the fire laughing heartily.

Next day the kindly robber took the little pig to the edge of the forest and said good-bye to him; and at the same time gave him a Christmas present about which you will hear later.

HOW THE LITTLE PIG GOT THE BETTER OF THE LANDLORD

YOU remember that the good robber, when he said good-bye to the little pig, gave him a surprising Christmas present. What was it? Well, he dived into his bag and produced a marvellous silver necklace, that he had taken from a fat Duchess, whom he robbed one evening. It was very beautiful and sparkled in the Christmas sunshine. "Give this to your old mother for a present," said the robber, and so they parted.

Of course the little pig was delighted. He went on merrily singing to himself. At last he came to the home sty. There were moss and ferns growing round the old wall and about the door hung ivy; and in the sty-yard were two large beds of Michaelmas daisies. It all looked very comfortable. Smoke came out of the chimney. The little pig knocked and his mother put her head out of the skylight of the sty. And when she saw who it was she rushed out and they embraced.

She was just getting the breakfast ready. The little pig showed her the handkerchief full of gold and silver and then presented her with the silver necklace. It just fitted her, so the Duchess must have been a fairly fat one anyway.

At breakfast the little pig observed that his mother seemed sad and anxious. So after breakfast he went out and bought her a large box of chocolates wrapped in silver paper; and with all this the humble little sty soon looked very bright and festive. But still the old mother pig was sad and anxious.

So the little pig asked her why.

At that a tear crept out of her eye and she said, "I'm so worried. I owe the farmer such a lot of rent."

"Why?" said the little pig. "Does the farmer charge rent?"

"Yes," she said. "He's a cruel mean man. He does no work, and makes all the animals pay rent. The horse has to pay rent now for his stables and the fowls for their hen-house, and the cows for the cowshed."

"Good heavens," said the little pig. "But where do they get the money from?"

His mother began to weep bitterly. "It's very hard," she said. "The fowls have to take their eggs to market to raise the money and the cows have to take their milk and the horse has to carry loads to and fro for the neighbours.

"But what can *I* take to market? I can't take sausages." And she wept so much that the silver necklace wobbled to and fro. "I owe him pounds of rent and I shall have to sell my beautiful necklace."

"No, you shan't," cried the little pig angrily, "and you shan't pay him any of the money I've brought you, which was to cheer your old age."

And then as they spoke they heard footsteps outside; and the mother pig said, "It's the farmer."

There was a knock at the door and the little pig hid behind a big vase of artificial roses in the corner, which his mother valued greatly. The farmer came in. He was thin with a long red nose and little mean eyes. The old mother pig had forgotten to take off her necklace and he saw it at once.

"Aha," he said. "So you have a silver necklace. That will just do to pay the rent you owe me. Otherwise you will be turned out in the cold this very afternoon."

The little pig was furious. He came out and said, "Fancy coming for your rent and on Christmas Day, too. You ought to be ashamed of yourself."

"Who are you?" said the farmer angrily. But the little pig was thinking very quickly how they could get the better of the farmer, who he saw was a cruel and greedy man. He suddenly hit on a clever plan.

"I see you have a perfect right to ask for your rent," he said very politely with a bow. "But you should leave this old lady alone on Christmas Day in peace. If you promise to do so, this evening you shall have the silver necklace. I promise you that."

The farmer's little eyes glistened with greed as he looked at the silver necklace. Then he said, "All right. To-night then. Where will you bring it?"

"I will bring it to those oak-trees over there," said the little pig. "You can meet me there at eight o'clock."

So the farmer said he would, and went away rubbing his hands with glee. And the little pig comforted his mother and told her all would be well; and they sat down by the fire, while he told her his adventures.

At last evening came on. Frost lay thick on the ground. A big cold full moon was rising. Then the little pig set about his plan. He went round to the horse's stable and asked the horse to lend him a rope; and the horse willingly did so.

Back in the sty that little pig made a noose at the end of the rope and then he did a clever thing. Very cunningly he took all the silver paper out of the box of chocolates and worked it round and round that rope till the noose was covered with silver paper. He carried it with him to the clump of oak-trees, and there climbing up into one of the branches, he hung up the rope in such a way that the silver noose dangled down; and it shone in the cold moonlight. He tied the other end of the rope to a branch.

Finally he gathered a little pile of five or six bricks and put them under the rope, and then fetching the carving-knife from his mother's drawer, he came out at eight o'clock and waited.

At last he heard the farmer coming; and there he was, with his long thin shadow dancing in the moonlight. He peered about him. He saw the little pig. "Ha," he said impatiently. "Here you are then. Come now. Don't keep me waiting. Where's the silver necklace?"

"I'm sorry, Sir," said the little pig, "but a jackdaw snatched it out of my hands and hung it up in the branches of the oak there. Look at it."

The farmer looked up angrily. He saw the silver rope.

"Doesn't it shine in the moonlight?" said the little pig.

The farmer hesitated. The wind howled in the hollow tree. It was very lonely. "How shall I get it?" grumbled the farmer.

"I've got a pile of bricks for you to stand on," said the little pig.

"I can't stand on them," said the farmer.

"But look how the necklace glitters in the moonlight," said the little pig.

And certainly it did look very attractive. The farmer grew greedier and greedier. At last he climbed on to the top brick and there was the silver rope within his grasp. He trembled with excitement. "It feels very light," he said. "Is it really silver?"

"That is only because your hands are cold," said the little pig. "Look how it shines. If you put it round your neck you would see it was real and strong."

So that foolish and greedy farmer put it round his neck.

And of course immediately that little pig knocked over the pile of bricks and there was the cruel farmer dangling and kicking at the end of the rope. "Help," he screamed. "Murder. Let me down! Let me go!"

"Will you promise not to ask any more rent from my mother?" said the little pig.

"Yes, yes," said the farmer, wriggling and kicking. "Never again. Let me down. I'm choking."

"Promise faithfully," said the little pig.

"Honour bright," cried the farmer. "I'm almost dead. Let me down."

"And never to ask rent from any of the other animals?"

"Never, never," sobbed the farmer who was indeed frightened.

So the little pig climbed up the oak-tree and with a carving-knife cut the rope, and down came the farmer with a bump. He staggered up and rubbed himself. After a while he hobbled away home, sobbing bitterly.

The little pig skipped joyfully back to his old mother in the sty, and they had a very festive evening together. The fire crackled on the hearth and the chocolates went down in twos and threes.

'THE BATTLE OF THE WHARF'

from *Hue and Cry*
Beaver Books/Chatto Educational, 1956

Written by Fielden Hughes

This extract comes from the novelization of a British film of the same name starring Alastair Sim which appeared in 1947 (produced by Michael Balcon; directed by Charles Crichton). The story revolves around a group of boys cracking a criminal gang's code that is being secretly published in a boys' comic. What was remarkable for a film of its time is that it was shot almost entirely on location in the streets of bombed-out London. In spirit as well as some of its plotline, it owed a good deal to Erich Kästner's *Emil and the Detectives* (English translation 1931), arguably the first children's detective story (Kästner's *The 35th of May* is discussed in Part Ten).

In cinematic terms, the German film of *Emil* (1931), with a script by Billy Wilder, was one of the first ever to be shot on location with 'synch sound', that is, with sound recorded as the cameras film the action, rather than being recorded in a studio later and 'dubbed' onto the film. In other words, a realist aesthetic attached to working-class youth culture runs from Kästner, to Wilder's screenplay, to synch location filming of the book, then to the same process with *Hue and Cry* (the movie) and on to its novelization, which was much enjoyed on its own merits in schools in the 1950s.

'The Battle of the Wharf' is the climax of both film and book, and involves the same motif found in *Emil and the Detectives*, of children (boys, actually), appearing from all over the city to corner the villains. There is a hint here of connecting young people to historical revolutionary moments that were regarded as important to socialists, such as the storming of the Bastille in 1789 and the Winter Palace in 1917, both of which have been depicted—some would say mythologized—many times since in literature, art and film.[1] There

1. Chapter 4 of Kimberley Reynolds's *Left Out: The Forgotten Tradition of Radical Publishing for Children in Britain 1910–1940* discusses in more detail the way past episodes associated with the fight for civil rights and liberties were retold for children of the Left.

is a parallel scene in a film often seen as 'progressive': *Le Ballon Rouge (The Red Balloon)* (directed by Albert Lamorisse, 1956) in which a group of 'bad' boys shoot down a balloon belonging to the main protagonist. In response, hundreds of balloons appear out of houses all over Paris, converge on the boy whose balloon was shot, and 'save' him.

The characters we meet in this chapter are the main protagonist, Joe Kirby, the boy who reads the comic and cracks the code; Larry, one of the crooks; and Nightingale, the chief villain and dissembler at the heart of the story.

Fielden Hughes (1899–1989)—full name Gwilym Fielden Hughes—was a schoolmaster, wartime broadcaster, and novelist who was commissioned by Chatto Educational to do the novelization job on the film.

CHAPTER 11

THE BATTLE OF THE WHARF

JOE's eyes were fixed in amazement on Nightingale as he lay on the floor after Larry's fist had struck him.

"Who are you?" demanded Larry once more, in even deeper tones.

Joe returned his gaze fearlessly to the big man.

"Elephant," he said promptly.

The password worked like a charm. The large face broke into a smile.

"That's more like it," said Larry. "You're young Smiler, eh?"

"That's right," replied Joe, smiling too.

Larry nodded contemptuously towards the fallen Nightingale.

"He's the boss of this warehouse, is he?"

"I think so," said Joe. "I was sent to hide here and open up for you all. He came in and caught me."

Larry turned to his followers, who were now crowded at the door, staring in.

"Tie him up and gag him, one of you. The others get on loading up the stuff."

These orders were being carried out, when it struck Joe that this was the moment for him to leave—if he could. He moved to the door, and called over his shoulder:

"I'll be keeping watch at the corner. If there's any danger, I'll walk by whistling 'The Lambeth Walk'. Pass that on to the others, will you?"

As cool as a cucumber outwardly, but shaking a great deal inwardly, Joe got out through the door. Two of the crooks were loading a lorry with the crates as he passed, but they took no notice of him.

He strolled as slowly as he could make himself till he was out of sight of the two men. Then he raced to a telephone box not far away. He dialled a number. It was the number of a public call box at Ballard's Wharf. In the box stood Arthur waiting patiently for Joe's call. The instant the bell rang he picked up the receiver.

"Elephant," he said quickly.

"The first lot of crooks have arrived," said Joe. "Tell the boys."

He peered through the glass of the box.

"The second van's pulling in now," he added.

"Right!" said Arthur joyously.

Ballard's Wharf was in a part of London where a great deal of bomb damage still remained. Tall windowless buildings stood around a vast open space where nothing remained except a few heaps of rubble.

The river flowed by, and there were a few ships at anchor near the Wharf. The telephone box where Arthur had been was on the edge of the damaged area. He came out hurriedly, and with his back to the box, put his fingers to his mouth and sent out a long shrill whistle.

Near the quay which was at the river edge of Ballard's Wharf stood a number of boys. As soon as they heard the whistle, they began to spread round a tall warehouse on the other side of the empty space cleared by the German bombs during the war. This party of boys, headed by Dicky, disappeared into the warehouse, and hurried down some dusty stairs into the cellars below.

Norman Pelley, on hearing the whistle, slipped just inside the door of the warehouse, and in a few seconds, no boys could be seen anywhere.

Meanwhile, Joe was still in his telephone box near Nightingale's warehouse in Covent Garden. He was ringing one number after another, giving orders to his forces. Fortunately for him, the crooks were too busy loading their plunder to pay any attention to him at all. If they had, this is what they would have heard:

"Is that you, Roy?"

"Yes. Go on."

"Get your crowd moving. The third van is on the job now."

Immediately, Roy slapped down the receiver in his call box, and rushed off to a park near him where several games of football were being played and watched by many boys. He raced onto the field waving his arms and shouting.

"Come on. I've got the word to move."

The news spread from one boy to another, from one game to another. Play stopped, and players and spectators began to race towards the entrance of the park, headed by Roy.

As soon as he had spoken to Roy, Joe dialled again. The telephone rang in a Post Office yard, and one of Joe's friends, a telegraph boy in uniform answered.

"All right," cried Joe. "Let 'em go."

The word was like the shot of a starter's pistol. All the telegraph boys in the yard, jumped on their bicycles and tore off down the road, headed for Ballard's Wharf.

In the same way, Joe started a crowd of boys with white coats and ice-cream tricycles. He even rang a friend who was a messenger at the B.B.C. with a mysterious message. The messenger grinned as he listened.

"All right, Joe," he replied on the telephone, "leave it all to me. It's dead easy."

With a sigh of satisfaction, Joe came out of the telephone box and went back to Nightingale's Warehouse. The two crooks were just handling the last of the crates. As he went in, Joe gave the password.

"Elephant," he said.

"Are you the boy who's been keeping a look-out?" asked one of the men.

Joe nodded and then pointed to the bound and gagged Nightingale.

"He might have heard where the stuff's going," he said. "It would be a pity if he was found before you got rid of it."

The man smiled and nodded agreement.

"You're right," he said. "We'll take him with us. And we'll cover him up with sacks so that he looks like potatoes."

They carried Nightingale to the lorry, quite helpless but also quite conscious, able to show his rage only with his glittering eyes.

Meanwhile, Joe's friend, the B.B.C. messenger had at that moment gone into the studio where the announcer was reading the news bulletin and handed him a piece of typed paper. The announcer took it without even looking at the messenger, thinking that it was—as indeed it certainly was—an extra item of news for the bulletin.

The young messenger stood by in the studio waiting for what would happen. When he had finished what he was announcing from the other papers before him, the announcer began to read from what he believed to be the special message.

"Here is a special announcement," he said, in that fine official voice of his. "All boys wanting a big adventure go immediately to Ballard's Wharf, Shadwell..."

Then he realized that something was very wrong, stopped reading, stared at the slip of paper in his hand, glared at the young messenger and took a threatening step towards him; but the boy swiftly and silently left the studio. The message—Joe's message—had reached thousands of boys. Whatever the B.B.C. now did, whatever the announcer now said, could make no difference. The call had gone out. And it was being obeyed.

Errand boys, newspaper boys, young waiters, schoolboys, boys still in short trousers, big boys in their first man's suit, boys in peaked caps, boys in all kinds of uniforms, boys from ten years old to young men of twenty heard the call to adventure, and hardly a lad within five miles of Ballard's Wharf did not drop whatever he was doing and rush away to the place mentioned on the radio, the now famous Ballard's Wharf. As they converged from all directions on the place, the roads leading to it became jammed with eager boys, shouting to one another, trying to see ahead what the adventure might be. People came to doors and windows to find out what on earth was going on in those usually quiet streets.

The vanguard of this army of boys now began to pour on to the waste space by the Wharf. They looked just like a human tide as they came, leaping over heaps of rubble, roaring in a stream between the bombed buildings, and laughing and shouting as they came, like the very sound of a great sea.

Meanwhile, the crooks had also arrived. Four vans stood on the open space in front of the warehouse. The fifth was just drawing up in line, all loaded with costly furs in crates of fruit. Some of the men were already unloading the vans, others sat in the driving seats, ready to drive off in case of need.

Larry the Bull and his man had finished unloading, and Larry was trying to start the engine of the lorry. The starter whirred but nothing else happened. Larry grabbed the starting handle and went to the front to wind. Seeing this, Joe stood up behind a heap of rubble and waved his handkerchief. It was the signal to his own party. From a dozen hiding-places the boys who had been with Joe throughout the whole adventure now rushed out, and made for the crooks at the lorries.

Larry stood up and wiped his brow. His engine would not start. But he saw the boys coming at him. To an airman up above them, it would have looked like a swarm of angry bees making straight for a large animal.

"Here!" said Larry, an ugly look coming on his face. "What's all..."

But he got no further, for in that moment, four boys sprang at him, and he was immediately very busy trying to shake them off. The others had split into groups of two or three boys and each small group made for one of the crooks. Instantly the open space was a battlefield, with strong men wriggling and punching to get themselves free of their young assailants. It might not have gone very well for Joe and his friends had it not been for the great army of boys now pouring all over the space. But they soon saw what the great adventure was to which they had been called.

With whoops of joy, they divided themselves into parties, each one consisting of many scores of boys, and joined in the fray, so that in seconds each crook found himself in the middle of a hot shouting crowd of boys, milling around, seizing his arms and legs, and giving him as good as he gave. If a crook managed to throw off one boy, three more leaped upon him at once. The men had not a chance. It was as if a handful of soldiers were trying to defend themselves against whole regiments. Besides, while the crooks hated it, the boys loved it. They had never had such a wonderful time in all their lives. Never had they dreamed of such tremendous doings. Most of them had not the faintest idea what it was all about. But one thing was perfectly clear to every boy, and that was that a number of very ugly-looking men were trying to knock a few boys about; and that was enough for them.

They did not get it all their own way. Sometimes one of the crooks would land a punch on a boy that sent him flying like a terrier from the kick of a horse. Noses bled, eyes got blacked, and lumps came up on heads. But Joe, that good general, had thought even of that.

Quietly seated on a heap of rubble was Clarry, watching the battle. Over her head was a rough notice on a pole. It said:

First Aid Post

On the ground at her feet were bandages and a large bottle of iodine, with a box of cotton wool. To her came the casualties, and like a good little nurse, she dabbed their wounds with the iodine, bound them up, murmured words of comfort and encouragement, and sent them back into battle.

Joe himself, aided by a dozen boys was dealing with the foxy-faced crook called Smoky Andrews. Suddenly in the struggle, Joe saw him draw a knife and raise it. Swiftly he picked up a piece of wood and brought it down on the back of Smoky's hand. With a yell of pain Smoky let the knife go, and collapsed under the crowd of boys. The knife flew through the air and stuck by the point in the tail-board of Smoky's lorry, by which he had been standing when he was attacked. And inside that lorry was Mr. Nightingale, bound and gagged but very much awake. He saw the knife, and knew it was his chance to get out of the terrible uproar. He edged forward on his elbows and back till he could cut his bonds on the upright knife. Once his hands were free, he swiftly freed his feet and took off his gag. Then he pulled aside the curtain behind the driver's place, got into the seat, started the engine, and the lorry lurched off. Joe saw it, pushed his way out of the crowd wrestling with Smoky Andrews, and with a yell of "Stop that van!" he tore off after it.

The lorry was increasing in speed, so Joe made a flying leap and landed on the tail-board. He was alone with Nightingale.

MICKY MONGREL, THE CLASS CONSCIOUS DOG NO. 2, 'WHITEWASH'

Daily Worker, 3 January 1930

Illustrated by 'Zelda' [pen name of Gladys Keable (née Main)]

This cartoon was part of a series about Micky Mongrel, which started in the *Daily Worker* right from its first days in 1930 (see pp. 147, 254, 322, 391, and 442 for the others). Notes on the 'Children's Corner', its editor, and *Daily Worker Children's Annuals* can be found in Part Five.

ADVENTURES OF MICKY MONGREL. NO. 2.

YESTERDAY WE LEFT MICKY MONGREL IN A BUILDER'S YARD, PINCHING SOME WHITEWASH.

MICKY took the whitewash home, and waited until it was dark. Then he set out and, under a lamp, wrote in large, though wobbly, letters "THE DAILY WORKER FIGHTS THE BOSSES." He felt pleased with this, so went right down the road writing different slogans on the ground. At the end was a nice blank wall. "What a lovely place for a slogan!" thought Micky. He was feeling very bold. But, take care, Micky! What is that light creeping along so near you?

This cartoon was part of a series about 'Micky Mongrel, the class conscious dog', which started in the *Daily Worker* from its first days in 1930.

PART TWO

THE WAR AGAINST WAR

INTRODUCTION

'Do not think that he who loves his own country must hate and despise other nations, or wish for war, which is a remnant of barbarism' (in Shortt, 1922 1).' So reads the ninth of the ten Socialist Sunday School (SSS) precepts learned by children who attended one of the 120 schools run by the National Council of British Socialist Sunday Schools. The SSS (background details for this movement can be found in the Introduction to Part One) feature in a 1922 memorandum on 'Socialist and Revolutionary Schools' produced by then Home Secretary Edward Shortt in response to concerns that the SSS and associated organizations and publications were seditious and blasphemous. Shortt concluded that the accusations could not be sustained, but the fact that he felt the need to investigate and report is evidence that the anti-establishment nature of these organizations for the young made the authorities uneasy. The SSS precepts underpinned the curriculum; arguably, the most problematic precept for an imperial nation that relied on the suppression of other countries for its wealth, security, and food supply was the ninth, with its rejection of war and enmity based on patriotism.

It is often claimed that in the years up to the First World War, children's literature was a form of military propaganda (see, for instance, Fussell, 1975, or Castle, 1996). There *is* evidence that some boys were inspired by the tales of camaraderie, heroism, and self-sacrifice found in mainstream war stories, but as the following extracts show, from 1900 to 1960 those on the left and unaffiliated pacifist organizations regularly produced counter-narratives that helped change public attitudes to war. In radical poems, songs, stories, pageants, picturebooks, personal accounts, novels, and in due course photojournalism in juvenile periodicals, children and young people were encouraged to focus on the way war enriched a few, but had devastating effects on the bodies and lives of ordinary people. Vivid descriptions of the grotesque and chaotic nature of the battlefield undermined traditional stories of the excitement, nobility, and glory of war. The ethics of manufacturing armaments and military aggression for the purposes of enrichment through colonization were also interrogated. Perhaps more worrying to many in authority, children's literature that opposed war questioned the very legitimacy of national governments and patriotism, and urged the young to resist attempts to recruit them in any future conflict. The SSS effectively waged a war against war, teaching scholars arguments against war, having them mount tableaux and performances on the theme of peace, and establishing the Young Socialist Citizen Corps whose motto was, 'The children of all lands shall unite for Peace.'

Throughout the period covered by this volume, children of the Left read eclectically, and many will have enjoyed popular war stories alongside the materials recommended by the SSS, the Young Communist League, the Woodcraft Folk, and the other left-leaning organizations that grew up in the early and middle twentieth century. In *The Intellectual Life of the British Working Class* (2001), Jonathan Rose documents this kind of reading pattern, a typical example being that of Percy Wall (b. 1893), who as a boy enjoyed reading mainstream writing for children such as the *Magnet* and the novels of G. A. Henty but also 'studied the *Clarion* [a weekly socialist newspaper], the *Freethinker*, *The Struggle of the Bulgarians for Independence* and *The Philippine Martyrs* for their politics' (332). The opportunity to read alternative accounts of war, especially in combination with instruction and discussion in youth groups, families, and communities, will have affected the extent to which such tales could impart a desire to join in military action or to see war as justifiable. Percy Wall, for instance, was a conscientious objector in the First World War.

Wall does not refer to any children's books, but even when he was a boy, children's literature offered young readers politically alternative perspectives and discourses. Among the first pacifist stories in wide circulation was Leo Tolstoy's 'Ivan the Fool', which was available in English translation from 1895. Tolstoy's tale offers a model of passive resistance in the face of military aggression and underlines the social and economic benefits of peace over war. Pacifist stories were a staple part of radical children's literature, but most left-wing organizations distinguished between the need to resist being co-opted into an unjust war and the possibility that there might be occasions when it was justifiable to take up arms (for some, this included supporting participation in the First World War). For example, number four of the ten maxims of the Proletarian School Movement, formed in 1918 as a breakaway group of the SSS, taught: 'Thou shalt not take part in any bourgeois war, for all modern wars are the result of the clash of economic interests, and your duty as an internationalist is to wage class-war against all such wars' (Shortt, 1922 3). Class-war was intended to be waged at the ideological level, but it did not preclude fighting; fighting in defence of one's country was also acceptable.

From the end of the First World War to the mid-1930s, anti-war activism permeated British culture, and young people and radical children's literature were fully involved. Although there were divisions among prominent leaders of left-wing organizations, all the associated youth organizations produced newsletters, leaflets, or magazines featuring anti-war articles and stories, reading lists, and announcements for and reports from peace rallies in the UK and abroad. With the rise of fascism in the 1930s, many who had previously renounced war accepted the necessity of fighting, though as Olaf Stapledon's vision of the future in Part Ten of this volume shows, lessons in the destructive nature of war continued. The end of the Second World War saw a return to anti-war demonstrations, now galvanized by awareness of the destructive potential of nuclear weapons. The final extract in this part was written in 1950, but its 'strange dream' of a world without war captures the vision imparted to children through radical children's literature across the first half of the twentieth century.

WAR IN DOLLYLAND

Ward Lock and Co, 1915

Written by Harry Golding. Photographs by Albert Friend

Published in the second year of the First World War, with its attack on the senselessness, bad management, and wasteful nature of war, this striking picturebook flies in the face of conventional war stories for children. Traditionally, juvenile stories about battlefields, such as those by G. A. Henty and Percy Westerman, were steeped in patriotic nationalism. Their pages feature military heroes and brave British campaigns. By contrast, in Harry Golding's (d. 1947) and Albert Friend's (n.d.) story there is little to rouse readers' pride. Albert Friend's photographs of toys against backdrops of cardboard, paper, and string, evoke children's art and play in ways that imply both that those in charge of fighting troops have failed to learn that war is not a game, and that their grasp of the complexities and ethical dilemmas posed by war is no better than a child's.

The book excoriates the established view of war. Brave, long-suffering soldiers are sent to their deaths in a conflict that is clearly pointless: the antagonists are fighting about the shape of their heads, although 'all their heads were precisely the same, so there was nothing whatever to quarrel about' (11). Illustrations include one of a doll-soldier before a firing squad that must have been particularly disturbing at a time when large numbers of soldiers were being shot as 'cowards' and 'deserters', especially since many of those required to form firing squads and some of those who stood before them were only teenagers who not long before would have been playing with their own toys. *War in Dollyland* goes on to show dead and injured soldiers on the battlefield; it also characterizes military leaders as buffoons, and points to the inadequacy of monuments to compensate for the sacrifices of those they memorialize.

War in Dollyland is a remarkable book, and remarkably little is known about its creators. Ward Lock and Co. was a mainstream publisher, probably best known for publishing Mrs. Isabella Beeton, the *Red Guides* for tourists, and a number of authors associated with children including R. M. Ballantyne, Daniel

Defoe, and Thomas Hughes. Their publishing and distribution networks suggest that the book would have been widely available; the firm went through many manifestations, and as far as can be ascertained, no print, production, or sales records relating to it survive. Harry Golding was one of their regular authors and editors, normally responsible for mass-market compilations and a best-selling series of *Wonder* books. He produced nothing else comparable to *War in Dollyland*, which was probably inspired by H. G. Wells's *Little Wars* (1913).

WAR IN DOLLYLAND

A Book and a Game

The war fever is catching—awfully catching. You'd never think it would spread to Dollyland, but it does, for dolls are just as stupid as human beings, which is saying a good deal.

The Flat Heads began it, but you couldn't blame them. Their heads were not flat really, though their caps were, so you can hardly be surprised that they objected strongly to being known as 'Fat Heads'. After that the Flat Heads said the Wooden Heads were 'Pudd'n Heads' and everybody knew that war was bound to come. It only made matters worse that really all their heads were precisely the same, so there was nothing whatever to quarrel about. But these are always the worst sort of wars.

The Wooden Heads were first in the field. Indeed it was the proud boast of their two famous regiments of Guards, the Wonder Brigade, that they were always 'Red and Ready'. But the Flat Heads had a very fine force of cavalry and could move more quickly.

'We'll wait for them', said the Wooden Head General. So he lined up his men behind a spiked barricade, and placed his artillery so that they could fire without killing their own side, which was a very clever thing to do, and led all the newspapers to say he was beyond doubt the greatest general since Napoleon Bonaparte. What he relied on chiefly was the great water-cannon, a new invention that had been carefully kept secret from the enemy. There were two of them really, but 'cannon' may mean either one or many. The word was purposely used to deceive the enemy.

The Flat Heads were rather careful at first, being afraid of a trap. Although they had only one cannon, they had a great advantage over the Wooden Heads in being armed with long, sharply-pointed pencils. After they had marched some way through the Wooden Heads' country without seeing a soldier, the General grew more and more nervous, and finally sent the Sergeant Major up a hill to have a good look round with the telescope.

'Ship ahoy!' reported the Sergeant-Major, who had once been in the Navy and could never sort out the proper terms.

'Ship be bothered,' said the General, charging up the hill at such a rate that the wind blew off his cap and he nearly capsized.

The Sergeant-Major was purposely looking through the wrong end of the telescope which of course made everything smaller.

'Very tiny force, sir,' he reported. 'They'll run directly.'

'Then forward!' cried the General, and waved his arms so violently that he nearly fell off his horse again.

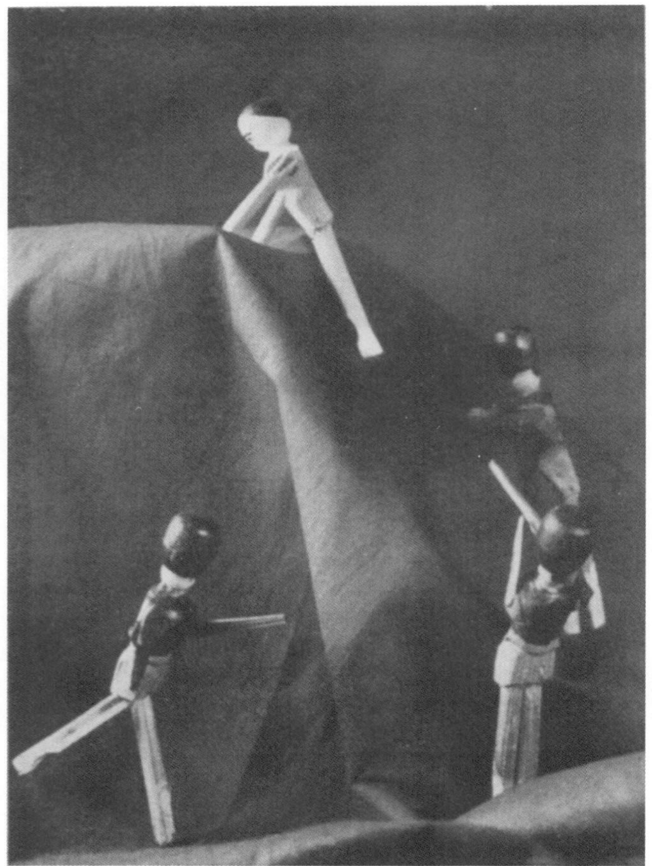

What had made him so uneasy was that he had sent out a spy two or three days before and the spy had not returned.

You can see why.

Perhaps the spy's life might have been spared under other circumstances. But he had been caught in the very act of looking down on the secret water-cannon, and the Wooden Heads rightly felt that no mercy could be shown.

The spy was led out at dawn…

He died as a brave man should.

Soon after the Sergeant-Major had reported, the whole army of Flat Heads declared that they could see the enemy with their naked eyes. That is the worst of red. If only the Wooden Heads had been less vain they would have worn khaki and avoided the bitter loss that now befell them. For the Flat Heads managed to approach quite unseen and instead of attacking from the front worked round to the flank and even contrived to get their big gun in position before the Wooden Head sentry was aware of their presence. The fact is, it had started to rain and the poor boy was afraid his paint would run, so he had taken shelter in the sentry-box and of course couldn't be expected to see out of the side, especially as the door was in the way.

'Halt! Who goes there?' he shouted, but by this time the Wooden Head General had seen the danger and given the order, 'Left Turn!' The Wonder Brigade turned as one man, in spite of the fact that they were half asleep. (You must remember they had been standing a long time and standing is very tiring).

'Present arms!' shouted the General, but before the order could be obeyed *Bang!* went the Flat Heads' cannon.

The aim was deadly. The stout Wooden Head Corporal made a first-rate target and the whole front rank fell with him.

'Hooray!' shouted the Flat Heads.

'Charge! My brave Pencillers', cried their General.

The gun was rushed to the rear and the Flat Head cavalry surged over the barricade. It seemed that nothing could withstand them.

But the Wooden Heads were now fully awake and poured volley after volley into the attacking ranks. Their coolness in battle, considering how warm were their coats, was amazing, and won the admiration even of their enemies.

None the less, the whole regiment would have been wiped out had it not been for the prompt action of Little Billy, who was described in the War Office List as the 'Royal Flying Corps'. He didn't really fly but ballooned. Anyway, he was soon high in the air, and to his great delight had no sooner focussed the telescope than he caught sight of the reserve battalion of the Wonder Brigade resting behind a hill. By frantic signals he made them understand the danger, and they rushed to the assistance of their sorely-tried comrades.

What were the obstacles and dangers to men of their spirit? A wide stream separated them from the field of battle, but the engineers seized a wash-tub from a cottage close by (it was washing day, too, and the lady badly wanted the tub), and in a very few minutes made a strong bridge, across which they passed in safety, Gunner Jim bravely leading the way with the other water-cannon. Unfortunately, the Commanding Officer got stuck in the mud, and couldn't be pulled out in time for the battle, though it would have made no difference if he had been.

Meanwhile the gallant first division of the Wonder Brigade were still holding their own against fearful odds. Man after man was bowled over, and at one time the General himself was in danger of being killed or captured. Although badly wounded in the left leg, one of his gallant men bravely jumped to the rescue, while another fired in the nick of time and in two rounds killed both the Flat Head General and the Sergeant Major.

Imagine, if you can, how busy the Hospital was all this time! A good stock of new arms and legs had been laid in, but it was soon seen that the paste would run short. The Medical Officer was in despair, when a few drops from the famous water-cannon fell in the paste-tub and the situation was saved. Yet the story that got into the Flat Head newspapers was that the Wooden Heads had actually fired on the Red Cross Hospital. A special word of praise should be given to the nurses, and the ambulance men were simply wonderful.

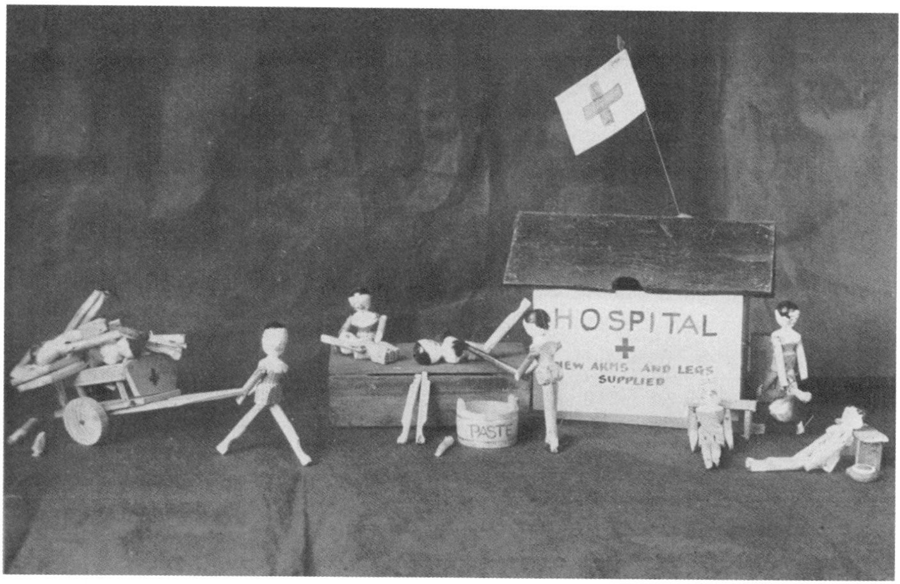

Just when things were at their worst the Wooden Head reinforcements rushed on the scene. They would have arrived sooner only they had forgotten (or never learnt) that a water-cannon is no good without water, and they had to go back to the stream for it (the CO—you know of course that CO is short for Commanding Officer and sounds much grander—was still stuck in the mud at that time).

'Charge!' shouted all the Wooden Heads together (they had agreed to do this to save quarrelling as to who should take the CO's place).

The noise alone struck terror in the Flat Head ranks, but it was followed by a full discharge from the powerful water-cannon and a heavy volley from the entire second division of the Wonder Brigade, and the hearts of even the bravest Pencillers sank within them.

It must be remembered that they had been fighting for fully five minutes, while the second Wooden Head division was quite fresh. The Flat Heads tried one final onslaught, but nothing could stand against that fearful cannon. Of all the brave host who had invaded the Wooden Head country but two returned to tell the tale.

The Wooden Heads rightly felt that so glorious a victory should be commemorated. A special medal was struck and given to every member of the Wonder Brigade. The few surviving members of the first division were also given a new coat of paint.

As for the fallen, a grateful country could only erect a worthy monument to their memory. To this day the Wooden Head children salute it as they pass.

You will be glad to know that in the hour of victory the Wooden Heads were merciful and remembered that, after all, they and the Flat Heads were members of the same great Doll Family.

'Forget and forgive,' they said and soon the blessings of Peace came again to the two distracted peoples...

'DON'T SHOOT YOUR CLASS!'

The Revolution, June 1918

Written by Tom Anderson

Though this piece is unsigned, the bound copy of *The Revolution* held by the Marx Memorial Library in London is annotated with the message that all unattributed work is by TA. Tom Anderson (1863–1947) was an active trade unionist who was involved in leading a major strike in Glasgow. As a result, he was blacklisted and unable to work at his carpenter's trade. He was rescued from this plight by a supporter who set him up in a draper's shop, enabling him to finance his own revolutionary activities. From the 1890s Anderson dedicated himself to the radical education of working-class children, claiming that he had set up the first Socialist Sunday School (SSS) in 1894.[1]

It soon became clear that Anderson's ideas about the kind of socialism to be taught were very different from those of the leadership of the SSS movement, and in 1910 he broke away to found a more radical Socialist School. Inspired by the February 1917 Russian Revolution, he changed the name to the Proletarian Schools and produced for it a set of rules known as the Proletarian Maxims, of which the fifth was 'Thou Shalt Teach Revolution'. The associated journal, *The Revolution*, was aimed at the young workers of the country. The first number appeared in June 1917, and from the beginning it mentioned events that were controversial under the wide-ranging Defence of the Realm Act (DORA), which reached into every aspect of social life and curbed the freedom of the press. Controversial subjects covered in *The Revolution* included references to Karl Liebknecht, imprisoned in Germany for his work against the war, and James Connolly, leader of the Easter Uprising in Ireland the year before.

The article printed here, which appeared in June 1918, the time of the German Spring Offensive, would have been considered particularly seditious as it actively campaigns for soldiers not to kill fellow workers fighting on the other side. This plea to workers was central to the class consciousness of the

1. As explained in the Introduction to Part One, the first Socialist Sunday School was in fact set up in 1892 by Mary Gray of the Social Democratic Federation in 1892.

international working-class movement. The First World War tested this principle and thereby split the movement, causing the collapse of the Socialist International, the Anarchist movement, and other working-class institutions. The success of the Russian Revolution in October 1917, and the mutinies and unrest amongst the ordinary soldiers during the last year of the war, meant that this call for international working-class solidarity was at the forefront of revolutionary thinking. The article comprises two pages of powerful rhetoric, and it can be assumed it was the reason why this issue was the last produced, as it almost certainly fell foul of DORA.

DON'T SHOOT YOUR CLASS!

YOUNG WORKER,—You will be asked, or forced, some day to don a hateful dress. With a rifle on your shoulder and a bayonet by your side, you will march under orders to slay and be slain.

Before you go, before your mind becomes a mechanical echo of the drill sergeant's voice, we ask you TO THINK.

You are a child of the working class. You were born of parents who toiled for a living. You own no land, no country, and no REAL wealth. The land, the country, and the wealth therein are all owned by a few men of another class. You cannot live without the permission of the men of the class who own these things, and because to gain that permission you must labour at the bidding of that class, it is truly a fact that you are a slave and your class a slave class.

Yet you, a slave, a member of a subject class, are ordered to don uniform and march away to slay.

To slay whom? The people who oppress you; the people who live in luxury whilst you toil and starve all your days?

NO! You will march away to shoot your own class your brothers who under another flag and speaking another tongue, will likewise march to war at their masters bidding to meet and fight you.

War! What is war? The capitalist class of all countries exists by and for the extraction of profits from the unpaid labour of the working class. The hunt for profits has speeded up the great wealth producing machines so that to-day we workers produce more than our masters can sell.

New markets are sought by the capitalists of Germany, France, Britain, America, Japan, etc. Their capital has grown so large, so international, that much of that capital cannot find room and means to reap profit for its owners. The owners of capital fall out and quarrel, each wanting to secure plenty of plunder. The owners of capital are grouped in different countries, and alliances are made between these different groups, and these alliances plot and scheme by secret diplomacy to beat their rivals and secure to themselves the sole right to exploit foreign countries.

This is what has occurred in Europe. In Europe two alliances of capital face each other as sworn enemies, each seeking the others' destruction, for they realise that there is not room for all.

One alliance is Germany, Austria, and Turkey, and the other is Great Britain, France, Italy, and America. German capitalists are seeking territorial aggrandisement, casting envious eyes on England's world trade. French capitalists want the rich lands of Alsace-Lorraine with its great mineral deposits, now held by Germany; British capitalists wish to maintain their world supremacy and to see their most dangerous competitor, Germany, vanquished. American capitalists want the dollars that are to be made from the sale of munitions to the Allies.

And you, young workers of Britain, France, Germany, Austria, and America are standing face to face maiming, slaying, and murdering each other.

And all for what?

That your masters may settle the ownership of the wealth that is not yours and has never been yours, although you created it.

Brother! wherever you are, no matter your nationality, is it not high time you began to think and act differently? We workers are brothers the wide world over; we share the same labour; we suffer from the same oppression—why should we hack, kill, and massacre each other? We are of the working class; we are international. Victims of the same capitalist system, we cannot afford to let the war drums of our masters stampede us to war, and to allow ignorance to blind ourselves to our own true interests.

Comrades! There is a great big happy world of freedom! Of joyous happiness, of true love, of equal rights for all to live and enjoy the fruits of their labour. There is a world where the crowded slums of the city hell and the weary grind of machine like toil are no more. Where starving children and overfed pet dogs do not exist, and where cringing workmen and overbearing slave-drivers are not met with. There is a world where the cannon stands in the museum along with cruel relics such as the rack and the whipping-post; a world where to slay or to slave shall indicate something lower than manhood.

That world is the future Socialist Commonwealth. It is the shining goal only to be reached by the solidarity of Labour!

Brothers of all lands! Think before you shoot your own class. Think before you go to war. Forget the cunning lies your masters have told you. Stop fighting to keep your chains fettered fast and start right here and now to strike a blow for the emancipation of yourself and your class.

All over the world we workers are one: white, black, brown, or yellow, English, French, German, Turk, or Africander; all are one despite difference of race and tongue. And if we are intelligent enough we will form a REAL International, sworn only to serve our own class, to achieve our emancipation, to achieve Socialism.

SOCIALISM! It is the new world vision of the workers.

Socialism! It is the only hope of the workers! It spells the freeing of the human race from the thrall of greed. It means the breaking of the bloodstained bayonet and the hoisting of the red flag of universal kinship.

This is an end worth striving for, living for, and dying for. And to that end, little comrade of the working class, we implore you NOT TO SHOOT YOUR CLASS.

NOT SO QUIET: STEPDAUGHTERS OF WAR

Albert E. Marriott, 1930

Written by Helen Zenna Smith (pen-name of Evadne Price)

Commissioned as a response to Erich Remarque's *All Quiet on the Western Front* (1929), *Not So Quiet* shows events on the front from a female perspective. Helen Zenna Smith is both the name of the central character and the pen name used by Evadne Price (1888?–1985), a journalist and writer of children's stories and romantic fiction.[1] The shared name implies that *Not So Quiet* is the first-hand account of a young voluntary aid detachment (VAD) ambulance driver; while Price herself had no experience of the battlefield, she claimed her novel was based on the diary (now lost) of ambulance driver Winifred Constance Young. *Not So Quiet* purports to speak for a generation whose parents sent 'their children to kill the children of other parents' (164). The account given by the narrating persona, Nellie, known at the front as 'Smithy', of the atrocities witnessed and experienced by those on or near the battlefield is set against pronouncements about the nobility and value of the war by her parents and other adults safely at home.

Although not written for children, the novel has many features characteristic of juvenile fiction. For instance, it borrows such tropes from the school story as midnight feasts, punishments, communal sleeping arrangements, bullies, insider slang, and a sadistic 'head teacher' in the form of the Commandant. Price's use of first-person address, the confessional nature of the writing, its dependence on colloquial speech, and its pitting of youth against the establishment are standard characteristics of Young Adult fiction, a category not yet created in 1930. It would certainly have spoken to young left-leaning readers.

These extracts capture Smithy's anger at the war, her parents' generation, and particularly women like her mother who think it is patriotic to send their sons and daughters to the frontline.

1. The ambiguity surrounding both Price's life and the origins of this novel are summarized in George Simmers's Research Blog, accessed at https://greatwarfiction.wordpress.com/helen-zenna-smith-and-the-disguises-of-evadne-price/.

CHAPTER I

NOT SO QUIET . . .

STEPDAUGHTERS OF WAR

WE have just wakened from our first decent sleep for weeks—eight glorious dreamless hours of utter exhaustion. The guns are still booming in the distance as energetically as when we fell on our camp beds without the formality of removing our uniforms, shoes, gaiters or underclothing. We have not had our garments off for nine days, but there has been an unexpected lull this afternoon; no evacuations, only one funeral, and very few punishments, though we feel the usual midnight whistle will break our run of luck any time now. That gives us ten minutes to dress and stand by ambulances ready for convoy duty. In the meantime we snuggle neck-high in our flea-bags and munch slabs of chocolate and stale biscuits. We have slept like logs through the evening meal—all except Tosh, who never misses a food-call on principle. It is her turn to make the Bovril. We gloatingly watch her light the little spirit lamp. We are hungry, but we are used to hunger. We are always hungry in varying degrees—hungry, starving, or ravenous. The canteen food is vile at its best; at its worst it defies description—except from Tosh. We have existed mostly on Bovril, biscuits, and slab chocolate since arriving in France, and when all is said and done it is a colourless, discouraging diet for young women of twenty-three—which our six ages average—who are doing men's work. Tosh is the only one who can systematically eat the canteen tack without vomiting or coming out in food boils; but she has a stomach as strong as a horse's. Also, she has been out longer than the rest of us and is more hardened. At first her inside used to revolt as ours still does, but she thinks that in another month or so she could eat what the food resembles without turning a hair.

The girl in the next bed, known as "The B.F.," objects to this remark on the grounds of coarseness, but Tosh only grins. The rest of us take no notice.... We know the B.F.'s protests are merely for refinement's sake. Tosh the sinner is not of the common herd. She is the niece of an earl. That, in the B.F.'s eyes, covers a multitude of Anglo-Saxon franknesses. [...]

...Tosh is the idol of the entire convoy, not only of this room. I have adored her since the first night I arrived, that ghastly first night I was shoved on to an ambulance and told to meet my first convoy of wounded. My nerves were on edge, and the first ghastly glimpse of blood and shattered men sent me completely to pieces. [...]

I whimpered like a puppy. . . . I couldn't go on. . . . I was a coward. . . . I couldn't face those stretchers of moaning men again. . . . men torn and bleeding and raving. . . . [. . .]

Tosh laughed a funny, queer laugh. "And the admiring family at home who are basking in your reflected glory? 'My girl's doing her bit—driving an ambulance very near the line.' . . . . You'll never have the pluck to crawl home and admit you're ordinary flesh and blood. Can't you hear them? 'Well, back *already*/You didn't stay *long*, did you?' No, Smithy, you're one of England's Splendid Daughters, proud to do their bit for the dear old flag, and one of England's Splendid Daughters you'll stay until you crock up or find some other decent excuse to go home covered in glory. It takes nerve to carry on here, but it takes twice as much to go home to flag-crazy mothers and fathers. . . ." [. . .]

"What was supper like, Tosh?" asks Etta Potato.

Tosh tells her in one graphic word, and The B.F. clutches her bosom dramatically and cries: "Tosh!" Tosh christened her The B.F., but we are quite convinced that, although flattered at being on nickname level with the niece of an earl, she hasn't the vaguest notion that the cryptic letters signify anything other than her own initials—Bertina Farmer.

The B.F. is quite liked. She is fearfully "refeened and neece," but we forgive her that: she is such a harmless ass. Her definition of a true lady is one who is ignorant of the simplest domestic details to the point of imbecility. She insisted on helplessly inquiring the first day she came over *however* one knew when water had reached boiling point. The servants at home had always boiled the family water, she said. She was very shocked at Tosh's coarse comment on this form of economy in the home.

The B.F. is like a Harrison Fisher girl on a magazine cover, and is frankly disappointed with the War. The War Office has not quite played the game sending her here. She had an idea being out in France was a kind of perpetual picnic minus the restrictions of home life. She saw herself in a depot, the cynosure of innumerable admiring male eyes. It seems such a waste of a well-cut uniform to be in a place where the men are too wounded or too harassed to regard women other than cogs in the great machinery, and the women are too worn out to care whether they do or not. She intends to transfer to the base at the earliest opportunity. "For," she said the other day, "surely you can do your bit just as patriotically in an amusing place where there are amusing officers!"

(The B.F. is very fond of talking about "doing her bit." She would go down terribly well with my parents.)

Tosh gravely advised her not to overdo "doing her bit" with the amusing officers, in case she was not so amused in the end.

The B.F. is pretty and soft and rather plump. She was comically like a ruffled doll as she drew herself up. "I can tell by your face, Tosh, you're being obscene, but I do *not* see the point."

"Oh, you'll see *that* if you overdo 'doing your bit,' " laughed Tosh. "Won't she, girls?"

"Do you know what she means?" inquired The B.F. piteously.

We did.

A few weeks ago we should not have known. [....]

If the War goes on and on and on and I stay out here for the duration, I shall never be able to meet a train-load of casualties without the same ghastly nausea stealing over me as on that first never-to-be-forgotten night. Most of the drivers grow hardened after the first week. They fortify themselves with thoughts of how they are helping to alleviate the sufferings of wretched men, and find consolation in so thinking. But I cannot. I am not the type that breeds warriors. I am the type that should have stayed at home, that shrinks from blood and filth, and is completely devoid of pluck. In other words, I am a coward.... A rank coward. I have no guts. It takes every ounce of will-power I possess to stick to my post when I see the train rounding the bend. I choke my sickness back into my throat, and grip the wheel, and tell myself it is all a horrible nightmare... soon I shall awaken in my satin-covered bed on Wimbledon Common... what I can picture with such awful vividness doesn't really exist....

I have schooled myself to stop fainting at the sight of blood. I have schooled myself not to vomit at the smell of wounds and stale blood, but view these sad bodies with professional calm I shall never be able to. I may be helping to alleviate the sufferings of wretched men, but commonsense rises up and insists that the necessity should never have arisen. I become savage at the futility. A war to end war, my mother writes. Never. In twenty years it will repeat itself. And twenty years after that. Again and again, as long as we breed women like my mother and Mrs. Evans-Mawnington. And we are breeding them. Etta Potato and The B.F.—two out of a roomful of six. Mother and Mrs. Evans-Mawnington all over again.

Oh, come with me, Mother and Mrs. Evans-Mawnington. Let me show you the exhibits straight from the battlefield. This will be something original to tell your committees, while they knit their endless miles of khaki scarves,... something to spout from the platform at your recruiting meetings. Come with me. Stand just there.

Here we have the convoy gliding into the station now, slowly, so slowly. In a minute it will disgorge its sorry cargo. My ambulance doors are open, waiting to receive. See, the train has stopped. Through the occasionally drawn blinds you will observe the trays slotted into the sides of the train. Look closely, Mother and Mrs. Evans-Mawnington, and you shall see what you shall see. Those trays each contain something that was once a whole man... the heroes who have done their bit for King and country... the heroes who marched blithely through the streets of London Town singing "Tipperary," while you cheered and waved your flags hysterically. They are not singing now, you will observe. Shut your ears, Mother and Mrs. Evans-Mawnington, lest their groans and heart-rending cries linger as long in your memory as in the memory of the daughter you sent out to help win the War.

See the stretcher-bearers lifting the trays one by one, slotting them deftly into my ambulance. Out of the way quickly, Mother and Mrs. Evans-Mawnington—lift your silken skirts aside . . . a man is spewing blood, the moving has upset him, finished him. . . . He will die on the way to hospital if he doesn't die before the ambulance is loaded. I know. . . . All this is old history to me. Sorry this has happened. It isn't pretty to see a hero spewing up his life's blood in public, is it? Much more romantic to see him in the picture papers being awarded the V.C., even if he is minus a limb or two. A most unfortunate occurrence!

That man strapped down? That raving, blaspheming creature screaming filthy words you don't know the meaning of . . . words your daughter uses in everyday conversation, a habit she has contracted from vulgar contact of this kind. Oh, merely gone mad, Mother and Mrs. Evans-Mawnington. He may have seen a headless body running on and on, with blood spurting from the trunk. The crackle of the frost-stiff dead men packing the duck-boards watertight may have gradually undermined his reason. There are many things the sitters tell me on our long night rides that could have done this.

No, not shell-shock. The shell-shock cases take it more quietly as a rule, unless they are suddenly startled. Let me find you an example. Ah, the man they are bringing out now. The one staring straight ahead at nothing . . . twitching, twitching, twitching, each limb working in a different direction, like a Jumping Jack worked by a jerking string. Look at him, both of you. Bloody awful, isn't it, Mother and Mrs. Evans-Mawnington? That's shell-shock. If you dropped your handbag on the platform, he would start to rave as madly as the other. What? You won't try the experiment? You can't watch him? Why not? *Why not?* I have to, every night. Why the hell can't you do it for once? Damn your eyes.

Forgive me, Mother and Mrs. Evans-Mawnington. That was not the kind of language a nicely-brought-up young lady from Wimbledon Common uses. I forget myself. We will begin again.

See the man they are fitting into the bottom slot. He is coughing badly. No, not pneumonia. Not tuberculosis. Nothing so picturesque. Gently, gently, stretcher-bearers . . . he is about done. He is coughing up clots of pinky-green filth. Only his lungs, Mother and Mrs. Evans-Mawnington. He is coughing well to-night. That is gas. You've heard of gas, haven't you? It burns and shrivels the lungs to . . . to the mess you see on the ambulance floor there. He's about the age of Bertie, Mother. Not unlike Bertie, either, with his gentle brown eyes and fair curly hair. Bertie would look up pleadingly like that in between coughing up his lungs. . . . The son you have so generously given to the War. The son you are so eager to send out to the trenches before Roy Evans-Mawnington, in case Mrs. Evans-Mawnington scores over you at the next recruiting meeting. . . . "I have given my only son."

Cough, cough, little fair-haired boy. Perhaps somewhere your mother is thinking of you . . . boasting of the life she has so nobly given . . . the life you thought was your own, but which is hers to squander as she thinks fit. "My boy is not a slacker, thank God." Cough away, little boy, cough away. What does it matter, providing your mother doesn't have to face the shame of her son's cowardice?

These are sitters. The man they are hoisting up beside me, and the two who sit in the ambulance. Blighty cases . . . broken arms and trench feet . . . mere trifles. The smell? Disgusting, isn't it? Sweaty socks and feet swollen to twice their size . . . purple, blue, red . . . big black blisters filled with yellow matter. Quite a colour-scheme, isn't it? Have I made you vomit? I must again ask pardon. My conversation is daily growing less refined. Spew and vomit and sweat . . . I had forgotten these words are not used in the best drawing-rooms on Wimbledon Common.

But I am wasting time. I must go in a minute. I am nearly loaded. The stretcher they are putting on one side? Oh, a most ordinary exhibit, . . . the groaning man to whom the smallest jolt is red hell . . . a mere bellyful of shrapnel. They are holding him over till the next journey. He is not as urgent as the helpless thing there, that trunk without arms and legs, the remnants of a human being, incapable even of pleading to be put out of his misery because his jaw has been half shot away. . . . No, don't meet his eyes, they are too alive. Something of their malevolence might remain with you all the rest of your days, . . . those sock-filled, committee-crowded days of yours.

Gaze on the heroes who have so nobly upheld your traditions, Mother and Mrs. Evans-Mawnington. Take a good look at them. . . . The heroes you will sentimentalise over until peace is declared, and allow to starve for ever and ever, amen, afterwards. Don't go. Spare a glance for my last stretcher, . . . that gibbering, unbelievable, unbandaged thing, a wagging lump of raw flesh on a neck, that was a face a short time ago, Mother and Mrs. Evans-Mawnington. Now it might be anything . . . a lump of liver, raw bleeding liver, that's what it resembles more than anything else, doesn't it? We can't tell its age, but the whimpering moan sounds young, somehow. Like the fretful whimpers of a sick little child . . . a tortured little child . . . puzzled whimpers. Who is he? For all you know, Mrs. Evans-Mawnington, he is your Roy. He might be anyone at all, so why not your Roy? One shapeless lump of raw liver is like another shapeless lump of raw liver. What do you say? Why don't they cover him up with bandages? How the hell do I know? I have often wondered myself, . . . but they don't. Why do you turn away? That's only liquid fire. You've heard of liquid fire? Oh, yes. I remember your letter. . . . "*I hear we've started to use liquid fire, too. That will teach those Germans. I hope we use lots and lots of it.*" Yes, you wrote that. You were glad some new fiendish torture had been invented by the chemists who are running this war. You were delighted to think some German mother's son was going to have the skin stripped from his poor face by liquid fire. . . . Just as some equally patriotic German mother rejoiced when she first heard the sons of Englishwomen were to be burnt and tortured by the very newest war gadget out of the laboratory.

Don't go, Mother and Mrs. Evans-Mawnington, . . . don't go. I am loaded, but there are over thirty ambulances not filled up. Walk down the line. Don't go, unless you want me to excuse you while you retch your insides out as I so often do. There are stretchers and stretchers you haven't seen yet. . . . Men with hopeless dying eyes who don't want to die . . . men with hopeless living eyes who don't want to live. Wait, wait, I have so much, so much to show you before you return to your committees and your recruiting meetings, before you add to your bag of recruits . . . those young recruits you enroll so proudly with your patriotic speeches, your red, white and blue rosettes, your white feathers, your insults, your lies . . . any bloody lie to secure a fresh victim.

What? You cannot stick it any longer? You are going? I didn't think you'd stay. But I've got to stay, haven't I? . . . I've got to stay. You've got me out here, and you'll keep me out here. You've got me haloed. I am one of the Splendid Young Women who are winning the War. . . .

"Loaded. Six stretchers and three sitters!"

I am away. I slow up at the station gate. The sergeant is waiting with his pencil and list. I repeat, "Six stretchers and three sitters." "Number Eight."

He ticks off my ambulance. I pass out of the yard. [. . .]

Oh, the beauty of men who are whole and sane. Shall I ever know a lover who is young and strong and untouched by war, who has not gazed on what I have gazed upon? Shall I ever know a lover whose eyes reflect my image without the shadow of war rising between us? A lover in whose arms I shall forget the maimed men who pass before me in endless parade in the darkness before the dawn when I think and think and think because the procession will not let me sleep?

What is to happen to women like me when this war ends . . . if ever it ends. I am twenty-one years of age, yet I know nothing of life but death, fear, blood, and the sentimentality that glorifies these things in the name of patriotism. I watch my own mother stupidly, deliberately, though unthinkingly—for she is a kind woman—encourage the sons of other women to kill their brothers; I see my own father—a gentle creature who would not willingly harm a fly—applaud the latest scientist to invent a mechanical device guaranteed to crush his fellow-beings to pulp in their thousands. And my generation watches these things and marvels at the blind foolishness of it . . . helpless to make its immature voice heard above the insensate clamour of the old ones who cry: "Kill, Kill, Kill!" unceasingly.

What is to happen to women like me when the killing is done and peace comes . . . if ever it comes? What will they expect of us, these elders who have sent us out to fight? We sheltered young women who smilingly stumbled from the chintz-covered drawing-rooms of the suburbs straight into hell?

What will they expect of us?

We, who once blushed at the public mention of childbirth, now discuss such things as casually as once we discussed the latest play; whispered stories of immorality are of far less importance than a fresh cheese in the canteen; chastity seems a mere waste of time in an area where youth is blotted out so quickly. What will they expect of us, these elders of ours, when the killing is over and we return?

'A LIFE WITH A PURPOSE—OR A GRAVE IN MALAYA: AN OPEN LETTER BY THE EDITOR'

Challenge, 26 February 1949

Written by Editor (Monty Cohen)

Challenge was, and still is, the journal of the Young Communist League (YCL), the youth wing of the Communist Party of Great Britain. It was founded in 1935, and at the time the editorial featured here was published, it appeared fortnightly. Members of the YCL were expected to read it and to sell it. *Challenge* was never intended for a very young readership—YCL members were generally fourteen and above. Indeed, its expected audience would be those who were eligible for National Service, *though Jane Rosen's mother used to read it during Religious Education lessons, which she was not required to join in because she was not Christian.*

The editorial takes the form of an open letter to the eighteen year olds who would be signing up for their National Service and who were likely to be involved in a war against the Malay people. This was one of many articles and editorials that campaigned against National Service and the enlistment of working-class youth in imperialist wars for the sake of big business interests.

Although it is aimed at a youth rather than a children's audience, in its tone, concerns, and presentation, *Challenge* is typical of the kind of material produced by the many left-wing youth organizations that were formed during these years, and especially between the two world wars (these are discussed in more detail in the introduction to Part Three). With its conviction that the young would and should be interested in political issues and needed to be informed in order to prepare themselves for responsible citizenship, *Challenge* typifies the ethos that underpinned radical children's literature.

A LIFE WITH A PURPOSE—*OR A GRAVE IN MALAYA?*

An Open Letter by THE EDITOR to the 18-year-olds signing on for National Service this Saturday

THIS Saturday you are signing on for National Service. Perhaps you have been affected by Government propaganda and think you are going to learn a trade in the Forces—in fact, any one of forty-three trades—according to the posters and adverts.

If so, you are in for a rude shock. A R.E.M.E. mechanic wrote to *Challenge* recently:

"I wanted to take a long course as a vehicle mechanic, but this was refused me as I was a conscript. So they sent me on a course as an electrician, which lasted fourteen weeks—how skilled can you become in any trade with less than four months' training?"

"O.K.", you may be thinking, "but even if I'm not going to learn a trade, at least I'll have the chance of going abroad."

Quite true. In fact, it's more than a chance.

Now that the Government has broken its pledge and increased the period of conscription from twelve to eighteen months, it is very probable that you *will* be going overseas. But where to? The *Daily Herald* let the cat out of the bag in its headline: "18 months or Quit Malaya".

There's the harsh truth. Unless the Government is quickly forced to change its policy—or make way for a government that will truly represent the people—you are likely to be sent to Malaya and instructed to fight our great war-time allies, the Malayan people who helped us so much in the fight against Japanese fascism. For whose sake? For big business interests with huge investments in Malaya's tin and rubber.

YET the period of conscription *could* be valuable.

Not only to learn how to use arms in the defence of Britain's working people. But with better officers, less wasted time, better education and trade training, a *year's* conscription *could* be a useful, happy and healthy time in the life of any young man.

Think it over, brother. You are eighteen. You were born in 1931. In that year MacDonald, Labour Prime Minister, went over to the Tories. Terrible suffering followed for the people.

Today, once more right-wing Labour leaders besmirch the fair name of Socialism. They pursue a Tory policy of lining up with big business at home, and selling us to the Yankee millionaires. You can read on page four ("Crazy") how this leads to their chucking overboard all their election promises, together with the housing and education plans on which many had pinned their hopes.

Don't let them get away with it.

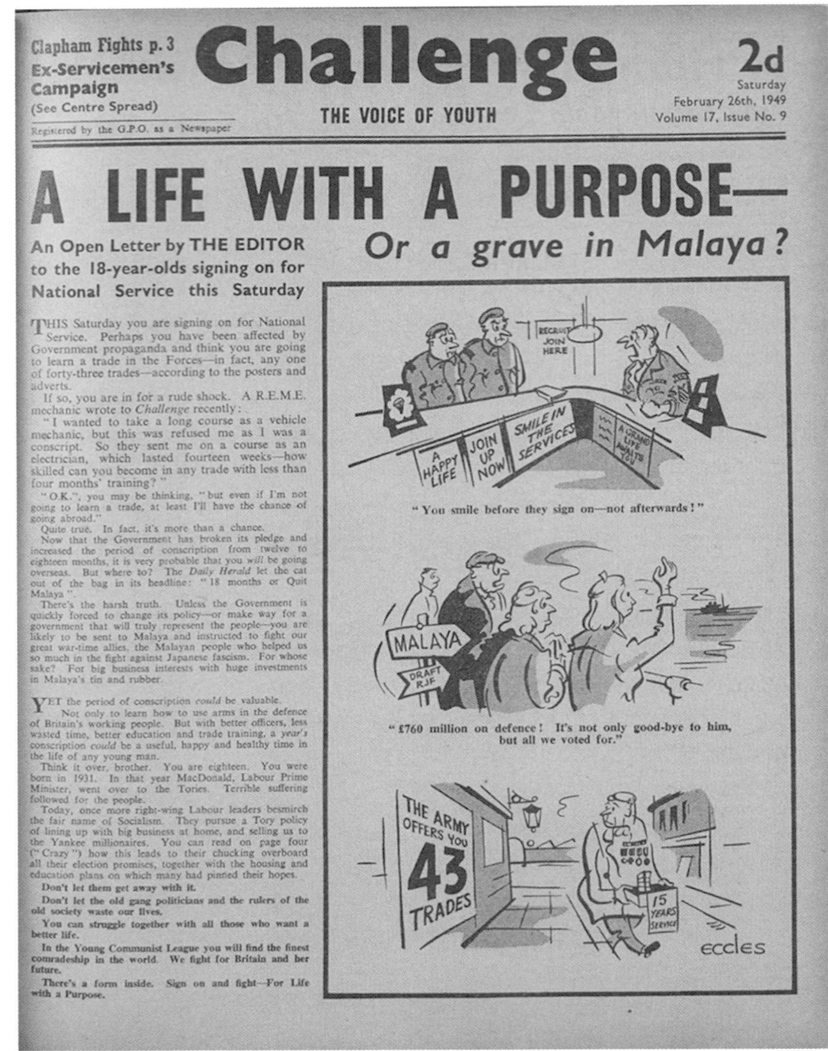

Clapham Fights p. 3
Ex-Servicemen's Campaign
(See Centre Spread)

Registered by the G.P.O. as a Newspaper

Challenge

THE VOICE OF YOUTH

2d
Saturday
February 26th, 1949
Volume 17, Issue No. 9

A LIFE WITH A PURPOSE—

Or a grave in Malaya?

An Open Letter by THE EDITOR to the 18-year-olds signing on for National Service this Saturday

THIS Saturday you are signing on for National Service. Perhaps you have been affected by Government propaganda and think you are going to learn a trade in the Forces—in fact, any one of forty-three trades—according to the posters and adverts.

If so, you are in for a rude shock. A R.E.M.E. mechanic wrote to *Challenge* recently:

"I wanted to take a long course as a vehicle mechanic, but this was refused me as I was a conscript. So they sent me on a course as an electrician, which lasted fourteen weeks—how skilled can you become in any trade with less than four months' training?"

"O.K.", you may be thinking, "but even if I'm not going to learn a trade, at least I'll have the chance of going abroad."

Quite true. In fact, it's more than a chance.

Now that the Government has broken its pledge and increased the period of conscription from twelve to eighteen months, it is very probable that you *will* be going overseas. But where to? The *Daily Herald* let the cat out of the bag in its headline: "18 months or Quit Malaya".

There's the harsh truth. Unless the Government is quickly forced to change its policy—or make way for a government that will truly represent the people—you are likely to be sent to Malaya and instructed to fight our great war-time allies, the Malayan people who helped us so much in the fight against Japanese fascism. For whose sake? For big business interests with huge investments in Malaya's tin and rubber.

YET the period of conscription *could* be valuable.

Not only to learn how to use arms in the defence of Britain's working people. But with better officers, less wasted time, better education and trade training, a *year's* conscription *could* be a useful, happy and healthy time in the life of any young man.

Think it over, brother. You are eighteen. You were born in 1931. In that year MacDonald, Labour Prime Minister, went over to the Tories. Terrible suffering followed for the people.

Today, once more right-wing Labour leaders besmirch the fair name of Socialism. They pursue a Tory policy of lining up with big business at home, and selling us to the Yankee millionaires. You can read on page four ("Crazy") how this leads to their chucking overboard all their election promises, together with the housing and education plans on which many had pinned their hopes.

Don't let them get away with it.

Don't let the old gang politicians and the rulers of the old society waste our lives.

You can struggle together with all those who want a better life.

In the Young Communist League you will find the finest comradeship in the world. We fight for Britain and her future.

There's a form inside. Sign on and fight—For Life with a Purpose.

"You smile before they sign on—not afterwards!"

"£760 million on defence! It's not only good-bye to him, but all we voted for."

A life with a purpose: cartoon accompanying the *Challenge editor's open letter A Life with a Purpose*. The artist is Eccles (Frank Brown), long-time cartoonist for *Challenge and the Daily Worker*, later the *Morning Star*.

Don't let the old gang politicians and the rulers of the old society waste our lives.

You can struggle together with all those who want a better life.

In the Young Communist League you will find the finest comradeship in the world. We fight for Britain and her future.

There's a form inside. Sign on and fight—For Life with a Purpose.

'LAST NIGHT I HAD THE STRANGEST DREAM'

1950

Written by Ed McCurdy

British children who went on Woodcraft Folk Camps in the 1950s and 1960s (see the discussion of the Woodcraft Folk in the Introduction to Part Six), or went on the 'Aldermaston Marches' to 'Ban the Bomb' (beginning in 1958), regularly sang this song around camp fires and while quite literally on the march. One person would lead off, usually on guitar, and the rest would join in, following a tradition most closely associated with the US folk and protest group The Weavers (founded in 1948). 'Last Night I had the Strangest Dream' was written by Ed McCurdy (1919–2000), who helped to create the New York City folk scene of the 1960s. He had an extremely successful singing, songwriting, and acting career.

This song belongs to a repertoire of newly composed, explicitly political material which followed or borrowed forms created by a mix of Irish and British migrants to the Appalachian Mountains, and African American slaves and their descendants. The most famous of these singer-songwriters is of course Bob Dylan, but before him there were Leadbelly (Huddie Ledbetter), Woody Guthrie, Pete Seeger, and even earlier, Ralph Chaplin and Joe Hill (Joel Hägglund). Other key figures who contributed to the vast resource of 'traditional' songs on which the radical songwriting tradition is based were John and Alan Lomax (1867–1948; 1915–2002).

The tradition of singing radical songs within the labour and socialist movements in Britain goes back at least to *Chants of Labour: A Song Book of the People*, edited by the pioneering British socialist Edward Carpenter in 1888 with illustrations by Walter Crane. In it, new songs by children's literature's E. Nesbit (1858–1924) and Charles Kingsley are found alongside 'The Voice of Toil', by that other early British socialist William Morris. Morris's song begins, 'I heard men saying', a phrase McCurdy echoes with his utopian image of what might happen.

'Last Night I had the Strangest Dream' also owes something to the pacifist mood behind the Pete Seeger and Lee Hayes song 'If I Had a Hammer' (1949) and others much sung by left-wing groups and anti-war protesters, including the song known both as 'Down by the Riverside' and 'I aint' Gonna Study War no More'. Although first published in 1918 in *Plantation Melodies: A Collection of Modern, Popular and Old-Time Negro-Songs of the Southland*, with lines such as, 'Goin' to lay down my sword and shield, down by the riverside' and 'I ain't gonna study war no more', this song spoke powerfully to those protesting against nuclear weapons and the escalating war in Vietnam. *Michael Rosen remembers singing it at Woodcraft Folk camps. It was one of those moments, he thinks, when adults took on a slightly grave air, as if to say, 'if only' and to convey to us young people that this was the big dream of the moment, particularly as nuclear weapons seemed so threatening at the time.*

LAST NIGHT I HAD THE STRANGEST DREAM

Ed McCurdy

Last night I had the strangest dream
I ever dreamed before
I dreamed the world had all agreed
To put an end to war
I dreamed I saw a mighty room
Filled with women and men
And the paper they were signing said
They'd never fight again

And when the papers all were signed
And a million copies made
They all joined hands and bowed their heads
And grateful prayers were prayed
And the people in the streets below
Were dancing round and round
And guns and swords and uniforms
Were scattered on the ground

Last night I had the strangest dream
I ever dreamed before
I dreamed the world had all agreed
To put an end to war.

PART THREE

WRITING AND REVOLUTION

INTRODUCTION

In 1917, the world turned upside down. After the revolutions in Russia that year, particularly the Bolshevik revolution in October, things were never to be the same again. It is difficult now, after years of Cold War propaganda, to appreciate the reaction around the world at the time. It was the first great victory of the working class. It was the beginning of a new world! There was hard work ahead, but the working class in Russia had achieved the overthrow of the tsarist regime. New ways of looking at things, including education and activism, had to be found. Children's literature, too, required reform. As Geoffrey Trease (1909–98) was to ask in 1935 in the journal *International Literature*: 'Where is our revolutionary literature for the young?... books which breathe the authentic spirit of the new world' (100).

This question had been asked before. As already discussed in Part One, the Socialist Sunday School (SSS) movement had many debates on the subject. The radical educator Tom Anderson, no doubt influenced by the 1905 Revolution in Russia, had stated in an article in May 1908 for the SSS magazine *The Young Socialist* that there could be no mending of the system; a revolution was required. To which the editor at the time responded, 'Our National Socialist Sunday School Movement stands for the teaching of *Socialism*—not Revolution... in no sense does the term revolution express our glorious ideal of Socialism. And to teach revolution is not to teach Socialism' (248, italics in original).

This disagreement led to Anderson's leaving the SSS and setting up his own schools with their revolutionary syllabus (see the introduction to Anderson's 'Don't Shoot Your Class' in Part Two for more on this). Yet, it was not until 1915 and the First World War that he started publishing his own revolutionary educational texts for his scholars. In June 1917, after the February Revolution in Russia, Anderson began producing periodicals for young workers starting with *The Revolution*, represented in Part Two.

The first truly revolutionary children's fiction came from abroad led, naturally, by Soviet Russia. There, as early as 1918, an article appeared stating the following:

> In the great arsenal with which the bourgeois fought against Socialism, children's books occupied a prominent role. In selecting cannons and weapons, we

> overlook those that spread these weapons. So focussed on guns and other weapons, we forget about the written word. We must seize these weapons from enemy hands. (Rosenfeld, 2009).

Soviet children's books are represented in this part by Valentin Katayev's (1897–1986) *A Lonely White Sail,* first published in 1936 and remembered by Michael Rosen in the Introduction. The Germans also produced a significant body of revolutionary writing for children. Germany had a strong revolutionary movement in the early years of the previous century, but in 1919 this suffered a bloody defeat with the suppression of the Spartacist revolt, which attempted to replicate the Russian Revolution. Despite its failure and the murder of three of its leaders—Rosa Luxemburg, Karl Liebknecht, and Leo Jogiches—the revolutionary tradition continued. Wieland Herzfelde, who founded the revolutionary publishing house Malik Verlag, in 1917, worked closely with members of the avant-garde. Herzfelde's books for children included 'Little Peter' (first published in Germany in 1921) reproduced here, and *Eddie and the Gipsy* (1931), represented in Part One.

It is clear that in Britain, publishers were experiencing difficulties in locating home-grown talent for their revolutionary stories. Anderson did publish 'The Experiences of a Russian Girl Revolutionist' in *The Revolution* (October 1917–March 1918). This serial story is set at the time of the 1905 Revolution and written by the Latvian revolutionary Alexander Sirnis. Several revolutionary periodicals for young people were also available in Britain during this period, mostly aligned with the Communist Party and the Third International. Amongst them were *Young Rebel* (1917); *The Revolution* (1917–18), represented in Part Two; *Red Dawn* (1919–21); *Proletcult* (fl.1922–4), represented in Parts Three and Nine; *The Young Comrade* (1924–8); and *The Worker's Child* (1926–8). Yet not until the publishing house Martin Lawrence, founded in 1927, started to print children's books was there much locally produced revolutionary fiction. In 1931 the firm published its first children's book, an annual called *The Red Corner Book for Children*. Some of the illustrations Michael Boland created for that volume are reproduced in this part. This was the beginning. In the years that followed, Martin Lawrence produced further children's books. The 1930s were its most productive period for juvenile publications and notably included launching Geoffrey Trease on his long career as a children's writer. Martin Lawrence also published a translation of *Eddie and the Gipsy*, produced books with International Publishers of New York, including a biography *Our Lenin* (1934) edited by Ruth Shaw and Harry Alan Potamkin, and issued *Martin's Annual* in 1935, from which comes the short story *Steel Spokes*, reprinted here.

Geoffrey Trease, represented in this part by extracts from his first children's book, *Bows Against the Barons,* was to produce four more books for Martin Lawrence and its successor, Lawrence and Wishart. These included *Comrades for the Charter* (1934), *Call to Arms* (1935), *Missing from Home* (1936), and *Red Comet* (1937), which features in Part Four. These books looked at the world in ways which were new to young British readers: they made revolution the ideal and an adventure; children were at the centre of the action and, most importantly, they were equal with their adult comrades, treated with respect, and consulted when decisions needed to be made. These books follow the Party line of the period by inspiring children not just to be useful and committed members of a new society, but to be part of making that new society, and making it through revolution.

The children's books produced by Lawrence and Wishart petered out as the Second World War began. After the war, in association with International Publishers, they produced two scientific books by Alex Novikoff relating to human biology and evolution. The last children's book they published was *Carpenter Investigates* (1950), by the historian Herbert L. Peacock, which is a strange selection of short stories, including non-revolutionary western tales as well as the story that gives the book its title. The eponymous Carpenter is an eighteenth-century investigator who looks into smuggling, Luddite riots, and who happens to be in the Bastille on the day that it is stormed in 1789. All very well, but no child revolutionaries or protagonists feature.

Little Tusker's Own Paper (1945), the last extract in this part, does have children at the centre of the action. These children learn the reality of day-to-day activism, producing news, and ensuring that the revolutionary voice continues to be heard. In the Cold War period that was to commence not long after this booklet appeared, this was arguably the best contribution they could make under the repression of that political wilderness.

'LITTLE PETER'

Proletcult, November 1922

Written by Hermynia Zur Mühlen. Translated by Eden and Cedar Paul

In March 1922, Tom Anderson (1863–1947), radical educator and publisher for children, launched *Proletcult*, his third periodical. His first two journals, *The Revolution* (discussed in Part Two) and *Red Dawn*, launched in March 1919 (it folded in September 1921), were aimed at young workers. Although children of twelve were part of the country's work force at this time, for the most part *Proletcult*'s content and the way it addresses readers point to an older audience.[1] No reason was given for the closure of *Red Dawn*, but there had been criticism of it. For instance, in their 1921 pamphlet, also called *Proletcult*, the writers and translators of socialist literature Eden and Cedar Paul observe, 'But the psychology of "Red Dawn", the monthly organ of the Proletarian School, is the psychology of the young adult, and not the psychology of the child'. Initially, however, as this story shows, Anderson's periodical did include material for younger readers.

As well as factual articles, *Proletcult* included short stories, and 'Little Peter' is from the first tale in a series by Hermynia Zur Mühlen (1883–1951), an Austrian countess who embraced the revolutionary movement and became a member of the German Communist Party. Zur Mühlen's commitment to the movement was perhaps best shown by her proletarian tales for children. The first and best known of these was *Was Peterchens Freunde erzählen: märchen* (What Little Peter's Friends Told Him: Fairy Tales). These were published in 1921 by Malik Verlag (the publisher of *Eddie and the Gipsy*, represented in Part One), with illustrations by George Grosz. In his editorial introducing the series (probably the first time they were published in English), Anderson describes the stories as 'the kind of lessons which interest the child mind'. In them, Zur Mühlen endeavours to describe the economic reality of capitalism to child readers.

1. Proletkult was a Soviet organization set up in 1917 to encourage the development of a new proletarian culture. Originally independent of the state, it was finally absorbed into the Commissariat for Education in 1920, and the movement fell out of favour.

Peter, the son of a poor woman, is forced to lie in bed after an accident. Bored, he listens to the conversations of the household objects in the room. This extract is the first of the tales; in it the pieces of coal describe their origins and the conditions that the miners must endure. In the other tales, different household items recount their own experiences and lament the way that the rich treat the poor and the fact that the poor do not unite. The tales end with this exhortation: 'But he who only thinks of himself will in the end be vanquished. This is an everlasting law.'

LITTLE PETER

Translated from the German for "Proletcult" by Eden and Cedar Paul. In Proletcult, *November 1922, Vol 1, No. 9*

Hermynia Zur Mühlen

NO. 1: WHAT THE COAL SAID

Little Peter had broken his leg, skating on the ice. Now he had to lie quite still in bed. He felt ever so dull: his mother had to go out to work and was away all day; his play-fellows were enjoying themselves outside in the snow, and it never entered their heads to visit their poor little comrade. During the daytime the boy could still amuse himself; then it was light, and the sunbeams came in through the window and threw funny shadows on the walls. But towards evening, when the narrow room grew darker and darker, Peter began to feel frightened, and longed for the sound of his mother's step on the stair. Besides, the little lad was cold, for the stove could not be lighted until mother was back.

All afternoon it had been snowing. From his bed Peter could watch the large, fluffy flakes as they fell to the ground. Now it was dark. He lay shivering, and felt both sad and frightened.

Suddenly he seemed to hear something that whispered on the floor. He listened. Two gentle voices came from the scuttle in which lay a few small pieces of coal. Peter was much alarmed, he hardly dared breathe. The room was so quiet that the tiny voices could be heard quite plainly now. The lumps of coal were talking to one another.

"How dark it is here," said the topmost coal. "One can see nothing at all."

"Where I come from it is darker still," answered another.

"Where do you come from?"

"Out of the earth, sister. I lay buried in the earth and I slept; it was warm and comfortable there. Pressing close up against me were thousands of my sisters. They, too, were asleep. One day our resting-place shook, and a great noise awoke me. The earth was rent asunder, and I rolled out. I fell into a small gallery; it was so narrow and so low that a man could not stand upright in it. A man was there; he was crouching, and hammered as best he might against the wall. He coughed and choked, and the sweat poured off his brow. He never rested, but hammered and hammered for many hours. Oh, but he was tired, poor fellow! His hands trembled; sometimes he groaned aloud, and rubbed his back as though it hurt him. But he was quickly at work again hammering on the wall. It was very hot in the gallery. Now that I know how human beings need fresh air to live, I can't understand how the man in the gallery managed to carry on in a place where there was no air to speak of, and where what there was had a foul and horrid smell. I thought that the man with his sad face must have done something wicked, and had been sent to work here for punishment. Later I was put in a little truck and was brought into the light of day. But I thought of that poor fellow down there who could not stand up straight, and whose back seemed to ache so terribly."

"You've hardly seen anything, sister," squeaked a tiny piece of coal that had fallen out of the scuttle and lay under the stove. "I've seen things that were far more dreadful than a man with a sore back! I lay in just such a gallery as the one you tell us about. It was low and narrow; ten men were at work there and each had a small lamp hanging down in front. 'What a queer smell,' said an elderly man. 'We'd better go back.'—'And be sacked for our trouble?' cried another. They continued work, for when a man is given the sack he and his wife and children can buy no food and have to go hungry. And if a worker does not do just as the master wishes, he is told to clear out. The lamps began to burn dimly; it was nearly dark in the gallery now. A man was peering in and the elderly miner spoke to him, saying: 'I'm uneasy in my mind, sir; hadn't we better quit?' But the other man answered angrily, and scolded the miner as if he were a schoolboy.

As soon as the foreman had gone, the men sighed and set to work again. I can't think why the miners were so docile and obedient. The foreman looked just like the other men, he was no larger or stronger.

"All of a sudden I rolled farther. I looked around, but the men had not touched me. Now I leaped into the air and at the same time a sound like thunder filled the gallery. The lamps went out; great blocks fell on all sides. In the darkness I could hear the men calling and groaning for many, many hours. One of them had fallen on top of me; I could feel him trembling; from his head something wet was flowing. How long we all lay there I cannot tell. After a while the men's voices grew weaker. Some one begged for a drop of water, but of course there was none to be had. After a very, very, long time other men came and carried the miners away. But they were all dead, the elderly one as well. At the pithead was a group of wives and children weeping. A tall, well-dressed gentleman stood there, too. As the elderly man was carried past his arm fell over the side of the stretcher and looked as if he were shaking his fist in the gentleman's face and saying: 'You knew that it was dangerous to work there; but your money is more to you than men's lives!' The gentleman did not heed him at all. I could see and hear everything for I was sticking to the clothes of the old miner."

At this point a third piece of coal interrupted, saying:

"You didn't see how in the evening, when the dead men lay in their cottages and the wives and the children wept, the rich man had a fine party up at his house. There was dancing, and the lovely ladies in their silk dresses never gave a thought to the little ones who had lost their fathers. The host was merry; yet he was really to blame for sending the men down the mine when it was not safe, and their death must be laid at his door. I cannot understand why human beings are so unkind to one another."

"I can tell you that," said a fourth piece of coal which was more than usually black and shiny. "I have lived for so long on the earth that I have seen a good deal. Besides I've always been reckoned the cleverest of the family and so of course I can take up meanings easily. There are two sorts of people in the world: the rich and the poor. Everything belongs to the wealthy; the poor have little or nothing. Just look at the lad lying over there in the bed. He is ill, and yet all day long he has to be alone; he has no toys, no soft comfortable bed, no good things to eat. His mother has no time to give to him, for from morning till night she works in a factory. Perhaps you think he has been naughty, and that is why he is having a bad time? Well, you are quite mistaken. He's a jolly little chap, works well at school—but he is poor. I can give you many more examples. For instance, once I was journeying in a ship over a vast spread of water. The rich had splendid airy cabins; they could pace the decks whenever they pleased; they had good things to eat and drink. But in the bowels of the ship the huge engines live, and they must be fed so that they may keep the vessel going. It is hot as hell down there and reeks of oil and soot. Day in, day out and all through the night men are at work shovelling coal into the glowing furnaces. They are stripped to the waist; the air is so heavy one can hardly breathe. Sometimes one of the men feels giddy, and rushes aloft to breathe the sweet, fresh air; but everything dances before his eyes, he can't see where he's going, he stumbles, falls into the water, and is drowned. Many are made ill by the terrible heat, but they have to go on shovelling coal all the same."

"But don't the rich ones come down and help sometimes?" piped the tiniest piece of coal.

The jet-black coal laughed: "Silly little thing! The rich keep the poor working for them so as not to have anything to do themselves, and so that they may lead beautiful lives."

"Are the poor so much weaker than the rich? Can't they keep themselves?" asked the inquisitive little coal.

"Oh, no," answered the wise and shining one. "There are many more poor than rich people. If the poor stuck together, if they were to unite, they could have all the things that now are enjoyed by the wealthy."

"Why don't they do it then?"

"You will have to put that question to mankind itself, little sister. I have never yet been able to understand why they don't."

Steps sounded in the stairway.

The pieces of coal were silent once more.

'STEEL SPOKES'

Martin's Annual, 1935

Written by T. H. Wintringham. Illustrator not identified

Tom Wintringham (1898–1949) has been described as 'the last English revolutionary'.[1] He was among the first to join the newly formed British Communist Party, and was arrested and sentenced with other Party activists for sedition in 1925, shortly before the General Strike. During the Spanish Civil War, he served as a machine gun instructor and later commanded the British Battalion during the Battle of Jarama in 1937.

'Steel Spokes' appears to be his only story for children. Geoffrey Trease called it a 'delightful story [in which] T. H. Wintringham deftly blends the modern child's interest in machinery with his primitive love of fantasy—and gives the whole a class significance'.[2] This radical tale, in which children are revolutionary protagonists, draws on Wintringham's knowledge of motorcycles, gained whilst serving as a motorcycle dispatch rider during the First World War. This experience perhaps also led to the story's depiction of an empathetic relationship between humans and machines. A broadly positive attitude to machinery and technology was characteristic of radical writing of this time (though see the entry on Eric Kästner's *The 35th of May* in Part Ten for more discussion of this), while in mainstream children's literature, things mechanical and technological were often perceived as threatening. This hostility is also evident in the work of some earlier socialist writers such as William Morris (1834–1896).

In 'Steel Spokes', the machines sympathize with their makers, involving themselves in the lives of their operators. The sympathy is reflected in the conversations the machines hold regarding the pressure the workers are under, leading to flawed work and to a strike for better conditions. This sympathy results in all the motorcycles enrolling Joey's gang in a sortie to participate in the strike. Allowing the machines of all nationalities to work together is a clear echo of radical writing's commitment to internationalism. The warmth and humour which cement the lessons suggest Wintringham could have been a fine children's writer.

1. See, for instance, Hugh Purcell's biography of Tom Wintringham, *The Last English Revolutionary* (2004).
2. In *International Literature*, 7 (1935).

STEEL SPOKES

ALMOST every night young Joey went to the garage that has motor-cycles in its windows. On Wednesdays he went early, after tea, because then there were men in black leather boots hanging round the door or working on their little shiny machines. These men had chins the colour of cinders. They rode on the dirt-track every Wednesday: right knee hooked under a special curved bar of the cycle; left toe, in a steel cap, skurring along the cinders. They were friends of young Joey's, and he fetched cigarettes for them if they asked him.

On Sundays Joey went late, after his real bed-time if he dared, hoping to see the club come in from a day's trials, or from a hill-climb. If he was lucky and the big machines came banging and razzing, and the little two-strokes snuffling and spitting, he would stay there till all good-nights were said, and the last tail-lamp went like a running red goblin up over the railway bridge and disappeared.

On ordinary evenings there was nothing to do except make his nose snubber on the plate-glass windows. He knew every bicycle in the shop-front, from the big yellow Harley, all elbows of pressed steel, with a side-car like a young bungalow, down to the baby New Imp, with its little curved magneto-fly-wheel that looked like a real baby's round belly.

One evening young Joey was pressing his nose to the window of the shop door. Four new machines had come in: one of them was hard to see. And the door opened.

Someone had left the door unlocked.

Joey went in.

First he looked hard at the new machines, and then he climbed into the saddle of his favourite, a Norton of the model that won the races in the Isle of Man.

He sat far forward on the saddle to reach the handlebars; his knees just came to the curved rubber pads on the side of the shiny petrol tank. He felt fine—rather high up, but as if he were a natural part of the lovely bike. And it seemed quite natural that the Norton should speak to him. When a man loves a machine and knows it and is a free part of it, of course the machine talks to him all the time.

"All very well, young-feller-me-lad," said the Norton, "but a real rider finds the brake first and keeps his heel near it. We Nortons never feel really happy unless the boy astride us is the sort that can put the model down—flat—in five yards."

Joey obediently felt for the brake pedal, gave it a friendly dig, and kept his heel near it. Then he asked, "What do you mean—put the model down flat?"

"Fall off," said the Norton, "without hurting yourself or the 'bus. If you see a herd of sheep just ahead round the bend, if a baby runs out on a narrow road, if you might kill an old dame—you've got to fall off quick. Brake with a kick and swing me with your knees; I'll stop flat on my side and you'll roll or bump the hedge. That's riding! Even if my clock" ("that's the speedometer," explained the motorcycle kindly) "is saying sixty-five, you can do it.... But excuse me; I have got to finish a discussion with my friend here. Do you mind?"

"Can't I hear the discussion? I'd like to," said Joey.

"Why not? Climb on the saddle of each machine here, and then you'll be able to listen," answered the Norton.

Joey started climbing on to saddle after saddle. On each machine he found the brake pedal and gave it a friendly dig. Then he patted the tank and swung down. When he was well started he began to realise what a babble of voices was going on; before he had finished he had caught enough scraps of talk to know why they were talking so warmly. They were fresh from a dozen factories, they were beautiful to look at, and they were beautifully made. But the men who made them in these factories were being rushed and speeded and bothered and worried and overworked and not paid enough and watched and bullied, until they were beginning to make little mistakes. The time was coming near, if this went on, when motor-bikes would be turned out with sprung frames and over-tight bearings, and wheels not perfectly round or balanced, and gears that sprang, and a wobble in the steering-head. "Then we shall kill our riders," said a big side-car machine, "and I'm built to carry three—him and her and a kid."

"Bad enough with only one," said a two-stroke. "And if we kill a rider we'll never be able to be safe again." All the machines murmured or clicked "Yes" to this. They knew that a motor-cycle which kills its rider ought—always—to be broken up and scrapped.

Joey broke the gloomy silence. "Can't we help stop it?" he said:

The discussion broke out again. A four-speed machine, one of the last arrivals, said, "They'll be on strike now, at Badstoke; it was near to that when I left the factory. Men on strike because they are rushed and speeded and bothered and worried and overworked and watched and bullied and not paid enough. And it shows in their work. I—" his voice became gruff—"I'm one of the sufferers. A little matter: a cotter-pin left riding sideways on the exhaust valve spring-ring. It hurts a bit...."

"Hurts? I should think it did," replied another bike. "They left one of my cotters jammed too, and it sheered through when I was on test. The valve dropped down into the cylinder, and everything blew up. I'm all new and stiff there still."

"Why can't we help to stop it?" young Joey repeated.

Then a bicycle spoke suddenly and quickly, so quickly that Joey could not grasp at first what was being said. (Each sort of bike spoke in its usual voice: little two-strokes in thin voices, big singles in deep notes with a bark in them, twin-cylinders in a sort of bubble like a man with a pipe in his mouth. But this machine was a Scott, and a Scott is a twin two-stroke, and so it talks four times as fast as any ordinary bike, in a shrill yelp.)

"Let'sallgothereandhelpthestrikepicket," said the Scott.

"Eh?" said young Joey.

Another bike explained: "he's saying we should all go there and help the strikers at this factory—help the men who stand at the factory gate to stop the people who don't understand from going in and working."

"Can we go there?"

"Most of us can ride ourselves...."

"I can't go: that cotter-pin," said the new four-speeder.

"We must have riders; it feels so much safer."

"Any sort of riders...."

The Scott spoke again:

"Joeygetyourgang!"

Other bikes took it up:

"Young Joey, get your gang!"

"JOEY, GET YOUR GANG!"

"Get the big ones and the little ones, the lads and the girls!"

And Joey went running down the street and after him through the shop door came the Norton and the Scott and the big bumping Harley, and they lay up against the garage wall or put their foot-rests on the kerb, and they waited, and all along the street the children came, some running, some walking, some big ones (including Bob, who had *really* ridden a motor-bike before, once) and some little ones (including three babies brought by bigger children and dumped all together on the Harley's side-car seat).

How all those children got away from mothers who had put them to bed, and even from mothers who were just washing their necks, I don't know. But they did.

The four-speed newcomer was still in the garage, cussing a bit because he couldn't go off with the others. So while the children were deciding who should ride which bike, and who should go on the pillion seats, young Joey explained the matter of the cotter-pin to Bob, and they got the heaviest hammer they could find and the softest punch (a light hit with a heavy hammer is *much* better than a heavy hit with a light hammer) and Joey punched the cotter-pin into its right place; Bob meanwhile held a weight against the valve stem so that it should not spring too much. And the four-speeder was happy and shot out of the door.

Meanwhile there was trouble about the babies; they would keep sliding and wriggling off the side-car seat, until a resourceful little girl got an enormous safety pin out of one baby's nappy. This she pinned through the cloth of the side-car seat, and then through a fold in each of three nappies, and then through the side-car seat again. (It was a *very* big safety pin.) That held them all fast, and they looked at the sky and blinked.

Soon they were all off, like a club outing, heading over the main road, taking the lamp-lit corners in swinging curves, their riders happy with the smooth power between their knees. Soon they were strung out, Bob in front on the Scott (because all could follow its shrill yelp, and because a Scott can find its way anywhere), young Joey on the Norton leading the main pack, the big American side-car just behind. (And there were other "foreigners" in the pack: a German B.M.W., cousin of the fastest motor-cycle in the world, went side-by-side with a Motosacoche, little and French and friendly.)

Young Joey listened to his Norton talking. The clear unhurried engine voice told him of a piston made of aluminium, going up and down within the cylinder forty times a second—faster than you can blink—and of a magneto in which platinum points, small as a match-head, were springing apart at exactly the right atom of time, so that punctually in each fortieth part of a second the throb of electricity leapt along a wire to the sparking plug, and at the plug points became the tiny cherry-red spark that is a motor-cycle's heart-beat.

Young Joey thought he could listen to that voice the whole night through. But soon he found there were other lesser voices, worth listening to, from the gears and the chain and the bearings and the wheels. Gears told him how their faces were cut to lock together perfectly, and how their teeth were as hard as steel can be, while their bodies were springy to absorb all shudders. The chain kept reckoning over difficult sums and algebra, somehow turning the engine's quick buzzing into slower movement of the back wheel. And the bearings explained how they lay in little steel beds, hugging so close to the spindles they controlled that there was no shake or tremble, and yet the spindles could turn smoothly all the time.

As each part of the bike explained the marvel of its making, the lovely usefulness of its shape, and the designer's skill and draughtsman's skill and turner's skill and fitter's skill embodied in it, Joey understood more clearly the reason for this night ride, for this raid on the factory.

And as he loved "his" Norton more and more, he began to hate more and more the men with money, the people who own factories, because these men keep their lovely bikes shut up—even for years, sometimes, till the mudguards are scratched and the bike is "shop-soiled"—and will not let boys and young men who have not much money get hold of them. He began to hate the bosses who use this making-skill and the clean metal not for good riding, good sport, but for money, more money, always money.

When they were well on the old North Road he heard the spokes in the wheel talking. At first they seemed to have a queer language; they said "Ennery, dennery, rin, tan, lintidan" and other words like that. Young Joey asked what they meant. The spokes explained: "it's the oldest way of counting. We count the times that the wheel goes round." (They were telling the truth: these counting words are older than Julius Cæsar. You can hear a Lincolnshire shepherd count his sheep that way, as they huddle through a gate. You can hear children in West Wales use almost the same words in a skipping game. You can hear fishermen in Cornwall count their catch in not quite the same words. But you'll never hear a banker or a millionaire use them. They are part of the old things that some ordinary people keep: the rich, who think they own everything and can know everything, have never learnt them and never will.) "We count the rods, poles, perches, furlongs and miles," said the spokes.

And the spokes explained that they lived a very strange life; when they stood on their heads, five hundred times a minute, their heads stopped moving for the smallest bit of time there is; when they were swung upright, their heads at the top of the wheel were moving forward in the same direction as the bike, but going twice as fast! (Look at a rolling wheel yourself, and see how the bit at the bottom stops still for almost no time, and the bit at the top is racing forward.) And the spokes told how they had grown out of an idea in men's minds, an idea older than King Solomon, older than any city that still lives. And the spokes told how tree-trunks used as rollers had grown into flat wooden wheels, and flat wheels had grown wooden spokes, and then steel wires had come.... And the spokes told him that each of them was separate from the others, and each only linked itself closely to one other spoke, and each leaned at a different angle, and pulled a different way, and slowed down or speeded up at a different time—yet they all shared their job; out of their different pulls there came no confusion but a strength; they were free and separate and different, yet united, woven together, equal.

And young Joey listening to them, knew that men could be and would be like the steel spokes, when the greed-grabbers have been stopped from twisting all the wheels of the world into loopy shapes.

* * *

The moon climbed: another hour and the wind Joey made by riding smelt of the north and the hills; his head-lights snatched at stone walls by the roadside: they were near Badstoke. At the top of a long hill they stopped; below lay the factory. They could see men of the night-shift picket at the factory gate; they could see the policemen.

As they watched, a leader of the picket was arrested by four policemen. But at once, from nowhere, appeared another leader—and a third. They did not quarrel who should be in charge, they took over together. And Joey remembered the steel spokes had told him how, if one of their number is broken, the two nearest the broken spoke share the extra strain. These men were like the steel spokes.

The picket remained. A little way up the hill, away from it, the police grouped, awaiting orders. They had two cars and two lorries, and thirty men.

Further up the hill the motor-cycles gathered. The children sat silent, rubbing cold fingers or stretching tired backs. The bicycles discussed their plans.

Before they had finished talking the police began to move. They started driving their two lorries side by side, one on the footpath and one in the road. They began to drive these lorries slowly through the crowded ranks of the picket. Men jumped out of the way, scattered, rushed and fell. But behind the lorries the picket closed up again. It was shaken, but it was still there.

"Jump off, kids!" said the Norton. "Not you, young Joey, but the others." And the children jumped out of the saddles and off the pillion seats. "What about my babies? What about my triplets?" said the Harley side-car; but no one listened. The babies were firmly pinned in, and they looked at the sky and blinked.

"Scott, Douglas, Calthorpe, Sunbeam—stop the lorries!" said the Norton. For the lorries were beginning to turn round, beyond the factory.

Off went the Scott, singing like bagpipes, leaping on the gear-change as an aeroplane leaps before it lifts. Off went the others. As their head-lights cut down along the road, young Joey saw the thirty policemen begin to move, from this side the factory gate, towards the picket.

Soon, over the noise of engines and gears young Joey heard, from far down the road, the high-pitched shriek of tyres hard-braked. He saw the Scott, sliding and skidding, both wheels yelping and bucking—then swinging, turning—and there it was turned completely round and in front of a police lorry! The lorry slowed down to avoid running over the bike. The bike slowed down too. Both stopped. A moment later and the other three machines were in front of the lorries, holding them up, dazzling the drivers with their head-lamps.

The police drivers were not going to be stopped that way, however. "Hi!" they shouted; "ho!" they yelled. They put the lorries' gears in with a grind and a clang; they put the lorries' clutches in with a squeal and a jerk; the lorries started and the bikes had to get out of their way. "If only this ham-handed, flat-footed Robbut knew how to change gear!" groaned the first lorry. "What am I? a steam roller?" grunted the second. Grumbling, and engines knocking, they moved towards the picket from one side. On the other side, along the road, moved the thirty police.

Scott and Douglas, one on each side of the first lorry's bonnet, spoke to it in its own language, which is their language too. Calthorpe and Sunbeam talked with the second lorry. What they said is a secret: very ordinary words, about the lorries' own troubles and grievances, made into a powerful magic that may not be printed. And the magic worked when the driver of the first lorry tried to change gear.

The lorry bucked, kicked and lurched. It almost stood up on its back wheels when the clutch went in. The driver fell off his seat. The lorry swerved away from the picket on to the other side of the road; its mate followed. Both the police drivers fell right out on to the road side. And the lorries came charging and banging along past the picket heading straight for the group of thirty policemen, who stopped in amazement.

"Our turn now," said the Norton up the hill. "If any coppers are spilled don't let 'em roll down the drain!"

The police saw driverless lorries coming at them from one side, wild motor-bikes from the other. They scattered and ran. And Joey, riding the Norton ahead of the pack, saw a very fat police sergeant fall over his own very big feet and sprawl right in the middle of the road.

Joey knew these policemen were only doing what the bosses made them do; he didn't feel like running over the police sergeant. He jabbed the brake on, gave a big swing with his knees, and the bike went sideways—down till a foot-rest touched the road, making a shower of sparks. Then it kicked up, almost upright again, and Joey flew out of the saddle up in the air and landed plonk on the very fat sergeant's soft round tummy. The sergeant gave a grunt and a whistle. A lorry missed him by inches, careering past on two wheels. After a bit the sergeant got up and bowled away muttering, "Oh, my ribs and brisket! Oh, my liver and lights!"

Joey picked up his bike, unhurt except for a bent foot-rest, just in time to see the Harley-Davidson push the nose of its sidecar gently into the back of a policeman who was holding the picket-leader as prisoner. The policeman jumped aside. The Harley picked up the "prisoner" neatly on the front of its side-car and went on down the road, singing "John Brown's baby's got a pimple on its nose."

Soon the men of the picket and the children—who ran down the hill as fast as they could—and the motor-cycles were all talking together, and all happy because the police were beaten and knew it.

The lorries had barged away; policemen had limped away; the very fat sergeant had rolled away holding his very fatness with both hands and groaning, "Oh, my ribs and brisket!" And after everyone had talked all at once, for twenty minutes, including the babies (one squawked, one chuckled, and one squeaked), the Scott made its last and best suggestion:

"Let'sgoandserenadetheboss!"

"Eh? What's that?" said several voices.

"He means we should go and give the owner a field-day farewell," said the Douglas, bubbling at the idea.

They were off again, led this time by the four-speeder, because he knew where the Big House stood among trees over the hill.

The boss was awake. And he heard motor-bike after motor-bike go by, and come back again, with the engines singing and shouting in a way they never do unless their riders are cheerful, and he recognised the songs and he got more and more worried, and tried to go to sleep and could not because of the Scott, and tried to think of something else and could not because of the tune of "John Brown's baby" out on the main road. And he thought: all the other factories are selling their bikes. And he wondered: how many would I have sold this week if it hadn't been for the strike? And he decided: I'll call it off—this time. I'll telephone to-morrow and give the men what they want—at least, part of what they want.

The strike was won.

As if they had heard his thought, the bikes turned homeward. And before the sky paled or the birds woke they were far off on the old North Road, singing very softly and steering very smoothly, for every child they carried was fast asleep (a good bike that you know well will carry you safely when you're asleep).

FRONTISPIECE AND 'A LOOK AT THE WORLD'

from *The Red Corner Book for Children*
Martin Lawrence, 1931

Written by Anon. Illustrated by Michael Boland

The radical publishing house Martin Lawrence was founded in 1927. Close to the Communist Party, it, first of all, produced books on Marxism, translations of novels from the Soviet Union, and books on culture, science, contemporary events, and history from a Marxist viewpoint. In 1931 it produced its first children's book, *The Red Corner Book for Children*. This is a collection of short stories, articles, and poetry. The un-named editor says in an introductory note:

> [it] is a departure from the ordinary run of children's books. It endeavours to spur their minds to the real issues life holds out—instead of drugging them with a false glamour over ugly things.

Contributors include the British historian T. A. Jackson, the Austrian writer Hermynia Zur Mühlen, one of whose stories is reproduced here, and writers from the United States such as the author Myra Page and the US trade unionist Frank Spector. Subjects covered range from strikes, socialist fables, historical events such as the Paris Commune, biographical sketches on Wat Tyler, James Connolly and Lenin, to articles on tramping and swimming. The contents are mixed in quality, but as Geoffrey Trease observed when reviewing it, *The Red Corner Book for Children* was 'the very first attempt in England to produce a Socialist storybook for boys and girls' (1937 *Worker's Monthly*, n.p.).

The major illustrator is Michael Boland (n.d.), who works mostly in black, white, and red and it is his work that is included in this section. There is little information about him, but he was responsible for many of the illustrations for Martin Lawrence's children's books including Geoffrey Trease's *Bows Against the Barons*, also represented in this section, and *Comrades for the Charter* (1934).

THE RED CORNER BOOK FOR CHILDREN

WE'RE marching towards the morning,
We're struggling, comrades all;
Our aims are set on victory—
Our enemies must fall.
With ordered step, red flag unfurled,
We'll build a new and better world!

FROM 'A LOOK AT THE WORLD'

6. His head he carries—oh, so high!
He doesn't see below the sky.
He's really king of all the land;
He's got all the money—you understand.

7. Here you have a working man,
Slaving as hard as he really can.
He must toil and sweat 'till he's weak and old,
Yet he never will have one piece of gold.
His home all broken down and small,
Has scarcely room in it for all;
It is low and dark, and damp and cold,
Compare it with the mansion bold.

8. Mother works the whole day through;
She washes and works and has to sew.
But still the cupboard is often bare;
The kiddies must starve, for there's nothing there.

17. The priests, they teach that God is Lord
(So be very quiet, say not a word).
Lord of ALL—both good and ill,
Sh-h-h-h-h, it is all the dear Lord's will.

18. The teacher says, "Now, listen to me,
And none of your cheek or trickery.
And if you doubt the dear good Pastor,
My cane will show you who is master."

19. The Bobbies blue they keep "the law"
So that things remain as they were before.
The working man, should he dare to fight,
Is batoned, and jailed for many a night.

20. The leaders of the workers' fight
Are often hustled out of sight.
Where, 'gainst the dark wall of a prison,
Are shot ere a new day's sun is risen.
Oft they are felled like slaughtered cattle,
These leaders of the workers' battle.
But is it murder? Not at all—
Tut, tut! Society's saved—that's all.

33. Working all unitedly,
Me for you, and you for me,
Swiftly comes the great new life,
Peace and calm, and end to strife.

'THE PEOPLE SPEAK'

from *Bows Against the Barons*
Martin Lawrence, 1934

Written by Geoffrey Trease. Illustrated by Michael Boland

In his autobiography *A Whiff of Burnt Boats* (1971), Geoffrey Trease (1909–98) explained how he came to write *Bows Against the Barons.* Struggling to find a publisher,

> I had approached a publishing firm whose sympathies were sufficiently indicated by its list composed mainly of Marx, Engels, Lenin and contemporary Soviet novels with such alluring titles as *Cement.* Would the firm be interested in a Robin Hood story that would be revolutionary in more ways than one? The response was more than I had dreamed of. By return post the publishers informed me that they had been looking for someone to do this kind of book for a long time. Would I submit a synopsis and three chapters? (145)

The result was his first children's book, a fast-moving adventure story about Dickon and his family's struggle to survive as peasants in feudal times. When Dickon kills a royal deer that is ruining the crops that feed his family he decides to join Robin Hood. But this is not the familiar figure from traditional retellings; Trease's Robin heads a group who speak in anachronistic radical language and have a revolution to win. The extracts here come from the chapter entitled 'The People Speak', describing an attempt by the people of Nottingham to release their comrades from gaol.

In the 1940s and (up to the 1970s), Geoffrey Trease was generally the first writer left-minded parents offered their children. Amongst Trease's work, *Bows Against the Barons* was seen as the radical ideal. This retelling brought together in one book several strands of thought within the Communist Party: it was, for instance, the job of communists in each nation to excavate, reclaim, and celebrate popular movements as signs of that particular country's continuous tradition of the struggle for freedom and equality. Additionally, this work was in line with the teachings of Georg Lukács, who maintained that the best examples of fiction belong to the genre of historical realism in which characters' actions spring from historically accurate class outlooks.[1] According to the precepts of socialist realism, fiction should offer heroic behaviour and optimistic outcomes; the fight for socialism was incomplete, if not doomed, if it did not attend to the minds and activities of young people.

We might ask how far Trease would have been aware of such formal and ideological requirements, and in his later years, when interviewed by Michael Rosen, he appeared to disavow any particular knowledge or wish to fit in with such official views of what constituted socialist literature. However, as discussed in the Introduction to this book, Trease spent some time in the Soviet Union at the very point at which the principles of socialist realism were becoming official policy. In response he produced the letter titled 'Revolutionary Literature for the Young', in which he argued for how and why such work could and should be produced for children.[2]

Bows Against the Barons was recommended in the left-wing press and found immediate and lasting popularity with its intended audience. Raphael Samuel found solace in it as a lonely young communist at boarding school (2006 74); a review in the underground public school magazine *Out of Bounds* (see Parts Seven and Nine) recommended it 'wholeheartedly' as 'an enthralling study of England in the Middle Ages' (2, 1934 41), while some forty years later *Jane Rosen recalls finding it in the children's section of her library and being told by her mother that Trease was a good writer. She agreed.* So did Chris Kaufman, a life-long friend of Michael Rosen's who remembers the impact Trease's book had on his imagination vividly to this day:

> *I was blown away by the book. Aged twelve in late 1950s London, teachers had got me reading. I found* Bows Against the Barons *at home. My parents were communists and didn't have much time for the ruling class. We lived in a council estate, but the real estates were the palatial houses nearby whose owners got the London County Council crest taken down as it 'lowered the tone of the area'.*
>
> *I imagined I was Dickon following Alan-a-Day's battle cry 'all men equal from sea to sea', taking on the lords, abbots and tyrants. An outdoor outlaw walking so carefully that they couldn't hear a twig snap under my feet. It took courage for me to scale their walls—to get my ball back!*
>
> *And how prescient was Geoffrey Trease over 80 years ago to have Robin Hood saying 'There are only two classes, masters and men, haves and have-nots. Everything else—*

1. For a detailed discussion of Geoffrey Trease's efforts to change British children's literature see Kimberley Reynolds, 'Firing the Canon! Geoffrey Trease's Campaign for an Alternative Children's Canon in 1930s Britain' (2017).
2. Lukács developed his ideas on fiction in two seminal works: *The Theory of the Novel* (1920) and *The Historical Novel* (1937). Lukács was in Moscow at the same time as Trease, and it seems almost impossible that Trease would not have encountered him at exactly the time when Lukács was developing his ideas around historical realism. At the very least, Lukács's ideas were the ones being accepted and approved by the official writers' and critics' organizations at that time.

> *Normans and Saxons, Christian and Saracen, peasant and craftsman—is a means of keeping us apart, of keeping masters on top'. He could have written that yesterday.*
>
> *In later life as a union official of T&G/Unite [Unite the Union is Britain's biggest trade union], I found myself representing the forestry workers from Sherwood. When I negotiated with the Forestry Commission for a pay rise, I imagined the skinflints on the other side of the table were put there by the Sheriff of Nottingham.*

The book itself went through several modifications; the one most commented on is the original edition of 1934 where the 'merry men' referred to each other as 'comrade', but this was removed by 1948. Similarly, the first edition's illustrations in the classic socialist realist mode, with hints of a hammer and sickle, were replaced. In *A Whiff of Burnt Boats*, Trease admits to the anachronism of the revolutionary language of his prose, and to the detrimental effect of the frontispiece of a hanged man on the sales of the book, though the illustration by Michael Boland was meant to call attention to the continuing oppression of workers throughout the centuries. Trease went on to write many novels and works of non-fiction for children and adults as well as a commentary on children's literature, *Tales Out of School* (1948).

'THE PEOPLE SPEAK'

Across the huge market-place of Nottingham ran a low wall, built to divide the Norman quarter from the Saxon. But to-day no one could see the wall except those who were tight pressed against it. On both sides an angry crowd surged slowly backwards and forwards, eddying and murmuring.

"One—two—three!" chanted the burly bridlesmith standing on the top of the market-wall. Thousands of voices took up the cry together.

"We—want—the—Sheriff!"

Dickon had become separated from his friend the weaver, and had wormed his way through the crowd until he was near the centre. In one hand he clutched a staff, while the other fingered the handle of his hunting-knife. He could see that most of his neighbours were armed in one way or another; butchers had brought their knives and smiths their hammers. Everyone had at least a cudgel. There was trouble brewing.

"We—want—the—Sheriff!" rose the shout again.

Dickon had not recognised a face from Sherwood, but he knew that they were all about him, disguised in the dust and rags of pedlars and pilgrims. When the signal was given, bows would appear from nowhere, and the King's men would fall as freely as the King's deer.

Hardly had the last word of that tremendous roar died away than a sudden hush fell on the throng. Like a forest fire the news sprang from lip to lip. The Sheriff was coming!

A double rank of pikemen was advancing slowly through the crowd on the Norman side of the wall. Sullenly the people gave back. Those who were nearest the pikemen were in no hurry to feel the sharp points between their ribs.

"Halt!" barked an officer. The two ranks turned, stepped back, and crossed their pikes, leaving a clear avenue fenced with two lines of steel. Down it rode the Sheriff.

He drew rein at the wall and stared at the bridlesmith on the top of it. Words passed between them, but few could catch what they were.

Suddenly the smith turned and cried to the waiting throng: "Friends!"

There was a roar of encouragement. When it died away, he went on quickly:

"Fellow workers, whoever you are, Normans or Saxons—COMRADES—!"

Once more the vast crowd shouted its agreement.

"The Sheriff will not listen to our demands. So the poor may go hungry while the rich eat themselves sick—and honest men may go to jail for saying so—"

The two nearest pikemen, at a signal from the Sheriff, lunged at him, but he hopped nimbly away. There was a rush of soldiers towards him, and he waited only to utter one last shout before leaping down into safety among the people.

"To the jail, my hearties!"

To the jail!

Suddenly every one was shouting again as though he was mad. There was a great surge forward, which carried Dickon along with it, as helpless as a twig in a rushing stream. Sticks and other weapons were brandished overhead.

Then the crowd surged back again, and Dickon with them, the breath almost choked out of his body.

I didn't know fighting was like this, he thought ruefully to himself. I can't draw my knife, I can't lift my stick, and I can't even see the enemy. I'm packed as tight as a fish in a barrel.

Slowly, fighting step by step, the people were giving back before the remorseless spear-points of the soldiers. Wool jersey and leather apron could not stand against such weapons, and sticks could make no impression on mail coats and steel helmets. Growling like a wounded animal, the crowd walked backwards before that unbroken line.

Part of the vast square was already cleared, save for a body here and there, or a wounded man crawling away with a shattered collarbone or a bleeding limb. The Sheriff rode backwards and forwards behind his men, hounding them on to further efforts.

Frontispiece, Geoffrey Trease's *Bows Against the Barons*. This is the Michael Boland illustration that Geoffrey Trease later described as a 'scarifying picture' that may have proved an additional handicap to the sales of the book.

"Whip them home to their kennels, the puppies!" He twirled his moustaches angrily—and at that moment an egg shattered itself on the nose-piece of his helmet, and spread over most of his face. "Get the man who threw that!" he screamed. "I'll have him dancing on air to-night!"

Where was Robin Hood?

Anxious looks were turning every way. He had promised his help, and in a few minutes, it would be too late. The crowd would be pushed back into the narrow streets and broken up.

Suddenly a horn rang out. Dickon's heart jumped. He knew that note.

Sixty men leapt on to the wall. They looked like honest country people come to market—one or two, even, wore the skirts and shawls of peasant women—but in every left hand was a six-foot bow, in every right hand a clothyard arrow. In a second, every bow was bent, a goosefeather tip drawn to each outlaw's ear.

The crowd had slipped back a little, leaving a clear space in front of the stupefied soldiers. It was safe to shoot.

"Let us pass in peace," came the high, bell-like voice of Robin Hood. "Otherwise—"

"Charge!" snarled the Sheriff, urging his horse forward.

"Shoot!" retorted the outlaw.

Sixty shafts gleamed for a moment in the sunshine. They rattled on chain-mail and steel, but some pierced the links and others struck the unprotected face and hand and leg.

The soldiers cowered before a second volley of shafts, and before they knew where they were, they were surrounded by a rush of men. Brawny hands wrenched their pikes from them, boys tripped them up, and others leapt on their backs from behind. There was no room to draw their swords. They were helpless and overpowered.

To the jail! [. . .]

After many adventures and attempts to capture them, the outlaws celebrate a victory where Robin sets out his 'Dream of England.'

"All men are equal in the forest," went on the outlaw. "They should be equal in the whole world. They should work for themselves and for each other—not for some master set over them. Let the ploughmen plough for all and the weaver weave for all—but let no lord step in to steal the harvest and no merchant-prince to take the cloth. Then the common people will have twice as much as they have now, and there will be no more hunger or poverty in the land. There must be an end of serfdom!" Robin's voice rang clear above the crackling fire. "An end of tolls and taxes! The land for the peasants and the town for the workers! No more castles, no more hired cut-throats in livery, no more war service, no barons, no bishops, no king!" [. . .]

And he sets out his plan for revolt—a unity of peasant and townsman against baron and in the winter when the roads are bad and the barons are less able to mobilise.

"We'll light the flame in the Midlands, comrades!" he cried. "But it'll spread, north and south, east and west, till all England's ablaze. The workers will rise in a great host, and no strong place will hold out against them. And when the last castle has hauled down its flag, we shall build the new England, the England of equality and freedom—Merrie England at last!" [. . .]

The rising fails and Robin is wounded. His comrades take him to a convent. Instead of assisting him the Abbess bleeds him in order to kill him to gain the reward and to stop his ideas from spreading. Outside, the outlaws realise that something is wrong and storm the convent.

Was it imagination, or was that the feeblest of horn blasts from an upper room? It had just the silver note, but it was so soft and weak—

Little John mounted the steps four at a time. He burst into the room to find Robin alone. The nuns had fled to hiding when the door was broken down.

Dickon was close behind. He stopped in the doorway, uncertain, half-ashamed. Because Little John was crying like a kid—

Dickon felt rather like that himself. His mouth opened and shut, but he couldn't speak.

It was Robin now who looked like a baby, because John had swung him up in his arms and was carrying him out and downstairs, as though he weighed no more than thistledown. Dickon sheathed his sword and followed, wondering what would be the end of it all.

They paused on the first hill-top and laid Robin down. He was dead. Gurth spat savagely. "So they got him in the end. They always do. Well, we've paid them for it." He glanced back at the Priory, from the roof of which smoke and flames were rising.

They buried him in a wood, cunningly, because his enemies would not let even his dead body alone if they could find it. Then they stood up, dusted their hands, and looked at one another.

"This is where we part I reckon," said Gurth. "I'm going south again."

"I'm for Barnesdale as before," said another.

"I'm sick of England. I'm going to try Ireland."

Little John and Dickon found themselves alone.

"Looks as though we're the only ones left who care much about Robin's ideas," said the boy wistfully.

"Yes. I reckon things will come about slower than we thought. Perhaps not in our time at all. But we'll do our best. Robin was *right*, dead right."

"An England without masters," murmured Dickon, looking towards the hidden grave. "Sounds daft, doesn't it? But he was right. Sort of *dreamed*, when the rest of us couldn't see further than our noses."

Little John put a hand on his shoulder. "Shall we go south together, Dickon boy? Back to the High Peak? I don't fancy Sherwood again now, somehow. What do you say?"

Dickon took the big hand and shook it. "Right, comrade. And we'll go on working to make Robin's dream come true."

Two figures slipped southwards, mere shadows in the wood, their faces set towards the Derbyshire hills.

CHAPTERS 14–16

from *A White Sail Gleams*
Foreign Languages Publishing House, 1954

Written by Valentin Katayev. Translated by Leonard Stoklitsku

First published as *Beleet Parus Odinokii* (Moscow-Leningrad, 1936), and first translated into English as *A Lonely White Sail* (George Allen and Unwin, 1937), this novel is set in Odessa, where its author, Valentin Petrovich Katayev (Kataiev or Kataev) (1897–1986), was born. Katayev had a fairly successful career in the Soviet Union, writing novels and plays, mostly for adults, and editing a new wave literary journal, *Yunost* (Youth) (1955–) which published such non-orthodox writers as Yevgeny Yevtushenko (1932–2017) and Anna Akhmatova (1889–1966). Given that much of Katayev's work in the early 1930s satirized contemporary events and conditions, his survival suggests both a degree of wiliness on his part and a reminder that even in the midst of draconian decrees and persecutions, some writers managed to work some flexibility into the system.

This novel owes its title to a line from the poet Mikhail Lermontov (1814–1841), in which the lonely white sail of a ship appears in the distance, leaving the poet to wonder about where it has come from and to conclude that the boat is neither looking for happiness nor fleeing it but is a rebel looking for peace in the storms.

This perfectly matches the theme of this novel, in which a sailor escaping persecution after the failed revolution of 1905 finds refuge in Odessa thanks to the actions of the two boy heroes. In so doing, Katayev combined socialist realism with early-nineteenth-century romanticism and late-nineteenth-century symbolism in ways that are unusual across the field of left literature for children at this time. *As Michael Rosen recalls, the effect on a reader could be a sense of harsh reality intertwined with a yearning for something ineffable.* In line with the spirit of radical children's literature, the novel also depicts a friendship—albeit with tensions—across classes between the working-class Gavrik and the middle-class Petya.

Katayev himself wrote of the book (as printed on the flyleaf of the 1958 translation):

> At the time of the Russian revolution of 1905 I was just a boy of eight, but I clearly remember the battleship Potemkin, a red flag on her mast, sailing along the coast past Odessa.[1] I witnessed the fighting on the barricades, I saw overturned horse-trams, twisted and torn street wires, revolvers, rifles, dead bodies.

Perhaps then, in addition to its combination of genres, the novel is also a *roman à clef* in which Petya is Katayev. His devotion to the writing of the screenplay for the film of the novel (*The Lonely White Sail*, 1937, dir. Vladimir Legoshin), and then to searching out locations and attending to the film's historical accuracy suggests a good deal of personal and emotional involvement.

1. The Russian Revolution of 1905 involved mass political action throughout Russia, and included strikes by workers and peasants, and military mutinies, most famously the mutiny on board the battleship *Potemkin*. The Tsar responded by establishing the 'Duma', Russia's first parliament.

14

"LOWER RANKS"

Although, as we have seen, Gavrik had a life of toil and cares, quite like a grown-up, we must not forget that he was, after all, only a boy of nine.

He had friends with whom he liked to play, run, scrap, catch sparrows, shoot with catapults and do everything else all Odessa boys of poor families did.

He belonged to the category known as "street urchins", and this gave him a wide acquaintance.

Nobody prevented him from going into any courtyard or playing in any street.

He was as free as a bird. The whole city was his.

Even the freest bird, however, has its favourite haunts, and Gavrik's were the seaside streets in the Otrada and Maly Fontan districts. There he was an unchallenged king among the boys, who envied and admired his independent life.

Gavrik had many friends, but only one real chum, Petya.

The simplest thing would be to go and see Petya and put their heads together about bread and meat.

Naturally, Petya didn't have any money, especially a big sum like fifteen kopeks. There was no use even thinking about that. But Petya could take a chunk of meat from the kitchen and some bread from the cupboard.

Gavrik had been inside Petya's house once, as his guest last Christmas, and he knew very well that they had a cupboard piled with bread and that nobody gave it any notice. It would be no bother at all to bring out as much as half a loaf. Those people didn't pay any attention to things like bread.

But the trouble was he didn't know whether Petya had come back from the country. He ought to be back by now, of course. Several times during the summer Gavrik had gone to Petya's yard to find out. But Petya had been still away.

The last time their cook, Dunya, said they would soon come. That was about five days ago. Perhaps they were already there.

From the market Gavrik set out for Petya's. Luckily, it was not far away: Kulikovo Field and the corner of Kanatnaya, just opposite the railway station and next to the Army Staff building. It was a big four-storey house with two front entrances. And a wonderful house it was; if you wanted to live like a lord, you couldn't find a better.

In the first place, it was just the thing for street fights because it had two gateways: one leading out to Kulikovo Field, or simply Kulichki, and the other to a marvellous vacant lot with bushes, tarantula holes, and a rubbish-heap; only a small rubbish-heap, true, but an exceptionally rich one.

If you dug properly in it, you could always collect a mass of useful things—from chemist's vials to dead rats.

Petya was lucky. It wasn't every chap had a refuse-heap like that next to his house!

In the second place, little suburban trains drawn by a tiny engine ran past the house, so that you didn't have to go very far to put a cap or a stone under the wheels.

In the third place, the Army Staff building was next door.

Behind its high stone wall facing the field lay a mysterious world guarded day and night by sentries. Behind that wall were the rumbling machines of the Army Staff printing plant. And what interesting scraps of paper the wind carried over the wall: ribbons, strips, vermicelli!

The windows of the staff clerks' quarters faced the field too. By standing on a rock one could look through the grating and see how the clerks lived, those extraordinarily handsome, important and dashing young men in the long trousers of officers but with the shoulder straps of privates.

Gavrik had learned from reliable sources that the clerks belonged to the ordinary "lower ranks", that is to say, were plain soldiers. But what a world of difference between them and the soldiers!

With the possible exception of the *kvass* vendors, the staff clerks were the most elegant, best-dressed and handsomest fellows in town.

When they saw a clerk the chambermaids from the nearby houses turned pale and began to tremble and looked as though they would faint any minute. They mercilessly scorched their hair and temples with curling-irons, they dabbed their noses with tooth powder and they rouged their cheeks with toffee paper. But the clerks paid no attention to them.

To any Odessa soldier a chambermaid was a superior and unapproachable being, but to a staff clerk she was no more than "a dull peasant" and not worthy of a glance.

In their rooms behind the grating the staff clerks sat on iron beds softly strumming guitars; they were sad and lonely. They sat without their jackets, in long trousers with a broad red stitched belting, and clean shirts with black neckties such as officers wore.

If a staff clerk appeared in the street of a Sunday evening, it was always arm in arm with two seamstresses wearing their hair puffed up high in front.

Staff clerks were unbelievably rich. With his own eyes Gavrik once saw one of them riding in a droshky.

But strange as it seemed, staff clerks belonged to the "lower ranks". At the corner of Pirogovskaya and Kuli-kovo Field Gavrik once saw, with his own eyes, a general in silver shoulder straps striking a clerk across the mouth and shouting in a voice that sent shivers down Gavrik's back, "Is that the way to stand, you dog? Is that the way?"

The clerk stood stiffly at attention and rolled his head, his light-blue peasant eyes bulging like a common soldier's. "Sorry, Your Excellency!" he muttered. "I'll never do it again!"

It was this dual position that made the staff clerks such strange, wonderful and at the same time pathetic creatures, like fallen angels exiled as punishment from heaven to earth.

The life of the ordinary sentries, whose quarters were next door to the staff clerks, was very interesting too.

These soldiers also had two natures.

One was when they stood in pairs, in full sentry uniform, with their cartridge belts, at the alabaster front entrance of the Army Staff building, springing smartly to attention and presenting arms the way sergeants did, that is, shifting their well-greased bayonets slightly to the side whenever an officer came in or went out.

The other was a plain, domestic, peasant nature, when they sat in their barracks sewing on buttons, polishing their boots or playing draughts—"dames", as they called it.

Bowls and wooden spoons were always drying on their windowsills, and there were many left-over pieces of black army bread which they readily gave to beggars.

They readily talked to boys, too, but the questions they asked and the words they used made the boys blush to their ears and run away horrified.

The two courtyards were asphalted and were just the place for playing hopscotch. Fine squares and numbers could be drawn on the asphalt with charcoal or chalk. The smooth sea pebbles slid across it wonderfully.

If the janitor lost his temper at the hullabaloo raised by the playing children and went after them with his broom, there was nothing easier than running into the next courtyard.

Besides, the house had wonderful and mysterious cellars with woodbins.

It was simply marvellous to hide in those cellars among the firewood and various junk, in the dry, dusty darkness, while out in the yard it was bright daylight.

In a word, the house where Petya lived was an excellent place in every respect.

Gavrik entered the yard and stopped under the windows of Petya's flat, which was on the second storey.

The yard, split diagonally by the distinct midday shadow, was absolutely empty. Not a boy in sight. Evidently they were all in the country or at the seaside.

Shuttered windows. The hot, lazy stillness of noon. Not a sound.

But from somewhere far away—perhaps even as far as Botanicheskaya Street—came the spluttering and popping noise of a red-hot frying pan. Judging by the smell, it was grey mullet being fried in sunflower oil.

"Petya!" Gavrik called, his hands cupped round his mouth.

Silence.

"Pe-et-ya!"

Closed shutters.

"Pe-e-e-et-ya-a-a!!"

The kitchen window opened and the white-kerchiefed head of Dunya, the cook, looked out.

"They haven't come yet." It was the usual reply, spoken quickly.

"When will they?"

"We expect them this evening."

The boy spat on the ground and rubbed the spittle with his foot. He was silent for a while.

"Please, ma'am, as soon as he comes tell him Gavrik was here."

"Yes, Your Honour."

"Tell him I'll drop round tomorrow morning."

"It'll be quite all right if you don't. Our Petya will be going to school this year. And that means good-bye to all your monkey-business."

"Never mind," Gavrik muttered dourly. "Only don't forget to tell him. Will you?"

"I'll tell him, don't cry."

"Good-bye, ma'am."

"Good-bye, you beauty."

Dunya, it seemed, was so fed up with doing nothing all summer long that she had descended to an exchange of banter with a little ragamuffin.

Gavrik hitched up his trousers and strolled out of the yard.

A bad business! What next?

He could, of course, go to his big brother Terenti at Near Mills. But in the first place, Near Mills was a long way off, and the walk there and back would take a good four hours. And in the second place, after the disturbances he didn't know whether Terenti would be at home or not. Quite likely he was in hiding somewhere or else had nothing to eat himself.

What sense was there in wearing out his feet for nothing? They were his own, weren't they?

The boy walked out on the field and looked in at the barracks windows as he passed by.

The soldiers had just finished their midday meal and were rinsing their spoons on the windowsill. A pile of leftover bread was drying under the hot sun.

The bread was black and spongy, with a chestnut-coloured crust that actually *looked* sour, and flies were crawling over it.

Gavrik stopped near a window, entranced by the sight of such abundance.

He was silent for a while, and then to his own surprise he blurted out roughly, "Give me some bread!"

But he immediately remembered himself, picked up his tank and walked away. "I didn't mean it," he said, showing the soldiers his gap-toothed smile. "I don't want any."

The soldiers crowded at the windowsill, calling and whistling to the boy. "Hi there! Where you running to? Come back!"

They stretched out pieces of bread to him through the grating. "Take it. Don't be afraid."

He stopped in indecision.

"Hold out your shirt."

There was so much good-natured gaiety in their shouts and in the fuss they were making that Gavrik saw there would be nothing humiliating about it if he did take some bread from them. He walked back and held out his shirt.

Chunks of bread flew into it.

"Won't do you any harm to try our army bread and get used to it!"

In addition to about five pounds of bread, the soldiers gave Gavrik a good helping of yesterday's porridge.

He stowed it all neatly into the fish tank, accompanied by earthy jokes about the effect of army rations on the stomach, [then] set out for home to help Grandpa mend the line.

Late that afternoon they put out to sea again.

15

"THE BOAT AT SEA"

When he saw that the steamer did not stop and did not lower a boat, but continued on her course, the sailor calmed down a bit and began to think clearly.

His first concern was to throw off some of his clothes; they interfered with his swimming.

The jacket was water-logged and as heavy as iron, but it came off easiest of all. He did it in three movements, turning over several times and spitting out the bitter, salty sea water.

For a while the jacket floated along after him with its sleeves spread out, like a living thing; it did not want to part from its master and tried to wind itself round his legs.

After the sailor had kicked the jacket a few times it fell behind and slowly sank, swaying and dropping from layer to layer until it was lost in the depths to which the cloudy shafts of the late afternoon light faintly penetrated.

The boots gave him the most trouble of all. They stuck as though filled with glue.

He furiously scraped one foot against the other to throw off those coarse navy boots with the rust-coloured tops which had given him away. Paddling with his arms, he danced in the water; one minute his head went under, the next his shoulders reared up over the surface.

But the boots would not yield. He filled his lungs with air and then, dropping his head under the surface, tugged at the slippery heel of one of the boots, mentally letting out a string of the vilest oaths and cursing everything under the sun.

At last he pulled off that damned boot. The second came easier.

However, the relief Rodion felt when he had got rid of his boots and trousers was accompanied by an overpowering weariness. The sea water, of which he had swallowed a good deal despite all his precautions, had set his throat afire. Besides, he had smacked the water painfully hard in his dive from the ship.

The past two days he had had hardly any sleep, had walked about forty or fifty miles, and had been under great nervous strain. Now everything was going dark before his eyes. Or was that because evening was falling fast?

The water had lost its daytime colour. The surface had become a bright, glossy heliotrope, while the depths were a frightening colour, almost black.

From where he was, the sailor could not see the shore at all. The horizon had narrowed almost to nothingness. The edge of the cloudless sky was touched with a transparent green afterglow, and a faint, barely perceptible star twinkled in it.

That showed where the shore was and which way he had to swim.

All he now had on was his shirt and underdrawers, and these were no hindrance. But his head whirled, and the joints of his arms and legs ached. With every minute he found it harder to swim.

At times he felt he was losing consciousness. At others he was on the verge of vomiting. Every now and then he was seized by a brief, sudden paroxysm of fear. His loneliness and the depth frightened him.

Never before had he felt like that. He must be ill, he thought.

His short wet hair seemed dry and hot and so coarse that he could almost feel it pricking his head.

There was not a soul in sight. Overhead, in the empty darkening air, a sturdy-winged gull with a body as plump as a cat's flew by. In its long bent beak was a small fish.

A new spasm of fear gripped the sailor. He felt that any minute now his heart would burst and he would go to the bottom. He wanted to cry out but he could not unclench his teeth.

Suddenly he heard the soft splash of oars. A few moments later he saw the black silhouette of a boat.

He mustered all his strength and struck out after the boat, thrashing his feet desperately. He caught up with it and succeeded in grabbing hold of its high stern.

Hand over hand he managed somehow to pull himself to the boat's side, which was lower, and with an effort he looked in; the boat tilted.

"Come now, none of your tricks!" Gavrik shouted in a threatening bass when he saw the wet head sticking out over the gunwale.

The boy was not at all surprised to see the head. Odessa was famous for its swimmers.

Some swam out as far as three or four miles from shore and returned late in the evening. This was probably one of them.

If he was such a hero he had no business catching hold of people's boats for a rest. He ought to keep right on swimming. They'd put in a good day's work and were tired enough as it is, without dragging him!

"Come now, stop fooling! Push off or I'll let you have it with this oar!"

To give more weight to his words he bent over as if to take the oar out of the rowlock, exactly the way Grandpa did on such occasions.

"I'm—ill—" the head said, panting.

Over the side stretched a trembling arm to which the sleeve of an embroidered shirt was plastered.

This, Gavrik saw at once, was not a swimmer: people didn't go swimming in the sea in embroidered shirts.

"What's the matter—your boat sink?"

The sailor was silent. His head and arms hung lifelessly inside the boat while his legs, clad in drawers, dragged in the water. He had fainted.

Gavrik and Grandpa dropped their oars and with difficulty pulled the limp but frightfully heavy body into the boat.

"How hot he is!" said Grandpa, catching his breath.

Although the sailor was wet and shivering, his whole body burned with a dry, unhealthy heat.

"Want a drink?" asked Gavrik.

The sailor did not reply. He merely rolled his glazed, unseeing eyes and stirred his swollen lips.

The boy offered him the water-keg. He pushed it aside weakly and swallowed his saliva in revulsion. A second later he vomited.

His head fell and banged against the thwart.

Then, like a blind man, he reached out in the darkness for the keg, found it and, his teeth chattering against the oaken side, managed to gulp down some water.

Grandpa shook his head. "A bad business!"

"Where are you from?" asked the boy.

Again the sailor swallowed his saliva. He tried to say something but only managed to stretch out his arm and then dropped it lifelessly.

"To the devil with him!" he muttered indistinctly. "Don't let anybody see me. I'm a sailor—hide me somewhere—or else they'll hang me—it's the truth, so help me God—by the true and holy—"

He evidently wanted to make the sign of the Cross but couldn't raise his hand. He tried to smile at his weakness but instead a film passed over his eyes.

Again he lost consciousness.

Grandfather and grandson exchanged glances but neither said a word.

Times were such that keeping mum was the best policy.

They carefully laid the sailor on the floor-slats, through which unbailed water splashed up, placed the keg under his head and sat down at the oars.

They rowed slowly, idling along so as to reach shore when it was altogether dark. The darker the better. Before landing they circled about for a while near the familiar crags.

Fortunately, there was no one on the shore.

It was a warm, dark night full of stars and crickets.

Grandfather and grandson pulled the boat up on the beach. The pebbles rustled mysteriously.

While Grandpa remained behind to guard the sick man Gavrik ran ahead to make certain the coast was clear.

He soon returned. From his soundless footsteps, Grandpa gathered that all was well. With great difficulty, but gently, they pulled the sailor out of the boat and stood him on his legs, propping him from both sides.

The sailor put his arm round Gavrik's neck and pressed him to his now dry and extraordinarily hot body. He did not realise, of course, how heavily he was leaning on the boy.

Gavrik braced his legs more firmly. "Can you walk?" he asked in a whisper.

The sailor did not reply but took a few swaying steps forward, like a sleepwalker.

"Easy does it, easy does it," urged Grandpa, supporting the sailor from behind. "It's not far. Only a couple of steps."

They finally made their way up the little hill. No one saw them. And even if anyone had, he would hardly have paid any attention to that reeling white figure supported by an old man and a boy.

It was a familiar enough scene: a drunken fisherman was being led home by his relatives, and if he wasn't swearing or bawling songs that was simply because he had taken too much.

The minute they got the sailor into the hot and smelly darkness of the hut he collapsed on the plank-bed.

Grandpa covered the tiny window with a piece of plywood from a broken box and closed the door tightly. Only then did he light the small, chimneyless paraffin lamp, turning down the wick as low as possible.

The lamp stood in the corner, on a shelf covered with an old newspaper.

On the same shelf lay the army bread wrapped in a damp rag to keep it fresh, a cup made out of a tin can, the soldiers' porridge in a tin bowl, two wooden spoons, and a big blue seashell with coarse grey salt in it—in a word, a poverty-stricken but neat household array.

An old smoke-blackened icon was nailed in the corner above the shelf: an oblong coffee-coloured stain that was the face of St. Nicholas the Miracle Worker—the protector of fishermen—looked down with glittering eyes painted in the manner of the old Kiev school.

A wisp of smoke and the lamp-light streamed up the ancient face from below. It seemed to be alive, to be breathing.

For a long time now Grandpa had believed in neither God nor the devil. He had not seen them bring either good or evil into his life. But in St. Nicholas the Miracle Worker he did believe.

How could he not believe in this saint who helped him in his difficult and dangerous occupation? Especially since this occupation, fishing, was the most important thing in Grandpa's life.

But lately, to tell the truth, the miracle worker had been falling down on the job.

When Grandpa was younger and stronger, when he had had good tackle and a sail, the miracle worker had been of some use.

But the older Grandpa became the less help did he get from his patron saint.

Of course, when there was no sail, when the old man's strength was waning from day to day, and when there was no money to buy meat for bait, the fish caught would be small and good for nothing, be he the most miraculous miracle worker the world had ever seen. And so there was no sense expecting anything of him.

Yes, even the miracle worker was stumped when it came to offsetting old age and poverty.

For all that, there were times when Grandpa felt bitter and hurt as he looked at the stern but useless saint. True, he was no expense and hung there in his corner without disturbing anybody. Oh well, let him hang there: perhaps he'd do a good turn some day. In time the old man had come to take a patronising and even somewhat ironical attitude towards the miracle worker.

Returning to the hut with a catch—and the catch these days was almost always pitifully small—Grandpa would grumble, looking at the embarrassed miracle worker out of the corner of his eye, "Well, you old codger, so we're empty-handed again, eh? This is such trash it makes me blush to take it to market. They're not bullheads but lice."

Then, so as not to hurt the saint's feelings too much, he would add, "It's only natural. Would a real big bullhead ever go for shrimps? A real, well-fed bullhead's ready to spit on a shrimp. What a real, well-fed bullhead wants is meat. But where'll we get it, eh? You can't buy meat with a miracle, can you? So you see?"

Now, however, the miracle worker was farthest from the old man's thoughts. He was greatly worried about the sailor. And not so much by his fever and unconsciousness as by his premonition of mortal danger from some unnamed source.

Naturally, Grandpa did have an idea of what it was all about, but to help the man he would have to know a little more.

As luck would have it, however, the sailor was unconscious and feverish; he lay sprawled out on the patchwork quilt, staring straight in front of him with open but unseeing eyes.

One of his hands hung down from the bed. On the other, which lay on his chest, Grandpa saw a blue anchor.

Every now and then the sailor attempted to spring up; moaning, the hot sweat pouring from him, unconscious, he would bite his hand as though trying to bite out the anchor, as if once the anchor were gone he would instantly feel better.

Grandpa forced him to lie down again and wiped his forehead. "Lie down, now," he urged. "Lie quiet, I tell you. And go to sleep, don't be afraid. Go to sleep."

Out in the vegetable patch Gavrik was boiling water in a cauldron to make the sick man some tea. Not real tea, that is, but a brew of the fragrant herb which Grandpa gathered in the nearby hills in May, and then dried and used instead of tea.

16

"TURRET GUN, SHOOT!"

They passed a fitful night.

The sailor tore at the shirt on his chest. He was suffocating.

Grandpa put out the lamp and opened the door to let in fresh air.

The sailor saw the starry sky but he could not understand what it was. The night breeze blew into the hut and cooled his head.

Gavrik lay in the weeds near the door, his ears attuned to the faintest rustle. He did not close an eye until morning. His elbow turned numb from lying on it.

Grandpa made a bed for himself on the earthen floor of the hut but he did not sleep either; he listened to the crickets, to the waves and to the moans of the sick man, who from time to time sprang up excitedly and shouted in a weak, colourless voice, "Turret gun, shoot! Koshuba! Turret, give it to them!" and other such nonsense.

Grandpa would take him firmly by the shoulders, shake him gently and whisper straight into his hot, feverish mouth, "Lie quiet. For the sake of the Lord God himself, don't raise a row. Lie quiet. What a trial!"

Little by little the sailor, grinding his teeth, would quieten down.

Who was this strange patient?

Rodion Zhukov was one of the seven hundred men of the battleship *Potemkin* who had gone ashore in Rumania.

He in no way stood out among the other men of the mutinous ship.

From the first minute of the uprising, from that very minute when the commander of the battleship dropped in horror and despair to his knees before the crew, when the first rifle shots rang out and the dead bodies of certain officers were thrown overboard, when the sailor named Matyushenko ripped off the door of the Admiral's cabin, that very cabin past which they still could not walk without a feeling of fright—from that very minute Rodion Zhukov lived, thought, and acted as did most of the other sailors: in a sort of haze, in a state of feverish exaltation until the time when they had to surrender to the Rumanians and disembark at Constantsa.

Rodion had never before set foot in a foreign land. And a foreign land, like useless freedom, is broad and bitter.

The *Potemkin* stood quite close to the pier.

Among the feluccas, freighters, yawls, yachts and cutters, and side by side with an emaciated-looking Rumanian cruiser, the grey three-funnelled battleship was absurdly huge.

The flag of St. Andrew, like a white envelope crossed with blue lines, still hung aloft, above the gun-turrets, boats and yards.

But suddenly it quivered, fell limp, and slid down in short spurts.

Rodion then took off his sailor cap with both hands and bowed so low that the ends of the new ribbons of St. George spread out gently over the dust, like those orange-and-black country flowers.

"It's a dirty shame! Twelve-inch guns, enough ammunition to last a month, and crack gunners, every mother's son of them. We ought to have listened to Dorofei Koshuba. He was right when he said we ought to throw the lousy petty officers overboard, sink the *Georgi Pobe-donosets* and land a force in Odessa. We would have roused the whole Odessa garrison, all the workers, the whole Black Sea! Oh, Koshuba, Koshuba, if only we'd listened to you! What a hell of a mess we're in!"

Rodion bowed to his beloved ship for the last time.

"Never mind," he said through his teeth, "never mind. We won't give in. We'll rouse the whole of Russia all the same!"

With his last money he bought a civilian outfit, and a few days later, at night, he reached Russian territory by crossing the estuary of the Danube near Vilkovo.

His plan was to make his way across the steppe to Akkerman, and then on a barge or a boat to Odessa. From Odessa it would be simple to reach his native village of Nerubaiskoye, and there he would decide his next move.

He knew only one thing for certain: that all the roads to the past were closed to him, that he was cut off once and for all both from the servile life of a sailor on the tsar's battleship, and from the hard peasant life at home, in the clay hut with the dark-blue walls and the light-blue window-frames, standing among pink and yellow holly-hocks.

Now it was either the gallows or going into hiding, starting an uprising, setting fire to landowners' manors, reaching the city and locating the revolutionary headquarters.

He began to feel ill on the road but stopping was out of the question and he continued on his way.

And now.... What's the matter with him? Where is he? Why are stars rocking in the doorway? And are they really stars?

Like a dark sea, night engulfs Rodion.

The stars gather into clusters, flare up, and form a low-lying row of Quarantine lights before his eyes. The city breaks into commotion. The trestle bridge in the port bursts into flames. Running men lose their direction in the raging fire. Rifle volleys smack down on the roadway like long steel rails.

The night is a rocking ship's deck. The bright circle of a searchlight skims along the winding shore, making the corners of houses glow white-hot and windows glare dazzlingly; and out of the darkness it snatches the figures of running soldiers, ragged red flags, ammunition-waggons, gun-carriages, overturned horse-trams.

And then he sees himself in the gun-turret.

The gunner glues his eye to the range-finder. The turret revolves smoothly, bringing the empty, shining, mirror-like, grooved barrel to bear on the city. Stop! Now it is directly on a line with the blue cupola of the theatre where an imposing general is holding a war council against the insurgents.

The turret telephone buzzes faintly and monotonously.

Or can that be crickets in the steppe?

No, it's the telephone. With a slow clang the electric hoist brings up a shell from the magazine. It sways on the chains and comes straight into Rodion's hands.

Or can that be a cool melon instead of a shell? Ah, what a joy to bite into a juicy melon! But no, it's a shell.

"Turret, shoot!"

That very same instant there is a ringing in his ears, as if some giant hand outside has struck the armour of the turret like a tambourine. There is a flash of fire. The smell of a burning celluloid comb pours over him.

The entire breadth of the roadstead shudders. The boats begin to rock. A strip of iron comes down between the ship and the city.

An "over".

Rodion's hands are flaming hot. Then again the crickets meander in a crystal stream among the close-set stars and the weeds.

Or can that chirping be the telephone?

Now the second shell crawls out of the hoist and into Rodion's hands. Now we'll finish off that general!

"Turret, shoot!"

"Lie down and stop your yelling. Want a drink? Lie quiet."

A second strip crosses the bay. Again an "over". But never mind, the third time we won't miss. And there are plenty of shells. A magazine full of them.

In his weary hands the third shell feels lighter than a feather and yet heavier than a house.

Fire it as quickly as possible, send smoke pouring out of that blue cupola—and then things'll roll along!

But why has the telephone stopped chirping, why have the crickets stopped tinkling? Have they all dropped dead there overhead?

Or is that the dawn, so quiet and so pink?

Smoothly the turret turns back. "Cease firing!" The shell slips out of his lowered hands and is carried back into the magazine, with a rattle of the hoist chains. But no—the cup has slipped from his fingers and water is trickling slowly from the bed to the floor.

And then all is quiet, oh, so quiet.

"What's this? They betrayed freedom, the damned swine! They turned cowards! Once you start fighting you've got to fight to the end! To leave not a single stone standing!"

"Shoot, turret gun, shoot!"

"Oh, Lord, oh, St. Nicholas, holy miracle worker! Lie down and drink some more water. What a misfortune!"

The pink quietness of dawn lays a tender and soothing hand on Rodion's inflamed cheek. Far away on the gilded bluff the cocks begin to crow.

'HOW TILL BOUGHT LAND IN LUNEBERG'

from *The Amazing Pranks of Master Till Eulenspiegel*
The Adprint Studios, London; Max Parrish and Co Ltd, New York, 1948

Written by Anon. Translated L. Gombrich. Figures, scenes and drawings by E. Katzer

The stories of the late medieval trickster figure Till Eulenspiegel are very well known by children all across the territories of what is now Germany, the Netherlands, and Belgium. The stories cover a set of episodes from Eulenspiegel's birth to his death, in which he plays tricks on whomever he comes across, escalating from his humble origins to tricking shopkeepers, landlords, aristocrats, kings, and great scholars. The earliest complete edition of Eulenspiegel's adventures dates from 1515, and some suggest the author to this collection of ninety-five tales could be Herman Bote, a fairly well-known writer of the time. However, it is clear that many of the stories predate Bote, who drew on oral sources, possibly relating to a fourteenth-century real-life figure of that name.

The route from 1515 to the 1948 edition represented here comes via Maxim Gorky, the Soviet writer who, along with Yuri Sokolov, did more than anyone else to lay down the theory which justified the adoption of folk culture as legitimate material for the Communist and socialist movements. His ideas are set down in one document in particular: a speech delivered in August 1934, at the Soviet Writers' Congress. Gorky was defending folk stories and songs from those who wanted to suppress this whole area of culture, which they perceived as representing reactionary ideas that were holding back the revolution. Gorky argued that the material represents working people's aspirations. 'The more the ruling class split up,' he wrote,

> the smaller did its heroes become. There came a time when the 'simpletons' of folklore, turning into Sancho Panza, Simplicissimus, Eulenspiegel, grew cleverer

> than the feudal lords, acquired boldness to ridicule their masters, and without doubt contributed to the growth of that state of feeling which, in the first half of the sixteenth century, found its expression in the ideas of the 'Taborites' and the peasant wars against the knights.[1]

At a stroke, Gorky provided a justification for the Left to celebrate this kind of literature; *this is exemplified in Michael Rosen's own experience by the fact that this 1948 edition of the book was given to him for his third birthday by a Communist friend of his parents. By then it had a place in the left canon.*

The extract is listed as Chapter 26 in the 1995 Oxford University Press translation of the 1515 edition, and Chapter 27 in this version. The translator is Lisbeth Gombrich (1907–94), who was born in Vienna, but left Austria in 1938. In England she worked for the Commonwealth Forestry Bureau and as a translator, including of works by her brother, the art historian E. H. Gombrich. The story deals with a key question from the European uprisings of the sixteenth and seventeenth centuries: who owns land?

1. Accessed at https://www.marxists.org/archive/gorky-maxim/1934/soviet-literature.htm

HOW TILL BOUGHT LAND IN LUNEBURG

TILL came to the capital of the Duke of Luneburg and here he amused himself at the expense of the citizens, until at length the Duke was displeased, and banished Till, forbidding him on pain of death to return. But somehow his wanderings soon brought him again to the frontier of Luneburg and his way lay across a corner of the Duke's domain.

Till was not a man ever to turn back, nor did he like to take a long way round to avoid the Duke's men. Yet he did not want to run the risk of being hanged either, and that was what the Duke had threatened to do if he ever found him on his land again.

Till sat down on the boundary stone, thinking hard. Then he had an idea. He walked up to a farmer who was carting manure on a nearby field and asked him, 'To whom does this field belong?'

'It is my own field,' said the farmer, 'I inherited it from my father, and he had it from his. We have always been free men.'

'If it is yours, you might sell me some of it. I shall pay you a fair price,' said Till.

The farmer replied that he was willing, and that he would just go and fetch a chain to measure the length and width of the strip to be sold. But Till said, 'You need not trouble over measuring implements. All I require is as much of your land as can be loaded on to your cart. And I should like to buy the cart and horse also.'

The farmer laughed at the strange request, but for a shilling filled the cart full of rich good loam. Till sat down on top, and thus prepared, he drove off into Luneburg.

He had not covered many miles before he was recognised by a group of the Duke's servants whom he passed on the road. They took hold of his horse and said joyfully, 'Now we've got you at last, you arch-rogue! Don't worry! You shan't escape.'

Till for once was silent, and allowed himself to be led off towards the castle. Not far from the palace they met the Duke himself mounted on a magnificent charger, on his way home from a day's hunting. As soon as he recognised Till, who sat quietly in his cart, half buried in the earth, his face grew purple with rage and he shouted:

'Till, have I not banished you for ever from my realm? I thought I made it plain that if ever I found you on my land again, I would hang you from the nearest tree! And I am going to do it; you need not think you can ignore my edict!' He turned to his men. 'Take this rogue and hang him on the highest tree you can find, and be quick about it.'

'At your service, my gracious lord,' was Till's calm reply. 'Of course you can do as you please, but you would be doing wrong, Sire, for I am not on your land. Look at me. I am on my own land, which I bought from a farmer whose freehold property it was. And a man has a right to be on his own land, hasn't he?'

At that the Duke could not help laughing, and he said, 'We will let you go this time. But take *your* land off *my* land as fast as you can, and never let me see you again, for if I find you here once more, I am going to hang you, horse and cart and all, land or no land.' Then he rode off, still chuckling.

Till, however, scrambled out of the cart, mounted the old cart-horse and rode away as fast as it would carry him.

THE LITTLE TUSKERS' OWN PAPER

Daily Worker League, 1945

Written and illustrated by Barbara Niven and Ern Brook

Wife and husband Barbara Niven (1896–1972) and Ern Brook (1911–93) worked together to produce this booklet. Niven, an artist, was the national organizer of the *Daily Worker* and later their Fighting Fund organizer. Brook was a landscape artist who made his living as a graphic artist and freely made his work available to the movement. The *Daily Worker*, the daily newspaper of the Communist Party, was first issued in 1930, and tales of its beginnings and fight for survival were familiar to members of the Party, the paper's supporters, and their children. The impossibility of finding distributors meant that initially the paper relied on supporters giving up their time to collect the newly printed issues and race them to all the London stations to catch the final trains to get them to their destinations around the country from the south west to the industrial strongholds of the West Midlands, the north west, the north east, and Scotland. Their dedication reflected the considerable pride and affection for 'our' paper felt by its readers.

This charming booklet captures this sense of pride as it follows a group of elephant children planning their own newspaper publication and going to the *Daily Worker* offices for advice and guidance. This is a junior version of *The Inside Story of the* Daily Worker*: 10 Years of Working Class Journalism* (1939), the story of the paper's daily work and struggle written by its editor, William Rust. The cartoons in *The Little Tuskers' Own Paper* echo the photographs in Rust's book, and with its simple text, provided the children of *Daily Worker* readers with an affectionate and realistic idea of the paper's—and their parents'—continuing struggle in an increasingly unfriendly atmosphere as the Cold War began to bite.

THE LITTLE TUSKERS' OWN PAPER

Little Tusker thinks about his paper. His Ma tells him not to worry.

All About Elephants

AN elephant is a kind, gentle, sociable and friendly animal. He loves his own kind. He works and plays and goes around with them.

He is also powerful and full of strength. And he never forgets what his enemies do to him, but bides his time and gives it all back.

In fact, in lots of ways, he is just like you and me and our pals.

Here's a baby elephant, ***LITTLE TUSKER*** is his name, who thought it would be fine to print a paper for him and his mates. He could talk to lots more that way.

He worried how to begin and went around with a wrinkled frown till his Ma told him, stroking the furrow off his iace with her trunk, "Silly boy—go and ask the editor of the Daily Worker. He'll tell you."

Little Tusker and his Ma

All About Elephants

AN elephant is a kind, gentle, sociable and friendly animal. He loves his own kind. He works and plays and goes around with them.

He is also powerful and full of strength. And he never forgets what his enemies do to him, but bides his time and gives it all back.

In fact, in lots of ways, he is just like you and me and our pals.

Here's a baby elephant, LITTLE TUSKER is his name, who thought it would be fine to print a paper for him and his mates. He could talk to lots more that way.

He worried how to begin and went around with a wrinkled frown till his Ma told him, stroking the furrow off his face with her trunk, "Silly boy—go and ask the editor of the Daily Worker. He'll tell you."

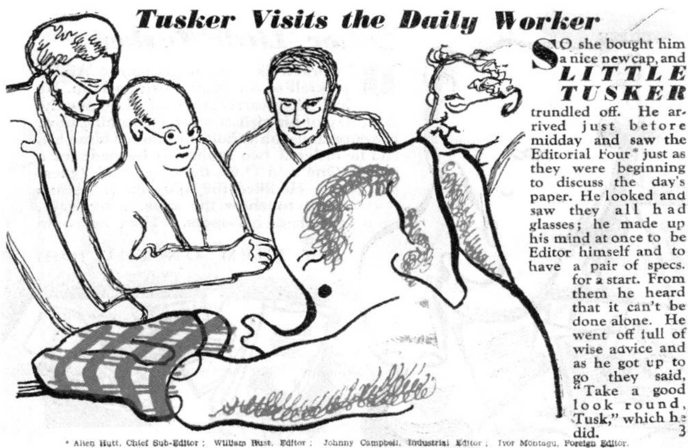

Tusker Visits the Daily Worker

So she bought him a nice new cap, and ***LITTLE TUSKER*** trundled off. He arrived just before midday and saw the Editorial Four* just as they were beginning to discuss the day's paper. He looked and saw they all had glasses; he made up his mind at once to be Editor himself and to have a pair of specs for a start. From them he heard that it can't be done alone. He went off full of wise advice and as he got up to go they said. "Take a good look round, Tusk," which he did.

* Allen Hutt, Chief Sub-Editor; William Rust, Editor; Johnny Campbell, Industrial Editor; Ivor Montagu, Foreign Editor.

Editor—Little Tusker

HE worked like mad to get going. All his pals rallied round and their pals too. He had taken careful note of all he saw the great day of his visit and forgot nothing now. His enormous job as Editor bothered him a bit, and he ordered two stamps to be made for a start. One said O.K., the other N.G. (guess that one). He liked the first better. Also a chart to show the sales, a secretary, and last—his specs. Then he could begin.

SEE THEM ON THE JOB.

Busy Corner

DO you know how the news from all the little working Tuskers comes in? Or from those snooping round for special bits (outside reporters)?

By lots of telephones. All day Bella, on the switchboard, pulls those little plugs in and out of holes, quicker than you can say "knife" and they can all speak to one another. A clever little elephant, Bella.

5

Busy Corner

Do you know how the news from all the little working Tuskers comes in? Or from those snooping round for special bits (outside reporters)?

By lots of telephones. All day Bella, on the switchboard, pulls those little plugs in and out of holes, quicker than you can say "knife" and they can all speak to one another. A clever little elephant, Bella.

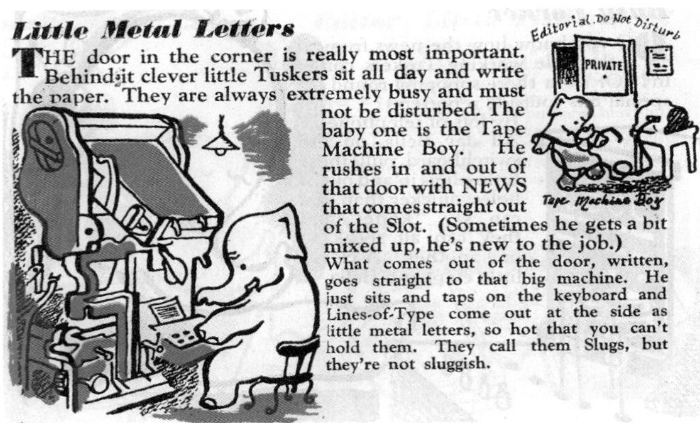

Little Metal Letters

THE door in the corner is really most important. Behind it clever little Tuskers sit all day and write the paper. They are always extremely busy and must not be disturbed. The baby one is the Tape Machine Boy. He rushes in and out of that door with NEWS that comes straight out of the Slot. (Sometimes he gets a bit mixed up, he's new to the job.)

What comes out of the door, written, goes straight to that big machine. He just sits and taps on the keyboard and Lines-of-Type come out at the side as little metal letters, so hot that you can't hold them. They call them Slugs, but they're not sluggish.

6

Little Metal Letters

The door in the corner is really most important. Behind it clever little Tuskers sit all day and write the paper. They are always extremely busy and must not be disturbed. The baby one is the Tape Machine Boy. He rushes in and out of that door with NEWS that comes straight out of the Slot. (Sometimes he gets a bit mixed up, he's new to the job.)

What comes out of the door, written, goes straight to that big machine. He just sits and taps on the keyboard and Lines-of-Type come out at the side as little metal letters, so hot that you can't hold them. They call them Slugs, but they're not sluggish.

The "Comps"

THE slugs, warm, are passed here. Each elephant has a "slug." They had to be taught to use their trunks for this, only skilful little Tuskers can manage it, even now. They have frames and build up a whole page in it with rows of slugs. They are so quick and clever they can do a page in 1 1/2 hours. When it's done it is called a FORME. Their gear is kept in those little holes at the back of the picture.

Queer Names

SEE where the FORME has got to? It stands on a solid table while a sheet of very special stuff (it has to be!) is laid on top. They call it a FLONG. The Tuskers like that because it's a fat little word which rhymes with BONG. But when it has been pressed down on the metal with a big machine that doesn't show, it comes off with the words written all over it and then it is A MOULD.

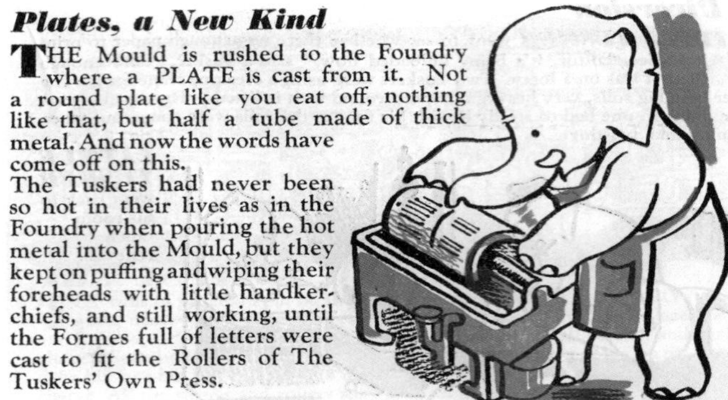

Plates, a New Kind

THE Mould is rushed to the Foundry where a PLATE is cast from it. Not a round plate like you eat off, nothing like that, but half a tube made of thick metal. And now the words have come off on this.

The Tuskers had never been so hot in their lives as in the Foundry when pouring the hot metal into the Mould, but they kept on puffing and wiping their foreheads with little handkerchiefs, and still working, until the Formes full of letters were cast to fit the Rollers of The Tuskers' Own Press.

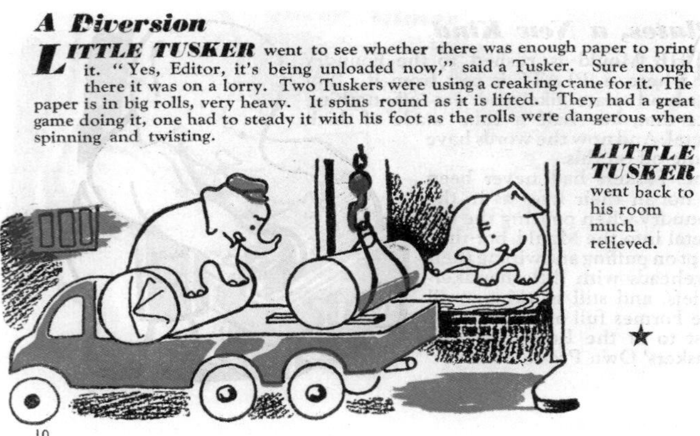

A Diversion

LITTLE TUSKER went to see whether there was enough paper to print it. "Yes, Editor, it's being unloaded now," said a Tusker. Sure enough there it was on a lorry. Two Tuskers were using a creaking crane for it. The paper is in big rolls, very heavy. It spins round as it is lifted. They had a great game doing it, one had to steady it with his foot as the rolls were dangerous when spinning and twisting.

LITTLE TUSKER went back to his room much relieved.

THE TUSKERS' OWN PRESS

THE rolls of paper are put on the printing machine, called A ROTARY (another queer name—it only means it rolls). The half-tubes of metal are placed on the Rollers. It's a great moment. The Little Tuskers are all excited and dashing about. Somebody has to put the ink in the Troughs—he gets some on his feet and dabs his face but he's too busy to notice. Go!—Switch on!—calls the Tusker in charge. All the wheels and rollers start to turn, and what a noise.
Every time ***Little Tusker*** hears them start up, he gets excited, too.

The Tuskers' Own Press

THE rolls of paper are put on the printing machine, called A ROTARY (another queer name—it only means it rolls). The half-tubes of metal are placed on the Rollers. It's a great moment. The Little Tuskers are all excited and dashing about. Somebody has to put the ink in the Troughs—he gets some on his feet and dabs his face but he's too busy to notice. Go!—Switch on!—calls the Tusker in charge. All the wheels and rollers start to turn, and what a noise.

Every time ***Little Tusker*** hears them start up, he gets excited, too.

12

"Daily Tusker" Runs Off

A CONSTANT stream of newspapers starts to flow off the rollers. The Tusker on his little stool is amazed. They keep coming. Printed and folded too, all ready to go out.
Every twenty-sixth paper is awkward and, instead of keeping in line, is crooked, so Tusker on the stool can scoop them up in bundles of twenty-six (they call it a quire—not the kind that sings). The papers have a ride along a belt to the Packers. It seems like magic, they go running right up to the gallery where they're waiting and never fall off.

"Daily Tusker" Runs Off

A CONSTANT stream of newspapers starts to flow off the rollers. The Tusker on his little stool is amazed. They keep coming. Printed and folded too, all ready to go out.

Every twenty-sixth paper is awkward and, instead of keeping in line, is crooked, so Tusker on the stool can scoop them up in bundles of twenty-six (they call it a quire—not the kind that sings). The papers have a ride along a belt to the Packers. It seems like magic, they go running right up to the gallery where they're waiting and never fall off.

Parcelling Ready For Off

EVERYONE's in a hurry in the Packers' Gallery. It is nearly half-past six and the papers have to be wrapped up and taken to the Railway Station for their trip to all the Towns and Villages. ***Little Tusker*** dashes in to see how everything is working. All the Tuskers are busy stringing the parcels with their trunks, pasting labels on.

A sticky label stuck to ***Little Tusker's*** feet and when he pulled it off with his trunk it stuck on the end. He gave it up and went around with a label saying "Birmingham."

Speed! Speed!! Speed!!!

Now into the Van with them, quick! The Driver is worried, there's no time to spare to catch the train for Scotland. You couldn't really see him it's so dark in the Yard.

The previous night was foggy. He got lost, and the Tusker with the bowler, one of the best, walked all the way to the Station in front of him with a lantern so he should catch the train. He's never missed it yet. It pays to worry about some things—for instance, about all the Tuskers who are waiting for their paper next day.

Fighting Fund

HAVEN'T you been wondering where they got the money from to do all this.

It came from all the Tuskers, little and big, who really wanted *their own paper*. They go on sending it because it's just the sort of paper they really do want. Everybody was prepared to help to keep it going.

Little Tusker learnt a whole lot from the Daily Worker Fund on that visit of his. He **longs** to make a paper that means so much to so many.

Home, with the first Copy!

Paint me
Produced by Daily Worker League
Done by Barbara Niven, Ern Brook
Printed by Illustrated Periodicals. Ltd., London, S.E.1.

ADVENTURES OF MICKY MONGREL. NO. 8.

Micky and his friends start out to push the DAILY WORKER.

THEY all set out together, Micky carrying the leaflets, because he is the biggest, and amusing the twins by telling them about his adventure with the whitewash.

They gave the leaflets to the people who passed, but they seemed to have such a pile. "Oh dear," sighed Tim and Tom together. "We shall never get rid of them all."

The wind was blowing very hard, and at that moment, an extra big gust came. Micky wasn't holding the leaflets as tightly as he should, and, horror of horrors—away they went, all too quickly.

This cartoon was part of a series about 'Micky Mongrel, the class conscious dog', which started in the *Daily Worker* from its first days in 1930.

PART FOUR

OF RUSSIA WITH LOVE

INTRODUCTION

Radical children's literature tended to be internationalist in its outlook offering, for example, heroic depictions of life in China, stories about the subsistence wages and poor conditions of miners and agricultural workers in the USA, and freedom fighters in Spain. These sympathetic stories were in marked contrast to the images in much popular fiction of Africans, Chinese, Indians, and 'natives' from various parts of the world as inferior and threatening. Interest in fellow workers around the globe never waned, but from the 1930s, one country dominated the pages of radical children's literature. In periodicals, non-fiction, biographies, and novels, children read about the daily life, key figures, and achievements in the Union of Soviet Socialist Republics (USSR). As a country, the USSR is invariably depicted as a grand experiment in which technology and the sciences were being used to plan and deliver a new and better way of managing society.

Radical publications treat the Soviet experiment as the 'most exciting adventure in the history of the world',[1] and a model that could address the instabilities and inequities of capitalism that many blamed for the series of wars that had punctuated the first decades of the twentieth century.[2] The empathetic nature of fiction made stories set in the USSR an effective way of planting the desire in young readers for Britain to become a socialist state. Their appetites for socialism were no doubt whetted even more by tales about how the Soviet state was investing in the young. Radical writing told of children being treated as full members of society, with important roles and responsibilities, as well as of state-funded amenities including massive children's theatres, libraries, and 'parks of culture' with parachute jumps, miniature railways, and buildings where children could practise skills that ranged from engineering to drawing. These accounts were not directed only at children; it was widely reported both in the USSR and abroad that Soviet children were happier, healthier, better educated and had more opportunities for play, creativity, and genuine participation in the affairs of the country than they did anywhere else in the world (Kelly, 2007 61).

1. This is how Olaf Stapledon describes the USSR in Naomi Mitchison's edited reference work, *An Outline for Boys and Girls and Their Families* (1932), 565. An extract from Stapledon's piece features in Part Ten of this volume.
2. Britons' optimistic interest in developments in the Soviet Union was mirrored in the USA, as Julia Mickenberg explains in *Learning from the Left: Children's Literature, the Cold War, and Radical Politics in the United States* (2006).

In fact, the reality for most Soviet children was far from ideal. Although from the 1920s the Soviet Union was visited by numerous official trade delegations, trade union excursions, political and scientific expeditions, and independent travellers from both the UK and the USA (Nicholson, 2009 67), the desire for socialism to prove successful meant that as a rule, the country was shown in the best possible light. What George Orwell called, in a 1940 essay on 'Boys Weeklies', 'the adulation of Soviet Russia' owed much to the way visitors were largely confined to officially approved routes that focused on showcase achievements: model factories, kindergartens, new housing designed for communal living, the Moscow underground, Pioneer camps, and parks of culture. With the advantage of hindsight, Geoffrey Trease concluded that the image of life in the USSR he painted in *Red Comet*, one of the texts featured in this section, was

> well intentioned and honest enough at the time, but in final effect, Stalinist propaganda. It contains many passages of accurately observed material, but I could not visit *all* the places, and, by relying on second-hand accounts I unwittingly produced a picture false in many respects.[3]

Although history showed that there was much wrong with the implementation of the succession of Soviet Five-Year Plans, as Britain and the USA endured the Great Depression and, particularly in Britain, the hardships of the post-war years, the idea of planned social and economic reform seemed very attractive. Radical children's literature was not only infused with the hope that the Soviets were leading the way into a future of achievement, comfort, and modern living, it also included children's books that originated in the USSR. Most famous of these are the many picturebooks produced as part of the Soviet drive to educate the masses. Reflecting the high priority children's books were given by Communist Party leaders, the Commissar of Education, Anatoly Lunacharsky, and his Deputy, Lenin's wife, Nadezhda Krupskaya, were given oversight of their production and the power to commandeer the services of leading artists and writers. As well as supporting the spread of literacy, these inexpensive books also explained and celebrated the way science and technology were being used to modernize Soviet society. Although their motivation was didactic and they were cheaply produced, these Soviet picturebooks are still recognized for their sophisticated, dynamic, and entertaining words and images.

Longer works also found their way to Britain, among the earliest being Mikhail Ilin's *Moscow has a Plan: A Soviet Primer*, discussed in Part Ten and which was based on the US edition entitled *New Russia's Primer: Story of the*

3. Quoted by Trease's granddaughter, Tamsin Grant, in correspondence relating to this anthology.

Five-Year Plan. Although some of these were republished by British publishing houses, most were imported from Moscow by the Communist Party of Great Britain and made available through the kinds of bazaars and friendship networks Michael Rosen recalls in the Introduction. Although the books represented approved values, they were read enthusiastically and remembered affectionately by many children of the Left, of whom Jane Rosen and Michael Rosen are representative. Figures such as punk guitarist Viv Albertine (b. 1967); Sheila Fitzpatrick (b. 1941), a historian specializing in Soviet Russia; *Guardian* journalists Martin Kettle (b. 1949) and Polly Toynbee (b. 1946); comedian Alexei Sayle (b. 1952); and Marxist historian Raphael Samuel (1934–96) are among those who are also on record as enthusiastic readers and performers of the kinds of materials featured in this anthology, not least those about Soviet Russia. Alison Light, who was married to Samuel until his death and who is currently writing about his life, recalls him talking about how 'books were passed on and between branch members':

> Raphael remembered seeing what the Party called 'Lit.', i.e. pamphlets about Basque children when he was three or four. I have Gorky's short stories which were Raphael's mum's, with her name in them from the Foreign Languages Publishing House, Moscow 1948—which Raphael kept and no doubt read (he would have been 14 then)—and there was much overlap of Soviet Classics; a volume of one act Soviet Plays.[4]

Samuel also read Arkady Gaidar's *Timur and his Comrades*, represented here.

4. Private correspondence from Alison Light to Kimberley Reynolds, 14 March 2017.

FROM *THE DIARY OF A COMMUNIST SCHOOLBOY*

Victor Gollancz, 1928

Written by Nikolai Ognyov. Translated by Alexander Werth

The fictional diary of Nikolai Ognyov, pen name of Mikhael Grigoryevitch Rozânov (1888–1938), was one of the first children's books from the Soviet Union to be translated for a British audience. It covers a year at school in the post-revolutionary period when the Bolsheviks were experimenting with education reforms as experienced and reported by schoolboy Kostya Riabtsov. Many of the reforms, at least in Kostya's eyes, are badly applied if not misconceived. The extracts include a typical example: the school's attempt to introduce the Dalton system. Developed in the USA, the Dalton system aimed to foster independence and self-reliance in school children by letting them work on individually agreed programmes of study. Classrooms were transformed into laboratories for exploring particular topics at their own pace. The system required well-trained teachers and ample resources, neither of which is available in Kostya's school.

The story shares some features with traditional school stories: it focuses on school hierarchies and rivalries, relationships between pupils and teachers, and reports pranks, misunderstandings, and punishments. There are, however, some notable differences. For instance, Young Pioneers rather than sporting captains are the leaders of the school, pupils wield considerable power over teachers, who can be denounced for teaching in pre-revolutionary ways, and there is a pervasive atmosphere of surveillance and threat. Ognyov periodically defuses this atmosphere through humour that for the most part stems from Kostya's naïve pronouncements.

Although he is initially critical of the new regime, Kostya gradually comes to terms with the new relationships among school, state, and youth organizations. At the end of the diary he is invited to become a leader in the Alliance of Communist Youth, one of the student groups involved in running of the school.

Diary of a Communist Schoolboy was followed by *Diary of a Communist Undergraduate*, which was published in the UK in 1929 with a preface by the translator Alexander Werth. Werth praises the book for its honest insider's version of what was happening in the USSR. By contrast, most accounts by British visitors, he observed, are ill informed:

> almost every week we have some new book by someone who has taken a ten days' trip to Moscow, and who is at last going to tell us 'the truth about Russia.' The fact that the . . . gentleman doesn't know a word of Russian and has seen no more of Russia than a gala show at the State Opera . . . doesn't deter him. . . . As information, these 'last words' are hardly worth the ink with which they are written . . . in almost every case, the 'last word' could have been written without going to Russia. (Ognyov, 1929 9)

The extracts here cover the beginning of the school year and a project in which pupils are involved in gathering and recording local information. This kind of project is described in Mikhail Ilin's *Moscow has a Plan*, discussed in Part Ten.

FIRST COPY-BOOK

SEPTEMBER 15TH, 1923

It's the middle of September already, but school hasn't begun yet. No one knows when we'll start. They said the school was being repaired, but when I went there this morning I saw no signs of it, and there was no one to ask. The doors were wide open, but no one was inside. On my way home I bought this copy-book from a youngster for three "lemons."[1] When I came home I didn't know what to do with myself, so I finally decided to start a diary. I shall write all kinds of things in it.

I want to change my name to "Vladlen."[2] Far too many people are called Constantine. But I went down to the militia yesterday, and they told me I couldn't change my name until I was eighteen. It's a pity to have to wait for two and a half years.

SEPTEMBER 16TH

I thought it would be difficult to know what to write in this diary, but I find there's plenty. Serezhka Blinov called for me this morning and told me school would begin on the 20th; but the most important thing was our talk about Lina G. He advised me not to be pally with her, as her father was a servant of the Cult,[3] and said it would be a disgrace if I, a son of the proletariat, were to attract general attention. I told him that, in the first place, I never attracted any general attention, and that Lina belonged to my group, and sat at the same desk as myself, and that it was only natural for me to be friends with her. But Serezhka said that the proletarian consciousness could not permit this, and that, in the opinion of the skworkers[4] and the pu-council,[5] I had already had a bad effect on her. That, instead of studying, she hung about the streets with me, and was quite likely to rot away in the ideological sense. And Serezhka also said that this palliness with girls ought to be stopped if one wanted to enter the A.C.Y.[6] Serezhka and I cursed each other, and I went home; and now I am writing what I hadn't time to tell him: Lina doesn't exist for me as a woman, but only as a comrade; on the whole, I look down on our girls with a certain amount of contempt. They are all interested in clothes and shoes and dancing, and most of all in gossip. If

1. Millions of roubles.
2. Vladimir Lenin.
3. i.e. a priest.
4. "School-Workers," i.e. teachers.
5. Council of the pupils.
6. Alliance of Communist Youth.

people were put in jail for gossip, not a single girl would remain in our group. As for having gone last year to the cinema with Lina, it's simply because I hadn't anyone else to go with. And Lina likes the cinema as much as I do. There is nothing surprising in that.[...]

SEPTEMBER 20TH

School has opened at last. It was fearfully noisy and rowdy. The same old fellows are in our group, but there are two new girls. One is fair, and has a pigtail with a bow like a propeller. She's called Sylphida, though she's pure Russian. The fellows at once called her Sylva. Her second name is Dubinin.

The other is dark and bobbed and dressed in black, and somehow she seems black altogether, and she never laughs. You say something to her, and off she goes like a railway engine—"Foo, ffoo, f-f-foo, f-f-f-foo." And she doesn't walk straight, and wanders about like a shadow. Her name is Zoya Travnikova.

SEPTEMBER 27TH

The Dalton Plan is being introduced at our school. It's a system under which the skworkers do nothing and the pupils have to find everything out for themselves. At least, that's what it looks like to me. There will be no more classes, and the pupils will merely be given "tasks." These will be handed out a month in advance, and may be prepared either at home or in school, and when your "task" is finished you get examined at the lab. There will be labs instead of classrooms, and in each there will be a *spesh*[7] in that particular subject. Almakfish, for instance, will be hanging round the maths lab; Nikpetozh will be in the sociology lab; and so on. They'll be the spiders and we'll be the flies.

We have decided to shorten the names of all the skworkers. Alexey Maximitch Fisher will be Almakfish; Nikolay Petrovitch Ozhegov will be Nikpetozh.

I don't talk to Lina nowadays, and she wants to move to another desk.

OCTOBER 1ST

The Dalton Plan has begun. All the desks have been crammed into one room, which will be the lecture-hall. Instead of desks we'll have long benches and tables. Vanka Petukhov and I loafed all day about these labs, and I felt silly. Even the skworkers don't seem very clear how to go about this Dalton business. As usual, Nikpetozh turned out

7. Specialist.

to be the most sensible among them. He simply walked in and gave the usual class, except that we had benches instead of desks. Sylphida Dubinin sat next to me, but Lina sat at the opposite end. Well, she can go to the devil.[...]

OCTOBER 3RD

The Dalton thing is a wash-out. No one can understand a thing, not even the skworkers. The skworkers discuss it every evening amongst themselves. The only novelty so far is that we have to sit on benches and have no place to put our books. Nikpetozh says there's no need for it, as there'll be special bookcases in the labs, with books on every subject, so that everybody can get whatever he needs. But what is to happen until we get the bookcases?

The boys say that this plan was invented by some Lord Dalton, of bourgeois stock. Now I wonder what the devil we need this bourgeois plan for? And they also say that while that lord was busy inventing he was being fed on goose's liver and jelly. I'd just like to see him do it on nothing but an eighth of bread, or going through the villages begging as we did in our colony. Anyone could do it on goose's liver.

Sylphida is always fidgeting, and it's uncomfortable sitting on the same bench. Several times I told her to go to hell, and she turned round and called me a skunk. I inquired about her social origin, and found that her father was a compositor. It's a nuisance, for, if she were a bourgeois, I would just *show her*.

OCTOBER 4TH

To-day there was a general meeting about self-government. They discussed last year's defects and the best ways to get rid of them. The greatest mistake is the penalty book. All the pu-councillors, even the best of them, threaten you with it on every occasion. And it doesn't do much good, anyway. In the end it was decided to suppress the book for a month, and to see how that would work. Everybody was very pleased, and shouted hurrah. Zoya Travnikova, as usual, made a nuisance of herself. She got up and said in a funereal tone: "For my own part, I think that the boys, especially, ought to be locked up in a dark cell. Otherwise there's no way of managing them." How they all booed and whistled! At first there was a general shout of indignation, and then she apologised and said she had meant it as a joke.[...]

After the general meeting there was a meeting of the new pu-council. It's been elected for a month.

OCTOBER 5TH

Our group was in a rage to-day. This is how it happened. Our new nat-history skworker, Elena Nikitichna Kaurova, known as Elnikitka, arrived. She began handing out tasks, and then said to the whole group : "Children——"

I then got up and said: "We're not children."

She answered: "Of course you are children, and I shan't call you anything else."

Then I answered: "Be good enough to be more polite, or else we may send you to the devil."

That was all. The whole group supported me, and Elnikitka grew quite red and said: "In that case, leave the classroom."

"In the first place," I answered, "This isn't a classroom, but a lab, and, in any case, you can't chase anyone out."

Then she said: "You're a rude fellow," and I replied: "You're more like a teacher of the old school, and only they were allowed to behave the way you do."

That was all. Elnikitka jumped out of the room as if she'd been burnt. There'll be some fuss now! The pu-council will chip in, and then the skworkers' meeting, and finally the school board. It seems perfect nonsense to me. Elnikitka is simply a damn fool.

In the old school the skworkers used to torment the boys any way they liked: but we shan't allow that now. I remember Nikpetozh reading us passages from *Stories of the Seminary*,[8] in which even grown-up fellows were flogged right in the classroom at the door; and I have also read how boys were made to swot, and how they were given all kinds of nicknames. But in those days the boys had no idea of the times through which we have had to live. For we've known famine and cold and anarchy; we've had to feed the whole family, and have travelled a thousand miles in search of bread, and some of us have been through the civil war. It isn't three years yet since the war ended. After the row with Elnikitka I thought about it all, and, to get my ideas straight, I tried to talk to Nikpetozh, but the lab was crowded and he was busy, so I went to the maths lab and told Almakfish what I thought of our life. He said that all we had lived through proved *quantitatively, the abundance of the epoch, and that, qualitatively, it stood beyond good and evil.*

I hadn't been thinking of that at all, and had only meant to show him that no one had any right to treat us as children or dummies; but we hadn't time to thrash it out, because some boys came in and began asking him questions about maths.[...]

8. By Pomialovsky, written in the early 'sixties.

OCTOBER 6TH

Well, we've got to do some work! In a month, or rather less—before November 1st—I'll have to read right through a whole pile of books, write ten reports, and sketch eight diagrams, and, in addition to all this, know how to answer questions in an oral; in fact, not merely answer, but talk about the things I've learned. And, besides, there are practical tasks in physics, chemistry, and electricity, and I'll have to stick in the phys lab for a whole week. To-day Sylphida and I were called before the pu-council. Serezhka Blinov and the others were sitting there. It appears that she had reported to them that I swear at her like people in a queue. I had done nothing of the kind. When we went out I pulled her bow; she howled and dashed off. No, to sit next to girls is intellectualism. To-morrow I'm going to change my seat.

OCTOBER 7TH

The skworkers' meeting decided to hand over the Elnikitka business to the school board, and proposed to have it discussed at the general meeting. This meeting takes place to-morrow. I don't know how it'll end, but we certainly shan't allow ourselves to be called children.

To-day the first number of a wall-sheet called the *Red Scholar* appeared. At first everybody was interested, but it all turned out to be bunk. The articles are stupid—all about studying and good behavior. [...]

I received a note: "It is no use your trying to look interesting; none of the girls want to have anything to do with you." I don't know what to "look interesting" means. I'm sure it's Lina. She has made friends with that new girl, Black Zoya, and they are constantly sitting together beside the stove and whispering to each other. [...]

GENERAL COPY-BOOK

JUNE 3RD

To-day Zin-Palna explained about the summer school tasks. We shall have to examine the Golovkino village, five miles out of town, from every standpoint, or, as she said, by the complex method. We'll have to get acquainted with the peasants, and we mustn't turn up our noses at them just because we happen to be townspeople. We'll also have to investigate their ways of living, measure their village geometrically, give them whatever help and information they may require, and generally serve as a link between them and the town; that's number one.

Then we are to listen to the songs, stories, legends, and superstitions of the peasants, and write them all down (and also make drawings of peasants' clothes—although this has more to do with their "mode of living"). To show us what is meant by popular epic poetry, Zin-Palna read some extracts from a Finnish poem called the *Kalevala*. There was a collector of folklore called Runeberg who walked through the whole of Finland and made a big collection of stories, and later there was a poet called Lenrot who turned them into a poem.

As if anyone could be interested in such wild superstitions as wood-ghosts and devils! I don't think even the peasants have much faith in all that bunk. Besides, there won't be much in the way of comparison, for in Finnish folklore there are giants. Three of them got together in order to find the Sampo treasure, and while they were searching for it they had to fight with every kind of evil power. Now, how can you compare this with old woman Yaga riding on a broom? All our witches and devils are ugly and terrible. And the Finns believe that you mustn't kill frogs, because frogs once were people, and that when teeth fall out they ought to be given to spiders. All this merely shows the ignorance of the people, and I don't see anything in it worth writing down.

They would be better to get on with the co-operation and electrification of the villages, and turn them Socialist. But Zin-Palna said that everything ought to be recorded, especially as all this folklore will disappear when the village is electrified, and then there will be no way at all of digging it up.

I don't think it'll be worth digging for, anyway.

I explained all this to Zin-Palna, but she said I had no love for my native language, the root of all our culture. I couldn't say anything in reply, and I had to take down all about Ukko the Thunderer, and Peyva the Sun, and Tjerems with the Hammer, the slayer of all the magicians. (Oh, my hat!)

Besides, we have to dig up all kinds of mounds for the district museum. Zin-Palna told us that there was an old subterranean camp eight miles away, consisting of eight sepulchres. The people at the district museum believe that ancient warriors are buried there, along with all their armour, horses, and wives. All this will have to be dug up and sent to the museum. That'll be fun; especially the armour. We'll dig it up and have a battle right there, near the graves. Only I'm afraid we won't manage it all, as the other skworkers will also have some tasks for us.[...]

JUNE 9TH

Yesterday we went to Golovkino for the first time. The peasants were busy working at their allotments, where they seem to grow chiefly vegetables. As I was told to investigate their manner of living, I walked up to a peasant woman planting potatoes and said to her:

"Let me help you, auntie."

"And who are you?"

"We've come on an excursion from town."

"Schoolboys, I suppose."

"That's right."

"Last summer some schoolboys went to Petrushkovo to measure the ground, and stole Aunt Arina's little hamper full of linen."

"We shan't pinch anything."

"I don't know what kind you are. You'd better run along and not bother me."

"Do you believe in devils, auntie?"

Here she got up and rubbed the earth off her hands, and yelled for all she was worth:

"Pe-ter! Pe-ter!"

And then a little peasant came out from behind a fence, carrying a pitchfork, and walked straight towards us. And the woman said: "Here's some fellow from the school crowd, and he talks about devils."

Here I pulled myself together and said: "Not about devils at all, but if you like I can tell you about electrification and wireless and help you in all kinds of ways."

"Oh, I see, it's the link,"[9] said the little peasant. "Well, well, we don't mind, if it's any good. Only, my lad, you had better come along on Sunday; our folks will have more time to waste then."

So I left that farm without learning anything, and walked along the allotments at the back of the farms, where the women and kids were busy digging, when a shaggy dog jumped suddenly at me, barking furiously. I bent down, pretending to pick up a stone, as I always do if a dog attacks me, but the beast wouldn't stop barking, and some other dogs came dashing out of the farms towards me. I had been told that the best way to get rid of a savage dog was to make water on it, but as there was a whole crowd of them, I started turning round and round, making water in every direction and aiming at the dogs." What's all this?" I suddenly heard a voice behind me. "More of the *link*?" And, as I turned round, I saw the same little peasant approaching me with his pitchfork. He chased the dogs away, and I walked on. But, after I had passed two farms, the dogs attacked me again, and one of them snapped at my trouser-leg. Then I got savage, and tore a post out of the fence to protect myself. "Chuck the stick, I tell you, or they'll tear you to pieces!"

I threw down the post; and a peasant came up and asked:

"What do you want?"

"I've come to inspect your village."

9. The official term for a *rapprochement* between industry and agriculture.

"There's nothing to inspect in our back yards. Always coming and inspecting. Why did you break that fence? You didn't put it up, did you? So what business had you to break it?"

And a woman popped up from behind a hedge and shouted:

"Get out, you villain! Always hanging round, and we've got to keep looking out all the time in case you pinch anything."

'A NEW KIND OF PARK' AND 'MAY DAY'

from *Red Comet: A Tale of Travel in the U.S.S.R.* Moscow: Co-operative Publishing Society of Foreign Workers, 1936; London: Lawrence and Wishart, 1937

Written by Geoffrey Trease. Illustrated by Fred Ellis

From the 1920s, the Soviet Union was a popular travel destination for official trade delegations, trade union excursions, political and scientific expeditions, and independent travellers. Geoffrey Trease's (1909–98) *Red Comet: A Tale of Travel in the U.S.S.R.* is one of many books for both adults and children generated by such visits.

The story begins with brother and sister Peter and Joy preventing the theft of *Red Comet*, the prototype for a revolutionary flying machine developed by their neighbour Jim, who invites them to travel with him to the Soviet Union. He hopes the Soviets will buy his plans, since no one in Britain is interested in them. The children meet a variety of youngsters who proudly tell the pair about their fulfilling lives and explain that a better new world is emerging from the ruins of the old. Their excitement about the future is in marked contrast to Peter's and Joy's situations in the Depression-era West. Peter has left school and, like his father, is unemployed, and the family cannot afford for Joy to continue her education. Their travels in the USSR also make Peter and Joy aware of how opportunities in Britain are circumscribed by class, sex, and poverty.

Red Comet is far from Trease's most accomplished novel and in later life he found it naïve in its optimistic view of life in the Soviet Union. Nevertheless, it is significant as the first book for children about life in Soviet Russia by a British writer. Like many others, Geoffrey Trease's initial enthusiasm for the Soviet experiment was dashed by revelations about Stalin's regime. He requested that *Red Comet* never be reprinted, but it should nonetheless be recognized as a groundbreaking work that captures the spirit of the times.

CHAPTER 5

A NEW KIND OF PARK

They went by Metro. Peter and Joy, who had faint memories of the London Underground, were amazed by the beauty and spaciousness of the new Moscow "tube."

Instead of London's single-line tunnels, with the roof arching closely overhead, they found both tracks running together, so that the tunnel was much bigger and the stations airy. In place of a jumble of differently coloured advertisements they saw walls lovely with tinted marbles, while here and there were graceful statues. At some stations the roof was upheld by rows of pillars like a cathedral.

It was funny to watch some of the people on the moving staircases. The young ones stepped off with confidence, but the bearded old men looked very nervous, and one elderly woman with a kerchief round her head had to be led gingerly on by her grandson.

"These escalators are still a novelty in Moscow, especially to peasants coming in from the country," laughed Nina. "This is the first subway in the Soviet Union, but foreigners tell us it is more wonderful than the ones in London, Paris or New York."

As they glided on under the city, she told them how difficult it had been to make the subway. The Russian engineers had had no experience of building underground railways. Some of the foreign experts who came to help said that the task was impossible, because the soil was unsuitable for tunnelling.

"But we have a slogan," said Nina. *"There are no fortresses which the Bolsheviks cannot conquer."*

The work of the Metro went on. The different gangs challenged each other, each saying they would dig more than their rivals. Most of the people in Moscow took part in building this first line—each gave up his holiday at one time or another and volunteered to work with a spade or a drill on the Metro. It was finished to time. The Bolsheviks had conquered.

"And now we're building a second line. After that there will be a third line and a fourth and a fifth."

They got out at the terminus. Here was the Moscow River again, curving round beneath the green slopes of the Lenin Hills. On the stone embankment was carved the slogan Nina had taught them, *"There are no fortresses which the Bolsheviks cannot conquer."*

"Soon," she explained, "our river will be much deeper here, so that big steamers can come to Moscow. You may have heard of our Volga."

"Yes!" cried Joy. "Longest river in Europe—2,325 miles long. Rises in Northwest Russia and flows into the Caspian Sea. . . ."

"All right," growled her brother. "We're not in school now. Don't show off."

"Anyhow," resumed Nina gently, "we shall turn the waters of the Volga so that they flow through Moscow and make our city a great river-port."

"Turn the Volga!" Joy's eyes goggled.

"You'll have to learn your geography again," cried Peter delightfully. "It seems the Bolsheviks are going to alter geography!"

Nina slapped him on the back enthusiastically. "A fine slogan, Comrade Peter! 'The Bolsheviks alter geography.' My father is an engineer. I shall tell him that."

By now they were at the gates of the park. Nina took tickets.

"Fancy having to pay!" said Joy. "We've got a fine park at home, and it's all free."

"What is it like?" asked Nina, interested.

"Oh, there's a pond—only it's a bit mucky—with diving ducks and swans. And lovely flower-beds and a band-stand and all."

"That sounds nice. What do you do there?"

"Oh, walk about, and feed the ducks. And Saturdays and Sundays there's the band or a sacred concert."

"Don't you play games?"

"Not there. You see you have to keep off the grass. When we've got a ball, we go on the waste land and play."

"Of course," put in Peter, "ours is a small town. In Manchester they've got real big parks. And in London, too."

"Well, our idea of a park is rather different," Nina said. "Perhaps you won't like it so much."

They didn't think much of the flower-beds, certainly, but as Nina said, spring came late to Moscow and it would be a month or two before the prettiest flowers would be out. Then they would be lovely. Meanwhile, it was interesting to see a full-length picture of Stalin made entirely of flowers and plants, and another bed like a calendar, with the year, month and day. The day-number was formed by purple pansies growing in a shallow wooden tray, which the gardener could change each morning for another.

But there were so many other things to look at.

A big cinema, close to the river bank. An immense circus tent, where there was always a circus—not just one which stopped a night or two and moved on. And a theatre. (Afterwards, at the far end of the park, they saw the Green Theatre, too—a vast open-air auditorium, seating 20,000 people. Nina told them of the great productions that were to be seen there on summer evenings, when hundreds of actors and actresses crowded the stage in their gay costumes, and even horses came galloping on from the wings.) As for band-stands and small stages for vaudeville, they seemed to be dotted all over the park.

One thing struck Peter especially—a tall tower like the helter-skelter he had seen in fun fairs at the Wakes. But at the very top, billowing in the light breeze, was what looked like a big parasol.

"That's the parachute-jumping tower," explained Nina. "People practise there before they jump from aeroplanes. It's quite safe, you see. The parachute is already open and it's tied by a rope running over a—a. . . ."

"Pulley?" suggested Peter. As he spoke, a young man jumped off the platform at the top of the tower and sailed gracefully down to the ground. "I'd love to try that," said Peter enviously. "Do you think they'd let me?"

"Why not? If you're touring in an aeroplane, you ought to practise your parachute-jumping."

"Well, I 'spect we'll be going home by train in a day or two. Still. . . ." And, quivering with excitement, Peter climbed into the harness they gave him and rushed up the stairs.

When he emerged panting on the platform, he didn't like the idea quite so much. The ground looked a long, long way below. Joy's and Nina's upturned faces were just pink blobs. Peter got a queer feeling low down in his stomach.

"Kharasho?" said the young man at the top, hooking him on to the parachute. Peter had learnt that word—it meant "all right." So he answered, between his teeth, *"Kharasho."*

Then the awful moment of jumping into space! And, a second later, the reassuring tug under his armpits, and the change from a stone-like fall to a gentle, feather-weight drifting earthwards.

Peter opened his eyes again quickly. His cap had fallen off. His four pennies (all he had brought from England) were raining on the heads of the people below. All too soon, he himself touched the ground, the parachute was unhooked and hauled up, and Nina was shaking his hand.

Joy, pale but determined, said: "I'm going, too."

So she did. But she kept her eyes shut nearly all the way down, and all she could say when she landed was: "Oo, did I show my knickers awfully?"

"Well done," Nina congratulated her. "Girls jump as well as boys here. Six girls made a world-record recently, all jumping together. And they fly aeroplanes, too, and some of them have even invented new types and built them."

"Seems to me," grumbled Peter, "that girls do all the same things as men, here. Tram-drivers and taxi-drivers. . . ."

"And sea-captains," cried Nina. "Our first Soviet woman sea-captain has just taken her master's certificate."

"And why not?" challenged Joy.

"Why not?" Nina echoed.

And Peter couldn't answer.

They walked on through the park. There were trees and lawns and flower-beds and statues, just like home. But there were also lots of things to do. Here, were pitches for volley-ball; there, nets and ladders and ropes for acrobatics; funny games, too, such as hobby-horses on which you mounted and fought a tournament with your friend, trying to get your lance into a ring which made his horse slide backwards in defeat; and fun-fair devices, like a big wheel which carried you aloft, level with the tree-tops, and many other amusements. In case you got hungry or thirsty, there were several big open-air cafés, as well as dozens of little huts for drinks, ice cream and fruit.

Peter and Joy were specially interested in the Children's City, a big corner of the park set aside for young people. Here too were all kinds of games, and you could play anything from volley-ball to bagatelle. There were several large buildings, and Nina led them from one to another.

Here was the House of the Young Technicians. Peter ran, chuckling with delight, from one workshop to the next. It was just Heaven for a boy who liked doing things with his hands. There was carpentry and every kind of model-making; chemical and physical laboratories; radio and photographic sections; and an automobile shop, where you could either build toy cars for the little children or tinker about with an old chassis to your heart's content.

"Boys and girls come here in their spare time," Nina explained. "Materials and instructors are always available. They hold exhibitions of their work, and they challenge each other to competitions. They even set themselves examinations to see who can get the best marks. But it has nothing to do with school and they do it all of their own free will, because they find it very interesting."

"Well, I'm hopeless at science and machinery," Joy said ruefully. "What should I find to do?"

"Come and see! There is the Artists' House where you could draw and paint. There are dancing and singing. If you are fond of books, they have literary circles, where real authors come and talk with the children. Up there on the hill is the Biological Research Station, where you can study live animals and plants. They have quite a little Zoo there, and all the work is done by the young people. Then, of course. . . ."

"Stop!" laughed Joy. "I'd never find time to do all the things I wanted to. It sounds great."

As they walked on, Peter inquired: "Aren't there *any* keepers? I haven't seen one yet."

"Keepers?" echoed Nina. "Why should there be keepers?"

"Well, don't people damage things?"

"Why should they damage their own property? They all know that the park and everything in it belongs to them. Only a fool would spoil what is his own."

"But they pay to come in," said Joy quickly.

"Yes—a few kopeks each—to cover part of the expenses for running the park and for the improvements that are being introduced all the time."

"But," persisted Peter, "there must be *someone* to look after things generally."

"Of course. And in the Children's City it is also done by the more active boys and girls themselves. You see that girl with a red band round her arm? She is an 'activist'—a keeper, if you like. She decides, if there is an argument, whose turn it is to have the hobby-horse game next. And she stops them if they play too roughly and look like hurting each other."

"And what if they take no notice?"

"Why shouldn't they take notice? Haven't they elected her to manage the games for them? Why did they elect her then? Sometimes, of course, when small children lose their tempers they do not obey the 'activist,' but then all the others tell them how silly they are, till at last they see it for themselves."

"Russia gets queerer and queerer," muttered Peter. "I know that *I* should tell her to boil her head!"

CHAPTER 6

MAY DAY

[. . . .] That night they met Mikhail Markov, who was to be their fellow-passenger in the aeroplane. Mikhail was short and plump. His round face was jolly and although he had a neat little black moustache he was just like a boy. He was twenty-seven, really, and a very important man in aviation.

He grasped their arms and marched them along the streets, now brilliantly illuminated and packed with people in holiday mood. Jim stalked behind, making his way through the crowds like a rather nervous crane.

"We must get acquainted, yes?" boomed Mikhail. For a small man he had a marvellously loud and resonant voice.

"Tea and cakes," went on Mikhail. "That is what I love. And especially I adore your English cake with currants and raisins. 'Angleesky keks' we call it here. So let us go into this café and get acquainted."

The café was packed to overflowing. A jazz band was playing at full blast and the noise was deafening. But somehow they fought their way to a distant corner, and Mikhail, with the air of a magician, displayed an empty table.

"And how do you like our city?" demanded their new friend when the tea and cake had safely arrived.

"I like the new parts," Peter said, "and of course the Kremlin, 'cos that's historical, but a lot of buildings are awfully tumbledown, and the roads all seem to be up."

"Heaps of drain pipes everywhere," chimed in Joy.

"Thank God for that!" said Jim briefly. "The old sanitation is ghastly."

"And there's a lot of scaffolding all over the place," Peter went on.

Joy added quickly: "As if the whole city was in splints after an accident!" Mikhail laughed at that, and beamed round at them, as if hoping for still more criticism.

"You are quite right, everyone of you," he answered with another of his jolly, gusty laughs. "Old Moscow is a rabbit-warren. It's not a city—it's an overgrown village. Fancy! One and two-storey houses of wood in a city of four millions! Streets like forest tracks, no drains to speak of—and what there are, not *fit* to speak of—this, comrades, is what the Tsar left to us. We know all these things. For every bad thing you can tell us, we can tell you a dozen more. But we are doing away with them every month. Have you seen our Metro? Our Park of Culture—which was the city rubbish dump before the Revolution! Our new apartment houses, our great stores, our schools, our factories? Have we not made a start? But listen—it is only a start."

And he began to tell them of the great plan for the complete rebuilding of Moscow in ten years. He made it all so plain and vivid that Joy could almost see the city of the future taking shape amid the clouds of cigarette smoke in the café.

Gone were the narrow streets, the low buildings, the jumble of factories. For the first time in the history of mankind a great city had sprung into being on a single, unified plan.

A new Moscow River, swollen by the waters of the Volga Canal, wound gracefully between granite embankments. Eleven new bridges linked the broad motor roads on either bank, and old bridges looked unfamiliar since their height was raised to let the big Volga steamships go by. Both banks were lined with ten-storey blocks of flats, glistening mountains of stone and glass, from whose sunny balconies the green forest looked very near.

And it would never be any farther away. No more would the country retreat before the town, making it harder and harder for the people to reach it. The population was fixed at five million. For that number there were ample houses, schools, shops, theatres, cinemas, and so on.

No building would be erected on the belt of wooded country which completely surrounded the city. Within Moscow itself were more parks and boulevards than ever before. Long avenues ran out from the very centre to the outer ring, like the spokes of a wheel. From Red Square you could walk to the proper country, your path shaded by trees and coloured with flowers. The houses, six storeys and higher, were spaced apart so that even the lowest rooms got plenty of sun. Between them were grassy quadrangles and paved courts, with statues and fountains and playgrounds for the children.

"Well?" boomed Mikhail through the haze of his cigarette. "What do you think of our plan?"

Joy came back to reality with a start. "I—I'd love to come back in ten years and see it all. Are you sure it will be just like that?"

"Sure. Only one thing can stop us."

"And what's that?" asked Peter.

Mikhail's face grew stern. "If the capitalist countries make war upon us! Then our dream may have to wait. But it will be realized in the long run all the same."

WASH 'EM CLEAN

Foreign Languages Publishing House, n.d. [first published 1923]

Written by Korney Chukovsky. Translated by E. Felgenhauer. Illustrated by A. Kanevsky

Korney Chukovsky (1882–1969) is the pen name of Nikolai Vasilevich Korneychukov and is still one of the most popular Russian children's poets. He started as a literary critic, and moved into the field of children's writing after the revolution. Foreign Languages Publishing House, later followed by its successor Progress Publishers, translated Soviet picturebooks into a variety of languages and distributed them all over the world. Like many children's books, they had a didactic purpose, in this case promoting the duty of cleanliness in society. *Wash 'Em Clean* was first published in Leningrad in 1923 by Raduga (The Rainbow), the revolutionary publishing house for children led by another popular children's poet, literary critic, and translator, Samuil Marshak (for more discussion of Marshak's work, see the introduction to *Black on White* in Part Eight). It is written with a sense of fun that is rather lacking in *What is Good and What is Bad* by Vladimir Mayakovsky, also represented here.

Until his death Chukovsky produced humorous verse for children which included *Cockroach* (1921), *The Telephone* (1926), and *The Crocodile* (1926). He also published *From Two to Five* (English translation 1963) for adults, which looks affectionately at the language of children, and received great acclaim in Britain. The sense of fun and word play that Chukovsky shares with Marshak ensures both poets' continuing popularity today.

WASH 'EM CLEAN

From my bed
The blanket fled,
And the sheet refused to stay,

And the pillow,
Like a billow,
Gathered up and flew away.

I got up to reach the light,
But it also took to flight.
I decided I would look
At my coloured picture-book—
In a twinkling it had fled,
Hiding underneath the bed.

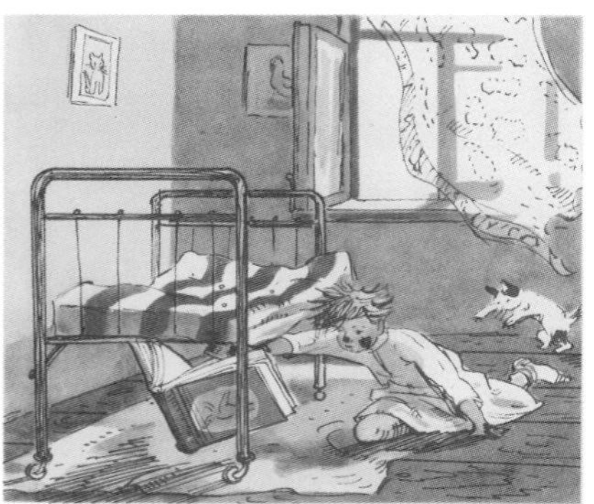

When I thought I'd have some tea,
Cups and saucers ran from me.
Teaspoons, teapot, cream and eggs
Ran as though they all had legs!

What has happened?
What's the matter?
What's the reason
For this rout?
What a tumult,
What a clatter!
Has the world turned inside out?
Mother's irons
                    chased
                              the dippers,

While the bird-cage
                    chased
                              the slippers,
And the slippers
                    chased the nippers,
And the poker
                    chased
                              the toys.
What a tumult,
What a racket,
What a horrid, horrid noise

Suddenly from Mummy's bedroom,
Crooked-legged, old and lame,
Straight towards me came the wash-stand,
And he scolded as he came:
"Oh, you nasty little slacker!
Oh, you naughty little squirt!
There's no chimney-sweep who's blacker,
There's no pig as fond of dirt!
Take a look into the mirror.
See the ink spots on your nose?
And your neck, your dirty fingers,
Never wash them, I suppose?
So no wonder even stockings
Couldn't stand a sight so shocking.

Every morning, bright and early,
All the little mice go washing,
And the kittens, and the ducklings,
And the ants and spiders, too.

All but you have washed this morning,
Cleaned their teeth and brushed their hair,
You're the only piggy-wiggy,
So you've nothing left to wear!

I'm a great and famous wash-stand,
'Wash 'em clean' is what I'm called.
I command the other wash-stands,
I have troops of sponges bold!

If I bring my foot down hard,
All the soldiers I command
Will come rushing to this room
With a great big bang and boom!
They will start to snort and howl,
They will stamp their feet and growl.
Though it won't be quite a whipping,
You'll be scrubbed until you gleam,
And a dipping,
And a dipping,
They will give you in the stream!"

Then he smote his bowl of brass,
And he cried: "Kara-baras!"

And at once a swarm of brushes
Chirped and darted round like thrushes,
And they scrubbed, and scrubbed and
scrubbed me,
Saying as they scrubbed and rubbed me:

"We will wash this little blighter
Whiter, whiter, whiter, whiter!
We will scrub this naughty mite
White, white, white, white!"

Then the soap jumped up, or rather,
Simply pounced upon my head,
And it covered me with lather,
Till I thought I'd soon be dead.

To escape the raging sponge,
In the ocean I could plunge
For it wouldn't let me be,
Everywhere it followed me.

I rushed out into the square,
Jumped across a railing there,
But it followed like a hound,
Biting me at every bound.

Suddenly around a turning
I saw dear old Uncle Croc,
With his twins he was returning
From an early morning walk.
And that sponge which dared to follow,
Like a bit of fluff he swallowed.

Then he turned and glared at me,
Then he stamped and flared at me.
"This is simply a disgrace,"
he exclaimed.
"Go and quickly wash your face,"
he exclaimed.
"If you don't, I'll beat you up,"
he exclaimed.
"If you don't, I'll eat you up!"
he exclaimed.

I ran homeward like a streak of lightning then,
Till in front of "Wash 'em clean" I stood again.
Soap and water,
Soap and water,
I applied with all my might.
Washed the dirt off,
Washed the ink off,
Till my face was beaming white.

Back my clothes came in a band,
Jumping straight into my hand.

And a pie stood up on end,
Saying: "You can eat me, friend."

Then an orange from the south
Landed straight into my mouth.

There's my picture-book returning,
All my toys, both small and big,
There's my book of sums and primer
Joining in a merry jig!

Then the great and famous wash-stand,
"Wash 'em clean," as he is called,
Who commands all other wash-stands,
Who has troops of sponges bold,
Ran towards me dancing, prancing,
Kissing me, he said and smiled:

"That's a darling! Now you're splendid,
Now that all your ways have mended,
All your nasty habits ended,
Now you look a decent child!"

* * *

Every morning, every evening,
We must play the washing game,
And to those,
Who're always dirty—
Lasting shame!
Lasting shame!

Hurray for towels and sponges!
Hurray for soapy foam!
Hurray for snow-white tooth-paste!
Hurray for brush and comb!

Then let us all wash every day,
Let's splash in the water and play

In bath-tubs, in wash-tubs, in basins and bowls,
In oceans, in rivers, with boats and with balls.

Washing is healthy for young and for old,
So glory to water, both steaming and cold!

WHAT IS GOOD AND WHAT IS BAD

Progress Publishers, 1971 [first published 1925]

Written by Vladimir Mayakovsky. Translated by Dorian Rottenberg. Illustrated by V. Kirillov

Vladimir Mayakovsky (1893–1930) was one of the foremost Soviet revolutionary poets. Throughout the Soviet Union his poetry was memorized and recited, among them 'All Right' (1927) and the epic poem 'Vladimir Ilyich Lenin' (1924). A supporter of the revolution and a founder of the Left Art Movement (LEF), he was involved in the production of the ROSTA window posters. These were propaganda posters displayed in windows and created by artists and poets for the news agency, the Russian Telegraph Agency, between 1919 and 1921. They dealt with current political events, were often satirical, and drew upon the Russian folk art tradition called Lubok. Critical of the policies of the New Economic Policy (NEP), he lost popularity in the late 1920s when his works were increasingly perceived as obscure.

Admired by Anatoly Lunacharsky, the People's Commissar of Education who was fully committed to a new children's literature for the new Soviet State, Mayakovsky turned his talents towards children's books. *What is Good and What is Bad* was published in 1925 in Leningrad by Priboi. English translations appeared from the 1940s onwards. Education was a primary consideration of the new state, and this didactic piece was a humorous endeavour to make sure that Soviet children were encouraged to behave well in regard to others. This meant not just behaving well for rewards or for pleasing adults, but as a way of preparing for a worthwhile life as part of a Socialist future.

After his death by suicide in 1930, Mayakovsky's poems for children, as well as his adult poetry, remained popular throughout the Soviet period.

WHAT IS GOOD AND WHAT IS BAD

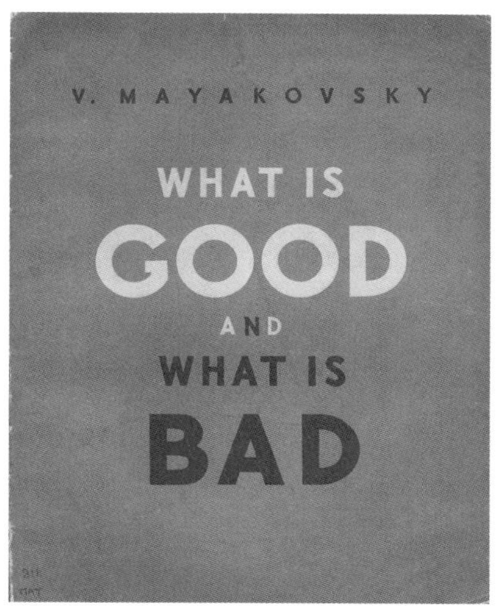

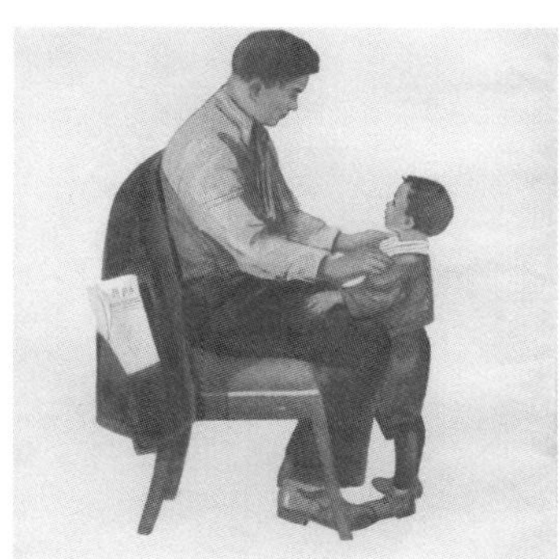

One fine day
a little laddie
came
and asked his dad:
"How am I to tell,
dear Daddy,
Good things
from the bad?"

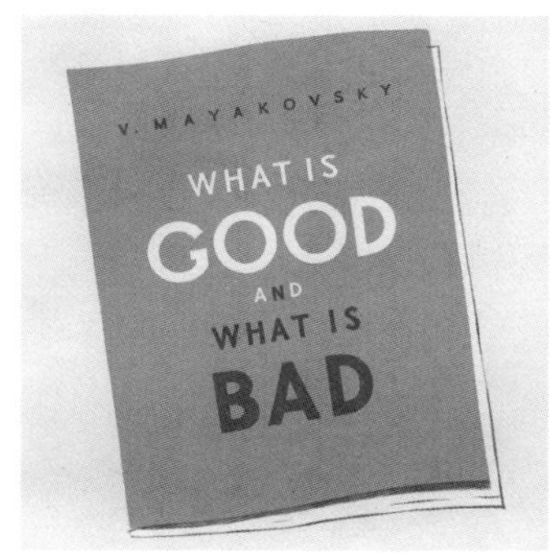

Father answered,—
and I heard.
Children,
listen well!
And his answer,
word for word,
In my book
I tell.

If the wind
behaves like mad,
Bringing rain
and sleet,
Everybody knows
it's bad
Walking
in the street.

After showers
comes the sun,
Driving off
the cold,
Then it's good
for everyone,
Whether young
or old.

When
a boy's as black as night—
Dirt on hands
and face—
We all know
that's bad, all right,
And a sad disgrace.

If
a boy
is clean and neat,
Washes
every day,
He's a lad
we love to meet—
He is good,
we say.

When a bully,
Tom or Billy,
Beats
a weaker lad,
Such a boy
is cruel and silly—
He
is very
bad.

This one cries:
"You mustn't touch
Smaller boys
than you!"
I admire him
very much.
Surely,
you do,
too!

If
you spoil
a book and toy
In
a single day,
"That's
a rather naughty boy,"
All the children
say.

This one likes
to work and read
And is never
bad.
He's the kind of boy we need,
He's
a good young lad.

This one's
frightened by a crow,
Shame
upon the lad!
He's called coward,
as you know,
And that is
very bad.

This one
stops the nasty bird,
Though he's just a mite,
He's a brave boy,
I have heard.
Now, that is good
and right.

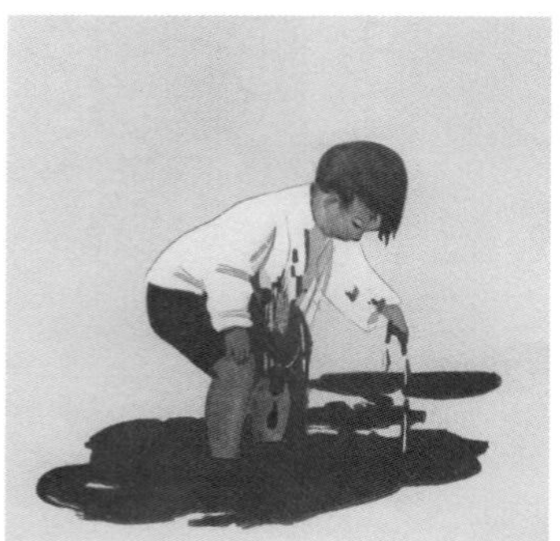

This lad
wallows in the dirt
With
the greatest joy.
Look at your
disgraceful shirt,
Bad, untidy boy!

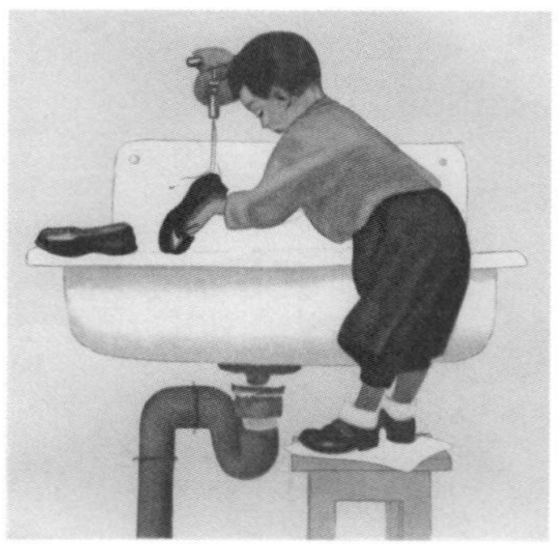

This one scrubs
his own galoshes,
Though
he's not so old,
Dirty hands
and face
he washes,—
He's quite good, I'm told.

Remember, son,
if you are now
A little pig
and bully,

Remember, son,
if you are now
A little pig
and bully,

You'll grow
into a great big one
When you are older,
truly!

You'll grow
into a great big one
When you are older,
truly!

Everything
he'd understood,
And he told his dad:
"I'll do always
what is good,
Never
what is bad."

TIMUR AND HIS COMRADES

Pilot Press, 1940

Written by Arkady Gaidar. Translated by Musia Renbourn. Illustrated by Donia Nachshen

Arkady Gaidar is the pen name of Arkady Petrovich Golikov (1904–41), who became a war hero at the age of sixteen when he commanded a regiment of the Red Army. Invalided out of the army aged twenty, Gaidar became a novelist and journalist, and eventually helped found Soviet children's literature. *Timur and his Comrades*, his most popular work, was required reading in the Soviet Union until the 1990s.[1] Written for Gaidar's son Timur, the book tells of a fictional group of children, organized by a boy also called Timur, who secretly help neighbours whose family members are fighting to defend the country or who have been killed.

Between 1940 and 1982, *Timur and his Comrades* was translated into English four times. The Marxist historian Raphael Samuel names it among the books passed onto him by family and friends in the party when he was a boy (see the introduction to Part Four). The first version published in the UK was featured on a list of Soviet children's books selected and translated by an official in the Russian Division of the Ministry of Information (Eve, 2003 79). Gaidar's story of responsible and capable young people was evidently seen as a model for the MOI's 'You Can Help Your Country' campaign, which urged young Britons to find ways to be useful such as helping around the neighbourhood, assisting the elderly with heavy work, helping with the harvest, and learning first aid and how to use the telephone efficiently—exactly the kinds of activities featured in *Timur and his Comrades*.

The extract features Timur telling a girl who has recently come to the village about the gang's activities.

1. See the entry for Gaidar in *Encyclopedia of Soviet Writers*, http://www.sovlit.net/bios/gaidar.html.

FROM *TIMUR AND HIS COMRADES*

Timur returned to the loft and related his encounter with Kvakin. It was decided that tomorrow they would send an ultimatum in writing to each member of the gang.

The boys jumped down noiselessly from the loft, and either disappeared through the holes in the fence, or climbed over it, and scattered in all directions to their homes.

Timur came up to Genya:

'Now do you understand everything?' he asked.

'In a way,' she answered, 'but please explain it to me more simply.'

'In that case, follow me. Your sister's not home, anyway.'

They climbed down from the loft and Timur put the ladder away.

They stopped by the small house where the old milk-woman lived. Timur looked around. There was no one about. He took a lead tube of oil-paint out of his pocket and went up to the gate with the red star painted on it. The top left-hand point was quite awry. With a sure hand, he altered, sharpened and straightened it out.

'Why did you do that?' asked Genya.

Timur put the tube back into his pocket. He wiped his paintcovered finger on a dock leaf and looking straight into Genya's face, he said:

'It shows that a man has gone into the Red Army from here. That house comes under our protection and care from the time he goes. Is your father in the army?'

'Yes,' answered Genya, with emotion and pride. 'He's a Commander.'

'Well, that means you come under our protection, too.'

They stopped by the gate of another house which had a Red Star heavily outlined in black on the fence. 'A man went into the Red Army from here, but he never came back. This is Lieutenant Pavlov's house; he was recently killed on the frontier. His widow lives here with that little girl who would not tell Gayka why she was crying so much. If you get a chance, Genya, do her a good turn.'

She was silent, her head bent, and it was only for the sake of saying something that she asked:

'Is Gayka a kind boy?'

'Yes,' answered Timur. 'He's a sailor's son. He often rags that little swanker, Kolokolchikov, but just the same, he always sticks up for him.'

A sharp, almost angry cry, made them turn round. They saw Olga standing near.

Genya touched Timur's hand; she wanted to introduce him to her sister. But another sharp call made her abandon the idea.

Guiltily nodding to Timur, Genya shrugged her shoulders and went up to Olga.

'Eugenia,' said Olga, breathing heavily and on the verge of tears. 'I forbid you to talk to that boy. Is that clear?'

'But, Olya,' muttered Genya, 'What's the matter with you?'

'I forbid you to go near that boy,' repeated Olga firmly. 'You're only thirteen, I'm eighteen. I'm your sister... I'm older than you. And when Daddy went away, he told me to....'

'But, Olya, you don't understand anything,' cried Genya in despair. She was very upset. She wanted to explain and justify herself, but could not. She knew she was in the wrong. So with a helpless little gesture she gave up trying to make her sister understand.

She went to bed at once, but could not sleep for a long time. She fell asleep at last and did not hear someone knock on the window during the night and deliver a telegram from her father.

* * *

Day dawned. The shepherd blew on his wooden horn. The old milkwoman opened the gate and drove the cow out to join the herd in the meadow. She was barely out of sight when five boys ran out from behind an acacia-tree, and trying not to make a noise with their empty pails, made for the well.

'Pump up!'

'Give it here!'

'Take it!'

'Here it is!'

Spilling the cold water over their bare feet, the boys ran into the yard and emptied their pails into the oak tub, then quickly ran back again to the well.

Timur came up to Sima Simakov, who was wet from continually pumping up the water, and asked:

'Have you seen Kolokolchikov? You haven't? That means he's overslept. Hurry up, get a move on; the old woman'll be back in a minute.'

Timur went along to Kolokolchikov's summer villa and, standing in the garden, under a tree, he gave a whistle. Without waiting for a reply he climbed a tree and looked into a room. He could only see half the bed, which was pushed up against the window, and a pair of legs covered with blankets.

Timur threw a piece of the tree bark on to the bed and called softly:

'Kolya, get up. Kolya!'

The sleeping form did not stir. Timur took out his knife, cut off a long branch, bent the end to make a hook, and pushing it through the window, caught up the blanket, which he slowly drew towards him.

The light blanket slipped out over the window sill.

A hoarse, surprised bellow came from the room.

Opening his sleepy eyes, a grey-haired gentleman leapt out of bed, caught hold of the disappearing blanket, and ran up to the window.

When Timur found himself face to face with this venerable old man, he quickly slid down the tree.

The grey-haired gentleman threw his recaptured blanket on to the bed, snatched a gun from the wall, put on his glasses as quickly as he could, and pointing the muzzle of the gun towards the sky, tightly shut his eyes and fired.

* * *

Timur was so frightened that he didn't stop running until he reached the well. He had mistaken the sleeping gentleman for Kolya. And, of course, the grey-haired gentleman had mistaken him for a thief.

Just then Timur saw the old milkwoman coming through the gate, carrying a pail to fetch water.

He disappeared behind the acacia-tree and watched.

Returning from the well, the old woman lifted her pail and emptied its contents into the tub, but she jumped back hastily as the tub was already so full that the water splashed all over her. Startled, and quite at a loss, the old woman looked around and examined the tub from all sides. She even put her hand into the water and sniffed it. Then she ran up to her house to see if the lock on her door was all right. At last, not knowing what to think, she knocked on a neighbour's window.

Timur laughed and left his hiding-place. He had to hurry. The sun was already rising. Kolya Kolokolchikov had not appeared and the wires still had to be repaired.

On his way to the shed, Timur glanced into a window which faced the garden.

Genya, wearing a sports shirt and a pair of shorts, was writing something at the table near the bed, and impatiently shook back her hair from her face.

When she saw Timur, she was not at all frightened, nor even surprised. She merely put her finger on her lips, so that Olga should not be wakened, then she pushed the unfinished letter into a drawer and tip-toed out of the room.

When she heard Timur's trouble, she forgot all Olga's instructions and readily offered to help him repair the wires which she had damaged.

When the work was finished and Timur was standing on the other side of the hedge, Genya said to him:

'I don't know why it is, but my sister dislikes you very much.'

'Well, that's how it is,' said Timur sadly, 'my uncle doesn't like you either.'

He was on the point of leaving, when she stopped him.

'Wait, do comb your hair, you look very untidy today.'

She handed him a comb just as Olga's indignant shriek came from the window behind them.

'Genya, what are you doing?'...

Her sister was standing on the veranda.

'I don't choose your friends for you,' said Genya, defending herself desperately. 'And look at your friends. Very ordinary ones. In plain white suits, who say: "Ah, how beautifully your sister plays!" Beautifully! He ought to hear how beautifully you lose your temper. You'd better be careful. I've written and told Daddy everything.'

'Eugenia! This boy is a ruffian and you're stupid,' said Olga coldly, trying to keep her temper. 'You can write to Daddy if you want to, but if I see you with this boy again, we'll go back to Moscow right away. And you know I mean what I say!'

'Yes, you... torturer,' answered Genya, in tears. 'I should think I do.'

'Now read this.' Olga put the telegram, which had come the previous night, on the table and went out. The telegram said:

'Stopping in Moscow few hours when passing through further telegram for date time Daddy.'

Genya wiped her eyes, kissed the telegram and murmured:

'Come quickly, Daddy! Dear Daddy! Your Genya's having a very hard time.'

* * *

Two cart-loads of wood were brought into the yard of a house. It was the house where the old woman lived who had beaten the lively little girl, Nurka, when she lost the goat.

Grumbling at the careless men who had thrown the wood down anywhere, and groaning and finding fault, the old woman began to put away the logs. But this work was too much for her. She sat on the steps to get back her breath, then taking the watering-can she went into the kitchen garden.

Then, Sima Simakov, who had been chasing the run-away goat, which leaped over bushes and ditches as gracefully as a tiger, left one of his group to watch out for it, and, with four others, came tearing into the yard.

Then the four boys hurried off to put away the logs while Sima Simakov went round the fence to make sure that the old woman stayed in her kitchen-garden. Stopping by the fence near some cherry- and apple-trees, Sima peeped through a crack.

The old woman had gathered some cucumbers into her skirt and was just going back to the yard.

Sima Simakov knocked softly on the fence.

The old woman pricked up her ears. Then Sima picked up a stick and rustled the branches of the apple-tree with it.

This made the old woman think that someone was stealthily trying to climb over the fence to steal the apples. She put the cucumbers on the ground, pulled up a big bunch of nettles, crept up to the fence and waited.

Sima Simakov looked through the crack again, but now he could not see the old woman. Feeling uneasy, he caught hold of the edge of the fence and began to draw himself up.

But at that moment the old woman jumped out from her hiding-place with a triumphant cry, and lashed Sima Simakov smartly over the hands with the nettles.

Waving his stinging hands, Sima bolted through the gate after the other boys, who had already finished their work.

When the old woman returned she stood in front of the neatly arranged piles of logs and stared.

'Who's been doing my work here?' she asked.

Then the milkwoman came into the yard and the two old women began to talk excitedly about the strange happenings with the water and the wood.

Nurka came in through the gate.

'Did you see anyone running into our yard just now?' asked the old woman.

'I've been looking for the goat,' answered Nurka, miserably. 'And running about in the wood all the morning.'

'It's stolen,' the old woman sadly complained to the milkwoman. 'And what a lovely goat it was! That goat was as sweet as a dove. A real dove!'

'Dove!' snapped Nurka, moving away from the old woman. 'When it started butting people they could hardly get out of the way quickly enough. Doves don't have horns.'

'Be quiet, Nurka! Be quiet, you stupid creature,' shouted the old woman. 'Of course it was a fine goat. I wanted to sell her little kid. Now, my darling dove isn't here.'

The gate flew open with a crash. In rushed the goat with lowered horns and made straight for the milkwoman, who caught hold of a heavy can and leapt on to the porch shrieking. The goat hit itself against the wall, and came to a dead stop. They all saw a plywood notice firmly fixed to the goat's horn, on which was written:

> 'I'm a goat, a goat,
> A terror to everyone.
> Whoever beats Nurka,
> Will have a bad time of it.'

On the other side of the fence, the boys were laughing delightedly.

Sima Simakov stuck a stick into the ground and dancing and stamping round it began to sing proudly:

> 'We're not a gang or a band
> Nor a horde of outlaws,
> We are jolly comrades,
> And dashing pioneers,
> Tra la la!'

Then, like a flock of birds, the boys swiftly dispersed.

* * *

Timur and his friends keeping watch and making plans in their meeting place

JOLLY FAMILY

Foreign Languages Publishing House, 1950

Written by N. Nosov

Nikolai Nikolaevich Nosov (1908–76), the son of an entertainer and actor, lived and worked in Kiev. From 1938 he devoted his writing life to children's literature and film. Most of his material was comic and reached English-speaking audiences from the early 1950s onwards. At this point in the Cold War, various agencies such as the Children's Crusade Against Communism of 1951 in the USA, with its 'Fight the Red Menace' campaign, depicted Soviet children's lives as totally restricted and unbearable. The Children's Crusade's bubble gum card number 72 warned its bubble-blowing readership that Russian children are 'told . . . what subjects they must master at school'. Without wishing to minimize the privations and persecutions of this time, Nosov's stories are a reminder that comic writing for children was not forbidden, and that the motifs of comic children's books throughout the world (such as the naughty boy) flourished in Soviet Russia and in the childhoods of British socialists. *One of the strong points of Nosov's books is their dialogue; it made them ideal for reading aloud, as Michael Rosen remembers his parents doing.*

Nosov's *Schoolboys, a story* (English version 1954) depicted children grappling with school grades, whilst getting distracted by out-of-school fun. The irrepressible quality of the boys in *Schoolboys* and *Jolly Family* allows for a far less domineering and authoritarian approach to childhood than was suggested in the West during the Cold War. This liveliness included elements of subversiveness, and must owe a good deal to the huge influence and protection of Korney Chukovsky (1882–1969), who successfully defended the place of fantasy and humour in children's books (see the introduction to Chukovsky's *Wash 'Em Clean* earlier in this part of the anthology).

Jolly Family is a set of loosely connected short stories about Kolya and Mishka as told in the first person by Kolya. In 'The Telephone', we get a strong sense of two boys who are far from being obedient, dutiful servants of the Soviet Union, and yet are not condemned by the story for being so wayward.

THE TELEPHONE

One day Mishka and I saw a wonderful new toy in a shop. It was a telephone set that worked just like a real one. There were two telephones and a coil of wire all packed neatly in a big wooden box. The sales-girl told us that you could use it between flats in the same house. You put one receiver in one flat and the other in the flat next door and connected them with the wire.

Now, Mishka and I live in the same house, my flat is one floor above his, and we thought it would be great fun to be able to telephone to each other whenever we wanted to.

"Besides," said Mishka, "it's not an ordinary toy that gets broken and thrown out. It's a useful toy."

"Yes," I said. "You can have a talk with your neighbour without running up and down stairs."

"A great convenience," said Mishka, all excited. "You can sit home and talk as much as you wish."

We decided to save up money to buy the telephone. For two weeks we didn't eat any ice-cream and we didn't go to the pictures, and by the end of two weeks we had enough money put away to buy the telephone.

We hurried home from the shop with the box, installed one of the telephones in my flat and the other in Mishka's and ran the wire through my window to Mishka's room.

"Now then," said Mishka. "Let's try it out. You run upstairs and wait for my call."

I dashed up to my place, picked up the receiver, and there was Mishka's voice already shouting:

"Hallo! Hallo!"

I yelled back "Hallo" at the top of my voice.

"Can you hear me?" shouted Mishka.

"Yes, I can hear you. Can you hear me?"

"Yes, I hear you. Isn't it wonderful! Do you hear me well?"

"Fine. What about you?"

"Me too. Ha! Ha! Do you hear me laughing?"

"Of course. Ha! Ha! Ha! Can you hear that?"

"Yes. Now listen, I'm coming up to you right away."

He came running in to my place and we hugged each other with joy.

"Aren't you glad we have a telephone? Isn't it grand?"

"Yes," I said.

"Now, I'll go back and call you up again."

He ran back. The phone rang again. I picked up the receiver.

"Hallo!"

"Do you hear me?"

"I hear you perfectly."

"Do you?"

"Yes, I do."

"Me too. Now let's have a talk."

"Yes, let's. What shall we talk about?"

"Oh, all sorts of things. Are you glad we bought the telephone?"

"Very glad."

"It would be awful if we hadn't bought it, wouldn't it?"

"Terrible."

"Well?"

"Well what?"

"Why don't you say something?"

"Say something yourself."

"I don't know what to say," said Mishka. "It's always like that. When you need to talk you don't know what to say, but when you know you mustn't talk you can't stop."

I said: "I know what: I'll hang up and think for a while, and when I think of something to say I'll call you."

"All right."

I hung up and started to think. Suddenly the phone rang. I picked up the receiver.

"Well, have you thought of something?" asked Mishka.

"Not yet, have you?"

"No, I haven't."

"Then what did you ring up for?"

"I thought you had thought of something."

"I would have phoned if I had."

"I thought you mightn't think of it."

"Think I'm a donkey or what?"

"Did I say you're a donkey?"

"What did you say then?"

"Nothing. I said you weren't a donkey."

"Oh, all right, that's enough about donkeys. We'd better stop fooling and do our lessons."

"Yes, so we had."

I hung up and sat down to do my lessons. I had just opened the book when the phone rang.

"Listen. I'm going to sing and play the piano over the phone."

"Go ahead."

I heard a crackling noise, then the thumping of a piano and suddenly a voice that didn't sound a bit like Mishka's sang:

Whither have you fled,
Golden days of my youth?...

What on earth could it be, I wondered. Where could Mishka have learned to sing like that?

Just then Mishka came in, grinning from ear to ear.

"You thought it was me singing? It is the gramophone! Let me listen too."

I handed him the receiver. He listened for a while, then suddenly he dropped the receiver in a great hurry and dashed downstairs. I put the phone to my ear and heard an awful buzzing and hissing. The record must have run down.

I sat down again to do my lessons. The telephone rang. I took off the receiver.

"Bow! Wow!" sounded in my ear.

"What're you barking for?"

"It's not me, it's Laddy. Can you hear him biting at the receiver?"

"Yes."

"I'm pushing the receiver against his nose and he's gnawing at it."

"He'll chew up your telephone if you're not careful."

"Oh, nothing will happen to it, it's made of iron. Ouch! He bit me that time. You bad dog, get down! How dare you bite me! Take that! (Bow! Wow!) You rascal. He bit me, did you hear that?"

"Yes, I heard," I said.

I sat down again to do my lessons, but the next minute the telephone rang again. This time there was a loud buzzing in the receiver.

"What's that?"

"A fly."

"Where is it?"

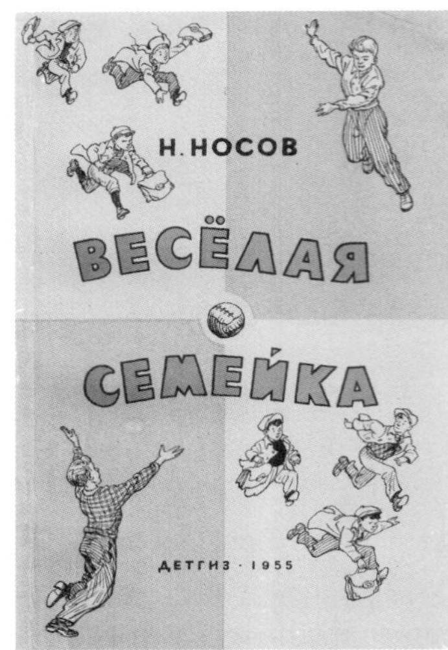

"I'm holding it in front of the receiver and it's buzzing and whirring its wings."

Mishka and I telephoned to each other all day long. We invented all sorts of tricks: we sang, we shouted, we roared, we miaowed, we whispered—and you could hear everything. It was pretty late before I finally finished my lessons. I decided to call up Mishka before going to bed.

I rang up but there was no answer.

What could have happened, I wondered. Had his telephone stopped working already?

I called again, but there was no answer. I ran downstairs and, would you believe it, there was Mishka taking his telephone to pieces! He had pulled out the battery, taken the bell apart and was beginning to unscrew the receiver.

"Here!" I said. "What are you busting the telephone for?"

"I'm not. I'm only taking it apart to see how it's made. I'll put it together again."

"You won't be able to. You don't know how."

"Who says I don't? It's easy."

He unscrewed the receiver, took out some bits of metal and started to pry open a round metal plate inside. The plate flew off and some black powder spilt out. Mishka got frightened and tried to put the powder back into the receiver.

"Now you've gone and done it!" I said.

"That's nothing. I can put it together again in a jiffy!"

He worked and worked but it wasn't as easy as he thought, because the screws were very tiny and it was hard to get them into place. At last he had everything put back except a small piece of metal and two screws.

"What's that thing for?" I asked him.

"Oh dear, I forgot to put it in," says Mishka. "How silly of me! It should have been screwed inside. I'll have to take it apart again."

"All right," I said. "I'm going home. Call me up when you've finished."

I went home and waited. I waited and waited but there was no call, so I went to bed.

The next morning the telephone rang so loudly that I thought the house was on fire. I sprang out of bed, snatched up the receiver and yelled:

"Hallo!"

"What are you grunting like that for?" said Mishka.

"I'm not grunting."

"Stop grunting and talk properly!" shouted Mishka. He sounded quite sore.

"But I am talking properly. Why should I grunt anyway?"

"Don't be a clown. I won't believe you've got a pig there anyway."

"But there isn't any pig here, I'm telling you!" I shouted, getting angry too.

Mishka said nothing.

A minute later he burst into my room.

"What do you mean by making pig noises over the phone?"

"I wasn't doing anything of the kind."

"I heard you quite plainly."

"What should I want to make pig noises for?"

"How do I know? All I know is there was someone grunting into my ear. You go downstairs and try it yourself."

I went down to his place, rang him up and shouted:

"Hallo!"

"Grunt, grunt, grunt, grunt!" was all I heard in reply.

I saw what had happened and I ran back to tell Mishka.

"It's all your doing," I said. "You've gone and busted the telephone."

"How's that?"

"You spoiled something in the receiver when you took it apart."

"I must have put it back the wrong way," said Mishka. "I'll have to fix it."

"How will you fix it?"

"I'll take your telephone apart and see how it's made."

"Oh no, you won't! I'm not going to let you ruin my telephone too."

"You needn't be afraid. I'll be very careful. If I don't mend it we won't be able to use the phone at all."

I had to give in and he got busy at once. He tinkered with it for a long time and when he had finished "fixing" it, it stopped working altogether. It didn't even grunt any more.

"What are we going to do now?" I said.

"I'll tell you what," said Mishka. "Let's go back to the shop and ask them to repair it for us."

We went to the shop but they said they didn't repair telephones and they couldn't tell us where we could get ours repaired. We felt pretty miserable all that day. Then Mishka had an idea.

"We *are* donkeys! We can telegraph to each other."

"How?"

"You know, dots and dashes. The bell still works. We can use that. A short bell can be a dot, and a long bell will be a dash. We can learn the Morse code and send messages to each other."

We got hold of the Morse code and started studying it. A dot and a dash stands for A, a dash and three dots for B, a dot and two dashes for C, and so on. We soon learned the whole alphabet and began sending messages. It went pretty slow at first, but after a while we were tapping away on our bell like real telegraphers. It was even more exciting than a telephone. But it didn't last long. One morning I called Mishka, but there was no answer. He must be sleeping, I thought. So I called later, but there was still no answer. I went down to him and knocked at his door. Mishka opened it for me.

"You don't need to knock any more. You can ring."

He pointed to the button on the door.

"What's that?"

"A bell."

"Go on!"

"Yes, an electric door-bell. From now on you can ring instead of knocking."

"Where did you get it?"

"I made it myself."

"How?"

"I made it out of the telephone."

"What?"

"Yes. I took the bell out of the telephone, and the button as well. And I took the battery out too. What's the use of having a toy when you can make something useful out of it."

"But you had no right to take the telephone apart," I said.

"Why not? I took mine apart, not yours."

"Yes, but the telephone belongs to both of us. If I had known you were going to take it to pieces I wouldn't have chipped in with you and bought it. I don't need a telephone that doesn't work."

"You don't need a telephone at all. We don't live so far from each other. If you want to talk to me you can come downstairs."

"I never want to talk to you again," I said and walked out.

I was so angry with him I didn't talk to him for three whole days. I was very lonely all by myself, so I took my telephone apart and made a door-bell out of it too. But

I didn't do it the way Mishka did. I made mine properly. I put the battery on a shelf near the door and ran a wire from it along the wall to the bell and the button. I screwed the push-button in properly so it didn't hang on one nail like Mishka's. Even Mum and Dad praised me for doing such a neat job.

I went down to tell Mishka about my bell.

I pressed the button on his door, but nobody answered. I pressed it several times but I didn't hear it ring. So I knocked. Mishka opened the door.

"What's wrong with your bell? Doesn't it work?"

"No, it's out of order."

"What's the trouble?"

"I took the battery apart."

"You what!?"

"Yes. I wanted to see what it was made of."

"Well, what are you going to do now without a telephone or a bell?" I asked him.

"Oh, I'll manage somehow," he answered with a sigh.

I went home feeling puzzled. What makes Mishka do such things? Why does he have to break everything? I felt quite sorry for him.

That night I couldn't sleep for a long time for thinking about our telephone and the bell we had made out of it. Then I thought about electricity and where the electricity inside the batteries came from. Everyone else was fast asleep but I lay awake thinking about all these things. After a while I got up, switched on the light, took my battery off the shelf and broke it open. There was some sort of liquid inside with a small black stick wrapped in a piece of cloth dipped in it. So that was it! The electricity came from that liquid. I carefully put the battery back on the shelf and went to bed again. I fell asleep at once.

PART FIVE

EXAMPLES FROM LIFE

INTRODUCTION

Part of the reading experience of most children in the period covered by this book included stories which children were encouraged to think of as true because they were based in real life. Among these were autobiographies, biographies and history, and accounts of scientific discoveries, along with some discussion of social and political theory: works of a kind that today would probably be classified as 'nonfiction' or 'information'. The main source for this body of material was usually school, but various authoritative agencies outside of school also offered it through the BBC, cinema newsreels (Pathé News), encyclopedias, and certain parts of the book trade, as well as more popular forms like magazines and annuals, and children's pages or strips in newspapers. Part of being the child of left-wing parents was to be told that most of this material was either not true or, in all sorts of ways, rigged or biased.

As a child, Michael Rosen remembers a running commentary coming from his parents whenever the radio was on, homework was to be done, encyclopedias were opened, mainstream children's magazines and comics such as Arthur Mee's Children's Newspaper *(1919–65),* The Boys' Own Paper *(1879–1967), and* The Eagle *(originally 1950–69) were spread out. He had a strong sense that his parents were always on the hunt for alternatives, so that something with the equivalent look of authority (usually in the form of a book or magazine) could be put in front of him and his brother.* Examples of these can be found both in this section and elsewhere in this book. On occasions, this meant that those from roughly twelve to sixteen year olds were given books aimed at adults as introductions to, say, Marxist approaches to history or politics (as noted earlier, Raphael Samuel recalled being given material about the Basque children who were being cared for in England when he was just three or four years old). *For example, before he was fifteen, Rosen remembers being given and reading A. L. Morton's* A People's History of England *(1938), Leo Huberman's* Man's Worldly Goods: The Story of the Wealth of Nations *(1936), and* Spokesmen for Liberty *(edited by Jack Lindsay and Edgell Rickword, 1941). Jane Rosen recollects quoting from Morton at school when the Irish Famine was being discussed. The book, at her own request, had been given to her as a Christmas present chosen, along with others, from the catalogues issued by Lawrence and Wishart and the London left-wing bookseller Collets.*

Michael Rosen's father, Harold (1919–2008), was brought up by a Communist mother and recollects in his memoir, *Are You Still Circumcised?: East End*

Memories (1999), that this oral addition to written sources was a part of his political education in the 1920s and 1930s. It was acquired by being taken to political meetings, reading the *Daily Worker* to his Yiddish-speaking grandfather, and the same kind of running commentaries from his mother on such events as Empire Day that Harold later delivered to Michael and his brother. Harold Rosen's other source for left-wing views of the world came from life stories recounted by relatives and strangers. Often these were told in such places as the local library in Whitechapel, London, which served a diverse, multilingual population, largely from Eastern Europe. Many of the tellers recalled pogroms, uprisings, and the Russian Revolution itself, which they were keen to share with others. *This sense that life was politics and politics was life carried over into Michael Rosen's childhood in the form of his parents' anecdotes, family history, and history as it is more conventionally understood, which was often finished off with a 'point' or a moral, along the lines of 'If we had lost at Stalingrad, we wouldn't be here now.' This could be part of family talk, the talk at informal gatherings, or interlaced into more formal talks and speeches at meetings, which children often attended. Even if as a child the significance was not immediately apparent, it was possible to get explanations—and plenty of them!—later.*

In these alternative histories, a pageant of heroes and villains was put before Michael and his brother: villains such as the charity that refused to provide winter shoes for Harold (as a child) because Harold's mother was technically still married, even though her husband was in the USA and not providing for the family; political heroes such as Georgi Dimitrov who, it was said, single-handedly stood up against the might of Nazi Germany when he successfully defended himself against the charge of having started the Reichstag Fire of 1933. Into this pageant went the villain and leader of the British Union of Fascists, Oswald Mosley, who had personally and through his organization threatened the community that Michael's and Jane's grandparents and parents lived in; the hero the great Czech long-distance runner, Emil Zatopek; the villains at the local education authority who had a blacklist of Communist teachers they would not promote; the hero and colleague 'Les', who successfully defended a boy against wrongful arrest; and so on. Mosley featured in the story most often repeated by those who had lived in London's East End in the 1930s, the Battle of Cable Street (1936). Equivalent stories around actions and flashpoints from the personal histories of parents and grandparents from anywhere in Britain or the world was a crucial way in which children were included in a political way of life and habit of thought.

All this and much more represented an oral history of life, struggle, persecution, opinion, migration, and settlement not covered directly by the printed material in this book, though thousands of equivalent and parallel stories were told by left-wing parents to their children throughout this period. *When, as a child, Michael Rosen stayed at a friend's house, he heard of the Armenian genocide; at another home, a parent of Woodcraft Folk members was admired for having been in the French Resistance and imprisoned in Dachau Concentration Camp.* Later, as an adult travelling round the British Isles, Michael became aware of left-wing parents and grandparents who had told their children stories of rent strikes, a TB epidemic in Birmingham, starvation in the South Wales coalfields, and the soldiers' parliaments in the Second World War.

One way in which an extended hearing of people who experienced working-class life reached the general public came in the form of Ewan MacColl's and Charles Parker's 'Radio Ballads', broadcast on BBC Radio 2 between 1958 and 1964. There was nothing specifically child-oriented about these but, *as Michael Rosen can testify from his own and his friends' experience, left-wing parents encouraged their children to listen to them.*

The extracts in this section represent the efforts by a group of people who thought that they should match the output of the education system, the BBC, the cinema newsreels, and the popular magazines and comics with an alternative view. Amongst their outlets were sympathetic publishers such as Martin Lawrence, the *Daily Worker*'s 'Children's Corner', and, for three happy years, the *Daily Worker Children's Annual.*

'SAFAR THE HERO'

from *Folk Tales of the Peoples of the Soviet Union*
H. Jenkins, 1945

Written by Gerard Shelley

The provenance of this book in the context of left literature is something of a curiosity. 'Fellow travellers' was a term used contemptuously towards people of left or liberal leanings who 'sympathized' with either the Soviet Union or the actions of the Communist Party of Great Britain (CPGB), or both. However, people in the party had mirror-image terms referring to people as 'sympathetic' or 'progressive' and who, it was thought, would therefore support campaigns led by the CPGB. This book found its way into the canon of left juvenile reading perhaps in part for its title, which includes the phrases 'folk tales' (rather than 'fairy tales') and 'Peoples of the Soviet Union', chiming exactly with the phraseology of Communist writing of the time.

Gerard Frankham Shell (1891–1980), who adopted the name Gerard Shelley, was a linguist, translator, and ultimately an archbishop in the Old Roman Catholic Church of Great Britain (founded in 1910). His relationship with Russia began socially in 1907 in Italy where he met émigré Russian aristocrats. He travelled to Russia, and was there throughout the Russian Revolution of 1917. Accused of being a counter-revolutionary, he escaped by dressing as a woman and hiding under the seats of a train from Moscow to Finland. He was employed as an interpreter at the Paris Peace Conference of 1919, and worked for the International Federation of Trade Unions in Switzerland. Politically, Shelley was attracted to anarchism and socialism, sympathetic to the Russian nation and its people, but hostile to Bolshevism, which he thought of as a cloak for Jewish aspirations for world domination.

Publishing the book with H. Jenkins placed explicitly Soviet stories amongst a list that ranged from many of the novels of the right-winger P. G. Wodehouse, through the 'progressive' educational ideas of A. S. Neill, to the political writings of William Beveridge, the liberal founder of Britain's welfare state. Only a few years later, at the height of the Cold War, it is unlikely that even a quirky, independent-minded publication house such as H. Jenkins would have taken on a book with this title, but the middle of 1945 was the high water mark for Anglo-Soviet relations. During the Second World War, British armaments ('tanks for Uncle Joe') had been sent to help in the fight against Nazi Germany, and few in Britain were unaware that Berlin had been won by Soviet soldiers following victory at the Battle of Stalingrad in February 1943.

Indeed, tales of Russian heroes such as this one of Safar coincided with the then current idea of Soviet military heroism, prior to the whole Soviet project being buried beneath a wave of fear and loathing as expressed by Western politicians and media during the Berlin airlift (1948–9), the Korean War (1950–3), Senator McCarthy's hearings (1950–4), and genuine or imagined Communist involvement in anti-colonial uprisings in Malaya (1948–60), Kenya (1952–60), and Cyprus (1955–9).

Behind the notion of 'folk tales of the Soviet Union' lay a long and bitter debate on whether the new society should reject folk tales. The writer Maxim Gorky and scholar Yuri Sokolov successfully defended the tales in a crucial speech to the Union of Soviet Writers in 1934, thereby laying down theoretical grounds for Communists and socialists all over the world to collect, retell, study, and perform folkloric material. In brief, Gorky and Sokolov argued that folk tales showed working people in a positive light.

In this tale, set during the Civil War following the Russian Revolution of 1917, Safar, a local partisan, fights the forces summoned by the landowners. Though he is defeated, he refuses to surrender, and in the course of the battle even the forces of nature, in the form of a cliff, try to help him.

SAFAR THE HERO

An Avar Tale

FOR forty days and forty nights the troops of that base hound Gotsinski[1] had been laying siege to the fortress of Khunzakh. News of this had crossed the snowy mountains, rivers and plains and reached the Headquarters of the Red Army. At the Red Headquarters was Commander Safar, a gallant jigit (horseman). He called together his men and said to them: "The dogs with the yellow fangs have surrounded the Red fortress of Khunzakh. Let us go and relieve it."

And all the troops answered as one man: "Let us go, Safar!"

And Safar set out for Khunzakh at the head of his men. No matter whether the mountain passes were high or low—they went forward without a halt. Safar himself dismounted from his horse and gave it over to the baggage train.

"I want to be the same as you," he said to his men.

And for two nights and two days Safar's troops moved on without halting.

The mountain people knew that Safar was on the side of the poor folk. Fathers sent him their sons, brides—their bridegrooms, sisters—their brothers. The mountain people knew what the villain Najhmuddin Gotsinski was after: he wanted to get back the cattle pastures which had been taken by the poor peasants, the flocks of sheep, orchards and plough-lands, of which he had been deprived. His men were robbing people at his command and for his benefit. They took the scanty crops from the barns and drove off the last asses. The poor peasants were full of woe; they cursed their lives and got their weapons ready.

As soon as it became known in the villages that Safar had come into the mountains with his troops, all hastened to join him. And on the third day Safar ordered the whole army to halt in a big valley.

They took the baggage off the horses: boxes of cartridges, baskets and bags of valuable supplies. They lighted campfires and posted sentries.

The night went by. Safar gave permission to sleep in turns, and he himself went the rounds of the watch. He went round the whole camp: all was quiet. Around were towering cliffs, and the sky was like a roof above them. There was a way out on either side of the valley, and one of these defiles was narrower than the other. Safar thought to himself: "If the enemy comes up on either side of these exits, what shall we do? How shall we get out of the sack we have entered?"

Safar returned to his commanders and held council with them. Meanwhile Gotsinski's curs surrounded Safar's troops and occupied all the exits and heights.

1. Najhmuddin Gotsinski—a landowner, leader of the White Guards during the civil war in Daghestan.

"Ho, Safar, surrender! You are caught like a mouse in a trap!" they shouted to him from above. "How are you going to get away now? We have closed all the defiles from the gorge with lead."

When he heard this Safar rose up.

"You lie!" he shouted. "We shall pass through the Arakan gates! Rise up, partisans!"

Safar had no sooner shouted than rocks were hurled down from above and shots rang out. The sleepers awoke; those who were lying down leapt to their feet. Those who had horses leapt into the saddles and galloped towards one of the defiles. They were met with bullets and gunfire. They rushed to the other defile and there too they were met with bullets and gunfire. Many were the men who fell there. They were in a trap. What were they to do? The men huddled together in the middle of the valley and waited. And the rocks came hurtling down from above, pounding the horses and crushing the men. The horses rushed about, dragging at the bridles and shuddering. And still the rocks came flying down.

"Let's force our way through!" said Safar. "After me, partisans!"

And he was the first to go forward. They could not see where the enemy were firing from, and more and more men were shot down.

"Ho, Safar, surrender!" the enemy shouted from above. "You won't get away."

It was a grievous insult, but Safar said nothing and thought to himself: "What is to be done?"

"Surrender!" they shouted to him. "Do you think you're a mouse that can get away under the ground? Or a falcon that can soar up into the sky?"

Then Safar made up his mind once again to get through the defile.

"Partisans, you heard what they are saying to us?" he asked.

"We heard!" the men replied.

"Since we are neither mice nor falcons, but Red partisans, is it possible we are not going to get out of here?"

The men dashed into the defile for the last time, but again they failed to get through. The enemy's bullets mowed them down. The enemy was everywhere!

The wounded horses broke the bridles and rushed along the valley screaming and snorting. The men tried to take cover but could find none, and many fell.

"Surrender!" shouted the enemy from above.

"We'll not surrender!" replied the men.

Rocks and bullets came whistling down.

"Ho, soldiers of October!" shouted Safar. "You remember how Shamil[2] taught his soldiers how to die?"

Then all who had remained alive took off their coats, tucked up their sleeves, bared their chests and began to sing an ancient war-song.

2. Shamil—the leader of the mountain peoples of the Caucasus who fought against the Russian autocracy in the middle of last century.

Gotsinski's curs surrounded the last group of brave men. They fired at these tired men point-blank and hacked at them with swords. The warriors fell, but Safar still stood by the cliff and slashed back at the enemy. And when he remained quite alone, he heard the cliff whisper to him: "You are surrounded, beware!"

He leaned his back against the cliff.

"Take care! They want to take you from the right. Defend yourself!"

Safar beat off the blow, but another was already waiting for him on the left. And he beat off the second blow.

"Surrender, Safar! If you don't surrender, we'll take you dead. You won't get away!"

"Take me, if your hands can reach me!"

"Bend down!" shouted the cliff.

Safar bent down, and a rock flew over his head. It struck against the cliff and fell at his feet.

The cliff shuddered.

"Are you strong?" asked the cliff.

"As strong as you," replied Safar.

He had scarcely uttered these words when a rock struck him in the chest. He did not quaver.

"Surrender!" they shouted to him again.

"Even dead I won't surrender!"

"We'll take you alive!"

The cliff hung lower over Safar and spread out its sides, as though Safar had entered a cavern.

"Stop! I know how to take him!" shouted one of the attackers.

He put his sword back into its sheath and commanded in a loud voice: "Ho, who has got any honey? Bring it here!"

They brought him some honey of the mountain bees. He tore a lump of wool out of his coat, dipped it in the honey and tossed it to Safar. The wool fell on Safar's wounded chest. Suddenly a cloud of flies flew up as though from nowhere. They covered his chest and clung to the open wounds. He threw the sticky wool to the ground. But a second lump of wool fell right into his eyes. Buzzing flies settled all around them. He shook his head, and the lump of wool flew off. His eyes grew dim, his body itched and smarted, as the flies swarmed over his wounds.

"Ho, jigits, who have you called in to help you? Flies!" Safar cried out in fury to the enemy.

"Are you going to surrender or no?" they asked him, as they got ready to throw a third lump of wool.

"Call in a jackal to help you, then I'll surrender!"

They threw the wool at Safar. It fell on the open wound near his heart. The flies swarmed over the red wound and began to suck the blood from it. Safar was about to drive the flies away with the hand in which he held his sword, but the enemy seized him.

The cliff staggered back.

"Where are you going to?" Safar called out to the cliff. The cliff leaned forward.

"Help me to get out of captivity," Safar whispered to it.

"How can I help you?" asked the cliff. "You are in the hands of the enemy."

"Stand firmer!" Safar said to it, and with all his might he dashed his head against the sharp side.

The cliff did not stir. Safar, the hero, fell dead at its feet.

TOMORROW IS A NEW DAY: A YOUTH EDITION

Puffin Books, 1945

Written by Jennie Lee

This book is one of the few examples in the first half of the twentieth century of a working-class, socialist woman's autobiography that was made available and accessible to children, and it remained in print in that format for many years. Autobiographies or fictionalized memoirs of working-class women's childhoods written specially for children are hard to find at any time, and a book like Gwent Grant's *Private Keep Out* didn't appear until after the time frame of this book (1978). In fact, it would be no easy matter getting one published today, making the publication and long life of *Tomorrow is a New Day* all the more remarkable.

Janet Lee (known as Jennie Lee; 1904–88) was born in Fife, Scotland. She was the daughter of a miner and after some struggle over financial support, studied education and law at Edinburgh University. After graduating with an MA, an LLB, and a teaching certificate, she worked as a teacher in Cowdenbeath. She served as an MP for the Labour Party from 1929 to 1931, and again from 1945 to 1970, and was instrumental in getting the Open University up and running when she served as Minister for the Arts in the Labour government of 1964. From 1934 to 1960, she was married to Aneurin Bevan, the person often regarded as the most socialist-minded of the ministers in the Attlee government.

Though the autobiography tells the story of a working-class childhood, there is no escaping the fact that one of the reasons for the story's success is that it fits an old and not-so-radical narrative: rags to riches. It may seem churlish to mention it, but it has always been much harder to publish and sell working-class autobiographical material to children if fame or fortune does not await the reader by the last chapter. Of course, this doesn't invalidate the experience itself, nor the writing of it, and by the 1950s the book was firmly established on the list of titles that left-wing parents recommended to their children to read. By then, Jennie Lee was a recognizable figure on the radio and TV; the fact that she was one of the few people to be heard with a strong Fife accent helped match the memoir to a person.

CHAPTER III

As we grew older unpleasant changes occurred. The sense of well-being that pervaded our childhood became exceedingly brittle. By the time we reached the secondary-school age, our wants had become expensive. It was no longer possible for our parents to buy us contentment for a few pence. Some class-mates had bicycles. Please could we have bicycles? Some class-mates had joined the local tennis club. Please could we have money to join the club and money to buy a racket and tennis-balls? Next it was golf or dancing lessons or a special outfit for gymnastics. In short, whatever we saw anyone else having we came home and clamoured for. Unhappily for us at the very time when our wants were mounting the family income was declining. Everything seemed to be declining. Partly, of course, we were beginning to look at the world more critically and with wider standards of comparison. But in addition there was a very real scaling down all round. We had moved from a four-roomed house to a three-roomed one. We hated that. It meant too much furniture cluttering up every corner and a much smaller living-room. But the heart of our discontents was that we were suffering from a kind of rash that breaks out sooner or later on most children from working-class homes who are sent to secondary schools. That is, we had become bitten with small-town snobbery. While this phase lasted we made life for our mother one long punishment. The family income was incongruously inadequate to meet even a quarter of our demands. Our mother peered at us anxiously over her spectacles and scraped and scrambled to meet us as far as she could. One day she came in beaming, carrying the much-coveted tennis-racket and an elegant net-bag holding six tennis-balls. The racket was presented to me. My brother borrowed it and in his enthusiasm straight away smashed it. The family fortunes never again enabled us to replace it so that was the end of our tennis careers.

About this same time an itch took possession of us to change round all the furniture in the house. We wanted to make it look smarter. The kitchen dresser was an obvious target. The shelves of the dresser were laden with useless ornaments climaxing in the inevitable 'China dogs'. I announced that I really must have these shelves for books. Mother was devoted to her miscellaneous crockery. Every week it was lovingly taken down, dusted or washed, and put carefully back in its place again. That week, reluctant but anxious to meet us as always, the china dogs, the remains of her wedding tea-service, weird shepherdesses, pink angels poised on sea-shells and all the other bric-a-brac, were taken down and not put back. I had won. Books, chiefly my father's and of not the slightest use to me for school purposes, arrogantly lined the dresser shelves. The household gods they had deposed were laid to rest in a large clothes-basket thrust out of sight under the bed. Next we turned our marauding eyes towards our father. He was no longer hero and superman. Why, if he had anything to him, did he remain a simple colliery fireman? Why did he not make more money? We measured him against the fathers of some of our friends who were richer than we were and decided he had more brains than they had. That just increased our exasperation. Why, why, did he not use any gifts he had to make more money so that we could become small-town swells? We had no patience with him and his socialist theories and the poverty we were condemned to by his obstinacy. Money, make money, lots of it, that was what counted.

With me this silly season lasted less than a year. My brother was smitten rather more severely. One day he helped to cure me by adding to our usual impossible demands on our mother a tone of bullying and contempt that was something new. I found myself flying to her defence, mad with rage. Henceforth I stood guard over her, waiting to tomahawk the boy if he should again forget himself. Not that she took his lapse as stormily as I did. Whatever we did she had a happy knack of finding a reason for or at least a good excuse. We were tired, overstrung, working too hard at school, just thoughtless.

Soon after I had recovered from this phase, I noticed something on coming in from school one day that stabbed me to the heart. The shelves above the kitchen dresser presented a droll sight. Two tiny clearances had been made in the midst of the books and a pink angel had been timidly inserted in each. Mother must have been under the bed looking at her china and had been tempted to reinstate these two pieces. In the quick-changing, adolescent moods that young people go through, I for the moment no longer wanted to have everything my own way. 'Let's put all the dishes back,' I volunteered. 'I think they look much nicer than books.' She knew I was lying and although bewildered as to the reason, sensed that I genuinely detested those pink angels on their fatuous sea-shells. As quick as quick, she turned down the proposal and stoutly insisted that she thought the books looked much nicer than dishes and she would rather that they were kept where they were. I knew she was lying just as she knew I was lying, but there the matter ended. The books remained on the shelves and the next day even the pink angels were again slumbering in the basket beneath the bed.

When I was nine years old I must have known every word of *Robinson Crusoe* off by heart. I had a very special reason for this. Our father had told us that Lower Largo was the birthplace of Robinson Crusoe. Our mother had booked a room in Upper Largo for the miners' holiday week. The whole town knew of these goings on. We babbled for months beforehand of this coming holiday by the sea.

Then came the deadly warning. We were cautioned not to build our hopes too high. There were rumours of a strike that was to be the biggest ever known in the history of mining. Every pit in the whole of Great Britain was to be brought to a standstill. If there was a strike, there could be no holiday. For days longer than years we hung around in an agony of suspense. As children it seemed a matter of life and death to us that no strike should take place just at that time. We pleaded with our parents, trying to make them understand that the most important thing in the world was that we should go to Robinson Crusoe's birthplace. We badgered all we dared. When our tongues were silenced our eyes went on campaigning.

Eventually the family conference was held where our fate had to be decided. Our mother looked inquiringly towards father. It was his place to give a lead. Two disconsolate children were hanging on his every word. He went on smoking his pipe in a slow, tantalizing way he sometimes has, then began very slowly and deliberately: 'As likely—as not—there will be—a strike. But nothing—is definite yet.—We might—as well risk it.'

Oh, the relief! That was all we wanted to know. We could run off now and prepare for our ascension straight into heaven.

I can always return to Largo Bay with a special feeling of intimacy and pleasure. Its old grey harbour is quite lovely. It is peaceful in the uplands behind the sea.

But that is not the Largo we knew as children. That Largo was a place of pure magic. The fishermen down by the harbour in their great blue jerseys filled us with bashful hero worship. Sometimes they let us sit in their boats. Once or twice we were taken a little way out to sea.

Then there were the Pierrots. Such Pierrots. We never willingly missed a performance. We liked the funny songs and we liked the sentimental ones. We liked everything. One day the favourite comedian caught sight of our parents. Without stopping his songs and patter, he lifted his hat and called 'How are you, Mr Lee?' A minute later in the midst of his fooling he sang out again, 'And how's our Mrs Lee? I am coming round to see'. No one in the audience except ourselves knew that these words had any meaning. But we knew. My brother and I nudged each other with pride and pleasure. Later, jingling the collection bag, he made his way to our part of the crowd. He really was a special friend of ours. He had stayed in the Arcade Hotel years before we were born.

On the second day of our holiday we got the news from somewhere that quite definitely there would be no strike. A settlement had been reached. That same day, trailing down to the beach together, my father and I stopped to buy a newspaper. He read it when we reached the shore, then stared gravely out to sea. So gravely that I knew something was seriously wrong. I was filled with dark misgivings. Perhaps there was going to be a strike after all. Perhaps we would have to return home that very day. Even if we could stay our whole week, perhaps there would be no pennies for ice-cream and everyone would be looking gloomy. I asked what was wrong. Would there be a strike? No, there would be no strike but the Germans—the German Fleet. Now I could breathe again. There was to be no strike. We could finish our holiday in peace. That was July 1914.

When the war began we collected all the broken dolls we could lay hands on and played at hospitals. Those with limbs missing were in special demand. And, of course, it was not possible for us to attend to our wounded until we had uniforms and white head-dresses like other nurses. When our mothers were not looking we confiscated old white towels and handkerchiefs and improvised magnificently.

We had lots of fine war games. But as the weeks passed I began to feel disquieted. My parents were not cheering with the rest of the crowd. They were opposed to the war. This was awkward. It was worse than that, it was frightening. I dared not confess it, but secretly I felt ashamed. Children are sticklers for convention. They hate their family to seem in any way 'queer'. Yet here we were meeting each Sunday evening in the open-air miles outside the town because the local authorities and someone called D.O.R.A.[1] refused to give us permission to hold meetings in the usual places like ordinary people. Then one Sunday evening I became happy and proud and spiritually at one with my family. It was one of those rare Sundays in Scotland when it is gloriously warm even in the evening. I had walked out to the Netherton Burn, where our meetings were usually held, along with my parents and two visiting I.L.P.[2] propagandists. They were to speak to us about the war. I don't remember a word of what they said but I recall very vividly a conversation I was holding with myself while the meeting was in progress. That week in school our history lesson had dealt with the persecution of the old Covenanters and their secret meetings on lonely hillsides. True, we were meeting at the side of a busy main road and beckoning to all who passed to come and listen. Nor had any of our members been put on the rack or tortured with thumbscrews. But the parallel was near enough. Were we not a persecuted minority? Were not some of our members in prison? Were we not forced to meet in the open country miles outside the town? We were the modern Covenanters, we were fighting for conscience' sake. There were only a few of us, but it was we, not the multitude, who were right. That conclusion made things much easier. Nothing could now make me feel ashamed. Indeed, I was now ready to go forth to battle and to slaughter everyone who stood in our way.

During the war years, Duncan Beaton, a local miner, Mrs. Watson, wife of the present Member for Dunfermline Burghs, and Mr. Garvie, the blind bookseller, conducted

1. Defence of the Realm Act.

2. Independent Labour Party.

a flourishing socialist Sunday School. I learned to recite with great gusto a poem called the 'Image of God'. It went something like this:

I slaughtered a man, a brother,
In the wild, wild fight at Mons,
I see yet his eyes of terror,
Hear yet his cries and groans.

Every one of us without exception was made word-perfect in the ten socialist precepts. I thought the one about war very reasonable. 'Do not think that those who love their own country need hate or despise other nations or wish for war, which is a remnant of barbarism.'

Mrs. Henderson, a miner's wife with a strong, sweet voice, attended every Sunday forenoon to help us with the singing. We learned to sing after her:

O beautiful my country,
Be it thy nobler care;
Than all thy wealth of commerce,
Thy harvests waving fair.
Be it thy pride to lift up
The manhood of the poor,
Be thou to the oppressed
Fair freedom's open door.

After that we all joined in the chorus:

We are children, but some day,
We'll be big and strong and say,
None shall slave and none shall slay,
Comrades all together.
We shall up and march away, march away, march away,
We shall up and march away, marching all together.

Another important part of my wartime training was a cartoon I picked up among my father's papers. It showed a monkey sitting in the tree-tops and looking quizzically down on a vast plain where men were fighting, maiming and killing one another. The caption underneath read 'Thank God civilization missed me'. I thought that very fine. I was now a politician and one with very definite views.

When the war had been on for some time and food rationing was at its strictest, my brother became ill. He needed more nourishment than the ration-cards allowed. My mother went to the Town House and applied for a permit for extra rations of meat and eggs. She was told that she must first get a doctor's certificate. The doctor called the following day. After a long examination he looked grave and said there was a small spot on one of the child's lungs. That way of putting it did not help. I knew that meant an early stage of consumption. The doctor then advised sending him to a sanatorium. I felt sick and panicky.

For the next three months the war was not important. I learned no more poetry and didn't care whether we were Covenanters or not. All that mattered was our weekly visits to a small boy lying in the bed fifth from the door in the children's ward of Thornton Sanatorium. He was made to wear a grey flannel night-shirt. I was angry and sad every time I saw that awful garment. It made me think of gaols and poorhouses. Why couldn't he wear his own clothes? I petitioned the nurses about it. They answered me civilly but firmly. It was a hospital regulation. And hospitals will be hospitals—when poor people are the inmates.

Each Saturday I walked through the fields to the sanatorium. The bus went only part of the way. When the snow was on the ground it was a bleak, tiring journey. I discovered that the best way of carrying parcels was in a net bag slung over my shoulder. I was too proud to arrive carrying it that way so, when the last corner was in sight, I swung it down and hung it nonchalantly over one arm. Once round the corner I could see the sanatorium and the glass door at the end of the ward. It was usually open. With any luck I could tip-toe right to the bedside without asking anyone's permission. And, knowing how I hated cold, my brother would thrust my hands and head beneath the blankets on his bed, and would have to be satisfied that I had thawed before he would even look at his parcels. To our great joy, three months later he was home again looking comically round and red and greatly improved in health. I could now go on with the war.

Shortly after this the war became almost real. My mother's youngest brother was killed in action. We all sat down together and wept, then, about a week later, the socks that had been knitted for him were sent to another uncle who was in the trenches. It became still more real when my closest friend at school arrived with red swollen eyes and wearing a black dress. Her father had been killed in action. All of us in the class tried in clumsy little ways to show our sympathy. I thrust before her all my answers in the arithmetic tests, although in the ordinary course of things it was arithmetic I depended on to pull me above her in our battles for first place in class.

But we were young and soon forgot those things.

The meetings held by the I.L.P. to explain the causes of the war and how to end it made a much more lasting impression on me than anything else I remember from those years.

One evening, greatly daring, it was decided to attempt an anti-war meeting some miles from home, practically at the gates of a military camp. David Kirkwood was the speaker. My father was in the chair. Before the meeting could begin a great hulking brute of a fellow caught my father in the ribs and threw him right over the heads of the crowd. Kirkwood immediately jumped on the chair that served as a platform and, brandishing a stout stick in the air, roared out: 'If there is a better man than me here, let him come and take this platform.'

Both soldiers and civilians in the audience enjoyed that kind of pacifism. Order was soon restored. A rough house of that kind seldom occurred when the audience was made up exclusively of miners. Experience varied in different coalfields. Here I am recording simply moods and circumstances as I recall them in our corner of Fife. And I am referring to public meetings, not to miners' lodge meetings.

Within the union, Grandfather Lee, then Disputes Agent for the Fife Miners' Union, was almost the only official who stood out against the war. I have heard since how the other officials, led by the late Mr W. Adamson, who were all violently pro-war, did everything in their power to make life Hell for him.

When the war began I was not yet ten years of age and when it ended I was barely fourteen, so its tragedies and controversies sat lightly upon me. But it made our home a very busy place. The few active local socialists who were campaigning against the war were constantly coming in and out for odd meals and discussion.

The week-ends were crammed with events. Very often we had a visiting I.L.P. propagandist staying with us. Usually he came from Glasgow, occasionally from London, and sometimes he was a young fellow on the run from place to place wanted by the police for his anti-war activities.

Those Saturdays when the speaker's train was due to arrive before father could be home from work; washed and changed, it was my job to go to the station. I liked that. It was always a tense moment waiting for the train to draw into the platform. If it was someone who had been with us before, then he was a friend and sure of his welcome. If it was a stranger arriving for the first time, it was a different, but equally pleasant kind of excitement. It was like putting your hand into a lottery bag and drawing out a ticket. You never knew what was going to turn up. Sometimes at first sight I was a little bit nonplussed. But I cannot remember a single one of those visiting propagandists who did not quickly become a friend we enjoyed having with us.

I think most of our guests enjoyed themselves as much as we did. Mother would bustle around, serving us all with unquestioning cheerfulness. Father sat by the fire explaining the local situation. The arm-chair on the other side of the fireplace was for the visitor. My brother and I were quite satisfied with this arrangement. It left for us the corners of the fender-stool where we could sit with our backs to the warm grate and our eyes glued to the stranger. Very occasionally he would ignore our existence and the room would echo with strange, exciting words—Nietzsche, Dietzgen, dialectics, Engels, Hegel——. But more often he would turn to us with all the usual wiles of a grown-up trying to make friends with children.

I can recall only one serious misadventure in our attempts to make our guests feel at home. The redoubtable Dick Wallhead had arrived for a series of meetings. He was an ace among propagandists and we were delighted to have him. We had also heard that he was fond of music. My parents felt, therefore, that he must have the pleasure of listening to me play the piano.

I could play 'Poet and Peasant', 'Tannhäuser', 'Il Trovatore', 'Rigoletto', and at least a score of other pieces with deadly accuracy. I swear to the accuracy, for Mr Garvie, who was blind and had a bookseller's shop in Cowdenbeath High Street, had given me very special facilities for practising.

In the parlour above his shop he had two pianos, an ordinary one and a mechanical one just like those in the ice-cream shops. He and I were very good friends and read together several volumes of *The Story of the Working Class throughout the Ages*. A group of Cowdenbeath Socialists had clubbed together to buy the series which at that time had quite a vogue. The books were stored in Mr Garvie's back shop. He was an eager, intelligent man, with a great faith in education. I enjoyed reading to him and hearing his sharp questions and criticisms. As an exchange in courtesies he invited me to use his pianos. I would wind up the mechanical one and, while it drummed out the scroll, keep perfect time on the other.

In preparation for Dick Wallhead's visit our mother moved the piano from the best parlour bedroom to our kitchen-living-room. All was in readiness for our guest. After supper was cleared away, my parents mildly announced that he must hear me play. I was egged on to begin.

Wallhead sat by the fire looking more and more gloomy and disgruntled. I could feel antipathetic currents of feeling swirling around the room. Finally, able to bear it no longer, he spluttered out in his cracked croak of a voice: 'That girl can't play the piano and never WILL be able to play'.

I don't remember what happened immediately after that. My parents must have felt a bit damped. To pay for piano-lessons, examinations and all, was a big drain on their tiny income. They had very great faith. My own sympathies were divided. I dimly realized that Wallhead was right. And I hated practising. Anyhow, before the end of his visit we were all good friends.

In fairness I must say that that was the only time when a guest had that kind of entertainment thrust on him.

When visitors were due, our mother had us carefully warned to sit quietly by the fire and go on working at home-lessons, or reading our story-books so as not to be a nuisance.

But there were regular old-timers who were special favourites with us and would not allow us to be quiet. James Maxton, for instance, would saunter in with a jaunty air and at once look challengingly around for someone to play with. At least that is how it seemed to us. His brother-in-law, the Rev. J. Munro, was another disrupter of the peace. Before he had been more than an hour in the house he had even my shy little brother on top of a chair shouting out Burns' poems. I was sorry he insisted on teaching him 'Fair fa' your honest, sonsie face, great chieftain o' the puddin'-race', for I thought the 'Address to a Haggis' the dullest poem Burns ever wrote. But my brother enjoyed it. 'Tam Samson's Elegy' was more to my liking. Munro enchanted us for ever by the gusto with which he used to recite it, especially the way he intoned the last three words of every verse—'Tam Samson's deed!'[3]

A less boisterous, but painstaking guest was the Rev. Campbell Stephen. He had no gift for stories but, as we grew older, we found that he was hot stuff on quadratic equations.

As I changed from childhood to adolescence I looked forward with increasing eagerness to these week-end visitors. I was grateful to those who did not try to talk down to us; to those who answered our questions with the same gravity with which we asked them. Maxton would never do that. Always urbanely charming, and with a delightful sense of humour, he would answer nothing seriously. I would tenaciously stick to my point as long as I could in spite of the charm and the humour. But in the end I was always turned away hungry and made to feel a fool for being so clumsily importunate.

As I grew older (I am now thinking of the years just after the war) it seemed a matter of life and death to have all sorts of questions answered.

The coalfields were in a ferment. The union had never been so strong and its morale was even stronger. Miners returning from active service joined in with the rest to demand better conditions. Hadn't the Government said that that was what the fighting had been about? To make life more spacious and gracious for the ordinary man? Lloyd George knew all the words. Our people were now bent on packing some content into them. Now was the time, father said. The sidings were empty. The returning soldiers were not in a mood to be played with. Every advantage lay with the miners.

The coal companies were in a state of funk. They knew the men were in a position to dictate terms. They saw themselves being compelled to disgorge some of the excessive wealth they had piled up during the war.

At this point the Government intervened, offering the Sankey Commission. The miners were to appoint half the commissioners, the coal companies the other half, and Sir J. Sankey was to act as chairman. It was a tempting offer. The more so as, in the same breath, the Government let it be understood that, if there was a national stoppage, soldiers would be drafted into the coalfields and any subsequent bloodshed would be upon the miners' own heads.

3. Dead

Our home, like thousands of others, rang with the controversy. To accept the commission and abide by its findings or to strike without delay and put the issue to a contest between the naked strength of miner and coal-owner?

Most of our lot were for striking. They did not trust Lloyd George. They did not trust any of the Government. They felt they would be tricked and they knew that by the virtue of their own strength they could at that moment have wrung solid concessions from the coal companies.

The most powerful voice for accepting the commission was that of Bob Smillie. Bob we loved, trusted and respected. We knew he was incapable of deceiving us. Every phase of his life he had been marked by lionhearted endurance. At that he was president of the M.F.G.B.[4] and at the height of his power. By the narrowest of margins the coalfields finally voted in favour of accepting the commission. Hurriedly an interim report was got out and the growling of the suspicious was drowned in promises of an immediate reduction of the working hours from eight to seven and some advance in wages. In addition, it soon became evident that Smillie, in his evidence before the commission, was putting an unanswerable case for the miners. Nationalization, a six-hour working-day, pit-head baths, improved wages, were just around the corner. The miners, to clinch matters, received the following letter from Bonar Law:

11, Downing Street,
Whitehall, S.W.
21st *March*, 1919.

Dear Sir,

Speaking in the House of Commons last night I made a statement in regard to the Government policy in connection with the Report of the Coal Industry Commission. I have pleasure in confirming, as I understand you wish me to do, my statement that the Government are prepared to carry out in the spirit and the letter the recommendations of Sir John Sankey's Report.

Yours faithfully,
A. BONAR LAW

We were getting on famously. It was an alive, bracing time. The union was strong. The I.L.P. was growing rapidly in numbers and influence. In our part of the world it was a close cordial fellowship proud of its anti-war record. It was succeeding so well that we forgot to remember, unless as good yarns to tell around the fireside, the

4. Miners' Federation of Great Britain.

harsher side of war-time treatment. It was quite true that many of our best people had been in gaol, that many more, such as my father, burned their calling-up papers and were not sent to prison by the mere accident of their occupations. There had, too, been many ugly incidents at meetings. But war memories faded very quickly. We were growing too fast to have time to look behind. Very soon now we would revolutionize the world. Our socialist hymns seemed to me to give a pretty good idea of what it was all about. I could never sing in tune, but I mumbled fervently to myself the words of the songs we were taught to sing every Sunday forenoon in our socialist Sunday school.

One of our favourite hymns seemed to me to contain the whole of history, and everything about the present and future that really mattered. It went something like this:

Lift up the people's banner, now trailing in the dust,
A million hands are ready to guard the sacred trust;
With steps that never falter and hearts that grow more strong;
Till victory end our warfare we sternly march along.
Through ages of oppression, we bore the heavy load,
While others reaped the harvest from seeds the people sowed;
Down in the earth we burrowed, or fed the furnace heats,
We felled the mighty forests, we built the mighty fleets.
But after bitter ages of hunger and despair
The slave has snapped his fetters and bids his foes beware.
We shall be slaves no longer, the nations soon shall know,
That all who live must labour and all who reap must sow.
So on we march to battle, with souls that shall not rest,
Until the world we live in is by the world possessed.
And filled with perfect manhood, in beauty it shall move,
One heart, one home, one nation, whose king and lord is love.

That sort of thing is not meant to be read in cold blood by grown-up people. They can see all its inadequacies. But our blood was warm, we were young, infinitely impressionable. Every line was real to us. 'Down in the earth we burrowed' meant our fathers working in the pits right under our feet. We had lots of friends working in the shipyards along the Forth and Clyde. It was they who 'built the mighty fleets'. And some of our cousins and uncles and brothers who had emigrated to Canada were sure to be among those who 'fell the mighty forests'.

I was now completely captivated by the socialist movement and well on the way to becoming a youthful socialist edition of Colonel Blimp. I had my prejudices. I had no doubts. I had not the slightest inkling of what went on under the skin of people who did not see things exactly as I did. Idealism, ancestor worship and a happy feeling that we were the people who would one day revolutionize the world so that 'none shall slave and none shall slay' seemed to me just about everything in philosophy, religion and economics that anyone need bother about.

One day, shortly after the war ended, my father announced that Clifford Allen was coming to stay with us. That was staggering news. Clifford Allen, a leading figure in the I.L.P. and in the No Conscription Fellowship, seemed to us the very embodiment of the martyrdom that some of our members had suffered during the war.

Before he arrived father told mother that he must be given most-favoured-nation treatment. That meant having a fire kindled in his bedroom. For husky young fellows, mother thought that unnecessary. But when the propagandist was elderly or not too robust, this extra little privilege was arranged. Clifford Allen, we were gravely told, had had a severe prison sentence and as a result was very, very ill.

I curled up as usual on the corner of the fender-stool and waited tensely for the stranger to appear. A hero was visiting our home. Everyone said that he had not long to live. That his health had been ruined by prison. I had to wait a long time. The local I.L.P. Committee had met the train and they had all gone directly to the hall. Half-way through the evening someone came in with the news that the meeting was a complete fiasco. Something had gone wrong with the timing or advertising and, anyhow, it was a Saturday evening, the hardest of all nights to assemble a crowd. I was wrung with pity. To think that a dying man had dragged himself all the way from London to Cowdenbeath only to be met by such callous indifference.

I settled myself for another long wait. At last I heard the front door opening and knew that the speaker, my father and the rest of the I.L.P. Committee were treading along the lobby towards the kitchen door. By the time the door opened, my eyes were hazy with excitement. I shall never forget the tall, ascetic face and figure of Clifford Allen framed in our kitchen doorway with half a dozen squat dark-looking miners grouped around him. I should not have been surprised if he had suddenly sprouted wings and a halo.

Later in the evening, when everyone else had gone, he won our hearts all over again by telling us how in prison he and another conscientious objector played an intricate game of chess, one move being made each day by signing to one another when as prisoners they were assembled and marched round and round the exercise-yard. It was all very elevating. Ours was a wonderful movement. All knights in shining armour who would never rest until the words in the songs of our socialist hymn-books had indeed come to pass.

I was wild with impatience when I thought of how much of this struggle I had already missed. I had been born so late that I could not even be a suffragette.

Mrs Helen Crawford, one of the old militant group, sometimes stayed with us as a visiting I.L.P. propagandist. Responding to our eager prompting, she would talk for hours about her window-breaking adventures and prison exploits. I longed to have broken windows and been sent to prison for the greater power and glory of the suffragette cause, and wondered ruefully if anything at all would be left to do by the time I had finished with school.

It was Grandfather Lee who cheered me most when I was in this mood. 'Lass,' he would say, 'there will be plenty left for you to do. It takes longer than you think.'

COME IN

Shakespeare Head Press, 1946

Written by Olive Dehn. Illustrated by Kathleen Gell

Olive Dehn (1914–2007) and Kathleen Gell (n.d.) had long careers in children's publishing. With the exception of *Come In*, neither produced anything out of the ordinary, though Dehn's *The Basement Bogle* (1935) is notable for introducing a likeable and competent working-class family before Eve Garnett's *The Family from One End Street* (1937), often thought to be the first attempt to do this in Britain.

Come In is a distorted version of Dehn's life: the family who live at No. 23 Pine Tree Lane are called Markham, and the father is an actor; Olive Dehn was married to the actor David Markham. At the time, Dehn had three children, like the mother in her story. However, far from living in a leafy suburb, she and her family lived as bohemian anarchists in a picturesque but very basic old cottage in the Ashdown Forest in Sussex.

The brilliance of this picturebook is the way, despite the fact that house and family seem to represent the epitome of suburbia, Dehn and Gell systematically question suburban lifestyles. Readers who respond to the invitation to 'come in' enter a 1940s house. The furniture is simply designed and functional; the bathroom is spacious and fully tiled, in line with the latest ideas about hygiene. There are no servants; the mother manages the house with some daily help and such modern gadgets as a telephone, vacuum cleaner, and refrigerator.

Come In depicts suburban living as over-regulated; most pictures incorporate the clocks that rule the day. The illustrations (it has not been possible to show them all) show different things happening in different rooms at the same time, creating a sense of modern life as hectic and tiring. It is a relief when the family goes to bed and the reader, like the artist and the family's cat, can walk out the door.

COME IN!

You see this house with the pine-tree in the garden and the cat tip-toeing about the roof? This is where the Markham family live. It is called No. 23 Pine Tree Lane. The cat on the roof is Sparkles Markham. He is black with very fat white cheeks. He is walking on tiptoe because he has just seen a sparrow in the pine-tree.

Once, Mr. Markham said he would cut down the pine-tree because the needles always dropped into his ears when he was gardening, but the postman said he mustn't because it was the only pine-tree in the district, and if it was cut down they might have to change the name of the lane.

Mr. and Mrs. Markham have three children. There is Susan, she is eight; and Stephen, he is four-and-a-half; and Sara, she is three months. Their names all begin with S because Susan's Granny knitted Susan three beautiful jerseys with S on the front, and Mrs. Markham wanted Stephen and Sara to have the benefit of them as well. You will see Susan's Granny a little later on when she wakes up. She lives at No. 23, too.

Mr. Markham is an Actor. He works in a Theatre where he pretends to be all sorts of different people. Sometimes he is an old man with a beard, sometimes he is a

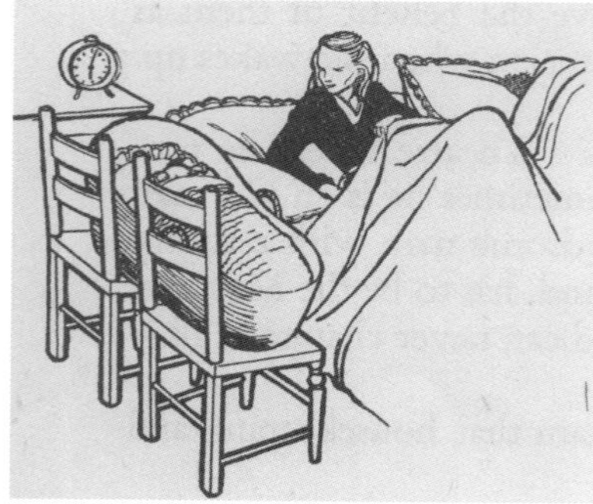

young handsome man with a twirly moustache. Mrs. Markham, on the other hand, has to be the Mummy of Susan, Stephen and Sara, all day long, and can never change at all—except into a clean dress.

One day Mrs. Markham told Mr. Markham that housekeeping and looking after children were the dullest work in the world. So Mr. Markham told her to write down everything that happened in the house from the time she got up to the time she went to bed, so that he could read exactly how dull it was. And Mr. Markham asked an Artist who worked in the Theatre, if she would mind getting up very early and going to No. 23 Pine Tree Lane and drawing all that went on there from morning till night, so that he could see as well as read why housekeeping and looking after children were so dull.

When you have finished looking at the outside of the house, you may come in, but you must come in very, very quietly because everybody in the house is fast asleep—except Sara.

Now you are in Mummy and Daddy's room, and that is Sara Markham in her Moses-basket. She is always the first to wake up at No. 23 and she is beginning to stretch herself and make little squeaky noises because it is six o'clock and time for her to be fed. The clock on the table is an alarum-clock, but Mummy never sets it because she prefers to tell the time by Sara. The sleepy-looking person in the dressing gown is Mummy. She is just wide enough awake to lean over, take Sara into her bed, feed her, change her nappy and roll her back into the Moses-basket.

Daddy hates getting up, so Mummy always waits until she has quite finished with Sara, and then she wakes him very gently. And when she has counted 20 several times, Daddy manages to get out of bed, and by seven o'clock he is more or less dressed and down in the kitchen.

This next bit is the only part of the book that has had to be written by Daddy because Mummy has fallen asleep again upstairs. He is not sure whether he has remembered the order right, but he thinks the first thing he did when he got downstairs was to draw the kitchen curtains and after that he let in Sparkles Markham who was mewing at the

back door. Then he put a kettle on the gas stove and filled the coal buckets. Sparkles followed him out and got shut in the coal-shed so Daddy had to let him in all over again and they had words about it. The fire was ticklish because Daddy forgot to put the chips to warm in the oven last night. When a person has to get into that position to light a fire it means he is nearly at his wit's end. Fortunately, Daddy did just manage, but he had to use eight chips and half a fire-lighter. Then he straightened up and began to clean the family shoes. Granny's were the best. Stephen's were terrible. Daddy thought it was a great blessing that Sara could not walk yet.

When he had done the shoes, he saw that the fire was roaring up the chimney and the kettle was on the boil. So he made three cups of tea, one for Granny, one for Mummy and one for himself. On his way upstairs with the tea-tray he pulled the morning paper out of the letter-box and then he popped his head round the children's door and told Susan and Stephen to get up as he went into the bathroom to shave.

The Artist, of course, comes upstairs after him, to draw the children's room and the children getting dressed. It takes her quite a while to draw the room because the walls have a border of swallows and woodpeckers, and the floor is covered with dressing-gowns and books and bedroom-slippers, and in Stephen's bed there is a red rabbit called Joyce, and in Susan's bed there is a doll with bushy hair called Fair Rosie. [...]

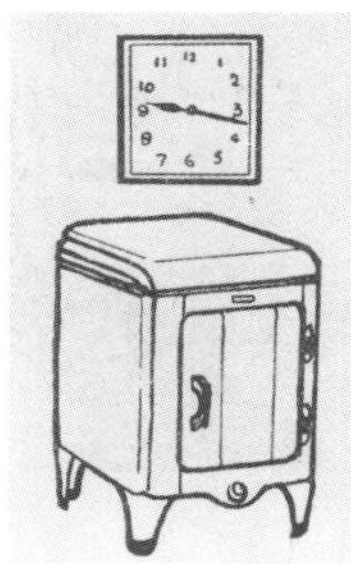

Good Gracious! It's a quarter-past nine, and all the breakfast things have been cleared away. In fact, Granny is actually washing them up in the scullery. Granny is very particular about washing up. She has what she calls a Special Method, and when she dries she uses three tea-towels, one for the glass, one for the silver

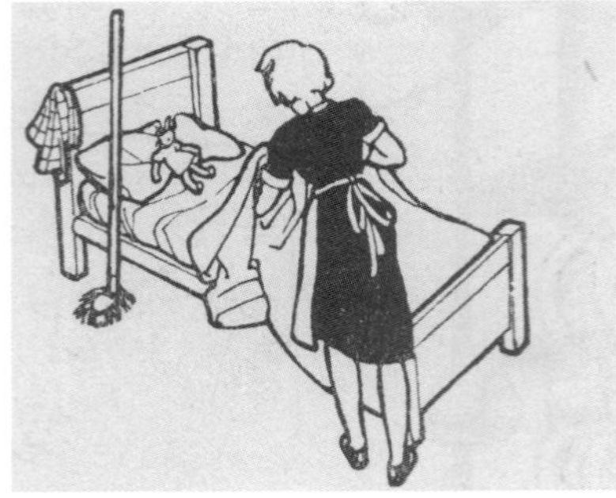

and one for the china! Mummy has a Method, too, but she only uses one tea-towel for everything. Daddy hasn't any Method at all and he has been known to dry plates with the oven-cloth.

Just as Granny was rubbing up the last fork, she remembered she had left the seven pints of milk on the back-door step. She goes to fetch them and this is where she puts them. It is called a Refrigerator. Everyone in Pine Tree Lane has one. They are very useful things because they make ice and you can store food in them for days and days. Once Mummy put some Cod in her Refrigerator and forgot about it for nearly a week, and when Daddy tried it he said it tasted as though it had just come from Iceland. And that is the highest compliment you can pay to a piece of Cod.

There isn't much food in the Markham Refrigerator to-day—only some butter and a few lettuces. That is because it is Monday and stores are running low. Someone will have to go to the shops. [...]

All the upstairs rooms have to be swept and mopped and dusted. Mummy thinks that on Sundays most houses sit quiet and hold their breath, but on Monday morning, they let it all out with a tremendous puff and snort, and that is why Mondays are such particularly dirty, dusty days.

Mummy opens the window to shake out the mop, and she sees Mrs. Sturch walking up to the back door with Pat. Mrs. Sturch comes every Monday morning to do the washing and turn out a room. She has to bring Pat because there is no other way, and, of course, if Pat gets mumps or a tummy-ache, Mrs. Sturch has to stay at home. [...]

And now that Mrs. Sturch is in the backyard, Granny at the shops and Sara in her pram, it's time somebody began to think about getting dinner ready. Mummy opens the larder door. Nothing but a hammer-shaped beef-bone and quantities of vegetables. The first course will have to be Vegetable Soup. Never mind, they all like Soup, except Stephen, and he can have his favourite pudding to make up. (Stephen's favourite pudding is Treacle-tart. What's yours?) The kitchen-table begins to look like a stall in the Market Place. Carrots . . . potatoes . . . turnips . . . the Treacle-tin . . . the pastry-board. Something's bound to fall in a minute. Yes, there goes the rolling-pin right into the scullery. Mrs. Sturch picks it up and tells Mummy it is eleven o'clock, and shall they have a snack of something before they start to turn out the sitting-room? Just look at them, all sitting round the kitchen-table as though they had the whole morning in front of them, with nothing to do but put their feet up. Yet, in five minutes, Mummy will be sweeping the stairs with the hoover and Mrs. Sturch will be pushing Daddy's mahogany desk into the hall. [. . .]

Mummy pokes her head round the door and wants to know the time. A quarter-to-twelve! She might just fit in the ironing before the children come back from school. In fact, she "must" fit it in, because if she doesn't, Sara won't have a frock for the morning, Stephen won't have any clean pyjamas and Susan won't be

able to wear her cherry-coloured dress with knickers to match, when she goes to tea with Pamela Sweeney tomorrow. Granny always used to help with the ironing, but, about a fort-night ago, she got muddled up over the switches, and the iron, which she thought was off, turned out to be on, and it set fire to the ironing-board and burnt one of Daddy's new striped shirts to a cinder. And now Granny can't look at an iron without trembling. So, when she saw Mummy open the ironing-drawer, Granny said she would go upstairs and give the bath a good clean, because they really ought to wash Stephen's hair tonight. Just as she went out there was a tremendous Tring-aring-a-ring-aring-a-rinng! from the hall. It is Mrs. Sweeney on the telephone. Can she speak to Mummy a moment? Mummy has just got to Susan's cherry-coloured knickers, but it can't be helped. Mrs. Sweeney says she doesn't think that Susan ought to come to tea after all because her Pamela has come out in some queer-looking spots this morning, and the Doctor thinks it may be chicken-pox. Whilst Mummy is answering, another bell rings.

Br-e-e-e-e-eng! That will be the back-door again. Mummy says the bells at No. 23 always ring in pairs, and at opposite ends of the house. Who is it this time? The window-cleaners, of all people, and on a Monday, too. [...]

And here, helter-skelter, come the children, back from school. And away go Mrs. Sturch and Pat to their dinners. Good-bye, Mrs. Sturch! Take care of yourself. Thank-you for all you have done for us. [...]

Now, what is Whittle [the gardener] getting into such a frenzy about? He has actually stopped mowing. One of the

chimneys is going to fall off? The pine tree is tottering? Mercy no! Far worse than that! It's RAINING! A regular cloudburst. Granny! Stephen! Come quickly! Bring in the washing! Put up Sara's hood. [...]

Half-past three and quiet at last. The house is having a breathing-space and everyone is doing what they like. [...]

Alas! The house is never quiet for long. Who is this little drowned rat, creeping in at the back door? Susan, soaked to the skin! Now what a fuss there will be. Her hair will have to be dried, her frock changed and her feet put in hot water. After that—a scolding. Why didn't she take a mackintosh? [...]

Whittle comes in, also very moist, and puts an end to the discussion. Whittle says, rain has got into the mowing machine and clogged the works. But don't worry, he will soon knock it into shape, only he must have a hammer. Also, Sara is crying fit to bust herself. [...]

And now comes the question, what shall she give the children for their tea? There is a Swiss roll and some of Sunday's Chocolate Mould; there might be fish-paste on toast; there "must" be plain bread-and-butter. But where are the children? The three of them have mysteriously disappeared—even Susan, who was in the kitchen a minute ago. Walk down the passage, open the first door on your left and you will find them, where all good children ought to be found—in the Nursery. [...]

There goes Sara upstairs in Mummy's arms. The first to wake in the morning, the first to go to bed at night. Singly, or in pairs, from now on, the family will move, gradually, from the ground floor to the top. [...] The children's time is coming to an end, the grown-ups' time is beginning. [...]

It is getting dark. Did you notice what time the clock said? A quarter past nine! And here, at this late hour, is a room you have never seen before. The sitting-room. [...] And Mummy? What is she doing? Why, writing this very book, as she promised Daddy she would. And who should the book be about but Susan, Stephen and Sara? Yes, it is the same three people, and here are the same three cups that Daddy carried upstairs this morning. [...]

The lights are going out all over the house. The sitting-room, that shone so brightly, is dark again. Only the kitchen

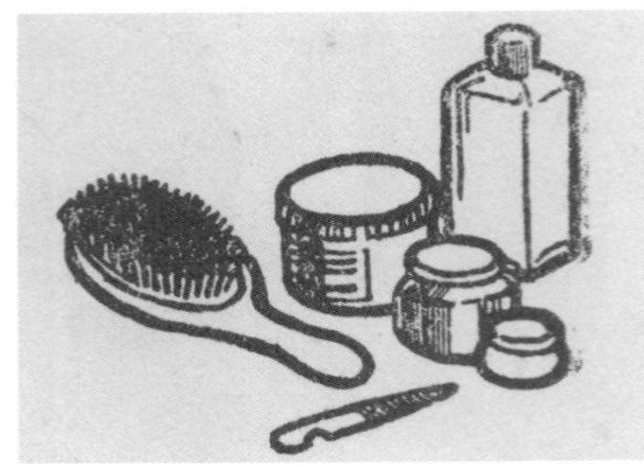

still blinks a weary eye. Cheer up, Kitchen, your work is nearly finished too. Wait but one more moment, whilst Mummy fills the hot-water bottles and Daddy makes himself a small, a very small piece of toast. There! You have boiled your last kettle and burned your last ember. Die down, fire. Save your energy until tomorrow morning. Tomorrow! We had quite forgotten about tomorrow, but the kitchen has a better memory than we have. See how the pattern repeats itself! The shoes have collected again; Sparkles is sitting on the hearth; the empty coal-bucket, the empty tea-cups. They are all waiting expectantly for tomorrow. Even Pleasant dreams! Let us tiptoe out and leave them.

Ah, but how shall we get out? Who will show us the way? For now the whole house is in darkness, and all the doors are shut. No, listen! There is someone still about. The Artist! At last her job is finished and she is getting ready to go home. Please, kind Artist, will you let us out at the back door? And who is this mewing so pitifully on the doormat? Sparkles! Have you too been forgotten? Never mind, the Artist shall let you out, also.

Away he goes, softly, silently, down the garden path. Hide, tits! Fly, sparrows! Field-mice, beware! Sparkles Markham is let loose once more! THE END IS UPON YOU!

Yes, children, it is the end. The end of the tits, the end of the garden, the end of the Lane, the end of the day and

THE END OF THE BOOK

'THE FIRST LABOUR M.P.'; 'HUNGER-STRIKE HEROINE'; 'IN GREAT-GREAT-GREAT-GRANDFATHER'S DAY'

from *Daily Worker Children's Annual*
People's Press Printing Society, 1957

Written by Anon.

The *Daily Worker Children's Annuals* built on the work of the paper's 'Children's Corner', edited for the first two years of the paper's inception by the keen Esperantist Gladys Keable (née Main; 1909–72) under the pseudonym of 'Zelda'.[1] The Corner was resumed in 1956, and lasted till 1970. Amongst Zelda's early creations was 'Micky Mongrel', the 'class-conscious dog' who would whitewash communist slogans on walls, do political leafletting, picket outside the dog biscuit factory, and fight class enemies such as 'Bertram Bulldog', the reformist Labour leader 'Lionel Lapdog', or the headmaster 'Mr Mastiff', who was fond of wielding the cane (Linehan, 2007; some of these Micky Mongrel cartoons appear at different points in this volume).

The Corner in the 1950s was a lively mix of stories, puzzles, competitions, cartoons, and nonfiction of different kinds, and this was reflected in the 1957 annuals from which these extracts are taken. Apart from politically focused articles like those included here, the annuals had articles and stories on a variety of subjects and themes ranging from 'The Story of Cricket' and 'A Memory Trick', to 'How the Goldfinch Got His Coat', 'Some Savoury Snacks', and occasional work by children such as 'The Lucky Kitten' by Michael Rosen (1946–), aged seven!

By offering annuals, the *Daily Worker* was consciously joining a long tradition in children's literature, its origins to be found in 1645 in Switzerland (Carpenter

1. Information about 'Zelda' can be found at http://www.grahamstevenson.me.uk/index.php?option=com_content&view=article&id=323:gladys-keable&catid=11:k&Itemid=112.

and Prichard, 26). In the nineteenth century, annuals of children's magazines did a roaring trade, whilst in the twentieth, the genre opened out into annuals based on sport, radio, cinema, and then TV and films. Exactly contemporary with these *Daily Worker* annuals (and in some ways in competition with them in the market of 'progressive' adults looking for Christmas presents for their children') were the *News Chronicle I-Spy Annuals*. These are full of 'Things to

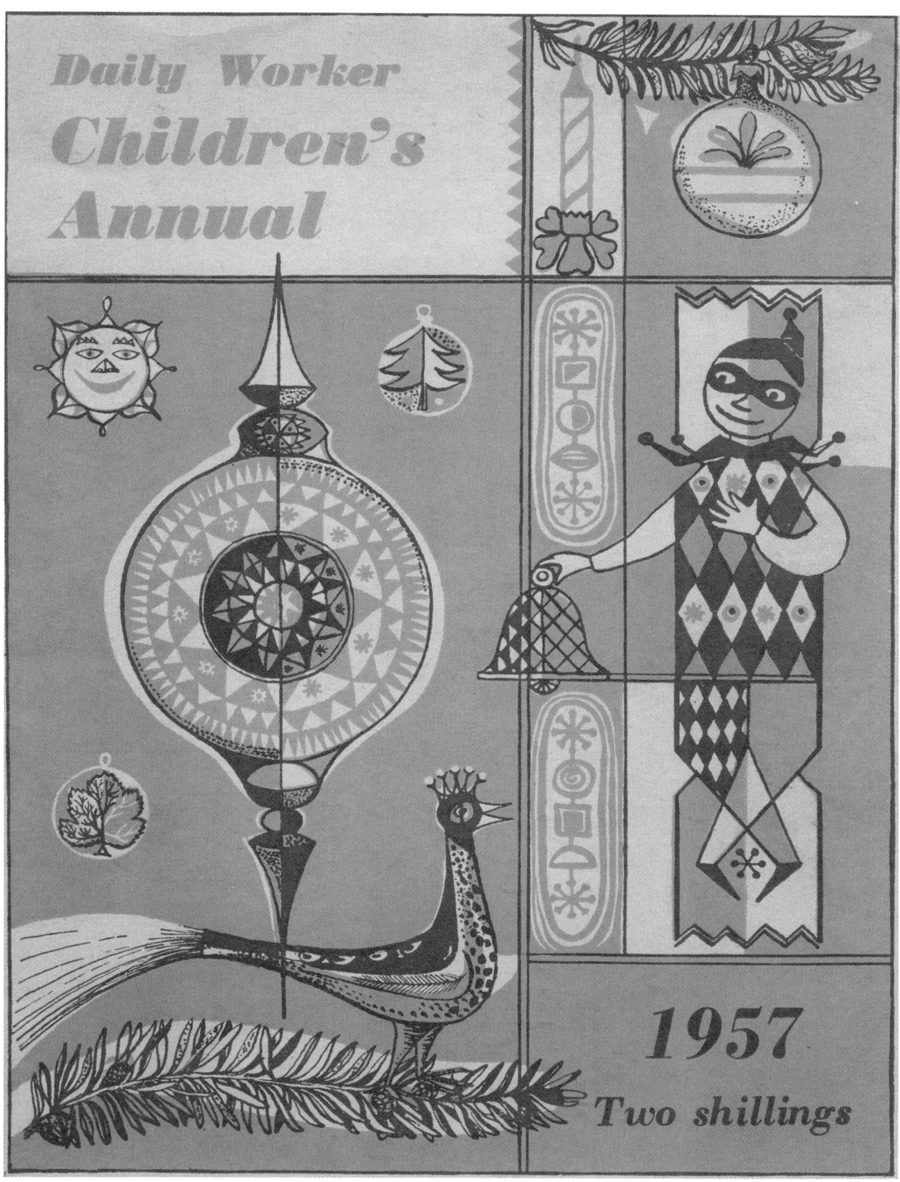

Do' and 'Things to Make', ideas for camping holidays, homes around the world, and the like, but scattered through them are assumptions about non-British people being, say, 'picturesque' or 'uncivilized'.

It was precisely in opposition to this sort of material that socialist and Communist parents relied on the *Daily Worker* or sympathetic publishers such as Lawrence and Wishart to provide alternative literature for their children.

THE FIRST LABOUR M.P.

The life story of James Keir Hardie, born 100 years ago in 1856.

THIS year we remember James Keir Hardie, founder of the Labour Party, who was born 100 years ago in Scotland, on August 15, 1856.

His parents were very poor, and young Keir had to go to work in a coal mine when he was only ten years old. When he grew up he organised a Trade Union for the Scottish miners, so helping them to win higher wages.

He became a Socialist, and in 1892 he was elected to Parliament from West Ham, in London. It was a great day when Keir Hardie went to the House of Commons, riding through London in a horse-drawn carriage filled with dockers from West Ham, to the tune of the "Marseillaise" played on the cornet.

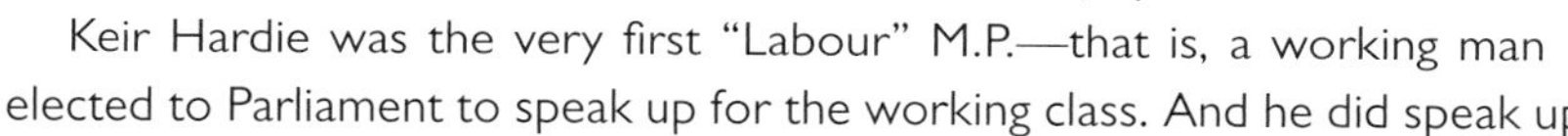

Keir Hardie was the very first "Labour" M.P.—that is, a working man elected to Parliament to speak up for the working class. And he did speak up!

When 260 miners were killed in a terrible explosion in South Wales, and the Tory and Liberal gentlemen in Parliament did not bother about it, Keir Hardie stood up and told them what he thought of them.

But one working man could not do very much by himself. Keir Hardie believed the working class should have a party of its own, to get more Labour men into Parliament. So he persuaded the Trade Unions to form the Labour Party.

Keir Hardie was always against War. He warned the working class of the danger of a war between Britain and Germany, and when that terrible war began in 1914 he spoke out against it.

He died in 1915, too soon to see the Russian Revolution which brought Socialism into the world.

Although Keir Hardie was never a Communist, he was a sincere Socialist. If the present leaders of the Labour Party were as good as its founder, our country would be a lot nearer Socialism and Peace.

HUNGER-STRIKE HEROINE

EVERY year on 6 February a number of old women with great records meet to celebrate the winning of votes for women.

Among those grand old women, both the ones who smashed windows and those who worked in constitutional ways, none has a prouder record than Charlie.

Charlie, as Miss Charlotte Marsh was always called from the day in 1908 when she decided to join Mrs. Pankhurst's Women's Social and Political Union, typified the

young girls of those days who faced every hardship to win the battle for the vote.

* * *

Now over 70—though you would never guess it from her tall, upright figure, unlined face and youthful smile—she recalls her part in the suffrage movement with spirit and humour.

"There were so many young girls in it, it was tremendous fun in spite of everything," she said.

Her first prison sentence—one month for obstruction—was after a great demonstration in Parliament Square in 1908.

The following year, when the Suffragettes were chasing Cabinet Ministers all over the country, Charlie and another girl climbed on to the roof of Bingley Hall, Birmingham, when Asquith was speaking there.

The two were drenched with water from hosepipes and finally dragged down the fire escape. "Don't think the hose was a hardship, it was deliciously refreshing. We were terribly hot after our climb," said Miss Marsh.

But what followed was downright torture, for Charlie and seven others got three-month sentences, went on hunger strike, and were the first women to endure forcible feeding.

When she was released—a week early to go to her dying father—after liquid diet had been pumped into her daily in an ice-cold cell, a sister did not recognize as she approached the house. She was then 22 years old.

Another spell of six months in 1912, after smashing shop windows in the Strand, completed Charlotte Marsh's criminal record, and added another bar to the hunger-strike medal which the Suffragettes had struck and presented to their members for valour. But it did not complete her work for the things she believed in.

* * *

"One of the reasons I went into the movement was that I believed if women had the vote they would stop war," she said. "Now I believe the unity of women and men stop it."

So today she supports all those who work for peace, and for equal pay for men and women.

IN GREAT-GREAT-GREAT GRANDFATHER'S DAY

A historian tells the story of the 'Battle of Peterloo'

AT different times in our history, the people of Britain have had to struggle for such simple things as the right to vote, the right to speak their minds, and the right to have trade unions.

The Governments of the day tried to prevent the people from having these things.

Then the people organised great outdoor meetings and petitions and processions—as we do nowadays to try to stop wars.

Some of these meetings were very exciting affairs, and huge crowds of people turned up.

In fact, so many people took part in these great struggles that I think all of us must have family ancestors who were actually there at the time and saw these things happening.

* * *

What a pity they didn't all keep diaries for us to read now! It would be such an exciting kind of history.

If some of your ancestors came from Lancashire they may have been at the Peterloo Massacre. This was in 1819, so you would have to put four or five "greats" in front of "grandparents" to get back to the right generation.

It was called the "Battle of Peterloo" because it was only four years after the famous Battle of Waterloo. But it was not really a battle at all. It was meant to be a peaceful meeting in "St. Peter's Fields", in Manchester.

On a lovely summer's day thousands of people walked in procession to the meeting. They were dressed in their best and sang as they went along.

* * *

They were going to hear a famous speaker called "Orator" Hunt, who was coming to speak about the right of working men to have the vote.

Suddenly, while "Orator" Hunt was speaking, a troop of mounted soldiers, armed with swords, came galloping into the crowd. They trampled over the people and slashed about with their swords.

When the "battle" was over, eleven people lay dead and hundreds more were wounded.

The people of England, when they heard of this terrible massacre, were extremely angry. There were great protest meetings all over the country, and money was collected to help the families of those who had been killed.

The Government still would not give in, and the struggle for the vote went on.

And no doubt Lancashire people who had been wounded on that summer's day in St. Peter's Fields were proud to show their "sword scars" to their grandchildren.

KARL MARX: FOUNDER OF MODERN COMMUNISM

Morrison and Gibb, 1963

By Arnold Kettle

One of the consequences of the Communist Party of Great Britain (CPGB) losing many members over (a) Nikita Kruschev's revelations in 1956 about atrocities and persecutions in the Soviet Union, (b) the Soviet invasion of Hungary in the same year, and (c) the party's rejection of the 'Minority Report' on inner-party democracy in 1957 was that a diverse range of people around universities, journalism, schools, and publishing felt free to develop socialist and communist ideas separately from both the Communist and Labour parties.[1] Sensing that there might be a new interest (or market!) developing, both independent socialist and more mainstream presses started to publish journals, books, and articles reflecting independent left-leaning work. Put more simply, it became possible to talk about Marx without referencing the Soviet Union. The extracts that follow come from a book which shows this transition in action; it represents the new independent Left, and yet it was written by a loyal Communist Party member who did not leave over any of the issues above, and did not appear to have any misgivings in that regard (see Kanwar and Kettle, 1987).

Arnold Kettle was born in London in 1916 and graduated from Cambridge University in 1937, not long after the infamous Cambridge communist spies Guy Burgess, Donald Maclean, Anthony Blunt, and Kim Philby. He became a successful academic, working at the universities of Dar es Salaam and then at the Open University until his retirement in 1981. Working in Tanzania and for the Open University very much suited his universalist beliefs. He died in 1986.

Along with such people as the historian Christopher Hill,[2] historian Eric Hobsbawm, and scientist J. D. Bernal, Kettle was regarded as one of the CPGB's

1. A nicely compact history of the CPGB, which provides details of the rapid decline in membership from 1956 (including a third of the party in a single night) can be found at https://www.marxists.org/history/international/comintern/sections/britain/history.htm.
2. Hill left the CPGB in 1957.

key intellectuals. His theory about the rise of the novel, set out in *An Introduction to the English Novel* (1951), for example, was taken up by critics who would never have described themselves as Marxist.

It is interesting that a mainstream publisher approached Kettle to write about Marx for a young audience as he was not especially known to be an expert on Marx or for relating to a readership younger than eighteen. That said, this book was clearly accessible to an interested person a few years younger than that. The extracts come from chapters called 'Marx's Philosophy' and 'Do Marx's Ideas Matter Today?'; the second passage reproduced here, in fact, appears earlier in the book, but in this context its definition is a useful way to introduce the material. It is worth noting that in the latter, by using a piece of English literature, Kettle follows the CPGB's favoured national approach as exemplified by its policy document, *The British Road to Socialism* (1951). This was a policy devised originally in the Soviet Union for all countries to develop separately, according to their own traditions, and developed in Britain by such people as A. L. Morton, Jack Lindsay, and Edgell Rickword. Other chapter heads give some idea of the scope and ambition of the book as a whole: 'Marx's Life', 'Marx as an Economist', 'Marx and History', and 'The Revolutionary', indicating that Kettle and those around him were convinced that a strong, direct approach was appropriate and timely. We think it is significant that the student rebellions of 1968 were only five years away.

FROM *KARL MARX*

The word communist has gathered round itself in the last hundred years so many emotions, so many prejudices and so much controversy, that one has to make a conscious and rather difficult effort if one is to try to examine fairly calmly and objectively what the word signifies.

The key idea behind the word is that of a society in which private profit has been abolished and where everything is organized for the common benefit. It was not an idea that began with Karl Marx. Three hundred years earlier the Englishman Sir Thomas More had outlined the idea in his book *Utopia*. It must have been fairly familiar to the Elizabethans, and Shakespeare in *The Tempest* makes old Gonzalo speak of his imaginary society or commonwealth of the future:

> All things in common Nature should produce
> Without sweat or endeavour: treason, felony,
> Sword, pike, knife, gun, or need of any engine
> Would I not have: but Nature should bring forth
> Of its own kind, all foison*, all abundance
> To feed my innocent people.

CHANGING THE WORLD

As we have seen, Marx's philosophy emphasizes all the time the question of change. It is not simply that Marx thought that many things in his time *ought* to change or be changed: his point was that everything in fact *does* change, whether we like it or not. The important question was, therefore, that men should ensure that things changed, in so far as possible, in the right direction. Everything is all the time either growing and developing or else decaying, moving towards extinction. Nothing stands still.

This applies, Marx insisted, to man himself. He argued that human nature is itself constantly changing. It is true, of course, that modern man has many things in common with primitive man. He needs to eat; he produces children; he feels pain and fear and joy. But what he eats, the way he feels towards his children, what makes him frightened or glad—these change as society changes. The fact that we control our appetite is just as important as the fact that we have appetites. And this very ability to control himself and his environment to a degree which even the most advanced animal cannot, is one of the things that makes man human, distinguishes his nature from

* The same word as the French *foisson*, 'harvest'.

that of other creatures. Human nature has changed considerably during the relatively short time that there have been men on earth, Marx and Engels argued, and either human nature will continue to change or else man himself will become extinct, like the dodo or the brontosaurus.

But the question remained: *How* does man change himself? And Marx's answer is clear, though it is not perhaps easy to understand. Marx maintained that man changed himself by changing the world. It was one of the great mistakes that previous philosophers and reformers had made to imagine that man could be changed by preaching. You do not change the world, said Marx, by first trying to change people's ideas. It is the other way round. In so far as you are able to change the world you are able to change man's ideas.

Marx did not deny, of course, that individual people could be changed or 'converted' by being preached to, or that they became, as a result of such conversion, able to influence the development of things. But he held that such conversion only became an effective force if the material conditions were already favourable.

It was true, for instance, that the preaching of socialist ideas and the spreading of socialist propaganda was a necessary part of the struggle to bring about the socialist revolution. But unless the working class was beginning to learn through its own experience, through its actions and its life, what capitalism was really like, the preaching and propaganda would fall on stony ground. Before you sow the seed you must have ground to sow it on and must also have worked to prepare the ground.

Marx believed that human beings were capable of tremendous change. He would have been bitterly and sardonically opposed to the idea, for instance, that you can measure a child's intelligence once and for all at the age of eleven and that this shows whether or not he is capable of receiving serious education. Marx considered every normal human being to be capable, *given favourable conditions*, of developing his abilities to a high degree. But he did stress that the important thing was the favourable conditions. He did not say that it was impossible to be good in a bad society. But he did believe that it is only in a good society that you can reasonably hope that most people will lead good lives. And in a bad society you cannot be good unless you struggle against the bad things in that society and try to change them.

The notion of changing the world is fundamental to Marx's philosophy. And it is linked up with the idea of freedom. It is hard to understand the one without the other. Marx and Engels did not believe that anyone is ever absolutely free. According to them a man's freedom of choice is always limited, limited by the hard facts of the situation he is faced with. But this does not mean that freedom is unimportant. On the contrary, it means that man becomes free to the extent that he is able to master and control the world.

Science was therefore seen by Marx and Engels as supremely important in man's struggles to be more free. For in so far as, through science, man comes to understand the outside world, he becomes master of that world and is free to use and extend his powers. And in so far as he masters the science of society, he can get control of social and human problems and is free to solve them.

Some philosophers see the ideas of power or control as being the opposite of the idea of freedom. But to Marxists, man's freedom increases with his power. You cannot be free in any situation unless you are in control of that situation. Or, as Engels put it, 'Freedom lies in the recognition of necessity'.

It is important to give full weight to this side of Marx's teaching, for otherwise it is impossible to understand why Marxist ideas have captured the imagination of millions of people and inspired them to live and work and sacrifice. Marx did not stress in his thinking only the things which are unsatisfactory in the world as it is. He held out the possibility of a far better world in which people would be able, he felt sure, not only to be better-off in the material sense, but to live better and more worthwhile lives.

Marx's is an optimistic philosophy because he saw men and women as free to take the world in their hands and shape it according to their needs and dreams. He did not think that this was something easy; he saw human life as involving tremendous battles for the overcoming of difficulties and ignorance, errors and false ideas. He was well aware of the weaknesses of human beings as well as their strengths. But he emphasized the strengths. He saw the world as a changing world, and men and women as capable, in changing it, of rising to new heights and glories.

ADVENTURES OF MICKY MONGREL. NO. 14.

Bertram Bulldog had tried to sack a worker for having a DAILY WORKER *leaflet, but the workers had all shown their leaflets and he had not been able to sack them all.*

So Bertram Bulldog, Esquire, drove off in his car, grinding his teeth while the workers laughed and cheered. He had thought he was everybody, but the workers had beaten him by sticking together. What a lesson for him! And what a lesson for the workers! "See what you get by solidarity," said Micky; "now let's sing the 'Red Flag.' " And they did. "Begorra," said Tom Tyke, "let's write about this for the DAILY WORKER." And that is how you are reading about it now.

This cartoon was part of a series about 'Mickey Mongrel, the class conscious dog', which started in the *Daily Worker* from its first days in 1930

PART SIX

PERFORMING LEFTNESS

INTRODUCTION

At one level, this topic encompasses the whole of the popular arts, which at various times in history have involved singing, dancing, putting on plays, pageants and parades, recitations and ceremonies. A snapshot of Elizabethan England, for instance, would find all these taking place, some in a carnivalesque tradition as described by Peter Burke in *Popular Culture in Early Modern Europe* (1978). In the twentieth century, a similar snapshot would take in a wide range of examples from both town and country. Some of these would be purely popular in the sense that a Mummers' Play or a singing, dancing May Day parade as in Padstow in Cornwall is not organized by any official association; some civic and organized by local authorities, and some coinciding with national events and commemorations. Likewise, for private functions such as weddings, wakes, and anniversaries, groups and individuals lay on performances of many different kinds, while specific organizations put on concerts and shows. At a more spontaneous level, people have for long socialized in pubs and clubs, singing songs, playing instruments, and on occasion performing poems and sketches.

This brief survey of popular performing arts includes the various ways in which, between 1900 and 1960, left-wing adults tried to adopt features of popular entertainment in the activities they thought appropriate or useful for young people. May Day was traditionally a festival in which children took part, and once it became an International Workers Day in the late nineteenth century, the way was open for trade unions and Labour, Socialist, and Communist parties and their offshoots to create pageants, floats, and parades in celebration of working people's labour and the need for solidarity and internationalism. *Children were involved in many of these activities: in 1921, Michael Rosen's grandparents and their children took part in just such a pageant in Brockton, Massachusetts, as part of the Boot and Shoe Workers' Union.* Our first extract shows something very similar occurring in Manchester, England in 1924 as part of the Co-operative movement affiliated to the Labour Party. Prior to the Second World War, popular theatre with a specifically left-wing flavour and which involved children is harder to pin down. One place where children were regularly involved in performances was at meetings of the Woodcraft Folk, founded in 1925. Its principles are democratic, practical, ethical, and non-militaristic, and many socialist and communist parents have found it to be a congenial and suitable place for their children. Since its foundation, the Woodcraft Folk has held local meetings and camps where all activities are mixed—boys and girls, young children, teenagers, and adults all together. These occasions always involve singing, dancing, and putting on plays and parades, whether at the local branch level, for national meetings, or at public events such as local fetes, May Day parades, peace marches, and drama competitions.

The Woodcraft Folk emerged out of various strands of thought and activity swirling around in what might be called the anti-Boy Scouts movement. These arguments originated in the two main strands of the Scouts movement itself: the one coming from Robert Baden-Powell, with its clear and explicit note of national allegiance along with military-style methods; the other coming from the Canadian writer and naturalist Ernest Thompson Seton, with its emphasis on outdoor skills and animal tracking, skills at least supposedly based on Native American knowledge. Hovering behind both these stands was Rudyard Kipling's *The Jungle Book*, with its concocted mythology of wolf packs, obedience, and a 'natural' hierarchy.

The Seton tendency gave rise to various organizations such as the Kibbo Kift, founded by John Hargrave, the Order of Woodcraft Chivalry, and eventually the Woodcraft Folk itself, founded in 1925 by Leslie Paul in South London, with strong links to the Co-operative Society, one of the key organizations which helped to found the Labour Party.[1] As new branches of the 'Folk' sprang up across England, this link to Co-operative Societies, themselves regularly replenished by the trade union movement and Labour Party members, enabled the Woodcraft Folk to expand into a national organization. Some adults who became involved in an organizational way did so as an explicit part of political activity, in what they called 'Youth Work'—a belief that a necessary part of developing socialism was to encourage the growth of a democratic, secular youth organization.

Michael Rosen was an affiliate member between 1958 and 1963, taking part in camps and Ban the Bomb marches with the 'Folk'. The branch he was attached to attracted precisely the kind of parents and children who circulated and discussed the books under review in this study: a mix of people from different backgrounds who were still in the Communist Party, those who had left in the 1950s, Labour Party members, people who were taking part in the Campaign for Nuclear Disarmament and the Anti-Apartheid movement, and members of trade unions. An important cultural aspect to this was that the Woodcraft Folk actively espoused the folksong revival which brought the politics of Pete Seeger and the Weavers into contact with the English Folk Dance and Song Society based on the work of Cecil Sharp.

1. The Co-operative movement and its associated societies are committed to the belief that workers should own, democratically manage, and share the economic benefits of the businesses where they are employed.

This was one of the attractions for Viv Albertine, former guitarist for the English punk band The Slits, who dedicates Chapter 13 of her memoir, *Clothes, Clothes, Clothes. Music, Music, Music. Boys, Boys, Boys.*, to her time in the Woodcraft Folk. As well as explaining the appeal of a group where she could mix with people whom she found pleasingly liberal, Albertine dwells on camping and singing folksongs around the campfire (and intimate encounters in tents afterwards!). Although Albertine joined the 'Folk' in 1967, so shortly after the time-frame of this book, she overlapped with Michael Rosen and her memories provide a sense of the continuity of interests and experience provided by the kinds of organizations and activities for British children of the Left discussed in this part of the volume. She recalls,

> *Woodcraft teaches us survival skills, how to make a campfire, hiking, how to save a life, is educational about global poverty, conflict and the peace movement—but for me, what it's really about is snogging boys.... Most of the boys are gorgeous, they have long hair and are a bit wild and lots of them play guitar. We go camping on weekends in a field in the middle of a traffic roundabout in South Mimms [they also went as far afield as Yugoslavia]. We all sit around the campfire at night, someone plays guitar—one guy who did this was Mike Rosen, later the famous children's author—and we sing protest songs about the Vietnam war, immigration and other social problems closer to home. My favourite are Ewan McColl's 'Dirty Old Town', Buffy Sainte-Marie's 'Welcome, Welcome Emigrante' and a folk song about the atom bomb, 'I Come and Stand at Every Door'.*

As Albertine suggests, various waves of political, folk, and protest songs have played a strong part in both performing and consolidating what it means to belong to the Left. After all, the easiest, cheapest, and most accessible popular art form which expresses feelings and opinions, puts these into people's memories, and unites everyone at any gathering is singing. It is hard to exaggerate the way in which these experiences offered participants a sense of identity and allegiance. It was a key way in which these young people lived 'leftness'.

As described in the introduction to Ed McCurdy's 'Last Night I had the Strangest Dream' (Part Two), the roots of political song in Labour and left-wing circles can be found at least as far back as the late nineteenth century. The movement was enriched by the activities of such folk song collectors as Cecil Sharp and, from the 1940s onwards, the researches of A. L. Lloyd and Ewan MacColl into what they called 'industrial song'—the ballads and broadsides produced by and for working people in towns and cities and which related to work and struggle. With new political songwriters in the USA and Britain such as Pete Seeger, MacColl, and many others, a huge repertoire of song developed, which the Woodcraft Folk and other young people participating in left-wing activity took up. Books, booklets, magazines, and songsheets proliferated. One of the offshoots of 'skiffle', with its use of improvised instruments backed up by acoustic guitars, was that thousands of young people in the 1950s discovered that they could accompany themselves on guitars with just three chords and a rhythmic strum.

Not all performance opportunities for those on the Left came under the aegis of an organization such as the Woodcraft Folk. From the 1930s onwards, small groups of actors and writers got together to create performances to support left-wing activity or, on occasions, to mount explicitly left-wing theatre productions. *Michael Rosen's mother recollected as a teenager seeing an Ernst Toller play in London's East End, and in 1938, the Unity Theatre in London put on a political 'panto',* Babes in the Wood, *which Rosen's parents recall was thought suitable for left-wing parents to take their children to.* Probably the first person to put on a left-wing play in a professional theatre and intended specifically for children was Joan Littlewood in 1955 (discussed in the introduction to *The Big Rock Candy Mountain*, later in this part).

Coinciding with these activities, something specifically Soviet occurred in the post-Second World War period. Performing companies from the Soviet Union and other Eastern Bloc countries began to put on shows in Britain. As well as the much-publicized visits of the Bolshoi Ballet, the Berliner Ensemble, and the Moscow Arts Theatre, troupes of dancers and singers visited with shows that children attended, alongside individual performers including the internationally renowned puppeteer Sergey Obraztsov, whose entertainment (at least as experienced by Michael Rosen) was geared towards children. These performances were not specifically left-wing, but because they were Soviet in origin they were intended in part to show that the Soviet Union could produce, develop, and celebrate such great artists.

Beyond the scope of this book, several performing traditions converged on film and left-wing ideas, and on occasions directed these at children. Up until the 1960s, Soviet film came into Britain via private film clubs, often under the auspices of the Co-operative movement. It was at film clubs organized by the Co-op that films directed towards children such as *A White Sail Gleams* (the original novel is discussed in Part Three), or the films of Maxim Gorky's childhood, first appeared. *That said, as Michael Rosen can testify, the children of left-wing parents also sat through plenty of cold winter evenings in upstairs rooms over Co-op stores watching such films as* Battleship Potemkin, Alexander Nevsky, *and* Ivan the Terrible *(all directed by Sergei Eisenstein in 1925, 1938, and 1944, respectively).* The work of the GPO Film Unit (discussed in the introduction to *The Magic of Coal* in Part Eight) notably included *Night Mail* (directed by Harry Watt and Basil Wright, 1936). This celebrates labour and our mutual needs and was inspired by the work of Soviet film-maker Dziga Vertov and the poetry of Vladimir Mayakovsky (1893–1930, whose work is represented in Part Four).

The film was co-opted by left audiences, and its suitability for children is reflected in the fact that W. H. Auden's poem of that name and which provides the narrative for the film has appeared in hundreds of school and children's anthologies since. German and English film adaptations of *Emil and the Detectives* were also produced (directed by Gerhard Lamprecht, 1931; Milton Rosmer, 1935), though these were not easy to find in the post-war era.

Hundreds of thousands of children and young people were affected by these popular arts and the left-wing ideas embedded in their content and style. Children were being taught every day through education, children's literature, radio, and TV about class, nation, war, empire, and race, so performing or spectating this oppositional material was intended to have a lasting balancing effect.

FROM *THE WORLD'S MAY DAY. A CELEBRATION*

Co-operative Union, 1924

Written by J. H. Bingham

This short play dramatizes the Left's views about work: in a healthy society, all people contribute their labour according to their means, all work is respected, and working conditions must never be degrading. Written for a large cast—nineteen girls and eight boys—the play is set in the future, when a visitor from Mars arrives to learn what is happening on Earth. The visit takes place on May Day—the day set aside to honour work and workers.[1] The Martian observes children representing many nations and forms of work coming together to create a happy, prosperous, equitable world.

Although children representing a number of countries are given speaking parts that display individual characteristics, the story shows that in an ideal future, nationalism will have given way to internationalism, and what people have in common will be more important than where they live or what they own. It is not just national barriers between people that have been dismantled in the play: the class system too has become irrelevant, so each May Day the global population celebrates 'the world's real nobility': the carpenters, builders, blacksmiths, millers, road menders, ploughmen, milkmaids, and all those who maintain society.

The World's May Day is typical of the performances mounted by children of the Left to spread the socialist message throughout their communities. In *Co-operative Culture and the Politics of Consumption in England, 1870–1930*, for instance, Peter Gurney describes individual performances and provides evidence that these plays were performed by a variety of groups, and often reached thousands of working people. He gives as one example the play *The Dawn* (1909) by Evelyn Pilkington.

1. The date commemorates what is known as the 'Haymarket Massacre': the shooting in Chicago on 1 May 1884 of workers agitating for an eight-hour working day.

Between February 1911 and December of that year at least eleven [Co-operative] societies—mostly in Lancashire and Yorkshire—performed the play. The Chester Society's drama group toured the district; it was estimated that over 4,500 adults and children attended nine performances. This type of activity was to flourish in the inter-war years. (70)

FROM *THE WORLD'S MAY DAY: A CELEBRATION*

(Mister Nevermove looks angrily at the scene, shakes his fist at the company silently and not obviously noticed by them, and then departs from stage, dragging Miss Understanding with him.)

MAY QUEEN (*Countries each put a finger up as if calling upon each other to listen*): Now that the King of Hearts has sway over all of you, I can enter. I am Queen because I am enthroned in your hearts; and the World CAN have a perpetual May Day when it WILL—for the World is really but a great big village green!

OPTIONAL.{(*With the closing words above, the stage lighting is subdued and a lantern slide showing the World as two hemispheres is projected to cover the whole company. The lantern slide lighting is gradually strengthened to its maximum, then silence for a moment to let the audience take in the illusion. Weaken lantern slide and light stage as before.*)

ALL: Let us crown the Queen!

KING OF HEARTS: Who shall crown the Queen?

(*Old Witch Machinery casually enters in background.*)

ALL (*pointing*): Old Witch Machinery shall crown the May Queen!

(*Craftsmen throw up caps and exhibit other signs of high glee. Old Witch Machinery shrinks terrified.*)

KING OF HEARTS (*addressing her*): The World bids you crown the May Queen.

OLD WITCH MACHINERY: I! (*angrily*) I, who have been its master these many years; must I become its servant?

ALL: Ay, ay, that you must!

OLD WITCH MACHINERY (*Stricken, succumbing; then rising to the occasion*): So be it; what the whole World wills I cannot refuse!

(*She takes the Crown from the King of Hearts—who has had it brought in by the two fairies—crowns her, then turns to address the Nations and the Craftsmen, bowing as she does so.*)

"Your servant henceforth!"

MAY QUEEN: For this you shall no longer be old witch, but fairy.

SOLO BY MAY QUEEN: "NOW IS THE MONTH OF MAYING."

(*Last verse repeated by Nations and Craftsmen and Fairies, who form a ring and circle round the Queen as they sing ad. lib. They then reseat themselves, except the Milkmaid and Craftsmen, who come to the foreground in a row with the Milkmaid in the middle.*)

MILKMAID:

I milk the cows that gently browse in *any* country's meads.
Think of the cheese, and butter please;
Think of the cream that's quite a dream;
But greater yet, please don't forget,
The milk for household and for babies' needs!

ALL *affirm by nods and excited ejaculations of* "Yes."

PLOUGHMAN:

I plough the fields; in *every* land I use the world's great spade;
From Russia to the Argentine,
The task of tilling—that is mine;
Potatoes, turnips, corn, and wheat,
That beasts and men must have to eat;
These are the harvests Earth has made,
But only by the ploughman's hand in *every* land!

ALL *affirm by nods and excited ejaculations of* "Yes."

ROADMENDER:

I'm the roadmender, I mend the roads,
Wherever roads there be;
The way from anywhere to anywhere,
In *any* land, that needs repair;
Well—it's repaired by me!

ALL *affirm by nods and excited ejaculations of* "Yes."

MILLER:

I am the dusty miller,
Who grinds for *all* the nations;
And if I stopped my ancient task
They wouldn't get their rations!
The oats and barley into meal,
The wheat into the flour;
For everybody's bread I grind,
Full many a dusty hour!

ALL *affirm by nods and excited ejaculations of* "Yes."

BLACKSMITH:

I am the blacksmith, all the world
Has me in many forms;
These later days, for melting, smiting, pressing, casting,
I make the things that must be hard and lasting.
And now the King of Hearts doth rule us

We are of one accord;
I make the hammer and the ploughshare—
But cease to make the sword.

ALL *affirm by nods and excited ejaculations of* "Yes."

CARPENTER:

I am the carpenter—
The type of all who work in wood,
Sometimes a wheelwright, sometimes cabinet-making,
And even, sometimes, undertaking—

(*Short pause, and horrified stage "Ohs" from all. Carpenter goes on, apparently oblivious.*)

To do small property repairs,
Put sash cords in, stop creaking stairs
And so on. One could go on—
But, to sum it all up—whenever woodwork's wanted anywhere,
Throughout the world you'll find me there.

ALL *affirm by nods and excited ejaculations of* "Yes."

BUILDER:

Bricks and mortar, wood and stone,
In *every* continent I put together,
For I'm a builder, by me alone
Folk are protected from the weather;
In short, wherever men may roam
I make the place that's known as "home."

ALL *affirm by nods and excited ejaculations of* "Yes."
Then, in rapid succession, staccato:

MILKMAID:	I milk the cows.	*Intoned, note: Doh.* (down scale)
PLOUGHMAN:	I plough the fields.	*Te.*
ROADMENDER:	I mend the roads	*Lah.*
MILLER:	I grind the corn.	*Soh.*
BLACKSMITH:	I do the ironwork.	*Fah.*
CARPENTER:	I do the woodwork.	*Me.*
BUILDER:	I make the houses.	*Ray.*

THE ABOVE SEVEN (*together, slowly*): For all the world. *Doh.*

THE NATIONS: Hurrah!

THE CRAFTSMEN and the MILKMAID (*again intoning, slowly, on notes as shown*):

(Up scale)	*Doh.*	We are the world's real nobility	(*Pause after each line.*)
	Ray.	For our lineage	
	Me.	Is more ancient	

Fah. Than blue blood

Soh. And our services

Lah. Are for all men

Te. And women—and children.

THE NATIONS (*a great shout on Doh*): That is so!

KING OF HEARTS: That *is* so. The millers, the smiths, the carpenters, and the masons are very, very much older families than the Vere de Veres. They are, in fact, the whole world's noblemen.

(*Fairy Machinery is now noticed at the wings very obviously carrying on a conversation with Mister Nevermove, who is making stage attempts to keep out of the picture.*)

MAY QUEEN (*in the manner of benediction*): May unity and peace, joy and abundance be with you. I shall be Queen so long as I reign in your hearts and minds. Now the world is one, to the Maypole with you.

FAIRY MACHINERY (*coming forward*): Madam!

(*The Queen lifts her hand to still the assembly.*)

Mister Nevermove is going to marry Miss Understanding!

(*A moment of surprise, then loud laughter.*)

He finds the world such a changing place that he cannot put up with his name any longer.

(*More laughter.*)

MAY QUEEN: But how will marrying alter his name?

FAIRY MACHINERY: He's adopting his wife's name. She was (*very clearly enunciated*) Miss Understanding, now they will be Mister and Mistress Understanding (*titters and clapping.*)

MAY QUEEN: Still more "unity!" Miss Understanding is of the past. Fairy Wildflowers, cast your treasures in their path. Fairy Open Country, stay with them and with the whole world of people.

To the Maypole all! The King of Hearts and the May Queen command it.

As for our visitor from Mars, she shall go with us; she will understand us—now we understand each other.

(*Concluding song, "To the Maypole haste away"; and they file out, boisterously, during last verse.*)

CURTAIN.

FROM *THE BIG ROCK CANDY MOUNTAIN*

First performed at Theatre Royal, Stratford, London, 26 December 1955–7 January 1956

Written by Alan Lomax

The inclusion of this piece owes something to the fact that Michael Rosen, aged nine, was taken to see this show during its London run. It was one of the first times in London that a committed socialist theatre director had addressed the question of how to offer children a Christmas entertainment. Joan Littlewood and the singer and playwright Ewan MacColl had developed Theatre Royal into a centre for world theatre presented from within the Brechtian tradition, though by this time MacColl had moved on. MacColl's acquaintance with the great folksong collector Alan Lomax (1915–2002) presented the team with the possibility of putting on what they called a 'folk musical' for children based on the popular songs of the USA. In the story, a boy (Jack) and a hobo (Mr Dofunny) travel together until Jack marries the daughter of a king, leaving the hobo to carry on to find the magical mountain. The form of narrative using popular song owed a good deal to the old ballad operas developed in the eighteenth century, the best known of these being *The Beggars' Opera* (1728) by John Gay.

The contemporary analysis of the US folk song tradition that had emerged in and around the 1940s folk revival by socialists and communists was that the 'people' or the 'folk' produced music which showed the essential creativity of ordinary people, and this included the people's production of what this new wave of collectors and performers called 'progressive' and 'rebel' songs. Lomax's knowledge of chain gangs and African American ex-slave culture about escaping and resistance was acquired from those with first-hand experience. For instance, he recorded 'Take This Hammer' from 'Leadbelly' (Huddie Ledbetter), an African American convict with whom Lomax worked for many years. Lomax and his father, John Lomax, recorded 'Long John' from a man identified as 'Lightning', who sang it with a group of his fellow African American convicts at Darrington State Prison Farm in Texas in 1934.

As a scene, this extract from *The Big Rock Candy Mountain* was probably unique in the history of children's literature of the time, in that it celebrates ex-slave/chain gang resistance along with utopian ideas of a land where everybody has enough to eat and respects everybody else. There is also a representation of white–black/black–white fraternization. The part of the Ballad Singer was played by 'Rambling Jack Elliott' (a Jewish New Yorker, Elliot Charles Adnopoz), who continues to makes his living from singing in the 'mountain' style collected, adapted, and perfected by such singers as the Carter Family (recorded as such, 1927–56) and Bill Monroe.

Michael Rosen dates the beginning of his interest in popular music, drama, and poetry to this show, which quickly became a favourite within his own family and a reference point for what popular socialist culture could be.

FROM *THE BIG ROCK CANDY MOUNTAIN*

BLACKOUT

LIGHTS UP

ENTER: Policeman 1 and Policeman 2

1: I drilled you till my throat is sore and my calm nature has been destroyed by your stupidity but I'm gonna try again. With the border guard we must keep fit.

[MOCK DRILL]

Now I'll go over our orders …

This border is sealed. Understood?

2: Yes sir

1: Just remember our order.

2: I shall never forget un. [Note: not sure what 'un' signifies there.—M.R.]

1: To keep everybody that's in—in.

2: To keep everybody that's out—out.

TOGETHER: And to put everybody else—in Jail.

ENTER JACK AND MR DOFUNNY

1: Where do you think you're going?

2: Where do you think you're coming from?

1: What do you think you're doing?

2: What do you not think of not doing?

DOFUNNY: Gentlemen, if you'll just release me, I will answer all your questions.

1: You'll answer our questions anyhow—won't he, pal?

2: Or he'll know the reason why.

1: Write down everything he says. What's yer names?

DOFUNNY: Mister William Dofunny.

JACK: Just Jack. I'm an orphan.

1: Put down—"Both give false names". Lemme see your passports.

dofunny and jack: Well, you see …

1: No passports.

2: No passports. Birth certificates?

JACK: We're both orphans looking for our people. Please Mister, will you help us?

1: Put down: "Refuse to give country of origin".

2: "Refuse to give country of origin." Occupation?

[DOFUNNY SPREADS HIS HANDS]

2: A couple of bums. What is your reason for a visit to this country?

JACK: We want to catch the Fireball Mail. It runs through here, don't it?

2: I'm not saying it does and I'm not saying it don't.

DOFUNNY: It does, Jack, it does... That means we can get it beyond Bagdad and then we're on our way to the Big Rock Candy Mountains.

1: But who says we're gonna let you get in to catch the Fireball Mail?

2: Not me. I'm not saying they can enter. They look like suspicious characters to me.

JACK: Please mister, let us in. We won't stay in your country long. Just long enough to catch the train. We're trying to get back to our country in the Big Rock Candy Mountains. It's a place where everybody is happy.

1: Write that down, mate. That's what I've been waiting for.

JACK: It's a place where everybody has enough to eat and enough to wear.

1: Are you getting it all down, P 2?

[Note: Perhaps Lomax intended 'P.2.' in this case to be a name or whatever appellation cops use to talk to each other in UK or USA.—M.R.]

2: Yes sir, yes sir.

JACK: It's a place where everybody treats everybody else right and you just have fun all the time. Please help us.

1: Have you got prisoners' statements?

2: Yes sir. It's clear that these are socilist agitators who are entering the country illegally.

[Note: not sure if Lomax meant 'socilist' as a deliberate cops' dialect or if it's just a typo!—M.R.]

1: Then I take it that entry permit is refused.

2: That's right.

JACK: Well, Mr Dofunny, I guess we'll have to turn back.

DOFUNNY: I guess so.

1: Just a minute there. Our orders read: "Keep everybody in that's in. Keep everybody out that's out."

2: And arrest everybody else.

1: Yes sir. It's into the chain gang with you fellows.

2: Into the chain gang.

BALLAD SINGER [who was seated at the side of the stage—M.R.]—sings the song, '*Take this hammer and carry it to the captain....*'

[Note: we should assume that the policemen retired out of earshot during the song.—M.R.]

1st prisoner: Old hammer weighs 1000 pounds.

2nd prisoner: My feet are full of lead.

1st prisoner: They drive us all day in the broiling sun.

[Note: I think these last three lines are sung too . . . or at least chanted—M.R.]

DOFUNNY: Anybody got a cigarette?

LONG JOHN: Here.

DOFUNNY: A match?

1st prisoner: Here you are.

DOFUNNY RETREATS INSIDE HIS COAT.

JACK: Remember the whisky springs.

DOFUNNY: Now you sir, the youngest and the strongest of the lot—can you run?

LONG JOHN: I can outrun an express train when I get warmed up.

DOFUNNY: Then here's our plan: when the signal is given, this fellow Long John will start to run and we'll all scatter in different directions.

1st prisoner: Funny thing about Long John, he can run faster if his magic song is sung good and loud.

2nd prisoner: But there's not enough of us to sing loud.

DOFUNNY: We'll get everybody in the world to help.

[TO AUDIENCE]

If you don't help us sing this song, we'll never get away from the Rock Gang and on the Fireball Mail to the Big Rock Candy Mountains. How about it? Will you help us to escape? Then we must hurry. The coppers are gone. You just have time to learn the tune—quickly! All you have to do is repeat the same words that Long John sings for you.

LONG JOHN: *"He's Long John"*

ALL: *"He's Long John"*

[And so it continued to the end of the song.—M.R.]

DOFUNNY: That's fine, that's fine, but don't forget to sing when we start running. Now what's the signal?

1st prisoner: Long John will be singing the hammering song and when he comes to the word "flying" . . .

2nd prisoner: Understand "flying" . . .

LONG JOHN: Get it: little man "flying" . . .

DOFUNNY: We fly, and when we fly the magic song will help us. Do you remember everybody? Do you? The one about Long John? Will you help us escape?

DOFUNNY: Shhhhhh, quiet now. I hear the police coming. Not a word, not a syllable . . .

ENTER POLICE

1: All right you big bums.

2: You big bozos.

1: Grab your hammers.

2: Pick up your instruments.

1: And slam into those rocks.

2: You hear what I say?

THE MEN BEGIN TO WORK AND SING

"Take this hammer and carry it to the captain...."

LONG JOHN: Goodbye old chain gang, I'm long gone...

DOFUNNY: Now everybody, help us! Long John must get away.

BALLAD SINGER:

"He's Long John

He's long gone...."

1: Gone gone.

COLLAPSES

2: Gone gone

COLLAPSES ACROSS HIM

BLACKOUT

SELECTED 'SONGS OF STRUGGLE' FROM *'IF I HAD A SONG', A SONG BOOK FOR CHILDREN GROWING UP*

Workers' Music Association, *c.*1954

Compiled by Alan Gifford

The Workers' Music Association (WMA) began life in 1936, when five London Labour Choirs, some of whom had taken part in the Crystal Palace pageant of Labour in 1934, met to perform together. Alan Bush was its leading light then, and until his death. As an organization, the WMA encompassed choral work, opera (three by Bush written specifically for children), folk songs, and new compositions intended to be left-wing and drawing on working-class, socialist, or campaigning themes. Topic Records, one of the chief exponents of British and Irish folk music, was an offshoot.

This small book (58 pages) includes songs that many schools as well as the various Scouting organizations sang at that time, such as 'The Wraggle Taggle Gipsies', 'My Bonnie' (as in 'My Bonnie lies over the ocean'), and 'Shenandoah'. In and amongst these, though, are songs that neither schools nor the Scout movement was then singing: a miners' folk song, for instance, and 'The Collier's Rant', which is accompanied by an explanatory note which says that it tells the 'story of our gallant miners', adding, 'The day the collieries passed out of private owners' hands—the day they were nationalized—a great assembly of miners sang this song at a Tyneside pithead.' It includes Pete Seeger's and Lee Hayes's 'The Hammer Song', 'Ain't goin' to study war no more', and 'Stand up, Diggers all' from the Diggers revolt of 1649.

The intention, then, was to include a mixture of popular songs of no particular political significance, folk songs with a rebellious flavor, and political songs of the past or present. This puts the collection in the tradition of Pete Seeger's live performances, at which he threaded in that same kind of mix. At the end of the collection, there is an article titled 'Making up Your Own Songs'

(57–8), which recommends putting new words to the tunes of old folk songs, a practice common among many left-wing groups and already discussed in relation to the Woodcraft Folk. Alan Gifford (about whom no information has been forthcoming) finishes the article by calling on readers to send in their new songs.

'The People of England' seems to be adapted from a song by the Irish activist Jim Connell, who most famously wrote the words of 'The Red Flag', the anthem of the Labour Party. The language is reminiscent of the English translations of the 'Internationale', the revolutionary anthem sung by communists and socialists all over the world, rather than popular or folk traditions.

INTRODUCTION

This little song–book has been compiled for boys and girls who are growing up and who will work together to make life happier for people everywhere. To do this we must join with people of other countries, so we have included songs that help to build friendship throughout the world.

Most of these songs have not been written by well-known composers or trained musicians, but by the people of different countries, who made them up and sang them for themselves and their children.

We have included some rounds. Singing rounds is great fun and is an easy way of making harmony with other people. At the same time it is a good way of getting used to singing in parts. One or two of the songs have been given an optional second part for those of you who would like to join together and sing them in harmony. [...]

We hope that you will take up the challenge on the last page and make up songs of your own. Please send them to us and also write and tell us what you think of this book. Then, some time in the future, with your help, we shall be able to print a bigger and better one for you.

GOOD SINGING!

THE CUTTY WREN

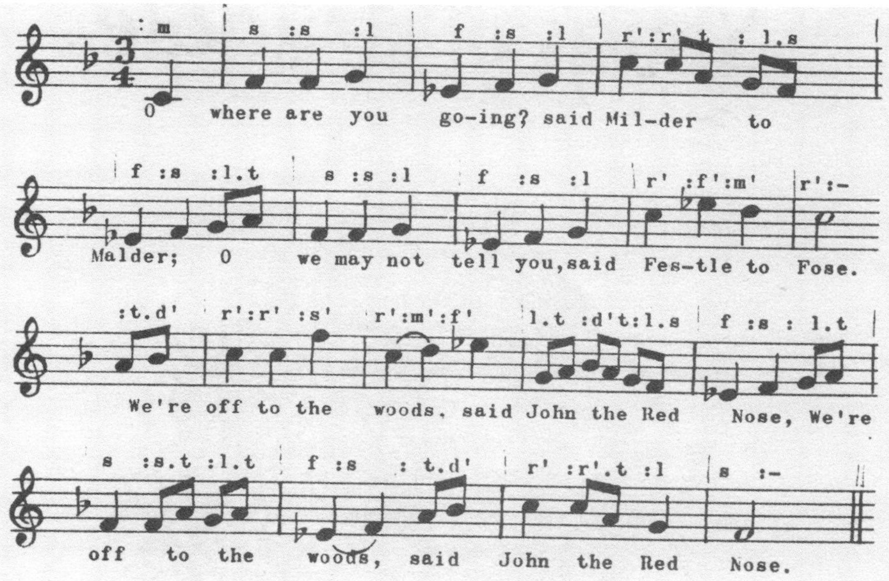

O where are you going? said Milder to Malder;
O we may not tell you, said Festle to Fose.
We're off to the woods, said John the Red Nose,
We're off to the woods, said John the Red Nose.

What will you do there? said Milder to Malder.
O we may not tell you, said Festle to Fose.
We'll shoot the Cutty Wren, said John the Red Nose. (Twice).

How will you shoot her? said Milder to Malder.
O we may not tell you, said Festle to Fose.
With bows and with arrows, said John the Red Nose. (Twice).

That will not do, said Milder to Malder,
O what will do then? said Festle to Fose.
Big guns and big cannons, said John the Red Nose. (Twice).

How will you bring her home? said Milder to Malder.
O we may not tell you, said Festle to Fose.
On four strong men's shoulders, said John the Red Nose. (Twice)

That will not do, said Milder to Malder.
What will do then? said Festle to Fose.
Big carts and big wagons, said John the Red Nose. (Twice)

How will you cut her up? said Milder to Malder.
O we may not tell you, said Festle to Fose.
With knives and with forks, said John the Red Nose. (Twice)

That will not do, said Milder to Malder.
What will do then? said Festle to Fose.
Big hatchets and cleavers, said John the Red Nose. (Twice).

Who'll get the spare–ribs? said Milder to Malder.
O we may not tell you, said Festle to Fose.
We'll give them all to the poor, said John the Red Nose. (Twice).

* * * * * * * *

NOTE: The Cutty Wren is hundreds of years old, belonging to the times of Wat Tyler and the Peasants' Revolt, when the common Englishmen suffered heavily under the hands of the rich and powerful barons, their feudal masters. In some parts the common people decided to put an end to their misery by overthrowing the master and sharing his property. It was a tremendous task and had to be planned and prepared with the utmost secrecy.

The Cutty Wren derives from a very old pagan song which was originally concerned with the sacrifice of a sacred bird. In the folk-tales of the common people the wren was always a tyrant. So, it also came to be used as a symbol of the power and the property of the rich feudal masters. You can now see how full of double-meanings was such a song, and how it would help to bring hope and strength to the poor who were to share the spare-ribs of that monstrous bird.

JOHN BROWN'S BODY

(American anti-slavery song, adapted from an earlier hymn tune).

John Brown's body lies a-mouldering in the grave,
John Brown's body lies a-mouldering in the grave,
John Brown's body lies a-mouldering in the grave,
But his soul goes marching on.

CHORUS:

Glory, glory, hallelujah!
Glory, glory, hallelujah!
Glory, glory, hallelujah!
His soul goes marching on.

He's gone to be a soldier in the army of the Lord,
But his soul goes marching on. (CHORUS)

John Brown died that the slave might be free,
But his soul goes marching on. (CHORUS).

They hung him for a traitor, themselves the traitor crew,
But his soul goes marching on. (CHORUS).

John Brown's knapsack is strapped to his back,
His soul is marching on. (CHORUS)

They will hang Jeff Davis on a sour apple tree,
As they go marching on. (CHORUS)

Now has come the glorious jubilee,
When all mankind are free. (CHORUS)

STAND UP, DIGGERS ALL

You noble Diggers all,
Stand up now, stand up now.
You noble Diggers all, stand up now.
The waste land to maintain,
Seeing Cavaliers by name

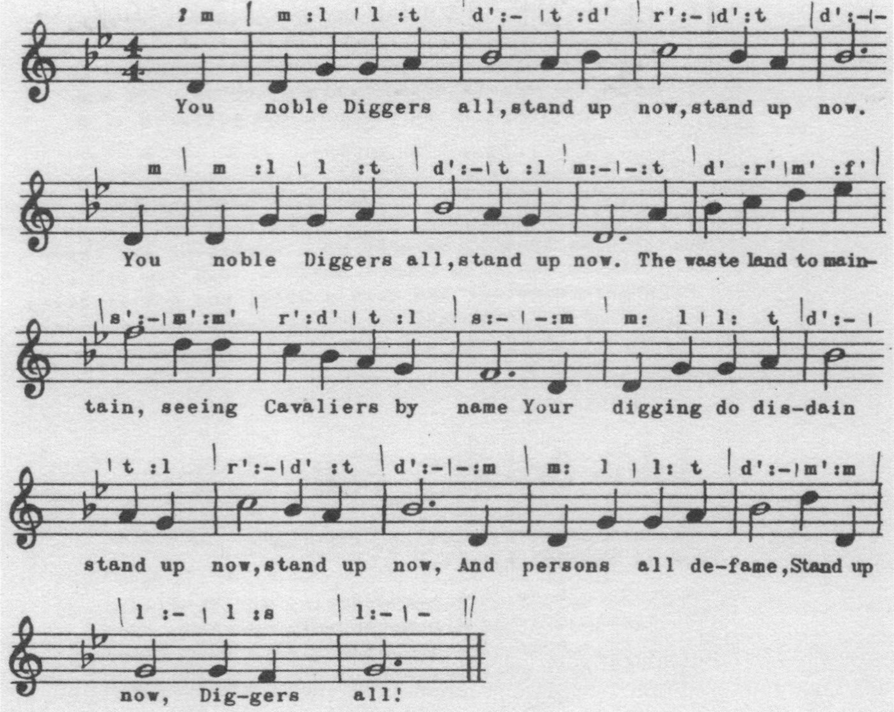

Your digging do disdain
  Stand up now, stand up now,
And persons all de-fame,
  Stand up now, Diggers all!

Your houses they pull down,
  Stand up now, stand up now.
Your houses they pull down, stand up now.
Your houses they pull down,
To fright poor men in town,
But the gentry must come down,
  Stand up now, stand up now,
And the poor shall wear the crown,
  Stand up now, Diggers all!

With spades and hoes and ploughs,
  Stand up now, stand up now.
With spades and hoes and ploughs, stand up now.
Your freedom to uphold,

Seeing Cavaliers so bold
Would kill you if they could,
  Stand up now, stand up now,
And rights from you withhold,
  Stand up now. Diggers all!

*****

NOTE: In 1649 a group of freedom-loving men, called the "Diggers", called on Parliament to "let the poor oppressed go free" and joined together to cultivate communally some waste land at Cobham. "Stand up now" became their anthem.

VAN DIEMEN'S LAND

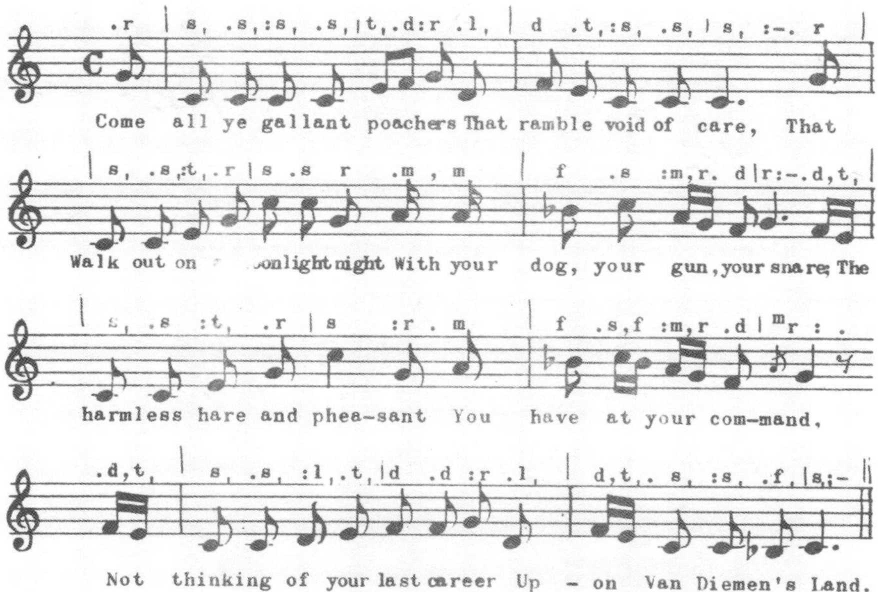

Come all ye gallant poachers, that ramble void of care,
That walkout on a moonlight night, with your dog, your gun, your snare,
The harmless hare and pheasant you have at your command,
Not thinking of your last career upon Van Dieman's Land.

'Twas poor Jock Brown from Glasgow, Will Guthrie and Munro,
They were three daring poachers the country well did know;

The keepers caught them hunting all with their guns in hand.
They were fourteen years transported unto Van Diemen's Land.

The very day we landed upon that fatal shore,
The settlers they came round us, some forty score or more;
They herded us like cattle and sold us out of hand,
And yoked us to the plough, my boys, to plough Van Diemen's Land.

Although the poor of Scotland do labour and do toil,
They're robbed of every blessing and produce of the soil;
Your proud imperious landlords, if you break their commands,
They'll send you on the British hulks to plough Van Diemen's Land.

*****

NOTE: During the second half of the 18th century the villagers who had lost their rights over the common lands organized poaching on the landowners' game preserves. Parliament, made up mostly of land-owners, passed severe laws against poaching.

Between 1827 and 1830 more than 8,500 men and boys were convicted as poachers and a great number of them were transported to places like Botany Bay and Van Diemen's Land with little hope of ever seeing house again, for no return passages were paid!

PEOPLE OF ENGLAND

People of England, why crouch ye like cravens,
Why live an existence of insult and want?
Why stand to be pluck'd by an army of ravens,
And hood-winked for ever by twaddle and cant?
  Think of the wrongs ye bear,
  Think of the rags ye wear,
Think of the insults endured from your birth;
  Toiling in snow and rain,
  Piling up heaps of grain?
All for the tyrants who grind you to earth.

Your brains are as keen as the brains of your masters,
In swiftness and strength you surpass them by far,
Ye've brave hearts that teach you to laugh at disasters,
Ye vastly outnumber your tyrants in war
  Why then like cowards stand

Using not brain or hand,
Thankful like dogs when they throw you a bone?
What right have they to take,
Things that you toil to make?
Know ye not, comrades, that all is your own?

* * * * * *

NOTE: This song was born out of the early struggles of the British working people in the 19th century; struggles for the right to vote and to be fully and properly represented in Parliament; struggles to put an end to the poverty and the appalling living and working conditions which they and their children were expected to endure. It was songs like this that helped to inspire the pioneers of our great Co-operative Movement, helped to build strong trade unions, helped to rally together and strengthen our forefathers who fought for the freedom and rights of which we in Britain are so proud.

FROM *SONGS FOR ELFINS*

The Woodcraft Folk, *c.*1950

Written by various.

The Woodcraft Folk is an ongoing organization (see the Introduction to this part of the anthology) but because the material here relates to practices from the years covered by this book, we have used the past tense. Some of the same songs and rituals are still in use today, but many have been modified to suit changing times.

Elfins in the Woodcraft Folk were children aged six to nine. This selection of ceremonial words and songs from a volume of *c.*1950 gives a flavour of how young children learned to say and sing a particular kind of political material. The first five pieces and the last one are about the organization itself and how it initiated newcomers, took leave of people, and how they kept the branch united and committed. These ceremonies usually took place in a circle with everyone joining in. At this time (and in the period before the Second World War) the Woodcraft Folks' emphasis was on a quasi-mystical relationship with 'nature' as expressed by such lines as 'I will grow strong and straight—like the pine' (5). At this stage in the history of the organization, the language of ceremonies still included gendered titles and expressions such as 'Headman' and 'your fellow men', though in many other ways Woodcraft activities tried to break down gender barriers. There are strong themes of peace, unity, and friendship in these pieces, representing the determination to mark out the organization as non-militaristic. Notably, there is no loyalty oath to the monarch or the country and uniform was restricted to the wearing of a green shirt with a Woodcraft badge on it.

'Black and White' has no author listed but it was composed by Richard Mitchell in the mid-1950s about the 1954 US Supreme Court's landmark decision banning racial segregation in what in the USA are called 'public' (meaning 'state') schools. The socialist and left-wing movements in the UK were active supporters of the US Civil Rights movement, although at the time there was no comparable movement in the UK. Perhaps significantly, this was a time when the UK was experiencing new levels of migration, much of it for economic reasons, from Commonwealth nations (Commonwealth citizens were automatically entitled to British citizenship until 1962). Migration from the British West Indies accelerated when in 1952 the USA restricted the number of people from the Caribbean who could settle there. Throughout the postwar years, Britons became increasingly conscious of the new minority population, with its links to Black American culture. Left-wing groups had a long-standing commitment to supporting those who had been disadvantaged and repressed and theoretically would have welcomed the new citizens, but while the membership of organizations such as the Woodcraft Folk broadly reflected that of the Communist Party and so included, for instance, many Jewish children, there is little evidence of West Indian participation in left-wing youth organizations before 1960.

'Family of Man' was written in 1955 by Karl Dallas (1931–2016) under the name of Fred Dallas. It was instantly taken up and sung on Aldermaston Marches organized by the Campaign for Nuclear Disarmament (CND) from 1958 onwards and is now often sung in primary schools in Britain.

'Long Time Ago' is a song that celebrates the movement itself and its founder Leslie Paul (1905–85). It will be noted that to the themes of peace and friendship, this song adds democracy and looks to a 'world without barriers'.

'Mighty Song of Peace' was another Aldermaston March favourite, with a rhythm that was useful to help people keep walking. No author identified.

'Who Are These Folk' is one of hundreds, if not thousands, of songs written to the tune of 'John Brown's Body', which was itself a political protest song. Here, the Woodcraft celebrates itself again.

Apart from the political dimension of these songs and rituals, it is worth remembering that like children in the Scout movement, Woodcraft Folk members had, through reading song-words and chants, an initiation into a good deal of literacy!

THE CAMPFIRE CAROL

Words by Leslie Paul

Leap high, O golden flame, the day is dead,
Give warmth and cheer, O flame, the sun has fled,
Stoutly your gleam maintain, youth's not abed,
Ring out the hearts' refrain, goodwill to all.

Now droops the crimson flower, 'neath silent skies,
Flickers the crimson flower, flickers and dies,
These merry singing hours, a swift-flown prize,
Pass whilst the soft dew showers, goodwill to all.

ENVOI

Peace to the strong, the thinking and the free,
Peace when the torch has set young Britain free,
Peace unto all, peace unto all.

ELFIN CREED

I will grow strong and straight—like the pine;
Supple of limb—like the hare;
Keen of eye—like the eagle;
I will seek health from the greenwood,
Skill from crafts,
And wisdom from those who will show me wisdom.
I will be a worthy comrade in the Green Company,
And a loyal member of the World Family.

INDOOR LEAVE TAKE CEREMONY

Commence with the "Creed."

FOLKMARSHAL:

Now the time has come when we must part and go our ways to our workshops and our desks.

May we remember the joys of kinship and look forward to our reunion.

Peace and Goodwill to all men.
Herald! Proclaim ye the Law.

HERALD:
List, O Woodcraft Folk, for it is the Law of Fellowship I proclaim.
Learn to grow strong like the pine.
Keep yourself supple and clean,
Read from the great book of nature, be hearty, happy and keen.
Work when there is work to be done, be helpful to all those in need,
Be faithful and true to your word, and pure in thought, word and deed.
I have spoken.

HEADMAN OR FOLKMARSHAL:
Go ye your ways, and may the Spirit of Woodcraft help you in all your works,
Be ye loyal to our cause and faithful to your fellow men.
Be Strong! Live Kindly! Love the Sun and Follow the Trail!
I have spoken.

(All finish with "Campfire Carol" or other appropriate song.)

INITIATION CEREMONY

HEADMAN:

Welcome young comrade.
Around you stand the Woodcraft Elfins;
Their hands link them in a circle.
Symbol of a wider friendship,
Between children of all nations
We would grow—in Peace—together;
Train ourselves in mind and body—
Build a better world to live in.
You would wish to join our circle—
Come then—take the hands of friendship.

(Headman leads the new member to a point in the circle between two members who, by pre-arrangement, loosen their hands and take the hands of the new member, thus bringing him/her into the circle).

Welcome to our Elfin Circle.
May the trail be broad before you.
May you grow in strength and wisdom.

(to all) Elfins, give our Woodcraft greeting—
Ish. Ash. Osh. "HOW."

LINK YOUR HANDS TOGETHER

Link your hands together,
A circle we'll make;
This bond of our friendship,
No power can break,
Let's all sing together
In one merry throng.
Should any be weary
We'll help them along.
(*Repeat last two lines*)

Let us then laugh lightly
If sadness should fall,
May joyous laughter
Spring from us all,
Helping each other
We'll lighten our load,
Arms linked with comrades
We travel the road.
(*Repeat last two lines*)

Let us march together
With firm step and strong,
As out from the darkness
We all go along,
All sorrow is banished
We march to the light,
Link your hands together,
We're strong in our might.
(*Repeat last two lines*)

BLACK AND WHITE

The ink is black,
The page is white,
Together we'll learn to read and write,

To read and write.
And now a child can understand,
This is the law of all the land—all the land.
The ink is black,
The page is white,
Together we'll learn to read and write.
To read and write.

Their cloaks were black,
Their heads were white,
The school-house doors were closed so tight,
Were closed so tight.
Nine Judges all set down their names,
To end the years and years of shame—years of shame.
Their cloaks were black,
Their heads were white,
The school-house doors were closed so tight,
Were closed so tight.

The slate is black,
The chalk is white,
The words stand out so clear and bright,
So clear and bright,
And now at last we plainly see.
The Alphabet of liberty—liberty.
The slate is black,
The chalk is white,
The words stand out so clear and bright,
So clear and bright.

The world is black,
The world is white,
It turns by day and it turns by night,
It turns by night.
It turns so each and every-one.
Can take his station in the sun—in the sun.
The world is black,
The world is white,
It turns by day and it turns by night,
It turns by night.

A child is black,
A child is white,
The whole world looks upon the sight.
A beautiful sight.
And very well the whole world knows.
This is the way that freedom grows—freedom grows.
A child is black,
A child is white,
The whole world looks upon the sight.
A beautiful sight.

FAMILY OF MAN

I belong to a family, the biggest on earth,
A thousand every day are coming to birth.
Our surname isn't Dallas or Hasted or Jones,
It's a name every man should be proud he owns.

Chorus:
It's the family of man, keeps growing.
The family of man, keeps sowing.
The seeds of a new life every day.

I've got a sister in Melbourne, a brother in Paree,
The whole wide world is dad and mother to me.
Wherever you turn you will find my kin,
Whatever the creed or the colour of the skin.
Chorus

The miner in the Rhondda, the worker in Peking,
Men across the world who reap and plough and spin.
They've all got a life and others to share it,
Let's bridge the oceans and declare it.
Chorus

From the North Pole ice to the snow at the other,
There isn't a man I wouldn't call brother.
But I haven't much time, I've had my fill,
Of the men of war who want to kill.
Chorus

Some people say the world is a horrible place,
But it's just as good or bad as the human race.
Dirt and misery, or health and joy,
Man can build or man can destroy.
Chorus

LONG TIME AGO

Long time ago a girl came along and no-one wanted to know
But a man named Leslie Paul listened on and knew what he must do
A children's group for girls and boys of any race and creed
Democracy will be its theme and the WOODCRAFT it will be.

Chorus:
Friendship, Peace and Democracy
are the Woodcraft aims today.
To live in a world without barriers
And to camp and sing and play.

Boys and girls in groups they met with a leader as their friend
They learned to hike and enjoy themselves no marching songs for them
For wars they hated and believed that soldiers have no place
In a world where people live in peace despite their creed or race.
Chorus

MIGHTY SONG OF PEACE

The mighty song of peace will soon be ringing
Soon be ringing, soon be ringing.
The mighty song of peace will soon be ringing
All over this land.

Chorus:
All over this land, this land.
All over this land, this land.
The mighty song of peace will soon be ringing
All over this land.

The mighty song of unity and peace will soon be ringing
Soon be ringing, soon be ringing.

The mighty song of unity and peace will soon be ringing
All over this land.
Chorus

The mighty song of justice, unity and peace will soon be ringing
Soon be ringing, soon be ringing.
The mighty song of justice, unity and peace will soon be ringing
All over this land.
Chorus

The mighty song of friendship, justice, unity and peace will soon be ringing
Soon be ringing, soon be ringing.
The mighty song of friendship, justice, unity and peace will soon be ringing
All over this land.
Chorus

The mighty song of freedom, friendship, justice, unity and peace will soon be ringing
Soon be ringing, soon be ringing.
The mighty song of freedom, friendship, justice, unity and peace will soon be ringing
All over this land.
Chorus

WHO ARE THESE FOLK

(Tune: John Brown's Body)

"Who are these Folk who dress in green,"
We hear the people say;
They ask if we're some foreign Scouts
Come here on holiday?
We answer all their questions in a very simple way.
WE ARE THE WOODCRAFT FOLK.

Chorus:
Hark the beating of our tom-tom;
See the sun upon our Totem;
And the Fire before our Wigwam;
WE ARE THE WOODCRAFT FOLK.

We are a happy band of folk.
  Our purpose we'll make known;
Our songs of freedom we will sing,
  Wherever we may roam,
For we like to wander o'er the hills
  And far away from home.
    WE ARE THE WOODCRAFT FOLK.
  Chorus:

Our girls and boys grow stronger
  As they step the Woodcraft way,
Our girls and boys grow wiser,
  As they study and they play;
For we are a virile Company,
  And we have come to stay
    WE ARE THE WOODCRAFT FOLK.
  Chorus:

PART SEVEN

FIGHTING FASCISM

INTRODUCTION

Eddie and the Gipsy, first published in 1931 and represented in Part One, clearly shows the political and class confrontations in German life at the time, and the hardships suffered by ordinary people trying to live their lives not only in poverty, but also with the fear of unemployment ever present. These circumstances meant fertile ground for the rise of fascism in Germany. Germany was not the only country that faced this menace, and indeed was not the first country to have a fascist regime; in Italy Benito Mussolini had come to power in 1922 at the request of the Italian king.

The Great Depression of 1929 caused further hardship everywhere, and Germany, already reeling under the crippling reparations demanded of them for their 'guilt' in the First World War, was particularly hard hit as inflation rose to extreme levels. Adolf Hitler's Nazi Party took advantage of this, appealing to the middle classes as it promised financial security and a return to German greatness. In common with all fascist parties, the Nazis had several scapegoats to blame. After a series of increasingly violent confrontations with Communist Party supporters, Hitler was appointed Chancellor in January 1933, and new elections were called for March. After the burning of the Reichstag, which the Nazis blamed on the Communists, and after a major trial, they were able to consolidate their victory and grasp of power. Their first attacks were against the Communists, banning the party and sending its members to concentration camps:

> In Germany they came first for the Communists,
> And I didn't speak up because I wasn't a Communist;
> And then they came for the trade unionists,
> And I didn't speak up because I wasn't a trade unionist;
> And then they came for the Jews,
> And I didn't speak up because I wasn't a Jew;
> And then ... they came for me ...
> And by that time there was no one left to speak up.[1]

Rescue in Ravensdale was the last to appear in print. Although published in 1946, it is set in the summer before the outbreak of war in September 1939. Quietly subversive in its overturning of the family holiday adventure genre, it

1. Martin Niemöller to the Bay Area Reference Center, San Francisco Public Library, 2 June 1971.

makes some important comments about the nature of fascism, where it can be found, and who will oppose it.

The extracts from the underground newspaper *Out of Bounds* give evidence of the concern of young progressives at the rise of fascism in this country and abroad. This understandable concern led to controversy in the Socialist Sunday School (SSS) movement (discussed in the Introduction). Much concern related to the movement's attitude to war, and there was great outcry when their periodical, *The Young Socialist*, printed an article in April 1936 describing a holiday to 'modern Germany', in which the author refers to meeting 'two charming Nazis', and describes her visit in laudatory tones. Although this article was highly condemned by many, there were other articles and editorials which criticized the International Brigades in Spain, who were supporting the democratically elected government against a nationalist military revolt that was supported by the fascist countries of Germany and Italy. The SSS Committee were reluctant to provide a lead in the matter, although there is no doubt that the rise of fascism in Italy and Germany meant difficult decisions for the traditional pacifists and anti-militarists of the SSS movement.

Of course, fascism also existed in Britain in the guise of Oswald Mosley and his blackshirts. Like Hitler, Mosley was influenced by Mussolini's success in Italy; his British Union of Fascists arranged meetings and marches that were notorious for their violence against any detractor. Also like the Nazi Party in Germany, blackshirts identified their enemies as the Communists and Jews. We have reproduced two items from the one-off volume *Martin's Annual*, produced for children by the left-wing publishing house Martin Lawrence, that deal with the blackshirts' overt use of violence. The cartoon 'Blacking His Shirt' does this through humour, using a familiar comic style that points to and undermines the bullying tactics of the fascist movement. The second example looks at resistance to fascism at the heart of its power. 'Red Front', by Michael Davidson, is particularly thought-provoking for its representation of German progressive youth, formerly members of the Communist youth movement, and the difficulties they experience resisting such a repressive regime. The point of the story is that there *are* resisters, in this case specifically those who recall the solidarity of the Communist movement. The two pieces from *Martin's Annual* also reflect the Popular Front policy agreed by the Communist International (Comintern), that Communist parties should work with a broad left front to oppose fascism.

The editors of this anthology debated whether to include Michael Davidson's short story. As stated in the introduction to 'Red Front', he was a well-known journalist who lived in Weimar Germany, became a Communist, and was a translator of anti-fascist German books. His memoirs also state that he was 'a lover of young boys', and disturbingly show that it was more than that. Although Davidson describes his relationships with boys as harmless, it is clear from his own accounts that some at least were exploitative, including of boys as young as twelve. In the end we decided to include the piece because history shows that whenever movements—artistic or political—have tried to fight against what they see as the restrictions of bourgeois life, some people in those movements have broken sexual taboos. With all we know today about power and exploitation, we understand that matters are very different when they take place between equal adults and when they take place between adults and children. Davidson clearly thought there was no difference. There will be no progress against exploitation and oppression through exploiting and oppressing others. Davidson didn't know that either. In his own way, he is yet another sad and awful example of one step forwards two steps back. We have included the piece in part to confront the problem rather than to ignore it.

'SIDE-LIGHT ON THE BLACKSHIRTS' AND 'FIGHT WAR AND FASCISM'

From *Out of Bounds: Public Schools' Journal against Fascism, Militarism and Reaction*
Parton's Bookshop, 1934

Written by 'T.P.' and Anon.

This short-lived magazine was inspired by a 1933 conference organized by the Federation of Student Societies, a group of university students committed to attacking militarism, reaction, fascism, and war. University students already had radical journals; *Out of Bounds* was created to engage pupils still at school in left-wing debates by showing how militarism and oppression operated in the public school system. Masterminded by Giles and Esmond Romilly, nephews of Winston Churchill and pupils at Wellington College, contributors to *Out of Bounds* came from across the public school sector.

Out of Bounds consisted of polemical editorials and opinion pieces on topics from peace and fascism to sex, critiques of public schools individually and as a system of education, and reviews of left-wing books and events. Priced at a shilling an issue, it was expensive, but by its second edition needed a print run of 3,000. The public school authorities and the conservative press denounced the magazine; Esmond Romilly was expelled, and the magazine ceased publication after its fourth number. Nonetheless, producing *Out of Bounds* shaped both its contributors and its readers. In the course of writing articles, reviewing books, advertising peace rallies, and inventing ways to circulate their magazine, they helped create an image of youth as resistant to authority. Many contributors went on to overthrow the conservative forces that had previously shaped their lives.

The extracts here focus on pupils' responses to the rise of fascism and include first-hand experience of a fascist rally. Shortly after being expelled, Esmond Romilly joined an International Brigade fighting in Spain, an example of how the political scene in the 1930s impacted on those who had worked to bring about an end to war.

"SIDE-LIGHT ON THE BLACKSHIRTS"

TO THE EDITOR, "OUT OF BOUNDS."

Dear Sir,

On June the seventh I had the interesting experience of accompanying a friend of mine to the meeting of the Fascists at Olympia. I thought it might be of interest to you to know my own personal experiences and the light they throw on the Fascist movement. I should state first of all that before the above date I considered myself a non-party man with considerable interest in both Fascism and Communism, but no definite leaning towards either. I am no longer in that position, and I hope that this letter will show clearly why I am not.

My friend and I arrived at Olympia about an hour and a half before the meeting was arranged to start. The Blackshirts were already marching up in well-ordered fours, but without any very definite tokens of either of admiration or of disrespect from the onlookers. The crowd was massed on the other side of the road to Olympia. Opposite them groups of Fascists, some in uniform, others in plain clothes, were gathered. I noticed at once the attitude of suspicious and pugnacious hostility with which they stared across at their possible opponents. Many were wearing gloves, a fact which, on such a warm day, could have only one meaning, knuckle-dusters. A little before 7 o'clock (Mosley's address was to begin at 8) a large body of working men arrived, escorted by mounted police, who marched them well down the road. The Blackshirts were arriving continually, and soon there was an enormous crowd of people massed on each side of the road. There was any number of police, some in plain clothes, some mounted, and all carrying batons.

Soon the whole crowd moved across to the Olympia side of the road, and spread right down to the entrance of the Addison Road Station. Fascist and Communist salutes were continually being given, and there was a very tense atmosphere of coming disturbances. The first outbreak came when a body of uniformed Fascists tried to force their way through the crowd in order to reach the side entrance. Pamphlets were hurled at them, there were many cries of "Boo" and "Mosley means Mass Murder," and finally, in spite of the active intervention of the police, their ranks were broken and they were thoroughly disorganised. The police adopted a threatening attitude and attempted (quite successfully) to quell the shouts and jeers.

Anti-Fascist pamphlets of various descriptions were circulated and copies of the "Daily Worker" offered for sale. The occasional Blackshirts who pushed their way through the crowd were jeered at, and seemed as nervous as one would expect. A red flag was raised and shouts of "One, two—three, four, five—we want Mosley, dead or alive." The flag was taken down by order of the police, and most of the crowd moved down to the main entrance.

Soon a long line of Blackshirts marched down the road, carefully guarded by mounted police. Missiles were hurled at them, the Red Flag was raised again and an organised march of the crowd began, and forced its way into the middle of the Fascist ranks. One of the flag-bearers was seized round the neck by a Blackshirt and a certain amount of fighting began, but was quickly suppressed by the police, who rode into the crowd at a trot, knocking many of them over. The flag was torn from its moorings by a Blackshirt, but was retrieved and pinned up again.

Expensive cars began to arrive and were treated with disrespect by the crowd, one attempt being made to overturn a Rolls-Royce. Pamphlets were thrust through the windows and the flag was again raised and marched between the cars. Finally a great effort was made by some of the crowd to force their way through the ranks of the police and reach the Blackshirts. The police rode up and down, knocking people over right and left. One horse slipped and fell, the policeman was kicked by a number of the crowd and completely lost control of himself, kicking out wildly. Finally the crowd was forced back again, three arrests being made.

At last the long line of Blackshirts began moving through the entrance. As they marched, the crowd sang the "Red Flag" and the "International." The solitary flag-bearer was jostled by the police and forced right out of the crowd by them, several times escaping being run down only by good luck. He was ordered to destroy the flag, and on refusing was threatened with arrest.

My friend and I joined the dense mass of people trying to get in, and at last found ourselves inside. In the crush by the gate one gentleman asked me to make room for his wife, so I did my best to hold the crowd back and to give her room. "You're a Blackshirt, of course," and a grateful smile, were my reward: a charge which I denied. The corridor outside the arena was thronged with Blackshirts, all extremely pugnacious in appearance. We found the way to our seats with some difficulty.

Soon we became the objects of any number of suspicious and hostile Blackshirt glances. An oldish man in uniform was sitting in front of us, so we talked loudly of the excellences of Fascism. There were many women Fascists in black shirts and bodices, several of them rather attractive in appearance. They distributed programmes and showed people to their seats with seraphic smiles. After a long delay a company of Blackshirts marched up the length of the building, carrying Fascist flags and Union Jacks. The whole audience rose, Fascist salutes were given and the party song chanted. Soon after, Mosley himself entered, walking in front of three flag-bearers with Union Jacks. There was considerable, though by no means universal, applause. Four vast lights were turned on him, and followed him up to the dais. Here he turned and saluted, and then began his speech. He had not been speaking more than two minutes when a cry was raised behind us of, "Mosley means war," and "Hitler and Mosley mean hunger and war." Blackshirts rushed up and a woman began screaming. The agitators were struck again and again, and finally hurled down steps into the outer corridor. I, by now an ardent anti-Fascist, tried to help them by thrusting all Blackshirts down that I could, but soon I was smashed in the face and pinioned. Accompanied by kicks I, too, was pushed down the steps. At the bottom about ten Blackshirts seized me and hit me again and again on the shoulders. I ran as hard as I could for the exit, but had to push through a mass of Blackshirts, all attempting to, but fortunately few succeeding in, hitting me in the face. Outside there was a courtyard with a narrow gate into the street which was packed with Blackshirts. I ran towards it, but was soon tripped up, and I honestly believe I should have been laid out if an officer had not arrived and protected me. Outside I found any number of ministering angels in the form of Communists who had not managed to get in. Do you wonder then, that I sign myself,

Yours faithfully,
"Anti-Fascist,"
T.P., Rugby

FIGHT WAR AND FASCISM

APPEAL FOR NATIONAL YOUTH CONGRESS AGAINST WAR & FASCISM TO BE HELD IN SHEFFIELD CITY HALL, AUG 4TH & 5TH

WE print here the manifesto of the National Youth Congress against Fascism and War. The appeal is signed by many prominent people, including Henri Barbusse, John Strachey, Storm Jameson, Ellen Wilkinson, Harry Pollit. James Maxton. It is supported by Trade Union branches, by unemployed organisations, by political organisations (branches of Labour Party League of Youth, Federation of Co-operative Youth, Young Communist League, etc.), by peace societies, by University students. The appeal has been signed by the Chairman of the Federation of Student Societies, which coordinates anti-war branches in seventeen Universities.

A message of support has been received by Georgie Dimitrov, the hero of the Reichstag Fire Trial.

To all young workers in factory, workshop and office—young unemployed—students in school, college and university—and young agricultural workers!

WAR IS BEING PREPARED!

Never has the preparation for war been so tremendous. Europe and the Far East are powder magazines. Driven to desperation by crisis, the antagonism and intrigue between all capitalist countries for markets and power, for a redivision of the world, was never higher.

War has raged in the Far East and South America for years. Plotting and intrigue for war is everywhere. Japan in Manchuria. France against Germany, Italy against France, Britain supporting Germany. Britain against the U.S.A.

Fascist dictatorship, terror and attack on working-class organisations has arisen in many countries.

Imperialist Powers continue their campaigns of lies and slanders against the Soviet Union on whom they aim to wage war.

WHAT DO YOU KNOW OF THE LAST WAR?

You have seen pictures and heard stories showing war as something adventurous and romantic; pictures and stories which are brought forward not by those who fought in the last war, but by the war mongers who herded the masses of young workers to slaughter in 1914! Ten million were killed, twenty million were horribly wounded in the last war. We don't want to die, we want to live and to work!

Why did it take place? It took place because wars are part of capitalism. It is the policy of capitalism to make war for markets and profits, to enslave and colonise whole countries, such as India, for raw materials and sources of exploitation—to destroy millions of young lives in the interests of profits.

We must vigorously oppose this policy; our enemy is not the workers abroad, but the capitalist class and the Governments who serve their purpose either in Britain or abroad.

The National Government and its capitalist supporters reduce our wages and speed us up in the factories, while they prepare war; have turned every industry into a blind alley occupation; they are starving the young unemployed, have destroyed our industrial future, and are forcing 100,000 youths into concentration camps for war and Fascism.

The National Government has increased war estimates; with their unemployment policy and propaganda they have driven thousands of youths into the Army. They are using increased Fascist measures to maintain their system and prepare for war. They mouth phrases about peace—but they have shares in armament firms. They are the representatives of British imperialism, of the British capitalists. They attack and oppress the colonial peoples. The struggle against war must be the fight against Fascism, the most reactionary nationalist and brutal dictatorship of finance-capital.

We must fight this system of Hunger, Fascism and War, fight the National Government and assist the colonial workers and peasants in their struggle for freedom.

THE WORKERS' MOVEMENT AND WAR

Most workers in the Labour movement recall with shame the support given by official Labour in the "Great War," and we cannot but feel concern and alarm at the recent declaration of the International Federation of Trade Unions, that working-class opposition to war must be directed to the "aggressor country," for the "aggressor" would be conveniently decided by the League of Nations machinery which is dominated by the British and French Imperialist Governments.

This policy is not working-class opposition to war, but could easily become working-class support for war; consequently sincere workers against war cannot support this policy.

We welcome the resistance to war expressed in the resolution of the Labour Party conference at Hastings, but we know that very little in "deed" has been done to give effect to its terms. We appeal to all, and especially to the Labour Youth, to support a militant struggle against war, to support the youth congress. Agitate in the branches for the wide, intensive campaign against war decided on by the Labour and T. U. Congresses; bombard the executive with militant resolutions for the special meeting against war.

HOW SHALL WE STRUGGLE?

It is not sufficient to say we are against war, to say "Never again." To prevent war means a bitter struggle against it, persistent day after day, with risk and sacrifice, against the war-markers. It is a battle against death and destruction.

It is often stated that war is inevitable. But for a nation to launch war it is necessary to have the support of the masses of the people, particularly the youth. Therefore, we have got to win the youth for the struggle against the imperialists, to prevent the war and to bring about the abolition of capitalism and the assurance of permanent peace. War is *not* inevitable.

However, it is just as wrong to say, "War won't come." "The world has learnt its lesson." Even now the capitalist powers have started their new war in the Far East. The deciding factor as to whether we shall be plunged into a new World War is the amount of anti-war work we can develop now. The National Youth Congress will hammer out a line of struggle of the youth against War and Fascism.

'RED FRONT'

from *Martin's Annual* (1935)

Written by Michael Davidson. Illustrated by Lucas

Published in 1935, by when the Nazi Party had gained control in Germany, this second annual issued by the radical publisher Martin Lawrence, in association with New York's International Publishers, reflects the Comintern's (Communist International) Popular Front policy of the 1930s, which encouraged Communist parties to work with a broad left front to oppose fascism. Much of the material in *Martin's Annual* deals directly with the threat of fascism, with many of the works encouraging direct opposition to oppression. 'Red Front' deals with fighting fascism in Germany.

Michael Davidson (1897–1976), who later in his career became a foreign correspondent of note, lived in Weimar Germany in the 1930s. On his return to England after the victory of the Nazi Party, he worked as a translator of anti-Nazi books. This short story, slight as it is, gives a small taste of what it might have meant to have been part of the political left in Germany before the Nazi takeover. The young protagonists remember their membership of the Pioneers—what they did and what they believed. They decide to keep that memory alive by performing small actions of opposition and resistance, though they are aware of the penalty if they are caught. True to the internationalist spirit of the radical working-class movement, the writer makes it clear that the enemy is fascism, not the German people. The story reflects the central idea of all the contributions to this annual—that children should be directly involved in resistance, and in opposing the status quo.

RED FRONT

HEINZ stood on the pavement by the market. He had been to his aunt's, hoping to get 50 pfennig for the pictures. But she had no money.

In one trouser pocket his fingers played with a piece of chalk—a nice big bit of red chalk—and he thought: Since Adolf came in there's never any money over for the pictures. Blast him.

Heinz glanced at the big Nazi flag with its hooked cross hanging outside a public-house, and at that moment he felt he hated that flag more than anything in the world. It meant no money for the pictures, and no more Pioneer camps—and it meant that ordinary workers like his uncle Willi and Otto's big brother Fritz were beaten and murdered.

The Ackerstrasse smelt of potatoes and bugs, and damp walls and too many people—smelt of the Ackerstrasse. The street lamps were pale and timid against the flat darkness of the tenement blocks; except for the beershops and the "Bio" cinema at the corner where the trams went by, the street was black, and the people hurrying along close to the walls were like shadows.

Three brown-uniformed Nazis came abreast down the pavement, their iron-heeled boots ringing; as they passed Heinz they jostled an old woman into the gutter. Great revolver holsters hung heavy on their belts. Timing himself with care Heinz spat neatly after them.

Suddenly there was a shout: "Kill the swine!" and a man, a young worker, fell, tottered out of a house-door. Three Nazis were on to him, kicking him, beating him. Heinz saw, like a blue spark in the lamplight, a knife flash.

The man lay in the gutter, and his gasps rose to a scream. "You murdering swine," he cried, "you can kill us if you like, but you'll never crush us!" Then he lay still.

The Nazis gave his body a couple of kicks. "The filthy Bolshevik," said one, and spat in his face. Again the iron heels of their boots rang down the pavement.

The people in the street stood silent, sullen, watching the body lying in the gutter, listening to the arrogant ring of the Nazis' step. But no one moved. No one dared move, with the great Nazi flag swaying over them and the gangs of Nazis lurking, ready to shoot, in the doorways.

Heinz was trembling with rage. "One of us," he said, half aloud, "that was one of *us*," and felt sick with fury and his own helplessness.

"You—Heinz—did you see?" His school friend Otto was beside him. Otto wore the brown shirt and shorts of the Hitler Youth, which all school children are forced to join. But Heinz would never wear the uniform—his mother could not afford it was the excuse he gave.

"Otto—that was one of us, d'you know—one of *us*. . . . " His fingers gripped on the chalk in his pocket till it snapped.

Otto gave a shrug. "Yes, foul. But it's like that now. . . . D'you remember last year, Heinz? Man, things were different then. D'you remember the Pioneer camp, and the swimming, and the propaganda marches into the villages, and the camp-fire songs? Man, I can still smell that burning pinewood. . . . "

"Course I remember. But Otto—what's the good of just remembering? Think of that—that just now. Otto—can't we *do* anything? . . . "

"Do anything? Man, don't be barmy. Want your head broken, too?"

"But the comrades—*they* do things, *they* aren't afraid. You know. . . . And Otto—we were, we *are*, Pioneers—and we are comrades, too. Listen, I've some chalk here, red chalk, pinched from school. Couldn't we? . . . "

Otto stopped dead. There was a laugh of excitement on his face, too, now. "Man, Heinz. But where? When? And if they get us—they'll kill us, you know."

"Let 'em—if they get us. At Koppenplatz, of course, the wall by the kids' sandpits. And right now—come on!" And he tore across the Elsasserstrasse, down into the little square with its round fountain guarded by great bronze toads, and its public lavatory by the children's playground.

Otto, in his brown Hitler uniform, sauntered on the pavement, keeping look-out, while Heinz, close under the shadow of the lavatory wall, worked feverishly with his chalk. Once the tread of heavy boots came by, and Otto on the pavement broke lightly into the melody of the Horst-Wessel song.

Heinz froze tight against the wall, holding his breath till the steps had passed. Then he went on working. In three minutes he was back with Otto.

"I've done it," he whispered, "but don't look now"—suddenly his mouth was quite dry, tasting a little sick. But in his mind he saw the foot-high red letters he had drawn: "HITLER MURDERS WORKERS—AND FILLS HIS OWN BELLY."

"Look out," whispered Otto—and round the corner from the Auguststrasse came a gang of young Brownshirts, harrying an aged, bearded Jew, a passing police-patrol looked laughingly on. Heinz spat skilully up at a street lamp. "Otto," he breathed, "to-morrow night—somewhere else." And they shook hands on it.

"So long," said Otto out loud, "don't forget the group evening to-morrow—talk on the old Prussian Army. Hail, Hitler!"

Heinz ran home. That's better than the pictures, he thought to himself—and in his pocket he felt the tiny bit of chalk left over. In the archway leading to his tenement he stopped.

It was pitch dark; there was no one about. The loud-speaker belonging to the Nazi house-porter was braying out a Nazi speech—"the Communist murder gangs in Germany have been smashed for good. . . ."

There was just enough chalk. Quickly he drew on the wall by the porter's door—RED FRONT LIVES—and paused just one second to give the Pioneer salute. Then he sped up the smelly, crumbling staircase. Must pinch some more chalk from school to-morrow, he thought, waiting for his mother to open the door.

‘BLACKING HIS SHIRT’

from *Martin’s Annual* (1935)

Written and illustrated by Anon.

Another example of the anti-fascist content of *Martin’s Annual* (see also T. H. Wintringham’s ‘Steel Spokes’ in Part Three); significantly, this time, the fascist is not foreign but British-born, reflecting the growing strength of Oswald Mosley’s blackshirts. This cartoon strip was produced the year before the blackshirts marched on the East End and were opposed and routed at the Battle of Cable Street.

Here we see working-class children, with patches on their clothes and wearing pioneer ties, flummox a bullying blackshirt who tries to ruin their game of football. The attack on a children’s game emphasizes the small-minded pettiness of rank and file fascists, and characterizes them as brainless bullies. The cartoon diminishes their importance and encourages young readers to believe that they can be opposed and defeated. It is an explicitly political comic strip and, unlike the politics of mainstream comics of the time, is not in support of the Empire, nor does it glorify war. In the second part, the unknown illustrator implies that the police are in cahoots with the fascists, though ultimately the blame for this behaviour is clearly placed on the real villain—capitalism.

BLACKING HIS SHIRT

Look what happened when a blackshirt tried to stop the boys playing football

What will the boss say when he finds the boys have made his two servants fight each other?

'I FOR INFLUENZA'

from *Rescue in Ravensdale*
Thomas Nelson and Sons, 1946

Written by Esmé Cartmell. Illustrated by Drake Brookshaw

'Esmé Cartmell' was the pen name of Leslie Barringer (1895–1968), who was a Quaker and, like the father in his book, worked as an editor for, amongst others, Thomas Nelson and Sons, prolific publishers of mainstream children's books.[1] Also like his character, Barringer had four daughters.

The novel-length story is set in August 1939, when Roger joins his uncle, aunt, and cousins for a summer holiday in Yorkshire. Roger's own family are conservative and traditional in their outlook with a tendency to find the positive in fascist Germany and Italy. This is a tendency that Roger does not share and is pleased to find that neither does his uncle's family. All, except the very young twins, are aware that war is about to break out and they want this holiday to be a peaceful and enjoyable one. On the car journey to Yorkshire the family decide what they do not want to have in their summer holiday. These include *s*mugglers, *w*ireless, *a*eroplanes, *s*pies, *t*reasure trove, *i*nfluenza, *k*idnapping, or *a*ccidents, an acrostic which means that they also reject SWASTIKAs. Of course, these, all of these, turn up!

They regularly run into a typical storybook hero, Ambrose Feirn, whom they christen Oswald Poop who has guns in the back of his car. They hear an announcement on the wireless that a German homicidal maniac has smuggled himself into England, is in the area, and is going by the name of Karl Kapp, a German anti-fascist artist that Roger's aunt and uncle have met. The manhunt is led by Oswald Poop. For reasons that become clear in the extract here, Roger and his uncle have to kidnap Karl Kapp, the alleged murderer.

1. Publication by Thomas Nelson makes it likely, though it has not been possible to find the evidence, that *Rescue in Ravensdale* would have had greater general distribution than many of the items featured in this anthology. Its dramatic cover aligns it with mainstream adventure stories from the period, and from the evidence of 'well-read' copies available second-hand, it appears to have been popular with readers.

Although set in 1939, *Rescue in Ravensdale* was published the year after the Second World War ended. At first glance it appears to be a run-of-the-mill combination of family adventure and spy stories featuring a British family that outwits foreign opponents. However, from the beginning, the novel challenges several of the traditions of these familiar genres. For instance, there is no main protagonist as the family act in unity. This ensemble approach reflects left-wing emphasis on both collaboration and the dismantling of traditional power hierarchies. In this novel, the adults are on an equal basis with the children. Decisions which carry some danger and could set family members at odds with the law and authority are discussed with the older children, and their thoughts are taken into account. Roger is an unusual central male character in being not athletic and instinctive, but thoughtful, intelligent, and politically aware.

The expected story line of good Britons defeat bad foreigners is also turned on its head, as the villains of the piece are revealed to be English supporters of fascist Germany. Unusually, Karl Kapp, the fugitive the family assists, is not a refugee because of his ethnic background, but because of his socialist beliefs. His encounter with Kapp helps Roger realize that although he hates war, fascist Germany must be opposed. This realization is not driven by an underlying nationalism and patriotism, but by Roger's recognition that such evil must be defeated and that all have their role in this fight.

'I FOR INFLUENZA'

Cover, Esmé Cartmell's's *Rescue in Ravensdale* (Thomas Nelson and Sons, 1946). The generic cover illustration reflects the book's appeal to a broad readership, its more left-wing message hidden in the pages of a traditional family holiday adventure.

The little man's eyes were closed. One grimy hand was flung sideways, with palm down and fingers spread as though he had clutched at the wire before losing consciousness. Beneath sunburn and a ruffianly growth of beard his face was gaunt and grey-white.

Roger stood above him, wary and shocked and curious. At last the holiday had produced something that might have come out of a story—something thoroughly unpleasant that meant police and telephones and reporters. One thing, though—there was no need to be sorry for this creature. You might as well be sorry for the pterodactyl in the dream.

"Have to meet Oswald Poop now," thought Roger. A wry amusement broke through his other sensations. He turned at the sound of footsteps, and saw his uncle coming up the cleft. Aunt Molly and Thelma were there too; that was not story-book style, but with the Levingtons it seemed natural enough. None of that "You'd-better-not-come-m'dear" stuff.

"Shall I fetch those chaps from the lead-mines?" he asked, as they neared him.

"Just a minute, "said Mr. Levington, and knelt down, setting his fingers on the artery in the fallen man's thin grey-brown wrist. For a moment he watched the still face carefully. Then his wife's shadow fell across it, and he looked up at her.

"Pulse going," he said, and added: "he certainly is like Karl Kapp as I remember him."

Mr. Levington dragged the limp slight figure from its resting-place and into the full shadow of the rocky shelf.

"Go on now, Roger," said Mr. Levington. "Ask one of those men to come up here while the other fetches the police. There'll be plenty of cars still on the road for him to get a lift along."

"Yes, Uncle," said Roger soberly, and turned to leave them.

Mr. Levington rose to his feet and spoke to Mrs. Levington.

"You and Thelma had better take the others—" he began, but she interrupted him.

"Wait a minute, Roger!" she called, her quiet voice suddenly stern. "Brand, I believe—*look at his hand. This* IS *Karl Kapp!*"

"Eh?" demanded Mr. Levington, as Roger spun round. "Which hand? What about it?"

"That scar," said Mrs. Levington, kneeling in her turn, clutching at her husband's sleeve and pointing down at the back of the fugitive's right hand.

There was certainly a scar there—a thin shining whitish line in the peat-grimed sunburn, curving from between the first two knuckles across the index finger tendon nearly to the base of the thumb.

"He had that scar at Swandyke," said Mrs. Levington simply.

"Molly, are you *sure?*"

"Yes, quite sure. Remember, I did that drawing of him. He sat with his hands crossed most of the time—I know I'm not mistaken. Have you that little cup in your pocket? Give it to Thelma to fetch some water in. We'll see if we can bring him round."

Roger's lips were parted to suggest that he had better go for help anyhow, when the man on the ground made a sound like a faint cough, came out of his half-swooning sleep, and opened dazed blue eyes. They did not look at all mad; he blinked, and gradually focused their gaze at the kind dark face bent over him. Baffled recognition flickered in them and suddenly changed to certainty. Their owner gave a kind of croak, licked his lips and said something hoarsely in German, and then something else in English.

"*Bitte—warum?* Mississ Levington, no?"

"Yes, Herr Kapp. Lie still a moment, and we will get you a drink. Don't try to talk yet."

To Roger the sunlight recovered its brightness. He stood, rooted and staring at the German exile, wondering how on earth such a mistake had been made.

"We'll have the police here in no time," said Mr. Levington soothingly. "Then we can clear up—"

"No, *no*!" whispered Karl Kapp, with a dreadful groaning urgency that shocked them all to stillness around him. "Your police—they will not believe you—they will hand me over to the Nazis!"

"Of course they'll believe us! You're in England now, you know."

"My friend I *do* know... you English, your innocence is the death of civilised Europe. I am hunted across your England, *on purpose*... it is *not* a mistake, it is a deceit, a deception, a frame-up... the kind of thing we are used to who are Hitler's enemies...

"My Dutch passport was in order, I was able to come ashore at Hull, I reported to the police, all correct... Then in the street a man saw me, an Englishman whom I have seen in Rotterdam with business men whom I know to be Dutch and German Nazis, spies, agents of the Gestapo....

"Since I was in England and met you," he went on, addressing Mr. Levington, "I have not been able to live by sculpture. I have drawn cartoons. I attracted the notice of those whose enmity is an honour; my cartoons were hostile to those who are ruining my country. They would like to drag me back to Germany, no doubt you know why. This Englishman in Hull... he recognised me."

This Englishman is Ambrose Feirn and Kapp convinces the Levingtons that he is in danger. Mr. Levington decides to hide him until he can get him to those who will protect him. Roger agrees to help and together they smuggle Kapp into the car in order to get him past his pursuers and into the house they are staying in.

Mr. Levington lit his pipe before he started the engine.

"Here goes," he said, and they began to move joltingly down towards the lead-mines.

One of the men was still standing among the huts.

"I say, I hope he doesn't ask you for a lift," muttered Roger.

The man only eyed them morosely, and presently they were out on the road again. There were still more cars and cyclists about than was usual at that time of day. A party of hikers turned in at the foot of Cracken Spout as Roger took a last glance in that direction.

"Pretty close call," he thought, and suddenly felt his spirits ride up on a wave of exultation. Whatever happened now, he was helping to take a crack at all the Hitler-isn't-such-a-bad-chap blighters who squealed: "We aren't ready to fight him!" and really meant: "We don't *want* to fight him because we rather like his ideas!"

"Are you all right, Herr Kapp?" he asked, as they neared the point where cars were still parked at the roadside.

"Yes, thank you," came the quiet reply.

"Quite still now. We shall have to slow down, and people may see into the car."

Roger draped his raincoat to hang over the back of the seat in front of him, further to hide the rug-covered shape that almost filled the floor-space. He leaned forward on the near side, with elbows on the raincoat, and looked interestedly out as though wondering what the crowd was there for. Presently a pang of excitement went through his middle; Mr. Levington had to stop altogether, because the scarlet-and-silver door of Oswald Poop's roadster was open for Oswald Poop to climb in.

For a second or two Karl Kapp and his chief pursuer were separated only by two car doors and a couple of feet of space. Then Mr. Levington drove on, and Roger let out the breath he had been unconsciously holding.

In the end, they manage to get Karl Kapp to safety, allowing him the time to prove himself an anti-Nazi refugee. Whilst doing so, Oswald Poop is killed in a car crash, and the holiday ends for Roger and the Levingtons, with Roger fully aware that he will soon be fighting against Fascism.

ADVENTURES OF MICKY MONGREL. NO. 46

THE other morning Micky and the twins were walking along when a posh motor-car whizzed by. They just had time to see a dog, beautifully brushed and wearing a top-hat, sitting inside. "Lord love us," said the twins together. "That's Lionel Lapdog, the Labour leader. Where can he be going to now? Not to help the workers fight against wage-cuts, I bet!"

"Let's follow as quickly as we can," said Micky. "I should like to give him a fright!"

This cartoon was part of a series about 'Mickey Mongrel, the class conscious dog', which started in the *Daily Worker* from its first days in 1930.

PART EIGHT

SCIENCE AND SOCIAL TRANSFORMATION

INTRODUCTION

The period of this anthology spans several difficult dilemmas facing socialists in relation to science, scientific education, and children. Throughout this time, people writing books or articles about science for children maintained a position of optimism towards the potential of science to liberate humankind whilst conveying forebodings about the misuse of science under fascism and through war. What supported them in this vein of thought owes its origins to two statements above all others: in 1880, Friedrich Engels, the Anglo-German Marxist, published *Socialism: Utopian and Scientific*; in 1920, V. I. Lenin, the Soviet leader, produced a report on the *Work of the Council of People's Commissars* in which he says: 'Communism = Soviet power + electrification of the whole country' (1975–9, vol. 36, pp. 15–16). At the heart of these two ways of thinking lies the rationale as to why communists, and many socialists, adopted, celebrated, and promoted 'science'. Engels refers to the view that Marx had developed an approach to society, economics, history, and revolution based on empirical study of production, profits, and wages. Progressive and socialist thought, therefore, should also rely on 'scientific' thinking. Lenin says that the development of communism, meaning a classless society in which workers would own and control the means of production, rested on workers having democratic control over production ('Soviet power') married to the latest and best in scientific production ('electricity'). It would follow, he argues, that the greatest possible productive capacity that science could think up would be used for the benefit of all humankind equally. The impact of these two arguments (or versions of them) resulted in the view that it was desirable to give children a picture of science as 'good'.

It should be noted that plenty of socialists were uneasy about 'science' because they felt it had been responsible for creating the terrible conditions many workers endured in factories and cities. As a consequence, they turned to various forms of pastoralism and small-scale artisan production as preferable to more scientific and technological development.[1] This was crucial in the development of some left literature and activity for children as it coincided with the idea that children are 'natural' (or at least nearer to 'nature' than adults) and so should be encouraged to think of 'nature' as better than the city. This lay

1. For a discussion of the conflict between ruralists and technophiles see Chapter 4, 'Radical Ruralism', in Kimberley Reynolds's *Left Out: The Forgotten Tradition of Radical Publishing for Children, 1910–1949*.

at the heart of the foundation of the Woodcraft Folk, for example (see the introduction to Part Six) and 'progressive' books, from Frances Hodgson Burnett's *The Secret Garden* (1911) to the 'camping and tramping' novels of Arthur Ransome and David Severn in the 1930s and 1940s.

The extracts in this section show a strong commitment to science on the grounds that it held within itself the potential to make life better for all. The problems around science, they argue, were not with the various branches of science themselves, but with how they had been applied in capitalist societies. As might be imagined, this posed enormous problems in relation to defence, armaments, and war. Many left-wing people in the 1930s switched from pacifism (which talked of the misuse of science) to demanding a strong military response to Nazi Germany's expansionism into Czechoslovakia. The peace movement, in particular, found ways to involve children. During the Second World War, the Soviet Union had to defend itself against the most scientifically advanced country in the world and only just succeeded—at enormous sacrifice. Many left-wing scientists in Britain and America joined the global struggle of the war and used their science to develop new materials, new methods of production, and new kinds of weapons. After the war, many of these were represented as heroes in publications and films that children read and saw.

In the post-Second World War era, the new scientific–military development of atomic and nuclear warfare again posed problems for left-wing scientists and promoters of science. The people running the Soviet Union took the position that it had to develop its scientific industrial base to the level of that reached by the USA. Vast amounts of gross domestic product were diverted by the Soviet Union into the production of rockets, missiles, and bombs (often disguised as the 'space race'), requiring a huge effort in training tens of thousands of children to become scientists. The Cold War locked children and scientists all over the world into science for warfare—or if you wanted to make it sound better, defence.

The problem for left-wing people who attacked the atomic and nuclear programmes of the West, as, for instance, on 'peace marches' *where, as Michael Rosen remembers, children happily walked along singing anti-war songs*, was whether they were equally bothered about those in the East? In relation to children, and the matter of popular science and education, were these problems of 'good' versus 'bad' scientific–military applications so complex that the best way to hold out hope to young people was by writing about science as if it were somehow purer than society? To do so, some maintained, would be to deny the connection between science and society that people such as Engels and Lenin had espoused.

The underlying optimism of this group of extracts lies in the way they regularly remind children and young people of the ingenuity of human beings in solving problems and improving life. This optimism sits uncomfortably with the knowledge that they were written in a period in which science was used to sterilize African Americans, exterminate Jews and Gypsies, obliterate many of the cities of Europe, and radiate hundreds of thousands of people in Japan. It should be remembered, however, that these were also the years that saw penicillin and other antibiotics, X-rays, radio, TV, air travel, birth control, mass production of plastics, the basis for computers, and mass immunization against polio, leprosy, TB, and smallpox. Socialists in local government hired the architects and planners to find new materials, engineering, and designs for the homes and schools which replaced slums and bombed-out streets following the Second World War. Books for children such as *Village and Town* (1942; discussed in Part Ten) expressed hope in these changes. Meanwhile, Engels's view on scientific socialism fed into left-wing sociology, which made the claim that improvements to society could come through empirical analysis of conditions, as shown in the groundbreaking work on equality and children in schools done by J. E. Floud, A. H. Halsey, and F. M. Martin in the 1950s.

'THE CHILD OF THE FUTURE'

The Young Socialist, 1913

Written by Margaret McMillan

Margaret McMillan (1860–1931) was a socialist propagandist and champion of Britain's poor city children. Through publications, projects, and political activities she was instrumental in developing the Left's interest in children and childhood. As well as using her position on the Independent Labour Party national executive board to make the case for children's needs and rights, McMillan produced fiction and journalism for children in which she explained or dramatized key socialist ideas.

Between 1900 and 1907 McMillan produced three studies of child development and the education of socially disadvantaged children in which she argued that children's physical bodies and living conditions were central to their intellectual and social development. This line of thought ran counter to ideas associated with Social Darwinism and the emerging science of eugenics, which maintained that the poor and weak represented a threat to the national gene pool.

'The Child of the Future' mingles fact and fiction. It is set in the Deptford Camp School, a project for poor children in London set up and run by McMillan and her sister Rachel. In real life the facility provided a nursery for infants and young children of working mothers by day, and a safe haven where children over the age of eight could wash and sleep at night. The fictional element of the piece takes the form of a glimpse into the future when, through good health care, living conditions, and education, all children in Britain thrive and contribute to the nation.

Margaret McMillan's efforts helped establish a welfare state in Britain, but 'The Child of the Future' reminds readers that child poverty was (and remains) a degrading waste of human potential across the globe.

THE CHILD OF THE FUTURE

WHEN THE STAINS ARE WASHED AWAY

Yesterday a wonderful thing happened. It was at the Evelyn Street Home, a humble little house where ambitious projects are entertained. "School clinics, indeed," cried the head of this house; "I will show you a Health Centre!" And as a kind of first fruits of the new order a little drill exhibition was given to which only one or two people were invited (on account of their being only room for two chairs when the girls were all dancing).

On the first landing a girl of thirteen stood. She is tall and graceful, and there is a peculiar shining quality in her young face and form that is like dew on a flower in the morning. During six months of last year she slept out in the camp and so did her companions upstairs. For, for more than a year they have been trained and treated in the Home till now every sign of disease, every trace of impurity, has been washed away.

"Come in," says this charming hostess, and in we go.

The drill-room is emptied of furniture, but filled with lovely young human beings. Ah! How beautiful girlhood is when one fairly sees it. Here are a dozen girls, ranging in age from nine to thirteen. They are dressed in cotton bodies with embroidered turn-down collars, and in serge knickers and shoulder skirts, and each wears a cardinal sash of coarse braid. Each girl has made her own costume and paid for the material in instalments. The costumes entire do not come to more than 2/- to 3/-.

Over every fair young brow the hair is parted and shines in rivulets of silky gold, and black, and auburn. How it shines! Between red lips the teeth, too, shine like pearls, and the hands and nails are as pure as flowers. Each walks in purity, and in every movement shows a keen, free-flowing joy. In their voices, a little husky yet but sweet already, this joy is also singing. It will sing more truly, more wonderfully when another year or two has gone by. Meantime a lady sits down to the piano and the girls form for drill.

There is nothing on this planet so lovely and eloquent as the movements of the young, well-nurtured girls walking in harmony. I look at them and try to recognise them, but the truth is I have never seen them before. True, this is Lily, who was operated on for adenoids in the room next door a year ago! Ah, Lily, in what misery were you plunged on that sad day on which none the less you faced the light for the first time. Your poor little body was not charming then. Your beauty was trampled under and hidden by the stains of disease and poverty. You were, perhaps, to be taken into a cripple's home, but *no* cripple's home would receive you now, for your limbs are straight and strong after all. Move on, sweet Lily, with your well-back little head, and light-stepping feet, and forget the dark past and all its sorrows.

Then is Alice—*is* it Alice? That dark-eyed young girl with the high, fair brow and beautiful features. Why did Nature give her every mark of high race if (as I know to be the case) her father never earned £1 a week in her lifetime? Not that we saw this grace very plainly in the old days when her hair was not silk and her limbs were hidden in a dozen garments. And yet it is impossible not to observe her now, so calmly and gently proud she is. And trooping behind her, and on either side, other girl-forms, almost as beautiful, almost as instinct with what is precious in our race. Deptford! Yes, this is Deptford—with the stains wiped away.

And now they are going to dance. The music strikes up again, the bright heads and cardinal braids are motionless for an instant. Then a light beat, one-two, they are off. This whirlwind of youth, and health, and beauty is turning round, and away. It is leaping from the smooth floor. It is meeting, turning, receding, linking itself in a wreath, and above it is setting your pulses athrob with a strange emotion and hope, with suggestions that even music itself can never offer, with visions that never swam below the grey horizon of every-day life. And in the midst of it all there is one figure that seems to gather all the beauty and joy and fix it in a dazzling point. Fascinated, you gaze on it until at last it becomes the centre, not merely of a dance, but of all the hopes and aspirations of life-times and of people. Is it possible that *all* children will dance one day as Alice is dancing now?

"Why! They are dancing like that already—thousands of them," a voice will cry. Alas! That is not *really* true. I have been in Canada and in the United States, in Germany, in France, in Switzerland. There is a great deal of dancing in all of these countries, but the workman's child does not dance like Alice in any country. And—let us wake now from our dream. This is a little room. This is not England.

Canada and the States follow England in social matters. And the same is true of Germany. Her "School Hygiene" is partly original, but it is just the original part we should not like to copy. The "fine organisation" and the "weekly school bath" are things we should respectively doubt and scorn. What we want is life itself, and an ideal, and while we are quickening and growing it is well to have as little "organisation" from the outside as possible. As for washing, how can one train children who have only one bath in a week? Mr. Chesterton says only Pharisees and English aristocrats go in for washing. He evidently has not read the Pentateuch in recent years. And as for the English aristocrats, of whom Alice is one, we cannot do better than make as many of them as possible. Let us go to, now, and make 36 millions of aristocrats in England, and initiate daily baths for every one.

'THE BEGINNING OF TRADE'

from *Pollycon: A Book for the Young Economist*
Basil Blackwell, 1933

Written by E. F. Stucley. With a candid preface by Stephen King-Hall. Illustrated by Hugh Chesterman

Today the subject of economics is not generally thought to be of interest to children, but during the first decades of the last century it was considered essential to building a new, more stable, and peaceful world, and so several writers tried their hands at making it interesting and comprehensible to even very young readers. As the popular children's broadcaster Commander Stephen King-Hall (1893–1966) observes in his Preface to *Pollycon*, 'I cannot tell you too often that *you* will be a stupid ass if you do not learn about Economics.'

E[lizabeth] F[lorence] Stucley (1906–74) uses stories, anecdotes, and vivid examples from history and everyday life to explain subjects ranging from the invention of money through want, effort, exchange, distribution, trade, foreign currencies, taxes, depreciation, borrowing, lending, capital, and strikes. Her short, often humorous examples are complemented by lively illustrations showing economics in action.

King-Hall's Preface is advertised as 'candid' on the grounds that it is not uncritical. After praising Stucley's style, he takes issue with her account of labour relations, and particularly her characterization of workmen as foolish for striking and factory owners as 'the kindest-hearted, most sensible chaps imaginable'. He directs readers to read the book and then ask a socialist for the other side of the story.

CHAPTER 1

THE BEGINNING OF TRADE

ONCE upon a time there lived a family of Early Britons. One day Mrs. Early Briton was sitting in front of her cave, nursing her youngest child. She wore her simple one-piece garment of fur. Mr. Early Briton was out for the day, hunting. At least, he *ought* to have been. So Mrs. Early Briton was very surprised when she saw him limping through the trees towards the cave.

'What is the matter?' she asked in very Early British.

Mr. Early Briton crawled to the cave and sat down with a groan.

'Hurt my leg. Pretty bad,' he grunted.

'And you've killed nothing to eat for dinner?'

'How could I, when I've got a bad leg?'

Mrs. Early Briton was very worried. There were no butchers' shops in those days, and no hunting meant no dinner. Luckily there were a few bones in the larder, but they would not last long.

You see, the Early Britons had already found out that in order to eat one must make an effort to get food, and until that effort was made there would be nothing to eat.

Look at the three pictures on the opposite page [not shown]. The first is a portrait of Mr. Early Briton feeling hungry. I shall call that picture WANTS.

The second picture shows him shooting an Early British animal. I shall call that picture EFFORT.

The third picture is very easy to understand. The Early British family are all very busy eating the Early British animal. Their table manners are not very good. I shall call that picture SATISFACTION.

Then Mrs. Early Briton had a bright idea. She took her husband's second-best bow and arrows round to the neighbour next door, and asked him to give her some meat for the bow and arrows.

As it happened, the next-door neighbour had a little spare meat which he did not want, because he knew that it would go bad. Also, he was quite glad of the new bow and arrows. Mrs. Early Briton took the meat home, and they all had a late breakfast.

After that, Mr. Early Briton made a great many bows and arrows and even when his leg got better he never went hunting again. He became so good at bow-making that he could work better and faster than any of his neighbours. People came from far and wide to get his bows and arrows, and he and his family lived on the food he received for them.

There is another picture of the next-door neighbour exchanging food for the bow and arrows. I shall call that EXCHANGE.

As time went on, the bow and arrow making became a very busy affair, and our friend, Mr. Early Briton, had to keep customers waiting because he had so much work to do. At last he had to get a man to help with the work.

Mr. Early Briton promised to give the man half of the meat they got in exchange for the bows and arrows they made. Every day Mr. Early Briton and his partner divided the meat which they got from the hunters.

The Mrs. Early Briton had another idea.

She said: 'I think it would be better if we had a few things besides meat in exchange for the bows and arrows. We want some fresh skins to make new winter furs for the children. And while the hunters are out in the forest, they might as well cut us some wood for the bows. We now get more meat than we can eat.'

Look at the next picture [not shown] showing the two partners dividing the meat, and the furs, and the wood between them, and call this picture DIVERSIFICATION....

THE RADIUM WOMAN

Puffin Books, 1953; first published 1939

Written by Eleanor Doorly

The Radium Woman, about Marie Curie, was the third in a trilogy of books about French scientists written by Eleanor Doorly (1880–1950), the previous two being *The Insect Man* (1936) about Jean-Henri Fabre, and *The Microbe Man* (1938) about Louis Pasteur. This is a substantial body of work, devoted to popularizing the life and discoveries of scientists so that children would acquire a sense of what pioneering work in science actually is. The three books first appeared while Doorly was Headmistress at King's High School for Girls in Warwick. *The Radium Woman* won the 1939 Carnegie Medal. *The Insect Man* and *The Microbe Man* appeared in paperback during the Second World War (1941, 1943) as some of the earliest books published by Puffin books, numbers 6 and 8, respectively. They were, then, part of director Allen Lane's social and political commitment to children.

Doorly was born in Kingston, Jamaica, but moved to England when she was seven and was then brought up by her great-aunt in Leamington Spa. She spent some time studying at a French lycée and had a lifelong interest in France and French culture.

Marie Curie's life was a mix of genius, persistence, heroism, discrimination, and tragedy, from some of which Doorly protected her young audience. By putting out the story of her life for young audiences, Puffin Books were making statements about both the need for the equality of women and the value and importance of science.

CHAPTER 15

WHATEVER HAPPENS

*

MARIE was born to have glorious courage. All her life she had had to call upon her valiancy, and it had grown strong and would not fail her. Moreover, she had truly loved a great man, and Pierre had left her a word to remember and to obey when her world fell to pieces around her. 'Whatever might happen,' he had said, one day when they were talking of death, 'Whatever might happen, and even though one might be like an empty body, whose spirit was dead, it would be one's duty to go on working all the same.' So Marie, fortunately, had to go on working. When a pension was offered her, she refused it, saying she was young enough to earn for herself and her children.

She found an odd little way of comfort which seems to make her all the dearer to us: she wrote her diary as if she were speaking to Pierre:

'They have offered to let me take your place, my Pierre: your lectures and the direction of your laboratory. I have accepted. I don't know if I have done right or wrong. You have often told me that you would like me to give a course of lectures at the Sorbonne. And I would at least like to try to continue your work. At one moment that seems the easiest way to go on living; at another I seem a fool to undertake it.'

'*May 7th*, 1906:

'My Pierre, I think of you all the time; my head is bursting with the thought of you, and my reason fails. I can't understand that I have to live without you and that I can't smile at my dear life's companion. The trees have been in leaf two days now and the garden is beautiful. This morning I was admiring the children in it. I thought how beautiful you would have thought them and that you would have called me to show me that the periwinkles and narcissus were out....

'*May 14th*: I want to tell you that they have nominated me to your chair of Physics at the Sorbonne and that there are people imbecile enough to congratulate me on it.' Marie was not too crushed to feel fierce rage at fools.

No woman had ever had the honour of a university chair at the Sorbonne; that is, no woman had been made head of a teaching staff in any subject. But there was no man in France capable of taking over Pierre's work, so it fell naturally to Marie. She alone of living scientists had the genius for it.

'THE FATE OF BOOKS'

from *Black on White: The Story of Books*
George Routledge, 1932

Written by M. Ilin. Illustrated by N. Lapshin

Mikhail Ilin (1895–1953) is the pen-name of Il'ya Yakovlevich Marshak and was the younger brother of the popular children's writer Samuil Marshak, who was involved in setting up the first arts complex for children in what is now Krasnodar. Samuil Marshak also helped to found Raduga (The Rainbow), a publishing house for children, recruiting a wide range of talented writers and illustrators. Later he became the head of the children's section of Gosizdat, the State Publishing House. As well as being a writer, Ilin was an engineer and so he was able to assist his older brother with his work in children's literature. According to the contemporaneous introductory notes to *Black on White:* 'Both brothers belong to a group of writers who are studying science and history and Soviet life and writing books not only for Russian children, but for workers in factories and for peasants.'

Ilin began by writing for Marshak's children's journal *Novy Robinson* (New Robinson) from 1924, and starting in 1926 he produced several titles in rapid succession. *Black on White* was first published in 1928 and translated into English in 1932 where it was published by the well-established firm of George Routledge, meaning it was widely available to families and educators. In it Ilin engages his readers in a dialogue on the subject of the history of communication, presenting his ideas vividly, and introducing his audience to the deciphering of ancient languages, the processes of printing, and the development of books as a permanent record of the knowledge of humankind. The final chapter is reproduced here. It deals with the survival of books and shows that even works thought to have been destroyed can sometimes be recovered. *Black on White* celebrates the importance of books, placing them at the centre of the education of the child, the adult, and the revolutionary.

CHAPTER VI

THE FATE OF BOOKS

THERE is a Latin proverb which says: "Every book has its fate." The fate of a book is often stranger than that of a human being. Take, for example, the works of the Greek poet, Alcman. This papyrus roll has come down to us in the strangest fashion. It would have perished long ago if it had not been buried. It was actually buried, just as people are. The ancient Egyptians had a custom of putting into the grave with a mummy—the embalmed body of a man—all his papers and books. Letters, learned books, and poems of people who lived thousands of years ago have lain on the bosoms of mummies down to our time.

Destruction of the books.

Egyptian graves have preserved many books which the libraries were not able to preserve. The largest library of Egypt, the Alexandrian library, was burned up when Alexandria was captured by the legions of Julius Cæsar. How many wonderful manuscripts perished when these millions of rolls were burned! All that has come down to us are some fragments of the catalogue of the library. Of all the books which once made readers laugh and weep, we have only the titles, like the names carved on the tombstones of people long since dead and forgotten.

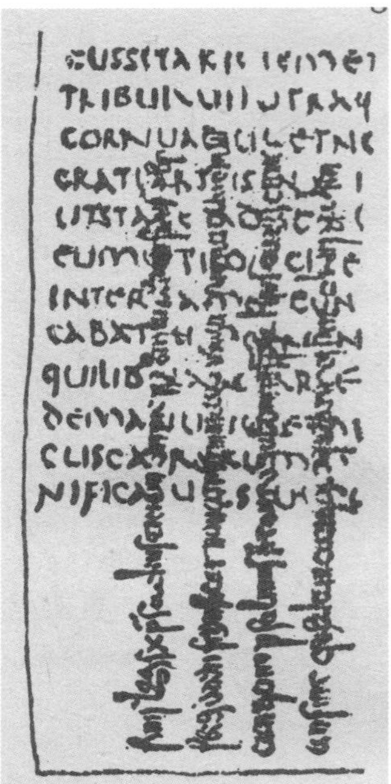

A manuscript showing two sets of writing.

Still more astonishing is the fate of those books which were saved because people tried to destroy them. Or rather, they tried to destroy the writing, not the book itself. In the Middle Ages, when parchment was very dear, they used to scrape off the original text with a knife and write the lives of saints in place of some Greek poem or work of Roman history. There were men who specialized in doing this scraping—this destruction of books. Many books would have perished at the hands of these executioners if we had not found a way, in our time, of restoring these ruined books—or *palimpsests*, as they were called.

The ink had penetrated so deeply into the parchment that even the most severe scraping could not remove all traces of the text. If the manuscript is soaked in certain chemicals the blue or red outlines of the old writing come again to the surface. But don't be too delighted with this, because very often the manuscript, after this treatment, begins to turn black very fast and in the end the text becomes so dim that it is impossible to read it. This was the case when they used the acid obtained from oak gall for restoring these palimpsests. In every great library there are several of these manuscripts which have suffered two deaths.

They tell the story of one scholar who was restoring some palimpsests who purposely destroyed some manuscripts to hide mistakes which he had made in his translation.

In place of tannic acid they have recently begun to use other substances which bring out the old writing for a short time. While the text is thus visible they quickly take photographs and then wash off the acids. The latest reports are that photographs of the hidden writing on the palimpsests can now be taken without any chemical treatment.

But if books had their enemies, they had also their friends who have hunted for them in Egyptian graves, under the ashes of Herculaneum and Pompeii, and in the archives of monasteries. There is an interesting story about how one of these booklovers, Scipio Maffei, found the Verona library.

There lay the oldest Latin manuscripts in existence.

All that was known about the Verona library, which had contained valuable Latin manuscripts, was found in notes written by travellers who had been in Verona many years before Maffei's time. The only thing that he knew about this library was that two famous scholars, Mabillon and Montfaucon, had searched for it and been unable to find it. Maffei was undaunted by their failure. Although he was not a learned paleographer, a connoisseur of manuscripts, he set eagerly to work on his search. Finally he did find the library in the very place where the former scholars had looked for it in vain—in the library of the monastery in Verona. The books were not *in the cases* of this library, and no one before Maffei had thought of climbing up on a step ladder and looking *on top of the cases*, where all these precious manuscripts had been lying in dust and disorder for many years. Maffei almost fainted with delight. There lay the very oldest Latin manuscripts in existence!

Some day I shall write a book about the adventures of books: about the books which were burned up at the time of the burning of the library of Alexandria, about the books which have been lost in monastery libraries, about the books which were burned in the fires of the Inquisition, about the books destroyed in times of battle.

I close the last chapter with a regret that I have told so very little about so wonderful a thing as a book.

The End

FROM *THE MAGIC OF COAL*

Puffin Picture Books, 1945

Written and illustrated by Peggy M. Hart

As Michael Rosen and Jane Rosen explain in the Introduction, there was much overlap and cross-fertilization of the books produced for and read by children of the Left and more mainstream children's literature. As works such as *War in Dollyland* (Part Two), *Rescue in Ravensdale* (Part Seven), and *The Magic of Coal* (Part Eight) demonstrate, mainstream publishers were affected by the Left, and children of left-wing parents were directed to read selected books from the mainstream. In truth, some people working in mainstream publishing were themselves sympathetic to the ideals of postwar reconstruction along socialistic lines as represented by the Labour government of 1945–50. From a publishing point of view, the story of Puffin Picture Books is intertwined with the Bloomsbury Circle, picturebooks in the Soviet Union, and the progressive ideas of 'New Education' emanating from Czechoslovakia and France. The story has been told in great detail in Joe Pearson's *Drawn Direct to the Plate: Noel Carrington and the Puffin Picture Books* (2010), where we come across Noel Carrington, brother of Bloomsbury's Dora Carrington, sitting in his office at the magazine *Country Life* in 1933, looking at a pile of Russian picturebooks brought to him by the socialist painter and illustrator Pearl Binder. The publishers of what would turn out to be the 'Père Castor' books in France were already tuned in to the artistic, technological, and social innovations of the Russian books, and through the late 1930s various publishers in Britain started to experiment along these lines too. The breakthrough for children in the UK came as a consequence of Carrington convincing Allen Lane, the director of Penguin Books, that he should follow suit.

The Magic of Coal was number 49 in the burgeoning Puffin Picture Book series, and it owes a good deal to a social and artistic movement which sought to portray industry as something of benefit to society and workers as honourable people without whom this benefit wouldn't happen. (The subtle placing of a tattoo of St George and the Dragon on the miner who appears on the cover subtly makes him a national hero.) By implication, then, production itself needed to be socialized—or, to use the term current in the 1940s, 'nationalized'. Strands of this movement can be found in the USA with Franklin Roosevelt's New Deal and in the songs that Woody Guthrie wrote as part of the cultural work around that initiative; they are also present in the most progressive work of the GPO (General Post Office) Film Unit in Britain (1933–40), and in the artwork commissioned by London Transport and displayed in trains and on the walls of London Underground stations.

In the Soviet Union, this approach was taken one step further, with workers being depicted as muscular heroes, fulfilling ever greater work 'norms' as part of the so-called Stakhonovite movement to meet the demands of the First Five-Year Plan.

The Magic of Coal takes a cooler approach whilst celebrating the coordinated labour required to get coal out the ground and the benefits that coal brings to society. By mentioning the Miners' Welfare Association, the book hints at the presence of a section of the Labour, socialist, and Communist movements that was significant in the development of socialist thought and culture in the twentieth century.

To date, no information about Peggy Hart has been forthcoming.

THE MAGIC OF COAL

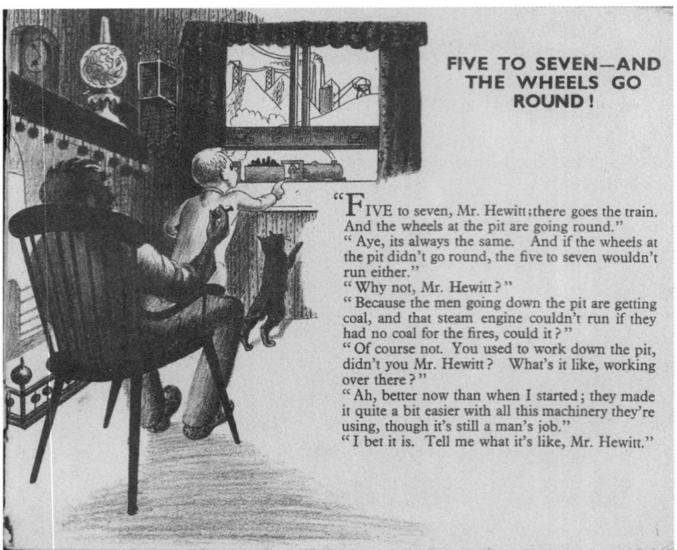

FIVE TO SEVEN—AND THE WHEELS GO ROUND!

"**FIVE** to seven, Mr. Hewitt; there goes the train. And the wheels at the pit are going round."

"Aye, it's always the same. And if the wheels at the pit didn't go round, the five to seven wouldn't run either."

"Why not, Mr. Hewitt?"

"Because the men going down the pit are getting coal, and that steam engine couldn't run if they had no coal for the fires, could it?"

"Of course not. You used to work down the pit, didn't you Mr. Hewitt? What's it like, working over there?"

"Ah, better now than when I started; they made it quite a bit easier with all this machinery they're using, though it's still a man's job."

"I bet it is. Tell me what it's like, Mr. Hewitt."

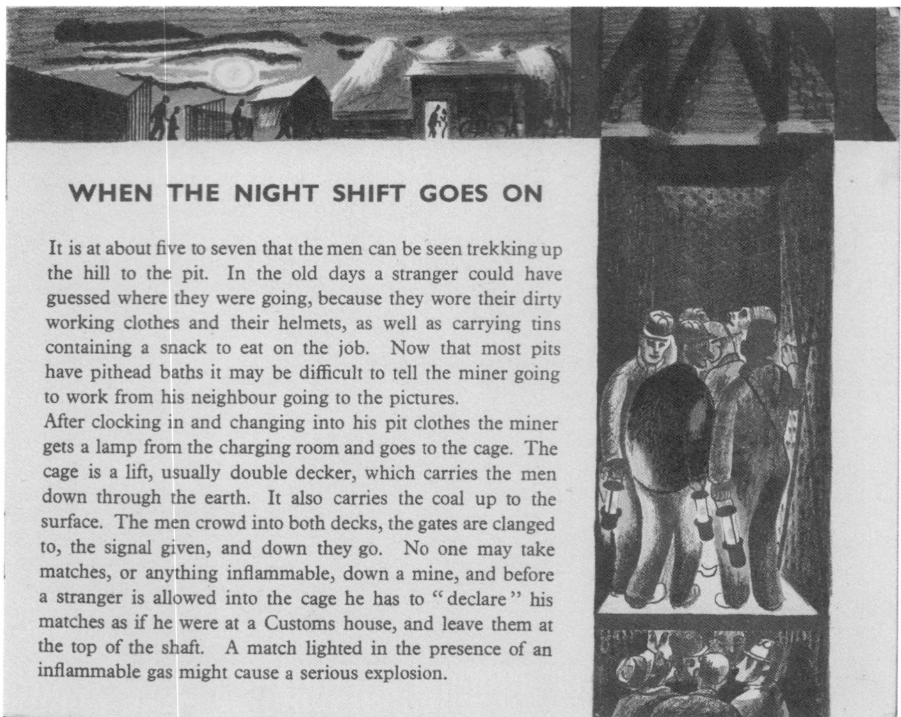

WHEN THE NIGHT SHIFT GOES ON

It is at about five to seven that the men can be seen trekking up the hill to the pit. In the old days a stranger could have guessed where they were going, because they wore their dirty working clothes and their helmets, as well as carrying tins containing a snack to eat on the job. Now that most pits have pithead baths it may be difficult to tell the miner going to work from his neighbour going to the pictures.

After clocking in and changing into his pit clothes the miner gets a lamp from the charging room and goes to the cage. The cage is a lift, usually double decker, which carries the men down through the earth. It also carries the coal up to the surface. The men crowd into both decks, the gates are clanged to, the signal given, and down they go. No one may take matches, or anything inflammable, down a mine, and before a stranger is allowed into the cage he has to "declare" his matches as if he were at a Customs house, and leave them at the top of the shaft. A match lighted in the presence of an inflammable gas might cause a serious explosion.

WHEN THE NIGHT SHIFT GOES ON

It is at about five to seven that the men can be seen trekking up the hill to the pit. In the old days a stranger could have guessed where they were going, because they wore their dirty working clothes and their helmets, as well as carrying tins containing a snack to eat on the job. Now that most pits have pithead baths it may be difficult to tell the miner going to work from his neighbour going to the pictures.

After clocking in and changing into his pit clothes the miner gets a lamp from the charging room and goes to the cage. The cage is a lift, usually double decker, which carries the men down through the earth. It also carries the coal up to the surface. The men crowd into both decks, the gates are clanged to, the signal given, and down they go. No one may take matches, or anything inflammable, down a mine, and before a stranger is allowed into the cage he has to "declare" his matches as if he were at a Customs house, and leave them at the top of the shaft. A match lighted in the presence of an inflammable gas might cause a serious explosion. [...]

PREPARING THE WAY FOR THE COAL FACE MAN

BEFORE the coal face man starts work, another shift of men prepares the coal for him. The cutters take their machine along the coal face, cutting a ledge five feet deep under the coal with the sharp little picks on the moving chain of their electric machine. One man works the machine while the other shovels away the coal dust which is formed during the cutting, and which piles up against the machine and would quickly stop it working if it were left there. This man has a very hard job, as he has to shovel very quickly indeed to keep up with the machine. Even this coal dust is not wasted, but is compressed into briquettes.

PREPARING THE WAY FOR THE COAL FACE MAN

BEFORE the coal face man starts work, another shift of men prepares the coal for him. The cutters take their machine along the coal face, cutting a ledge five feet deep under the coal with the sharp little picks on the moving chain of their electric machine. One man works the machine while the other shovels away the coal dust which is formed during the cutting, and which piles up against the machine and would quickly stop it working if it were left there. This man has a very hard job, as he has to shovel very quickly indeed to keep up with the machine. Even this coal dust is not wasted, but is compressed into briquettes. [. . .]

Tubs of coal and tubs of shale come up the shaft. There is no use for shale, the rock surrounding the coal, so it is emptied on to the slagheaps, either by overhead cables, or by being lifted by hydraulic power and carted away by ponies. Shale also comes here from the screen house.

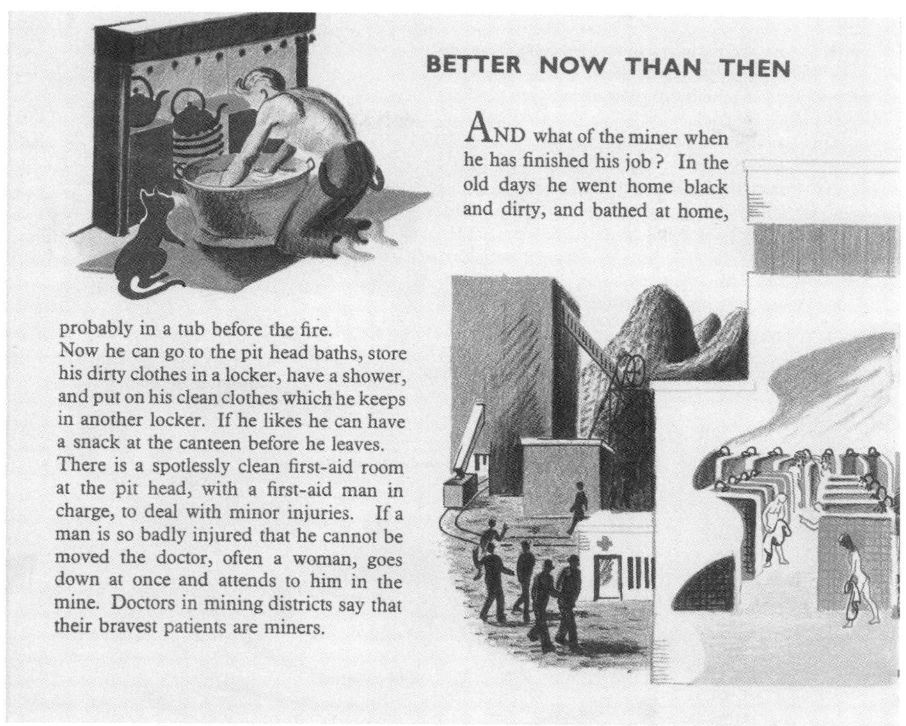

BETTER NOW THAN THEN

AND what of the miner when he has finished his job? In the old days he went home black and dirty, and bathed at home, probably in a tub before the fire.

Now he can go to the pit head baths, store his dirty clothes in a locker, have a shower, and put on his clean clothes which he keeps in another locker. If he likes he can have a snack at the canteen before he leaves.

There is a spotlessly clean first-aid room at the pit head, with a first-aid man in charge, to deal with minor injuries. If a man is so badly injured that he cannot be moved the doctor, often a woman, goes down at once and attends to him in the mine. Doctors in mining districts say that their bravest patients are miners.

BETTER NOW THAN THEN

AND what of the miner when he has finished his job? In the old days he went home black and dirty, and bathed at home, probably in a tub before the fire.

Now he can go to the pit head baths, store his dirty clothes in a locker, have a shower, and put on his clean clothes which he keeps in another locker. If he likes he can have a snack at the canteen before he leaves.

There is a spotlessly clean first-aid room at the pit head, with a first-aid man in charge, to deal with minor injuries. If a man is so badly injured that he cannot be moved the doctor, often a woman, goes down at once and attends to him in the mine. Doctors in mining districts say that their bravest patients are miners.

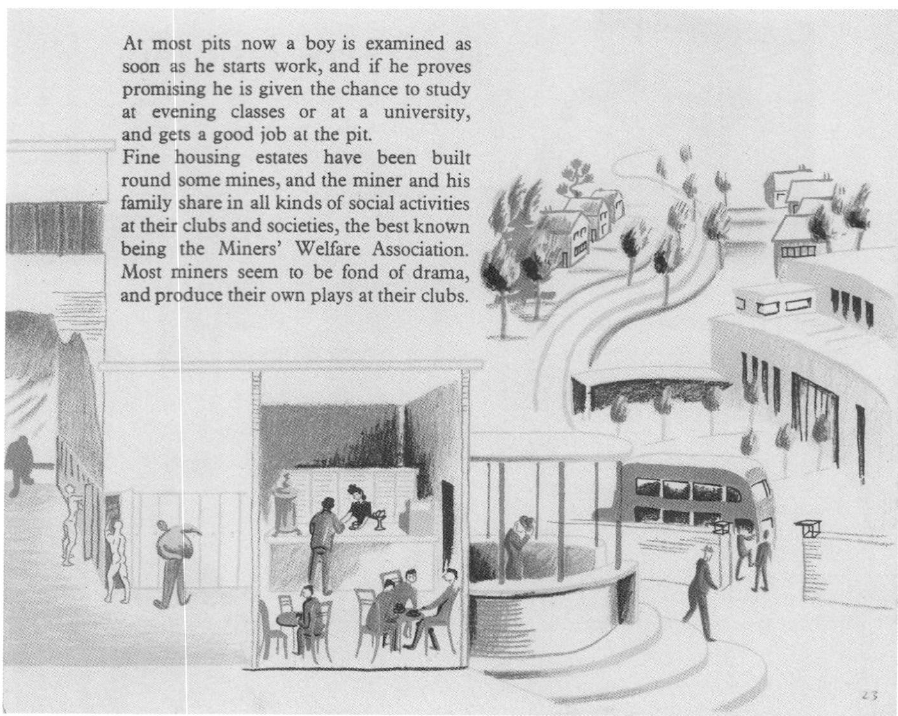

At most pits now a boy is examined as soon as he starts work, and if he proves promising he is given the chance to study at evening classes or at a university, and gets a good job at the pit.

Fine housing estates have been built round some mines, and the miner and his family share in all kinds of social activities at their clubs and societies, the best known being the Miners' Welfare Association. Most miners seem to be fond of drama, and produce their own plays at their clubs.

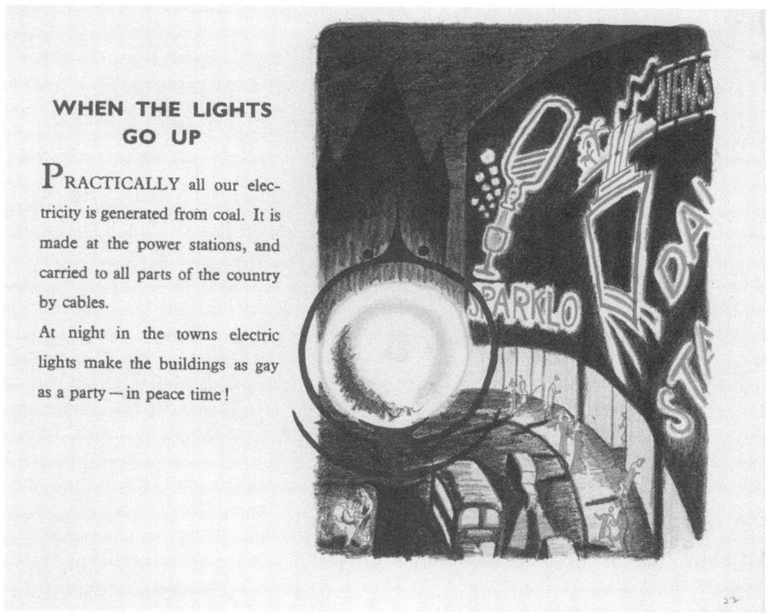

WHEN THE LIGHTS GO UP

PRACTICALLY all our electricity is generated from coal. It is made at the power stations, and carried to all parts of the country by cables.

At night in the towns electric lights make the buildings as gay as a party—in peace time!

WHEN THE LIGHTS GO UP

PRACTICALLY all our electricity is generated from coal. It is made at the power stations, and carried to all parts of the country by cables.

At night in the towns electric lights make the buildings as gay as a party—in peace time!

'NUMBERS AND NOTHING'

from *Man Must Measure: The Wonderful World of Mathematics*
London: Rathbone Books, Adprint House, 1955

Written by Lancelot Hogben. Art by André, Charles Keeping, Kenneth Symonds. Maps by Marjorie Saynor

Lancelot Hogben (1895–1975) was an experimental zoologist and medical statistician. He liked to describe himself as a 'scientific humanist', but he was known more specifically to be a socialist, having been, in his early years, in the Independent Labour Party. As well as being an academic, Hogben published a series of books aimed at popularizing science, most notably *Mathematics for the Million* (1936) and *Science for the Citizen: A Self-Educator Based on the Social Background of Scientific Discovery* (1938). In post-war left-wing circles, he was an example of how socialists and communists would take on people as 'one of ours', so when *Man Must Measure* appeared, it was a book that could be given to children in the full knowledge that it had an approved provenance.

In its time, *Man Must Measure* was also a luxury book, as it was hardback, large format, and full colour on every page, with a superb mix of pictures ranging across historically accurate scenes, pastiches of period art seemingly taken from ancient and medieval art, and illustrated diagrams. It told the story of mathematics from prehistoric times, through Ancient Egypt, Babylon and Assyria, the Phoenicians, Greece and Rome, the Moslem Empire, Western Europe, and the industrial world. This was clearly a conscious effort to show how mathematics belongs to all of humanity, and the pictures are careful to represent peoples with skin colours other than white, and in local and regional dress. On every page the social narrative includes examples of mathematics (some of it quite complex) developed from within societies and cultures across the world. As an illustration of how political this was, one need only look forward to October 1987, when Prime Minister Margaret Thatcher said mockingly to the Conservative Party Conference, 'And children who need to be able to count and multiply are learning anti-racist mathematics—whatever that may be.' The answer to her question had been available for the thirty-two years since *Man Must Measure* was published.

NUMBERS AND NOTHING

ONE OF THE world's oldest civilisations grew up in the valley of the River Indus, in India. Like those of the Nile and the Euphrates, it learned its first lessons in mathematics through astronomy, the gateway to time-reckoning and to temple-building. Several centuries before Rome rose to power, the mathematicians of India had found a close value for π. In the arithmetic of trade, the merchants of India were the equals of those of Mesopotamia.

Until about two thousand years ago, they probably used numerals made up of horizontal strokes. But when they began to use dried palm leaves as writing material and developed a flowing style of writing, they also began to join up these strokes, so that = became Z and ≡ became Ƶ. In this way they gradually built up different signs for each number up to nine. Each sign could conveniently be used to indicate the number of pebbles in *any* groove of the abacus.

Had progress stopped short there, it would not have amounted to much. If ZZ merely stands for two pebbles in any two grooves, it can have many different meanings, such as twenty-two, two hundred and two, two thousand and twenty, and so on. We need to be told not only how many pebbles in a groove, but also which groove they are in.

Somewhere in India, some unknown person, probably a counting-house clerk, hit on a device which does this for us. He used the figure on the extreme right to stand for pebbles in the units groove, the next figure to the left to stand for pebbles in the tens groove, and so on. To indicate an empty column, he used a dot, just as we now use a zero. Thus Z Z could mean only 22. Z.Z. could mean only 2020. With this system, we no longer rely on space-consuming repetition; and we can record the same number on any groove of the abacus by using the same sign. But saving space is only a small advantage, as the later Greeks must have learned. The great advantage of the Hindu system is that it enables us to *calculate* with numerals.

The ancient systems of writing—Egyptian, Babylonian, Greek, Roman and Chinese—all relied on the use of different symbols for the same number of pebbles in different grooves of the abacus. Before you could do written or mental calculations with them, you would therefore need to learn a different table of addition and of multiplication for each groove. When you have only nine different signs, each of which can show the number of pebbles in any groove, and a zero to indicate empty grooves, you need learn only one simple table, once and for all. You can carry over in your head because there is only one simple table to remember. The Hindu number-language quickly led to a revolution in the art of calculation. The mathematicians of India began to think of fractions and to write them in the way that we do. By 500 AD

India had produced mathematicians who solved problems which had baffled the greatest scholars of antiquity. The mathematician, Varahamihira, was able to calculate how to forecast the positions of planets; Aryabhata stated a rule for finding square roots and gave a value for π which is still good enough for most purposes today—3.1416.

By about 800 AD, Indian traders, following the age-old caravan route which passed through Persia into Mesopotamia, brought news of the new numerals to Baghdad which was then rapidly becoming the world's greatest city of learning.

Early in the seventh century, Mahommed, founder and prophet of the Moslem religion, united the whole of Arabia under his leadership. For more than three centuries after his death, his followers carried the new religion across the whole of North Africa, into Spain and Portugal, and eastward through Asia beyond the River Indus.

About 762 they founded the city of Baghdad and made it the seat of government of a rapidly-growing empire. About forty years later, under the Caliph, Harun ar-Rashid, it became the capital of learning of the western world, just as Alexandria had been during Greek and Roman times.

In learning, Baghdad made the best of both worlds, East and West. Merchants and mathematicians from the East brought with them the new number signs and the arithmetic of India. Heretics, who had fled from the West, brought copies of scientific works written while Alexandria was still at its prime. These included treatises on astronomy and geography and Euclid's geometry. By order of the Caliph, Moslem scholars translated such works into Arabic, the language of their sacred book, the Koran. Thus, the science and geometry of Greece became available throughout the Moslem world, now equipped with an arithmetic far better than the best the Greeks had known.

To this growing body of knowledge the East made two other contributions. Chinese prisoners, captured during a skirmish on the frontier, taught Baghdad the art of paper-making, while Persian astrologers, who added a spice of eastern magic to a sound knowledge of the heavens, gave the Caliph's court a keen interest in astronomy.

In observatories built by command of the Caliph, astronomers advanced the science of map-making far beyond the level it had reached in Alexandria. In the schools of Baghdad trigonometry flourished. Because they had mastered the new arithmetic of India, Moslem mathematicians could make much fuller use of the geometry of Euclid and of Archimedes. The astronomer equipped the mariner with nautical almanacs for navigation by sun and stars and gave him improved instruments, designed in the observatories. The geographer had new and better tools for land-survey.

Never before in history had knowledge advanced in a single century as it did between 800 and 900 AD, where East met West in Baghdad.

PART NINE

SEX FOR BEGINNERS

INTRODUCTION

The sexual revolution is associated with the 1960s and the availability of the contraceptive pill, but radical children's literature had been helping to change attitudes to sex since the beginning of the twentieth century. During decades when even books for adults were likely to be prosecuted for obscenity if they included descriptions of sexual activity, *The Young Socialist* was calling for writing for children and young people that provided information about the sexual aspects of their bodies and desires. In 1913 it carried a review article of 'Books on Delicate Subjects' which declared

> Sex subjects, for growing people, need to be handled carefully and delicately, but they need to be handled. Until such matters are dealt with openly, in sympathetic and intelligent fashion, we may expect nothing but unhappiness to come as a result in years after.... Prudery and calculated ignorance are responsible for a thousand evils in our land. There is no room for either of them in the socialist movement. (220–1)

The reviewer's condemnation of prudery and ignorance captures the view of many on the Left that ignorance about sex was responsible not just for unwanted pregnancies and sexually transmitted diseases, but for feelings of guilt and frustration that could feed violence and antisocial behaviour.[1] This attitude owed much to the theories of Sigmund Freud and his followers, such as Wilhelm Reich, who argued that sexual repression was a cause of personal and social illness, juvenile delinquency, and the rise of fascism in the interwar years.[2] The noted sexologist Havelock Ellis, whose six-volume *Studies in the Psychology of Sex* was completed in 1927, argued that healthy sexual relationships were just as important in the creation of a successful, civilized, modern society as good genes. Ellis specifically identified 'the absolute necessity of taking deliberate and active part in [young people's] sexual initiation' (1927 n.p.). By this he means neither encouraging young people to be promiscuous nor concentrating on the possible consequences of sexual activity, but what the Eugenics Education Society called 'responsible reproduction'. Responsible

1. The Left did not have a monopoly on wanting to provide sex education for children, but as a rule they set about it more directly and comprehensively—providing materials for children of all ages—than did more conservative bodies.
2. Richard Overy provides a discussion about the perceived relationship between social ills and sexual repression in *The Morbid Age: Britain and the Crisis of Civilization, 1919–1939* (Penguin, 2010).

reproduction requires managing the urge to have sex. Effective—responsible—management, Ellis maintained, required accurate understanding of the body and its urges. Young people's desire for information is clearly articulated in the extracts from the underground magazine *Out of Bounds* included in this section. Here pupils write about the way lack of information—or worse, misinformation—can lead to vulnerability, guilt, and abuse.

Radical children's literature included a cluster of books that set out to provide up-to-date, matter-of-fact information intended to alleviate guilt and anxiety, and to impart the benefits of responsible reproduction. In other words, these publications were attempting to change the whole way of thinking about sex and reproduction with the aim of improving health, happiness, and social relations. These goals, and the associated doctrine of encouraging children to regard their bodies and sexual feelings as normal and natural, may now seem unproblematic, but the regulation of sex and sexuality had for long been a central activity and source of authority for British legal, religious, and governmental bodies. Writing about sex implicitly challenged religious teaching, social convention, and legislation on blasphemy and decency, making it a highly contentious area of radical publishing for children. For this reason, publications that provided sex education had to tread carefully.

The most common strategy for flying beneath the cultural radar while avoiding confusing euphemisms was to emphasize the scientific nature of the information provided. Reproduction was presented as a bodily function like any other, and generally discussion of reproduction at the level of cells, lower organisms, and other creatures preceded that in humans. This approach inevitably took the form of information books, though as seen in the extracts from 'Sex Knowledge' and *How You Began* in the following pages, attempts were made to enliven material and make it more personal by interjecting questions, stories, and observations beyond the strictly factual.

Non-fiction is a good way of providing information, often supported by diagrams, but when it comes to explaining feelings and emotions, fiction is more effective. Finding a way to convey accurate information and realistic descriptions of sexual desire and behaviour between young people without rousing the censors was a particularly difficult task. One solution was to set stories in the distant past, when it was accepted that ideas about both sex and childhood were different. This approach is used by Naomi Mitchison (1897–9) in novels such as *Cloud Cuckoo Land* (1925). Set in antiquity, it not only acknowledges that young people are sexual beings but also that there are many kinds of sexualities. The story includes young characters involved in both homosexual and heterosexual relationships.

As the works that make up this section show, radical writers found ways to provide young readers with information about the sexual organs, sexual drives, and the sexual act from biological, psychological, and emotional perspectives. Readers of these works were told that sex is natural, important, and enjoyable for those who are well informed and responsible in their actions. How far readers could act on the information they were given depended to some extent on their educational, economic, and material circumstances, but the publications opened up aspects of behaviour that had long been secret and which were central to tackling the challenges of population control, disease, women's health, and family finances that affected the whole population. These books also offered insights that their authors hoped would make future generations happier, more creative, and less aggressive. In their efforts to liberate thinking and change behaviour, they epitomize radical children's literature. And if what is read in childhood affects thinking in later life, a case can be made for saying that the seeds of the sexual revolution were sown in their pages.

'SEX KNOWLEDGE'

Proletcult, March–May 1923

Written by Margaret Dobson

Margaret Dobson was the pen name of Tom Anderson, who has been mentioned at several points in this collection, and what follows is a second piece of writing by him which shows yet another side of the revolutionary education he promoted. This extract from *Proletcult*, launched by Anderson in March 1921 and discussed in the introduction to 'Little Peter' in Part Three, introduces another interest of Anderson's: sex education. Like many from left-leaning and progressive parts of society, Anderson was influenced by the teachings of the sexologist Havelock Ellis, discussed in the introduction to this part of the anthology. Like Ellis, Anderson was convinced that children—and, indeed, many adults—would benefit from the lucid and practical explanation of sex. He was in many ways in advance of his peers, certainly in his belief that sex was to be enjoyed equally by both men and women, and that children should be taught the facts of life at a very early stage.

'Sex Knowledge' was planned as a series of short articles directed at mothers to provide advice on how to deal with children's questions regarding sex, and it gives very clear instructions on how to do this. The central theme of the series is the exhortation to be honest with the child. Although the pronouncements against masturbation alongside the preoccupation with the pure child are disturbing to twenty-first century ears, these would not have been extraordinary to readers at the time. To understand its tone and origins, it is perhaps necessary to take into account the Christian background of the Glasgow working class. Revolutionary many of them may have been, but most would almost certainly have been brought up with strict Catholic or Presbyterian beliefs. What is remarkable in this text is the level of honesty that Anderson demanded that his reader exhibit on the subject, alongside his view that women are the equals of men in a sexual relationship. This is a belief that he expresses elsewhere in the journal in an article on morality. There he notes that the mainstream press decry the morality of the movement. His response is that 'our morality is not theirs. [W]e have said that "a girl in sexual matters should be on the same plane as a man." '

Printed here is the full text of the three instalments that were published before the series was brought to an abrupt end. Anderson's comments on this cessation make it clear that he was under pressure to stop producing the series. It was, of course, appearing in a periodical that had specifically been launched to appeal to younger children.

Anderson promised a pamphlet based on the articles, and that duly appeared in 1924. When it did, the material was regarded as so controversial that questions were asked about it in the House of Commons, and a case was brought against those responsible for its publication in the Glasgow Sheriffs' Court. Once an undertaking was given by the accused that publication would stop and that all copies in their possession would be destroyed, the proceedings were dropped. Although this caused immense financial problems, Anderson managed to carry on teaching and publishing revolutionary material until his death in 1947.

SEX KNOWLEDGE

NO I CHILDREN

Knowledge to all children is pure; it is only when we lie to them that we leave the imprint on their sub-conscious being that there is something impure or wrong in what we have told them. Thus we do a most grievous wrong by telling the child a pernicious lie about our sex life.

We cannot at the same time blame the mother for the telling of the lie to the child; all we grown-ups tell the same lie when we are asked by the child the same question. This lie is primordial in our being. Thousands of years ago the human did not understand the mystery of procreation, and so it was deified—it was sacred—it was the work of the gods, and there gathered round it a mystery which humans had no right to question. In every religion this is made manifest by their virgins and saviours. Our Christian story of the "Fall" only equals a mother telling her child that the little stranger that has come to the home "was brought by the fairies."

Nearly everyone of us can remember the episode in our life of the little sister or brother, as the case may be, coming to our home. We may have been five years of age, or seven or nine, when this event occurred, and as the friendly neighbour (I am writing of working-class life) was washing the little one we came on the scene. We were awe-struck. A beautiful little baby, larger than a doll and it was living and kicking and making faces. Its wonder to us was so great that we had to speak. And the first words we uttered would be: "Oh where did the beautiful baby come from, Aunt?" The aunt would smile and parry the question, and we kept looking at the baby and feeling its hands, and then its little toes. We look up again into Aunt's face and say: "Where did the baby come from, Aunt?" Then the aunt would look serious and say: "The doctor brought it to your Mammy in his black bag." The child was satisfied. It was thinking of "the doctor and his black bag." And when dear mother was getting better and nursing the little one, we look at it again and again, and the "black bag" would come up, and then we would say to mother: "Where did little Rosa come from?" Our little one by this time having been given a name. Mother would say: "The fairies brought it, my child." We were crest-fallen. Aunt had said the doctor brought it in his black bag. And we would look hard at mother, and poor mother felt somehow that we knew she was telling a lie. But to distract us she would say: "Kiss little Rosa."

This I think is a common example of every working-class home. The names told of the different fairies and bags and cabbages and flowers, etc., vary according to each district; but they are all in substance the same. The first pernicious lie we tell our child.

A week or so passes and, say, we are a little girl, and mother is washing the baby; and he is called little Dan. We are looking on, and we see something different from little Dan and ourselves, and we ask, "What is that?"—pointing to Little Dan's penis; and poor mother says, "You are not to be naughty girl and ask such questions." The child feels that there is something wrong but it cannot grasp it. "There's the doctor's black bag" and the fairies; and so the child moves away, but it is thinking all the time. The little one unknown to itself has entered the vale of that deceptive mystery—Sex.

We grown-ups think that our answers are quite sufficient for the child. But we lie both to the child and ourselves. The child knows now there is a mystery and it also knows mother has told a lie, and the child feels ever so uneasy.

COULD WE NOT TELL THEM THE TRUTH?

Most of us are unable; the past holds us too strong in its clutches, and we, the members of the working class have been so many generations in servitude that we look on it as quite natural. We may not know we are slaves, but we know we lie, our conscious knowledge of life tells us so. And many of us know the awful price we have paid for not being told the truth and it is this very thought that haunts us when we grow old.

Should we not tell the truth? I know all the objections used as an argument against telling the truth. And I also know they are all lies; and when they are not lies, it is cowardice or superstition. If you are a real man, or a real woman, you must tell the truth. Because you know that nothing but the truth will give you rest. Then, what does the truth mean?

I will try and tell you, mothers and fathers and children as I see it. And I will tell you in all reverence; for I believe the sexual union of a man and a woman is the greatest treasure on earth. But they must both be pure in the sexual sense. For the man or woman who has abused their sexual powers before mating can never hope to enjoy the blessedness of true sexual union. It is an impossibility. You might as well expect the habitual drunkard to be a man that a woman could love; and a sexual degenerate is lower than the lowest drunkard.

Supposing, then, a little baby boy comes to your home, and you have a little girl of, say of 5 or 9 years of age. In many cases the other child may only be two or three years old. The questions and answers will be slightly different, but the fundamentals will be the same.

The first thing you have got to do is to warn your nurse or your neighbour, as the case may be, who is attending you, that you want to tell your little girl where baby comes from, and just say to your friend "I want to tell the little one the truth and say, should she ask you, 'Mammy will tell you.' "

This makes your friends aware they cannot tell your little girl the fairy stories that are usually told. A good way would be to put this little article in their hands, it would save you a lot of trouble. And just by the way, let me tell you we mean to publish these articles in pamphlet form to be sold for 2d, and we think every man and woman of the working class should read them, and also every girl and every boy, for we shall deal with the trials and troubles of girls and boys starting on their sexual life, which generally begins about 14 years of age.

Supposing then you are washing your little boy, and supposing again you have given him his name, and you call him Dan. Your little girl comes to your side and she looks at the little one, and you can see from her that she is full of wonder: A real live doll, it can kick, squeal and throw up its arms, and do quite a number of wonderful things that is ever so amusing to the child mind.

Your little Rosa has been looking on all the time and she is in a very wonderland; and her little brain is bursting, and so she says to you in all innocence, touching your arm: "Mammy, where did little Dan come from?" You should just take your little girl's hands in yours and kiss her and say—Daddy and Mammy made little Dan.

CHAPTER 2—QUESTIONS AND ANSWERS

The answer which you have given your little girl, that "Daddy and Mammy" made little Dan, will appear to the child as the most natural thing in the world. Every child looks on its mother as the greatest of all on earth. But you will have to prepare yourself to answer further questions, for such a wonderful thing as a baby never leaves the child's mind.

Many mothers would say when asked the question, "God made little Dan." This is no better than saying that "the doctor brought it in his black bag." In fact, it is even worse. A child cannot understand God no matter how much you may teach it. Like the "black bag" God to the child is unknown. Your child only learns of God as it grows older. Then it succumbs to the superstition of its elders. But in childhood God is only taken on trust by the child just in the same way as the other stories. In all our Schools the children are taught that "God made them." The children listen to this in a far-off sort of way. They don't know and they try to think, but the problem baffles them, so they just let it go by. If the children were told that the King made them, and that the Queen was their godmother, they would be quite well pleased for, every child likes a fairy story, and somehow by an intuition, every child knows that a "fairy story" is only a "fairy story." They will tell you that if you ask them. Oh, they say, it was only a "fairy story," meaning by that they did not expect it to be real. "It was only about fairies," they say. But one day your little Rosa will say to you, just as you are dressing little Dan, "Where did you make little Dan, mammy?" or she may say, "Where did you keep little Dan, mammy, before you brought him here?"

This is a very difficult question to answer the child so that it will understand, but you must take courage in your hands and tell the child in the simplest way possible.

If you have a flower pot in your house with any kind of flowers growing, just ask her to bring it to you. A child perceives very quickly when it is given something to reason by. You say, to the child, "Was that flower always this size?" and in all probability the child will have noticed its growth, and she will answer "No." Then "It's growing," you say, and you explain that daddy planted a few tiny seeds in the flower pot some time ago, and they were ever so small, just about the size of a pin head, and so they grew and grew and came up through the soil you see in the flower pot. And just like humans they will grow to their full height, to their full bloom, and then they will grow no more. "That, my little Rosa, is a law of Nature."

"Daddy and I made little Dan the same way. A small tiny seed from daddy, not so large as a pin head, was planted in my body by daddy, and it grew and grew for nine long months, and at the end of that time little Dan was born."

"And I was made the same way, mammy?"

"Yes, my child. Every child that is born into the world is made by their parents in the same way. That is the reason I am your mother and daddy is your father."

"Mammy, the teacher at the school told our class that 'God made us.' "

"Yes, Rosa; your teacher was afraid to tell the truth."

"But, mammy, everyone in the class believes 'God made them.' "

"That is so, Rosa, but you must remember that at one time everyone thought our world was flat, because their priests and teachers told them so, and yet the world is not flat; it is round, and every child is taught so now."

"Does our teacher know, mammy, that he was made just in the same way as little Dan?"

"Yes, my child."

"Then why does he tell a lie about it, mammy?"

"He does so, my child, because his mother and father and the priest and the doctor told him the lie, and so he tells you the lie, just as he was told himself."

"But why should he not tell the truth, mammy?"

"He has not the courage, my child."

"Is it wrong to know who made you, mammy?"

"No, my child; I am telling you so that I might keep you pure."

"Should the teacher ask me, mammy, who made me what will I say?"

"I will write you a letter to give to your teacher, telling him what I have told you."

"But, mammy, will the teacher believe it?"

"Yes, my child. Your teacher is a coward as well as a liar, and when he knows that you know the truth he will never ask anyone again who made them."

"Mammy, should I tell anyone what you have told me?"

"Yes, when you grow a little older you may tell, and by and by I will tell you when you come to be a girl of twelve or thirteen years of age some wonderful things about yourself. These truths I am telling you now are the most precious truths in the world, and I want you to grow up a pure and noble girl, and to remember what I have told you, and never to speak in a slighting way about them, and you are only to speak of them to others so that you may be made purer and better."

Your little girl will understand all you have said by this little lesson, and the effect of it on her will be one of great reverence for you. She will be perfectly satisfied, and the knowledge she has gained from you will make her reverence what you have told her, because children are remarkably quick in perceiving a truth when it is told to them.

Weeks may pass before she asks you another question, but of a certainty she will ask one relating to baby Dan.

And if she should be watching you washing baby Dan, she will come to your side and look and take his little hand, and she will do just much the same as you do yourself. When you take baby Dan on your lap and you are rubbing him up with the towel (readers will understand I am writing of the working class, the rich don't wash or nurse their children, they have slave women of the working class to do that for them), your little Rosa will notice something different in little Dan from herself, and she has been looking and looking. Yes, her little brain is trying to formulate a reason for the difference; but she is beat, and every little girl is the same, and every little girl asks the very same question.

Your little Rosa will say, and say it in all innocence, "Mammy, why has little Dan got that there?" pointing with her finger to little Dan's penis.

Nearly every mother when she is asked this question says to her little girl, "You are a naughty girl to ask such questions; shame on you!" and she goes on with her rubbing the baby, and the result—it's another "black bag".

Now why should anyone tell a lie about their little boy's penis, or say their little girl was talking rude when she asked what it was? No woman would marry a man if she knew he had no penis, in fact, no man would ask to marry a woman if he had no penis for the simple reason that he would not be a man, and he would know it. What then should you tell your child who asks this question? You should say in a simple unaffected way, "That's little Dan's penis," just as that's little Dan's big toe, only the difference between Dan's toe and his penis is not clear to your little girl. She also has a toe just the same as Dan's, but she has not a penis, and your little girl is thinking, and that is the reason she has asked you the question. Ask your little girl to bring you the dictionary, and in most of cases girls of eight or nine years of age have one for school use. Now ask her to turn up the word penis. She does so, and spells out the word penis—"the characteristic external male organ." This answer to your little girl, taken from the dictionary, will give confidence from the fact that she can tell anyone the meaning which she has taken from the dictionary.

And so your little Rosa will be much further advanced in her knowledge now, and she may in quite a natural way ask you a further question or she may not, but sooner or later you will have to tell her, and if you think your child is not satisfied you should just say that it is through the penis the seed comes to make a little baby, and that is why a boy has a penis and a little girl has none. Your little girl will be quite satisfied with this answer.

Nearly everyone who objects to the children being told these things say it is hurtful as it lets the children know too much. The very reverse is the case. We have all in our beings a primordial inheritance, which acts for us unknown to ourselves, and the more we learn of ourselves the purer we become. There is not a man or woman in the world who has a true knowledge of their sexual natures that ever abuses them.

Our two million syphilitic men and women in our country to-day are the result of gross ignorance and superstition regarding sexual matters. There are millions of men to-day lower than the beasts. Go to any garrison town if you want to see an inferno, and if you go with your eyes open you will be astounded.

III—SEXUAL LIFE OF THE CHILD

The answers which you have given to little Rosa will be the means of quieting that stimulus which arises in every child, and especially in girls—the stimulus of sex. The life of the child and the sexual life of the child has only within recent years been studied by our physicians, but now all our leading physicians are all agreed that the sexual life of the child starts very early in life. They have divided childhood into two equal periods. The first period, from birth until the end of the seventh year. The second period, from the beginning of the eighth year until the end of the fourteenth year. This period ends childhood, and the next (or third period) starts with the fifteenth year up till the eighteenth year, and is called youth. At the end of this period, in normal children, full sexual growth has been acquired.

In all normal children, from the ninth year up till puberty, a detumescence impulse is growing, and that is the sexual impulse, and is accounted for by the growth of genital organs. So, when your little girl asks you a question which may surprise you, and a question which you yourself up to your marriage would have been unable to answer—you may be surprised, but you need not be dismayed; and both for your own good and for that of the child, you should answer the question honestly.

The average grown-up thinks a child of nine or ten years knows nothing about sex questions, and in this they are vastly mistaken. Children are very quick in picking up points in relation to sex. You must never forget that children at this age have sexual sensation; they may not quite comprehend them, but they are ever on the alert to find out.

Nearly every observant mother has noticed erection of her little boy's penis many a time during the first period of childhood, and in the same way she has also noticed her little girl rubbing her genital organ. The child is quite unconscious at this age, but after it enters the second period of childhood, a marked change takes place. The subconscious is always growing, and anatomical growth likewise, so that a propelling force is given to the child outside of any conscious knowledge on its part.

Thus children in the second period of childhood ask those questions of their mother which surprised their elders. It may be noticed that the development of boys sexually at this period is more passive; the reasons are obvious. Boys never become mothers; they have not the same inborn tendency, say, to nurse a doll, or play at being the mother; they don't clean up the house and set the table, or nurse baby, intensively as girls do.

There are many differences in sex which become apparent from the second period of childhood, but that does not come within the province of these short articles on Sex knowledge. We only want to give an elementary knowledge to every girl and boy on the difference of sex, so that we might be able to save them from falling into the pit falls of the several evils which surround them. There is no greater error than supposing that if you do not tell, the children will grow up pure and unconscious until they come to maturity. The evidence which our medical men have given to us on this subject repels such an idea. Many think that if girls and boys had a strict religious education that it would save them from degrading themselves. I am sorry to say that this is not borne out by fact. The sexual life of the child overcomes any religious instruction. Let me quote to your what Dr Albert Moll says on his "The Sexual Life of the Child.":

"By many persons an especial stress is laid upon the value of religious education, for the purpose of directing in proper paths the sexual life of the child and of giving help in the mastery of the temptation. But notwithstanding the fact that I value most highly a genuinely religious education, I feel that for the purposes first mentioned we cannot place reliance upon that which in our schools of to-day passes by the name of religious education."

"I have been personally acquainted with too many persons brought up on 'strictly religious' lines, adherents of the most diverse creeds, but chiefly Protestants, Catholics and Jews, whose religious education has been of remarkably little use to them in this respect.

"Among children I have known some who masturbated (self-abuse) immoderately, and yet their progress in religious studies is extraordinary. I have known serious epidemics of masturbation (self-abuse) in some cases of mutual masturbation in boarding schools in which the day's work was always begun with prayer and hymns. I note recently, another case has been reported to me of a so-called exemplary school, where the educational methods had a strong religious trend, and yet seduction to mutual masturbation played a great part."

From this statement of an eminent doctor, who himself is of a religious temperament, one cannot doubt that in so far as the sexual life of the child is concerned, religion is of no avail. Any number of cases could be quoted, and of evidence where called for, no better account could be placed before any court than the sexual immorality of the clerics. It is a standing monument of sexual degradation; we have authenticated proof of a bishop who was the father of 70 illegitimate children.

If Christianity cannot control grown-up men and women, what hope have we then of it having any effect on children? Absolutely none.

Children in the second period of childhood have often sexual dreams of which they had no previous consciousness, and the sensations are those akin to the voluptuous sensations which the grown-up enjoys; these dreams are of a very varied character, but they all demonstrate the coming of puberty. The child cannot understand them, and no one tells them, and so they carry the secret till some companion who has learned of masturbation seduces them, and so they are lost to the beautiful in life.

There are children who have been known to menstruate from one year upwards. We have had cases at all ages up to normal period of 14 years. In like manner we have abnormal boys.

Breschet, in the year 1820, reported the case of a boy three years of age who exhibited all the signs of puberty. "His voice resembled that of a young man. The length of the flaccid penis was 3 ¾ inches, its diameter at the root, 2 ¾ ins; the length of the penis when erect was 5 ¼ ins."

From this you will see what an enormous factor the sexual impulse is in the life of the child, and mothers should in every case try to get the sympathy of the child by taking it into her confidence; by doing this the barrier is broken down and the child is able to overcome those difficulties that it is sure to meet later on.

A classical description of her first nocturnal orgasm (wet dream) is given by Madame Roland in her "Memoires Particuliers, written during the last months of her life in prison in Paris at the time of the "Terror." She menstruated for the first time, she informs us, soon after she had been partially enlightened regarding sexual matters by her grandmother. Even before menstruation began she had experienced sexual excitement in dreams.

"I had sometimes been awakened from a deep sleep in a most remarkable manner. My imagination played no part in what occurred; it was occupied with far more serious matters, and my tender conscience was far too strictly on guard against the deliberate pursuit of pleasure for me to make any attempt to dwell in imagination on what I regarded as a forbidden province of thought. But an extraordinary outbreak awakened my senses from their quiet slumber, and my constitution being a very vigorous one, a process whose nature and cause were equally unknown to me, made its appearance spontaneously. The first result of this experience was the inset of great mental anguish: I had learned from my 'Phitothea' (the introduction to a 'Devout Life' by St Francis of Sale, published early in the 17th century) that it was forbidden to enjoy any bodily pleasure, except in lawful wedlock; this teaching recurred to my mind; the sensation I had experienced could certainly be described as pleasurable; I had there committed a sin; and indeed, a sin of the most shameful and grievous character, because it was the sin of the most of all displeasing to the Lamb without blemish and without spot. Great disturbance of mind, prayer and penances, for how to avoid a repetition of the offences; for I had not foreseen it in any way—but in the moment of the experience I had taken no trouble to prevent it. My watchfulness became extreme; I noticed that when lying in certain positions I was more exposed to the danger, and I avoided these positions with anxious conscientiousness. My uneasiness became so great that ultimately I came to wake up before the catastrophe, when, unable to prevent it, I would jump out of bed and, notwithstanding the cold of winter, stand barefooted on the polished floor, crossing my arms, and praying earnestly to God to guard me from the snares of Satan."

This is the experience of every normal girl and boy who has not been seduced.

SEX KNOWLEDGE

The articles on Sex Knowledge, owing to objections, will not be continued in 'Proletcult'. We have, much against our will, agreed to this so as to save our utopian friends. But the articles will be published in due course in pamphlet form, and all interested may secure a copy by writing to our bookstall or to Comrade I Nicholas.

HOW YOU BEGAN: A CHILD'S INTRODUCTION TO BIOLOGY

Gerald Howe Ltd., 1928

Written by Amabel Williams-Ellis. Preface by J. B. S. Haldane

Amabel Williams-Ellis (1894–1984) lived on the edges of a group of English aristocrats and bohemians who, over several decades, contributed to liberal or left opinion and artistic activity. Much of this is summarized by the single word 'Bloomsbury', a circle of friends, writers, thinkers, and artists who at times became more famous for their sexual and emotional experimentation than their political thought or art. The circle included such influential people as Virginia Woolf, E. M. Forster, John Maynard Keynes, and William-Ellis's cousin, Lytton Strachey.

Williams-Ellis was born into the Strachey family, though her mother, Henrietta Mary Amy Simpson, under the pen name Amy Strachey, was a writer and reviewer in her own right. Williams-Ellis's father edited the independent but generally right-wing magazine *The Spectator*, while her brother, John Strachey, was a Labour MP and co-founder of the Left Book Club (1936–48), an engine for socialist thought at this time. By marrying the architect Clough Williams-Ellis, Amabel took part in the extraordinary experiment of Portmeirion, a pastiche Italianate village in North Wales.

The Preface to the extracts is written by J. B. S. Haldane (1892–1964), who at various times and at various universities was a professor of physiology, genetics, and biometry. He was also the author a children's book *My Friend Mr Leakey* (1937). Haldane joined the Communist Party in 1942 and produced a stream of books and articles about science and society from a Marxist viewpoint. It is clear from this Preface how embattled the group of people writing about sex for children felt—and small wonder, given that mainstream British culture (along with that of many other countries) had developed its ideological outlook in relation to sex under the auspices of dissenting Protestantism. This body of opinion owed its origins to a view held by some seventeenth-century dissenters that all people are born with original sin, acquired through Adam and Eve's disobedience, sexual awareness, and, by implication, the sexual act to begin the human race and all sexual acts from then on. This idea, adapted, modified, and revived in Victorian times, lived on into the twentieth century in the form of highly restrictive attitudes to sexuality and the human body itself, in particular those directed at girls and women. It is no coincidence, then, the new frankness about sex came in part from an aristocratic wing of the Left and progressive movement (Bloomsbury), as the upper classes had mostly avoided Puritanism, Methodism, and dissenting Christianity. Even someone like D. H. Lawrence, the proletarian evangelist for new attitudes to sex, owed much of his frankness to his relationship with the aristocratic Frieda von Richthofen and outliers of the Bloomsbury group.

Williams-Ellis's text has a strong interrogative quality, as it tries to overcome the monologue of authorship. We find this feature across many of the non-fiction texts in this field, and in left and progressive texts even more so. It is also noticeable that Williams-Ellis uses children's questions, which might be seen as part of the movement to observe empirically children's speech and questions being pioneered by Susan Isaacs at this time.[1]

1. See, for example, Susan Isaacs' *Intellectual Growth in Young Children* (Routledge, 1930), which includes several years' study of children's questions.

PREFACE FOR GROWN-UPS

THIS BOOK HAS made me very angry, not with its authoress, but with the remainder of the human race, and particularly the biologists, including myself, who did not write it. For it is the only book of its kind, so far as I know—which is a scandal. If every child in Britain were to read this book, their average expectation of life would probably be increased by about a year, for hygiene is applied biology, and you cannot act hygienically if you have not learned to think biologically.

As this book is the first of its kind, I should have to commend it even if it were rather bad, just as I should commend an animal which learned to live at the South Pole, even if it was rather a poor sort of animal otherwise. As a matter of fact, however, the account of evolution given by Mrs Ellis strikes me as being more nearly correct than either of those two recently published by well-known scientific men. There are, of course, things that I should have put differently, and I should have stressed certain embryological facts which Mrs Ellis has omitted. But then no child would have read my book.

There are one or two ideas in the book which might well appeal to a grown-up biologist. For instance, it is a very good account of embryology to say that we spend the first six months of our lives in playing at being extinct animals. For there is a certain lack of seriousness about the changes in bodily form which we undergo. Our gills are not very good gills, for example. We play at being fish, but it is only play. We are inadequate fish at four weeks, just as we are inadequate savages at nine years.

The opinion is widely spread that biology is unsuitable for young children. I do not agree with it. I knew the differences between the main types of animal, and the names of most of my bones, when I was seven, long before I knew any but common-sense physics or chemistry. And, in my limited experience, children find it just as easy to understand simple things about animals as about machines.

CHAPTER IV

I

WE SAID AT the end of Chapter II that when you had been growing for four weeks you did not seem very likely to become a person because of your tail and your gills.

You had not got real eyes or ears, and there was not much difference between your head, and your neck, and your body. Your arms and legs were getting on, though.

By the end of another week your arms and legs would bend in the middle where your knees and elbows are now. You were growing a nose and lungs, too, but you could not bear quite yet to throw away your gills, but kept them a little longer as if they might come in useful.

You had not got proper nostrils, though, but only dents that did not lead anywhere.

Your eyes were fairly big, but only made of a sort of puckered skin. There was no beautiful hard eyeball, with lids and lashes and pretty colours. You grew these afterwards.

At that time, when you had been growing for about five weeks, you might quite easily have been mistaken for a pig at the same age—not for a grown-up pig, of course.

You had got only one lot of joints in your arms or legs, which were still very short.

All your bones were still soft. Your backbone was the best.

There still seemed quite a chance that your arms and legs would turn into flippers, and you be a seal, and swim in the sea, and flop about on the rocks, and have beautiful long whiskers.

Still, it was clear you were not going to be a fish, because of your nose and your lungs.

Your tummy and heart were getting on, too.

Nowadays you have a very grand tummy, with all sorts of pipes and tubes in it, and a regular factory going on of all sorts of things that you need—it is much grander than a fish's inside, but still quite like a pig's or a seal's tummy.

2

And now, what were you like after you had grown for about eight weeks?

You were still extremely small for one thing, not much bigger than a big horse-chestnut.

But you had decided some more things.

You were not going to have hoofs. Your tail had not quite disappeared; but you had begun to have fingers and toes.

So now you were not going to be a goat or a seal or a sheep or a deer; but something either with paws, or with hands and feet.

By now you had got eyelids, and a short nose. [...]

4

So now, in every little bit of you, thin, delicate white threads were beginning to grow, and to join together, and to reach along, either straight to your brain or to the big nerves inside your backbone:

Nerves for smelling.

Nerves for feeling hot and cold.

Nerves for hearing.

Nerves for feeling whether what your hand was touching was hard or soft.

Nerves for tasting.

Nerves for seeing.

These nerves take messages from all the different bits of you, and tell your brain what is going on.

Another lot of nerves, from your brain to the different bits of you, tell your toe or your hand what to do about it.

Smell nerve says to the dog: 'There's a delicious bit of meat close to me,' and quick as winking, brain flashes back to teeth, tongue and throat: 'Snap it up and swallow it!'

If you have got a dog you will see how quick that can be done. You can do it pretty quick yourself.

Or try another thing—to see how well the telegraphs work. Shut your eyes, and let somebody prick you gently with the point of a pin. You will feel the prick and can pull your hand away before the other person can count up to one.

By the way, the place where the person pricks you makes a small difference. You feel a little quicker with your toes or fingers than with your leg or back. This is because your toes and fingers have the most nerves. [. . .]

7

Several of the children who had the book read to them, said different things about what is in it.

A little girl of about seven . . . made a very sensible remark. She said: 'Why, you were once like everything!'

That is nearly true. We were once like everything in our line. We were not like ants or bees ever. But I thought it was a good way of putting it, which I had not thought of.

A boy called Joe, who was eight, said that a grown-up person's heart, with its four rooms and its doors, was just like a house.

Another little girl felt very sorry that she had shed her fur before she was born; and when the teacher came to the part about the fur-coated creatures keeping their babies inside them until they had been growing for some time, she said: 'Yes, how nice! Then, if a lion ran after the mother, she wouldn't have to go hunting about for the baby.'

Some of the children wanted to know whether other mammals, such as tigers, were jellies before they were born. The answer is, yes, they were. Every creature has to act through the whole history up to the sort that it belongs to. If it is only going to grow into a dog-fish or a lamprey, it does not act through very much of it.

'HERO-WORSHIP ADRIFT: FILM-STAR HERO OR GAMES MISTRESS?' AND 'MORNING GLORY (SEX IN PUBLIC SCHOOLS)'

from *Out of Bounds: Public Schools' Journal against Fascism, Militarism and Reaction*
Parton's Bookshop, 1934

Written by Phyllis Baker and Giles Romilly

Both of these articles for the underground student magazine *Out of Bounds* (see also Part Seven) are concerned with the effects of single-sex education and lack of information about sex on pupils in public schools. They stand out for the way they capture young peoples' voices and the open way in which they write about bodies and emotions, from crushes to masturbation and sexual experiments with other pupils. Together the articles show how different the atmospheres and attitudes were in public schools for boys, and those for girls.

Phyllis Baker details the over-heated emotions and excessive behaviours displayed by schoolgirls whose only available love objects were attractive young mistresses (no mention is made of girls who have crushes on other pupils). A more detailed and angry account of what happens when young people are kept ignorant about their bodies and desires is provided by Giles Romilly, one of the editors of *Out of Bounds*. 'Morning Glory' describes how teachers' warnings and oblique references created the kind of confusion and anxiety that led to sneaky searches for information in literature, and any other available source, resulting in cycles of desire, action, guilt, and despair. Unlike Phyllis Baker, Romilly discusses the tendency in single-sex schools for attraction between pupils and the possible consequences if these were acted upon and discovered—'beastliness' in boys was deemed deviant and greatly feared. The long-term damage caused by growing up in repressive environments is central to Romilly's argument, though the assumption in both pieces that co-education would of itself bring an end to misinformation and repression is unexamined.

HERO-WORSHIP ADRIFT FILM-STAR HERO OR GAMES MISTRESS?

By Phyllis Baker (Ashford High School)

GIRLS' Public Schools are notorious for "incidents." And seeing that they are allowed so few interests, it is scarcely to be wondered that the effects of their segregated education show themselves so remarkably on their unfortunate inmates. The latter have to find some object on which to concentrate their sex-emotions. This object is usually a film hero or a member of the staff.

If the object chosen is a film hero, the girl is not likely to be so degraded as in the case where she develops a "pash" on someone with whom she comes in daily contact. Nevertheless, a state of mind is produced which can hardly be called healthy. As film books are not allowed, the adoration must go on in secret.

There is a certain type of film star chosen by girls. He has a pleasant voice with a decidedly English accent, dark hair and eyes, wide shoulders, slim hips, a slouching walk and a dimple; in fact, he has sex-appeal.

...

But really this film star adoration is not more than childish romance, and cannot in any way be regarded as tragic. The other effect is far worse, that of developing an adoration for a member of the staff.

A certain type of teacher appeals to most girls. She is practically always a games-mistress (which speaks for itself); but she must also be young, fairly short, and essentially "sporty"; she must have fair hair, a good figure, shapely legs, and a very short gym tunic. She is followed about all over the school by a worshipping crowd of girls. They carry her hockey-stick or her tennis racquet, swimming costume, towels, games-registers, lists, and other sports gear. Another crowd, armed with cameras, goes ahead, stopping at frequent intervals to take photographs. Large bunches of flowers are picked, and expensive presents bought for this mistress; even her shoes are cleaned by the lucky one who secures them first.

These girls are absolutely sincere in their adoration; they mean everything they say or do, however hysterical or ridiculous. It is, to them, a great tragedy if they are punished or lectured by this particular mistress. They exaggerate it to such proportions that it becomes quite heart-breaking. Incredible though it may seem, there are cases on record where girls have committed suicide for this reason.

The authorities do nothing to stop this particularly dangerous form of "hero-worship." In fact, they are rather proud of it. They murmur complacently: "She is so popular with the girls, my dear Mrs. ________; I am sure your daughter will *love* having extra gym. with her. I will put her name down."

This article was not written as an advertisement for co-education. But surely, it needs very little intelligence to realise what a lot of anguish would be saved by educating the two sexes together.

MORNING GLORY

(SEX IN PUBLIC SCHOOLS)

By Giles Romilly

WHEN I first went to _________ I was totally uneducated in sex. The headmaster of my prep. School had told me the physical facts; but he had told them without comment of any kind. "You will develop a natural desire to embrace a woman," he had said. You may say it could not have been more lucidly put. True, but by themselves these facts seemed to bear so little relation to what I did and felt that they made no impression on my mind, and very quickly I forgot them. Beyond a—to me—meaningless warning against the dangers of Public School life my parents also told me nothing. The consequence was that I went to _________ knowing only that there was something called SEX—in holy capitals—about which one could not be too careful.

My knowledge was not increased by the additional lectures and admonitions I received during my first term. The Headmaster's address to new boys, although awe-inspiring, was hardly more than an injunction to avoid being found out. If its object was to impel us to mind our step without satisfying our curiosity as to the dangers we were likely to encounter, it was, I imagine, fairly effective. I, at least, came away wondering, frightened, and determined to be good. My tutor, an austere disciple of the Public School code, was also wary and reticent; his remarks on the mysterious Subject became so attenuated as to mean, for practical purposes, almost nothing. "There are men here," he told us, "who will try to take advantage of a man because a man is a new man." We listened with puzzled attention, and I doubt if any of us, if he had been previously as ignorant as I was, would have known that the subject around which he was so diffidently hedging was the same as the Headmaster had talked to us about in Chapel.

This was the sum total of my official sex education; the rest I had to find out for myself. Except for a sentimental attachment to senior boys, which hardly ever went beyond admiring glances in Chapel, I was not much troubled, my first year or so, by desires of the flesh; my contemporaries appeared as ignorant and apathetic as I was—we never discussed the subject—and so I was slow to add to my little store of knowledge. But at about the age of fifteen my latent sensuality began to be roused in three ways.

First, a boy was expelled from my dormitory; I had no idea what it was all about until my tutor spoke on the subject one evening after Prayers. He said it was always painful to him to see a boy expelled, especially one from his own dormitory, but the boy had been guilty of "grave self-abuse," and the surgeon's knife had been necessary in order that the dormitory might become whole again. These impressive words did not clear up my confusion, but they roused my interest and made me think. At last the dreaded "thing" had happened. At last someone had blundered. Why had the Headmaster been compelled to take the step he so much regretted? I had known the boy slightly, and found him pleasant; I could not imagine what was the terrible difference between us which had brought on him so horrible a fate. What had my tutor meant by "grave self-abuse"? Could it have anything to do with a "secret practice" in which I had myself indulged for years? I was extremely frightened, and sin-conscious for the first time. I vowed that I would cease this wicked practice altogether, or, failing that, I would take such precautions as to ensure that I should never, never be found out. I wondered whether the prefects had caught the boy red-handed, or whether the doctor had examined him, and discovered something disgracefully wrong; I was terrified of being suddenly summoned to the sanatorium myself; I could see the doctor sternly scrutinising my person, on which the tell-tale facts would be recorded, and my imagination played havoc with this unpleasant scene.

Secondly, since I was intellectually a precocious boy, I began to have friendships with boys two or three years older than myself, who were my companions in work; two especially I associated with. Their conversation was pure filth, and mine was as disgusting as I knew how to make it. Soon I knew a great deal; fundamentally, of course, I was ignorant, but I had picked up enough scraps and fag-ends of knowledge for a glib and precocious opinion on almost anything. I learned, for example, to fall in love with boys younger than myself; for a whole term I had a quite insincere passion for a boy who was similarly "loved" by the entire Army Sixth; I was fifteen at the time, and he was fourteen and a half. I kept a diary about him; it was a feverish piece of work, and entirely lacking in sense of humour. The last time I read it, about a year ago, it displeased me so much that I tore it into very small pieces, and put it into the waste-paper basket.

Thirdly, I was a precocious reader; I got hold of a portentous book called "Fiction and the Reading Public," by a woman called Mrs. Leavis; it became my literary Bible. Under its guidance I began to read Lawrence and T. F. Powys, and my sexual appetites were thoroughly aroused. At the same time one of my friends came on the mat before the Headmaster, and was asked to leave. In addressing him, the Headmaster had said: You young men think too much about your bodies; you read too much Proust and D. H. Lawrence." The remark might well have been applied to me; for Proust was another of my authors, and I supplemented him with Robert Graves, whose book, "Goodbye To All That," was banned from the local newsagent.

These three factors combined to create in myself a demand for satisfaction; it was a demand to which ________ could give no answer. Not only were all signs of sexual activity sternly suppressed, but many of the masters went out of their way to make trouble by opening letters, rummaging in drawers, and following their charges on walks. A few became notorious for the catlike way in which they would play with their unsuspecting victims, and then suddenly pounce when the horrid chain of evidence was complete. Naturally we suspected them of sadism and repressed homosexuality; their names became a symbol of obscenity. Their presence was an encouragement to flout them. We were indignant that such men should have charge of our education; we admitted that our approach to sex was probably not a healthy one, but at least, we said, we represented an intelligent reaction. For any defects in our own attitude we blamed the system.

...

Public School men are notoriously awkward and idiotic in front of women; they tend to idealise them or to regard them as prostitutes, and to be incapable of a sensible personal relationship. It cannot be doubted that this is the fault of the system, which separates boys from girls, and prefers that they should get their knowledge surreptitiously (through dirty stories, limericks, “Razzle,” etc., etc.) rather than by intelligent instruction.

'PHYSIOLOGY'

from *An Outline for Boys and Girls and Their Parents*
Victor Gollancz, 1932

Written by Winifred Cullis and Evelyn Hewer. Edited by Naomi Mitchison. Illustrator not identified

Victor Gollancz conceived the idea for the reference work from which this extract is taken. It was meant 'to help forward the new world' by introducing the 'citizens of the future' to the most up-to-date information about all the branches of knowledge he believed they would need to know to help solve the problems and challenges facing the world (Gollancz 1932 catalogue). He commissioned Naomi Mitchison (1897–1999), a new but already successful writer of historical fiction for children, to edit it. Mitchison was well connected politically (her husband became a Labour MP) and socially. She was also scientifically trained, and both her father and brother were distinguished scientists (her brother, J. B. S. Haldane, provided the Preface for Amabel Williams-Ellis's *How You Began*, reproduced earlier in this part). She used all her networks to persuade leading figures from all the arts and sciences to tell readers the current state of thinking in their disciplines.

Naomi Mitchison was herself a political activist with an interest in women's rights—particularly as these related to female bodies and reproduction. She spoke to groups of women about contraception and wrote a novel about abortion. Mitchison was one of those who believed that sexual repression was responsible for many of the ills of the world, and she wanted men, women, and young people to feel comfortable about their bodies and to enjoy their sexual lives when the time and circumstances were right. This meant having knowledge about how bodies work, how to avoid disease and pregnancy, and that there are many kinds of sexualities.

Her determination to have women's rights to sexual knowledge and pleasure recognized may lie behind the choice of two women to write the section on the body for *An Outline*. Winifred Cullis was the Professor of Physiology at the London School of Medicine for Women as well as a broadcaster and journalist. Evelyn Hewer was a medical doctor. Together they find a way to talk fully about how the human body works and refer to the pleasure of sex without becoming sensational or romantic or ideological.

FROM 'PHYSIOLOGY', SECTION V: GROWTH - REPAIR - REPRODUCTION

THERE is another difference between a young animal and a grown-up one besides the differences in weight, size, and proportions: an adult can reproduce its own kind. All living organisms have this power of reproduction, otherwise in the struggle for existence they would soon become extinct.

Many of the simplest organisms, consisting of only one cell, merely divide into two offspring; but except in these very lowly forms of life two different cells are necessary. The two cells fuse together into one, which then divides repeatedly, and in the end grows into a new organism like the original: this process of fusion is called fertilisation.

Sometimes both the cells needed are produced by one animal, but much more often they are produced by two different animals, which are then called male and female. Usually the male cell is deposited inside the body of the female, and here it meets the female reproductive cell, and the two fuse: this new cell, the "fertilised ovum," then ultimately gives rise to a new animal like its parents [...]. The fertilised ovum is sometimes deposited as an egg: in this case it has a protecting covering within which it divides and increases until it has become an organism capable of taking care of itself; then it breaks the shell and comes out. This happens in fish, amphibia (like frogs), reptiles (like snakes), and birds. While the egg is developing it is usually carefully protected, and in warm-blooded animals kept warm: this is why most birds prepare a nest for the eggs and then sit on the eggs until they are hatched.

But in the mammals the fertilised ovum develops actually within the body of the mother until the baby animal reaches a stage when it can live by itself if looked after, and then it is passed out of the mother's body—i.e. it is born. Some baby animals, such as guinea-pigs, can run about and feed themselves almost at once; others, like kittens and puppies, need their mother's care for some time after birth; human babies are like this. A kangaroo mother has a neat way of tucking all the family into a pouch in the front of her body, where they are quite safe and warm and can be carried about easily.

In the human the fertilised ovum grows into a little baby within the womb (or uterus) of the mother. Only mature organisms can produce the sex cells, and this development into maturity is what we call growing-up, or puberty. Until this time the differences between girls and boys are not very strongly marked, but at puberty all the changes occur that ultimately distinguish a man from a woman, and these bodily changes are controlled by special hormones. At puberty special activity of the nervous system usually occurs, and the sense of "sex" is developed in the girl or boy with the growth of the reproductive organs. All the changes that take place are really designed in a most wonderful way for the production of the sperm cells, for their meeting within the body of the mother, and for the development of the new baby within her body, and all these processes are intimately bound up with pleasure-giving emotions [. . .].

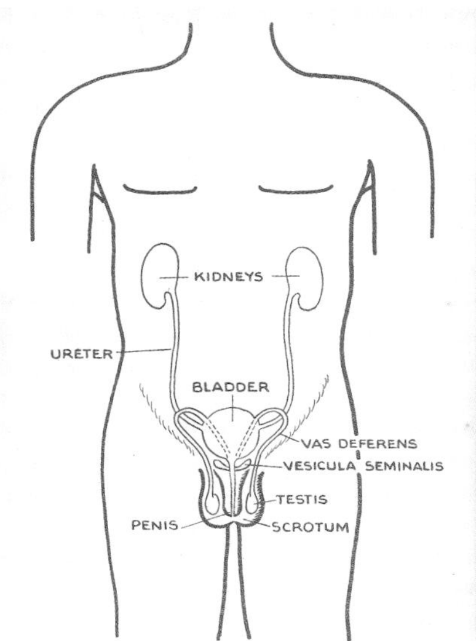

Diagram of male reproductive system

In the male at puberty there are certain obvious changes in the growth of the skeleton and of the hair, and also the "break" of the voice: but more important still is the development of the special sex organs, of which the most important are the two testes (see Fig 27). At this time the testis becomes much larger: it is an olive-shaped little body in the scrotum that at this time becomes capable of making and setting free the special sex cells. These cells, which are called spermatozoa, are very minute; each has a small head containing the nucleus and a long vibratile tail which enables it to move rapidly in a fluid medium. The spermatozoa are continually formed and set free in large numbers: they leave the testis by its duct, the vas deferens, and are temporarily stored: then periodically they are involuntarily passed down the remaining part of the duct or urethra (which also receives the urine from the bladder), through the penis, to the exterior. This sometimes happens in the night, giving rise to "wet dreams," and is simply nature's method of getting rid of the collected cells. The spermatozoa are mixed with secretions from the vesiculæ seminales and from the prostate gland, which are poured into the urethra. The penis is usually quite limp, but when the spermatozoa are to be implanted within the mother's body it becomes engorged with blood (by a reflex mechanism), and this makes it stiff, so that it may be introduced without injury into the female tube. The change in the penis is known as erection, and the coming together of the male and female for the purpose of introducing the spermatozoa into the female is called coitus.

In the female there are also changes at puberty in the form of the skeleton which adapt her for child-bearing later on; in addition there is the development of the breasts (or mammary glands) to provide food for the baby after birth, and there is the special development of the uterus.

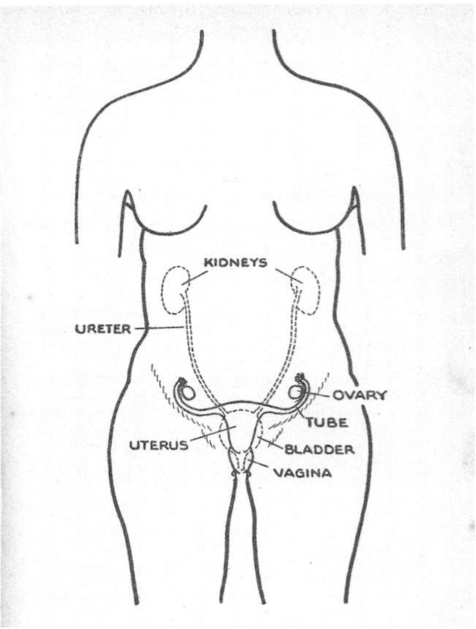

Diagram of female reproductive system. Note: The kidneys, ureters, bladder and its passage to the exterior are in dotted outline. The reproductive organs are seen in continuous line. The bladder and its passage lie in front of the uterus and vagina.

The uterus is like a nest in which the fertilised ovum will grow into a little baby, and a wonderful provision is made whereby the nest is newly prepared every time there is a possibility of an ovum requiring it (see Figs. 28 and 29). Every four weeks a female reproductive cell is set free from the ovary and passed down the female tubes, ready to be fertilised if it should meet a male cell. Every four weeks, also, there is an increased growth of the lining wall of the uterus, and an increase in the blood-vessels: then this extra tissue breaks down into the cavity of the uterus and the debris of cells and blood are passed out from the body as the menstrual flow: at once the lining is renewed, and at this stage it offers a newly prepared bed for the fertilised ovum. If such an ovum is present, it settles into the nest and is firmly fixed there by the healing growth of the uterus lining, and is thus provided with nourishment while it is developing into a little baby: during this period of development it is known as a fœtus.

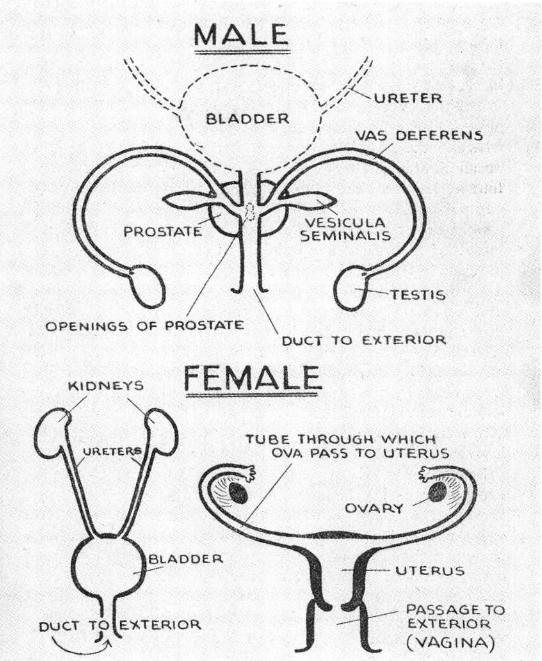

Male and female reproductive systems: explanatory diagram

So it comes about that menstruation usually occurs every four weeks, the changes involved being controlled by hormones, and represents nature's preparation for a developing ovum. If a fertilised ovum does become implanted, then menstruation ceases for a time, and the developing ovum is nourished by the mother's blood. The close connection between the fœtus and the mother is maintained by the development of a special arrangement of blood-vessels belonging partly to the fœtus and partly to the mother's uterus: this structure is called the placenta, and is attached to the fœtus by a cord carrying blood-vessels, and called the umbilical cord. The fœtus continues to grow within the mother's uterus, and in forty weeks' time it has developed into a little baby. Then it is born, i.e. it is expelled from the mother's body by strong contractions of the muscle of the uterus, and the umbilical cord is then cut, and the baby begins to breathe for itself. At the same time hormones are liberated into the blood stream that stimulate the mammary glands, and milk is secreted as food for the new-born child. After the birth of the baby the placenta is expelled as the "afterbirth," the process of menstruation gradually begins again, and possibly another little baby begins to develop.

It is very important that while the baby is growing within the mother's uterus the mother should have plenty of rest and plenty of good and suitable food, as her blood has to provide food for the baby as well as for herself. [...]

SECTION VI

FROM LIFE AND DEATH

The male places the sperms within the body of the female, and they swim along a tube to the eggs. Both sexes have a strong instinct to come together for this purpose, and in the higher animals the act of transferring the sperms gives a great pleasure to both which can be compared to the pleasure of eating. If eating were not in the slightest degree pleasant, a dog would not eat, and he would starve. If the transferring of sperms were not pleasant, he would fail to reproduce himself, and his race would die out. In the lower animals we have no proof of the existence of pleasure and pain, and quite possibly the transference of sperms takes place without consciousness.

ADVENTURES OF MICKY MONGREL. NO. 335

LAST week Micky's class at school went to see the Air Display at Hendon. Oh, what fun it was to be taken out for the afternoon instead of learning lessons, thought all the pups. But Micky was wiser. He knew that this was as much a lesson as any other—only this was a lesson on the glory and wonder of war instead of reading and writing.

This cartoon was part of a series about 'Micky Mongrel, the class conscious dog', which started in the Daily Worker from its first days in 1930.

PART TEN

VISIONS OF THE FUTURE

INTRODUCTION

Concern with the future is fundamental to radical children's literature; its makers and disseminators were dedicated to exposing the exploitation and injustices on which the existing world order was built. Their gaze was firmly fixed on a peaceful future world in which resources were shared equally, machines relieved humans of degrading and tedious labour, and people everywhere had access not just to the necessities of life, but also to recreation, culture, and the kind of education required to give people the skills they would need to inhabit a technologized future. Writing in 1934, Geoffrey Trease's *Bows Against the Barons* captures this sense of optimism with its vision of a time when 'the common people will have twice as much as they have now, and there will be no more hunger or poverty in the land' (102). This promise of better times to come may have been set in the Middle Ages, but its aspirations and expectations belong to the early decades of the twentieth century.

Trease was writing historical fiction; today readers are more likely to find visions of the future in speculative fiction such as science fiction and fantasy. There has been a distinct turn away from the optimism of early radical writing, however; in recent decades forecasts for the future have tended to be dystopian. Much recent young adult fantasy, for instance, imagines life after disasters brought about by human actions that usually stem from misuse of science or technology. Another difference in attitudes to the future is that between 1900 and 1960, most radical writing that forecasted what the world would be like in years to come took the form of non-fiction and, at least until work began on the development of nuclear weapons, it generally gave credit for improved ways of living to new scientific discoveries and labour-saving inventions. Far from seeing innovation as dangerous, as Part Eight illustrates, scientists, inventors, and engineers were often presented as heroic figures who improved life for the many. The philosophers, economists, and social scientists who argued for and offered new kinds of social relationships, new attitudes to work, and a new economic system were similarly celebrated.

For a time, it seemed that this new future was in the process of becoming a reality, and that the population of Soviet Russia was living the dream. This is certainly the impression given in the extracts from Mikhail Ilin's *Moscow has a Plan: A Soviet Primer* (1931), which was based on the US edition entitled *New Russia's Primer: Story of the Five-Year Plan*, and Olaf Stapledon's 'Problems and

Solutions', both reproduced in this final section. But by 1933, Adolph Hitler had seized power, Winston Churchill was issuing public warnings about German rearmament, civil war in Spain was brewing, the world learned about famine in Ukraine, and fears of a second, highly technologized global conflict likely to obliterate civilization seemed increasingly well founded. The effect of these developments on ideas about the future for those who had supported socialism, extolled the virtues of the Soviet model, and who found themselves accepting that it was necessary to join the fight against fascism after years of opposing war were profound. As Michael Rosen recalls in the Introduction, these events did not immediately sway those who for long had been intellectually, ideologically, and emotionally committed to the principles of communism and socialism, but by 1960 many on the Left in both Britain and the USA (where fear of communism was most obviously manifested in the McCarthy trials of 1954) had become disenchanted with the Soviet Union and no longer saw communism as a possible way forward. However, many of the hopes and aspirations for the future that had been laid down in the children who grew up between 1900 and 1950 were deeply rooted.

This takes us to a final and crucial difference between the radical works represented in this volume and mainstream writing for children. Both represented children as the innocent inheritors of a damaged world. In mainstream writing this tended to rely on a prelapsarian notion of a child's ability to heal and reform simply by virtue of its goodness; as a consequence, the passage from childhood to maturity was lamented. In radical writing, however, children's innocence was seen as offering a fresh start. With the right education, opportunities, and mindset, these works suggest, the rising generation would be capable of changing not just a few individuals, but the whole world for the better. And maybe, to some extent, they did. By 1960, those who were children in the first decades of the twentieth century had become adults with responsibility for making the future they had been encouraged to believe in, not least through radical books, songs, performances, and periodicals. The generation for whom these radical texts were written was responsible for seeing that the young Welfare State flourished, for making Britain part of Europe, and for placing it at the centre of popular youth culture and fashion. While the hopes and ambitions for lasting peace and global government may not have materialized, the vision of a more socially just, inclusive, and progressive society that lies at the heart of radical children's writing shaped Britain at the start of the new millennium. In the second decade of the twenty-first century, however, it is hard not to think that it is time for a revival in radical thinking—and the production of radical texts in every form and format, for young people.

'THE SORRY-PRESENT AND THE EXPELLED LITTLE BOY'

from *The Story of the Amulet*
T. Fisher Unwin, 1906

Written by E[dith] Nesbit. Illustrated by H. R. Millar

One of the earliest and most optimistic visions of the future in writing for children from the first decades of the twentieth century is found in E. Nesbit's (1858–1924) *The Story of the Amulet*. The story features the adventures of four children who discover one half of an ancient amulet that transports them to different moments in time as they seek its missing half. Most of the book tells what happens when they are taken to moments in the past, but in the final chapter they travel to the future, where they find everything much improved. For instance, instead of the notorious 'pea-souper' fogs associated with early-twentieth-century London, they discover a world of sunlight, blue skies, and beautiful gardens. Nor is this attractive future blighted by arbitrary rules or social divisions based on sex, class, or wealth.

Nesbit was a founder-member of the Fabian Society, which sought to introduce socialist reforms through education and consent rather than revolution. The hopeful vision of the future she offers at the end of *The Story of the Amulet* is grounded in the belief that life for the masses could be made more beautiful, less restrictive, more pleasurable, and more rewarding by combining better policies, planning, and practices with new technologies and scientific developments.

Nesbit's glimpse of what the future could be like comprises only a short interlude in a book which is primarily about the past. As the children hunt for the missing piece of the amulet they meet a variety of people from previous eras and come to understand that, unlike what they are taught at school, history is as much about the everyday lives of ordinary people as it is about rulers and key events. Their experiences subtly convey the understanding that the way things are is not the way they must be, and that humans of all ages, cultures, backgrounds, and races are responsible for what Nesbit's friend, the novelist H. G. Wells, called, the shape of things to come.

CHAPTER 12

THE SORRY-PRESENT AND THE EXPELLED LITTLE BOY

'LOOK here,' said Cyril, sitting on the dining-table and swinging his legs; 'I really have got it.'

'Got what?' was the not unnatural rejoinder of the others.

Cyril was making a boat with a penknife and a piece of wood, and the girls were making warm frocks for their dolls, for the weather was growing chilly.

'Why, don't you see? It's really not any good our going into the Past looking for that Amulet. The Past's as full of different times as—as the sea is of sand. We're simply bound to hit upon the wrong time. We might spend our lives looking for the Amulet and never see a sight of it. Why, it's the end of September already. It's like looking for a needle in—'

'A bottle of hay—I know,' interrupted Robert; 'but if we don't go on doing that, what are we to do?'

'That's just it,' said Cyril in mysterious accents. 'Oh, *bother*!'

Old Nurse had come in with the tray of knives, forks, and glasses, and was getting the tablecloth and table-napkins out of the chiffonier drawer.

'It's always meal-times just when you come to anything interesting.'

'And a nice interesting handful *you'd* be, Master Cyril,' said old Nurse, 'if I wasn't to bring your meals up to time. Don't you begin grumbling now, fear you get something to grumble *at*.'

'I wasn't grumbling,' said Cyril quite untruly; 'but it does always happen like that.'

'You deserve to *have* something happen,' said old Nurse. 'Slave, slave, slave for you day and night, and never a word of thanks....'

'Why, you do everything beautifully,' said Anthea.

'It's the first time any of you's troubled to say so, anyhow,' said Nurse shortly.

'What's the use of *saying*?' inquired Robert. 'We *eat* our meals fast enough, and almost always two helps. *That* ought to show you!'

'Ah!' said old Nurse, going round the table and putting the knives and forks in their places; 'you're a man all over, Master Robert. There was my poor Green, all the years he lived with me I never could get more out of him than "It's all right!" when I asked him if he'd fancied his dinner. And yet, when he lay a-dying, his last words to me was, "Maria, you was always a good cook!"' She ended with a trembling voice.

'And so you are,' cried Anthea, and she and Jane instantly hugged her.

When she had gone out of the room Anthea said—

'I know exactly how she feels. Now, look here! Let's do a penance to show we're sorry we didn't think about telling her before what nice cooking she does, and what a dear she is.'

'Penances are silly,' said Robert.

'Not if the penance is something to please someone else. I didn't mean old peas and hair shirts and sleeping on the stones. I mean we'll make her a sorry-present,' explained Anthea. 'Look here! I vote Cyril doesn't tell us his idea until we've done something for old Nurse. It's worse for us than him,' she added hastily, 'because he knows what it is and we don't. Do you all agree?'

The others would have been ashamed not to agree, so they did. It was not till quite near the end of dinner—mutton fritters and blackberry and apple pie—that out of the earnest talk of the four came an idea that pleased everybody and would, they hoped, please Nurse.

Cyril and Robert went out with the taste of apple still in their mouths and the purple of blackberries on their lips—and, in the case of Robert, on the wristband as well—and bought a big sheet of cardboard at the stationers. Then at the plumber's shop, that has tubes and pipes and taps and gas-fittings in the window, they bought a pane of glass the same size as the cardboard. The man cut it with a very interesting tool that had a bit of diamond at the end, and he gave them, out of his own free generousness, a large piece of putty and a small piece of glue.

While they were out the girls had floated four photographs of the four children off their cards in hot water. These were now stuck in a row along the top of the cardboard. Cyril put the glue to melt in a jampot, and put the jampot in a saucepan and saucepan on the fire, while Robert painted a wreath of poppies round the photographs. He painted rather well and very quickly, and poppies are easy to do if you've once been shown how. Then Anthea drew some printed letters and Jane coloured them. The words were:

'With all our loves to shew
We like the thigs to eat.'

And when the painting was dry they all signed their names at the bottom and put the glass on, and glued brown paper round the edge and over the back, and put two loops of tape to hang it up by.

Of course everyone saw when too late that there were not enough letters in 'things', so the missing 'n' was put in. It was impossible, of course, to do the whole thing over again for just one letter.

'There!' said Anthea, placing it carefully, face up, under the sofa. 'It'll be hours before the glue's dry. Now, Squirrel, fire ahead!'

'Well, then,' said Cyril in a great hurry, rubbing at his gluey hands with his pocket handkerchief. 'What I mean to say is this.'

There was a long pause.

'Well,' said Robert at last, '*what* is it that you mean to say?'

'It's like this,' said Cyril, and again stopped short.

'Like *what*?' asked Jane.

'How can I tell you if you will all keep on interrupting?' said Cyril sharply.

So no one said any more, and with wrinkled frowns he arranged his ideas.

'Look here,' he said, 'what I really mean is—we can remember now what we did when we went to look for the Amulet. And if we'd found it we should remember that too.'

'Rather!' said Robert. 'Only, you see we haven't.'

'But in the future we shall have.'

'Shall we, though?' said Jane.

'Yes—unless we've been made fools of by the Psammead. So then, where we want to go to is where we shall remember about where we did find it.'

'I see,' said Robert, but he didn't.

'*I* don't,' said Anthea, who did, very nearly. 'Say it again, Squirrel, and very slowly.'

'If,' said Cyril, very slowly indeed, 'we go into the future—after we've found the Amulet—'

'But we've got to find it first,' said Jane.

'Hush!' said Anthea.

'There will be a future,' said Cyril, driven to greater clearness by the blank faces of the other three, 'there will be a time *after* we've found it. Let's go into *that* time—and then we shall remember *how* we found it. And then we can go back and do the finding really.'

'I see,' said Robert, and this time he did, and I hope *you* do.

'Yes,' said Anthea. 'Oh, Squirrel, how clever of you!'

'But will the Amulet work both ways?' inquired Robert.

'It ought to,' said Cyril, 'if time's only a thingummy of whatsitsname. Anyway we might try.'

'Let's put on our best things, then,' urged Jane. 'You know what people say about progress and the world growing better and brighter. I expect people will be awfully smart in the future.'

'All right,' said Anthea, 'we should have to wash anyway, I'm all thick with glue.'

When everyone was clean and dressed, the charm was held up.

'We want to go into the future and see the Amulet after we've found it,' said Cyril, and Jane said the word of Power. They walked through the big arch of the charm straight into the British Museum. They knew it at once, and there, right in front of them, under a glass case, was the Amulet—their own half of it, as well as the other half they had never been able to find—and the two were joined by a pin of red stone that formed a hinge.

'Oh, glorious!' cried Robert. 'Here it is!'

'Yes,' said Cyril, very gloomily, 'here it is. But we can't get it out.'

'No,' said Robert, remembering how impossible the Queen of Babylon had found it to get anything out of the glass cases in the Museum—except by Psammead magic, and then she hadn't been able to take anything away with her; 'no—but we remember where we got it, and we can—'

'Oh, *do* we?' interrupted Cyril bitterly, 'do *you* remember where we got it?'

'No,' said Robert, 'I don't exactly, now I come to think of it.'

Nor did any of the others!

'But *why* can't we?' said Jane.

'Oh, *I* don't know,' Cyril's tone was impatient, 'some silly old enchanted rule I suppose. I wish people would teach you magic at school like they do sums—or instead of. It would be some use having an Amulet then.'

'I wonder how far we are in the future,' said Anthea, 'the Museum looks just the same, only lighter and brighter, somehow.'

'Let's go back and try the Past again,' said Robert.

'Perhaps the Museum people could tell us how we got it,' said Anthea with sudden hope. There was no one in the room, but in the next gallery, where the Assyrian things are and still were, they found a kind, stout man in a loose, blue gown, and stockinged legs.

'Oh, they've got a new uniform, how pretty!' said Jane.

When they asked him their question he showed them a label on the case. It said, 'From the collection of—.' A name followed, and it was the name of the learned gentleman who, among themselves, and to his face when he had been with them at the other side of the Amulet, they had called Jimmy.

'*That's* not much good,' said Cyril, 'thank you.'

'How is it you're not at school?' asked the kind man in blue. 'Not expelled for long I hope?'

'We're not expelled at all,' said Cyril rather warmly.

'Well, I shouldn't do it again, if I were you,' said the man, and they could see he did not believe them. There is no company so little pleasing as that of people who do not believe you.

'Thank you for showing us the label,' said Cyril. And they came away.

As they came through the doors of the Museum they blinked at the sudden glory of sunlight and blue sky. The houses opposite the Museum were gone. Instead there was a big garden, with trees and flowers and smooth green lawns, and not a single notice to tell you not to walk on the grass and not to destroy the trees and shrubs and not to pick the flowers. There were comfortable seats all about, and arbours covered with roses, and long, trellised walks, also rose-covered. Whispering, splashing fountains fell into full white marble basins, white statues gleamed among the leaves, and the pigeons that swept about among the branches or pecked on the smooth, soft gravel were not black and tumbled like the Museum pigeons are now, but bright and clean and sleek as birds of new silver. A good many people were sitting on the seats, and on the grass babies were rolling and kicking and playing—with very little on indeed. Men, as well as women, seemed to be in charge of the babies and were playing with them.

'It's like a lovely picture,' said Anthea, and it was. For the people's clothes were of bright, soft colours and all beautifully and very simply made. No one seemed to have any hats or bonnets, but there were a great many Japanese-looking sunshades. And among the trees were hung lamps of coloured glass.

'I expect they light those in the evening,' said Jane. 'I *do* wish we lived in the future!'

They walked down the path, and as they went the people on the benches looked at the four children very curiously, but not rudely or unkindly. The children, in their turn, looked—I hope they did not stare—at the faces of these people in the beautiful soft clothes. Those faces were worth looking at. Not that they were all handsome, though even in the matter of handsomeness they had the advantage of any set of people the children had ever seen. But it was the expression of their faces that made them worth looking at. The children could not tell at first what it was.

'I know,' said Anthea suddenly. 'They're not worried; that's what it is.'

And it was. Everybody looked calm, no one seemed to be in a hurry, no one seemed to be anxious, or fretted, and though some did seem to be sad, not a single one looked worried.

But though the people looked kind everyone looked so interested in the children that they began to feel a little shy and turned out of the big main path into a narrow little one that wound among trees and shrubs and mossy, dripping springs.

It was here, in a deep, shadowed cleft between tall cypresses, that they found the expelled little boy. He was lying face downward on the mossy turf, and the peculiar shaking of his shoulders was a thing they had seen, more than once, in each other. So Anthea kneeled down by him and said—

'What's the matter?'

'I'm expelled from school,' said the boy between his sobs.

This was serious. People are not expelled for light offences.

'Do you mind telling us what you'd done?'

'I—I tore up a sheet of paper and threw it about in the playground,' said the child, in the tone of one confessing an unutterable baseness. 'You won't talk to me any more now you know that,' he added without looking up.

'Was that all?' asked Anthea.

'It's about enough,' said the child; 'and I'm expelled for the whole day!'

'I don't quite understand,' said Anthea, gently. The boy lifted his face, rolled over, and sat up.

'Why, whoever on earth are you?' he said.

'We're strangers from a far country,' said Anthea. 'In our country it's not a crime to leave a bit of paper about.'

'It is here,' said the child. 'If grown-ups do it they're fined. When we do it we're expelled for the whole day.'

'Well, but,' said Robert, 'that just means a day's holiday.'

'You *must* come from a long way off,' said the little boy. 'A holiday's when you all have play and treats and jolliness, all of you together. On your expelled days no one'll speak to you. Everyone sees you're an Expelleder or you'd be in school.'

'Suppose you were ill?'

'Nobody is—hardly. If they are, of course they wear the badge, and everyone is kind to you. I know a boy that stole his sister's illness badge and wore it when he was expelled for a day. *He* got expelled for a week for that. It must be awful not to go to school for a week.'

'Do you *like* school, then?' asked Robert incredulously.

'Of course I do. It's the loveliest place there is. I chose railways for my special subject this year, there are such splendid models and things, and now I shall be all behind because of that torn-up paper.'

'You choose your own subject?' asked Cyril.

'Yes, of course. Where *did* you come from? Don't you know *anything*?'

'No,' said Jane definitely; 'so you'd better tell us.'

'Well, on Midsummer Day school breaks up and everything's decorated with flowers, and you choose your special subject for next year. Of course you have to stick to it for a year at least. Then there are all your other subjects, of course, reading, and painting, and the rules of Citizenship.'

'Good gracious!' said Anthea.

'Look here,' said the child, jumping up, 'it's nearly four. The expelledness only lasts till then. Come home with me. Mother will tell you all about everything.'

'Will your mother like you taking home strange children?' asked Anthea.

'I don't understand,' said the child, settling his leather belt over his honey-coloured smock and stepping out with hard little bare feet. 'Come on.'

So they went.

The streets were wide and hard and very clean. There were no horses, but a sort of motor carriage that made no noise. The Thames flowed between green banks, and there were trees at the edge, and people sat under them, fishing, for the stream was clear as crystal. Everywhere there were green trees and there was no smoke. The houses were set in what seemed like one green garden.

The little boy brought them to a house, and at the window was a good, bright mother-face. The little boy rushed in, and through the window they could see him hugging his mother, then his eager lips moving and his quick hands pointing.

A lady in soft green clothes came out, spoke kindly to them, and took them into the oddest house they had ever seen. It was very bare, there were no ornaments, and yet every single thing was beautiful, from the dresser with its rows of bright china, to the thick squares of Eastern-looking carpet on the floors. I can't describe that house; I haven't the time. And I haven't heart either, when I think how different it was from our houses. The lady took them all over it. The oddest thing of all was the big room in the middle. It had padded walls and a soft, thick carpet, and all the chairs and tables were padded. There wasn't a single thing in it that anyone could hurt itself with.

'What ever's this for?—lunatics?' asked Cyril.

The lady looked very shocked.

'No! It's for the children, of course,' she said. 'Don't tell me that in your country there are no children's rooms.'

'There are nurseries,' said Anthea doubtfully, 'but the furniture's all cornery and hard, like other rooms.'

'How shocking!' said the lady; 'you must be *very* much behind the times in your country! Why, the children are more than half of the people; it's not much to have one room where they can have a good time and not hurt themselves.'

'But there's no fireplace,' said Anthea.

'Hot-air pipes, of course,' said the lady. 'Why, how could you have a fire in a nursery? A child might get burned.'

'In our country,' said Robert suddenly, 'more than 3,000 children are burned to death every year. Father told me,' he added, as if apologizing for this piece of information, 'once when I'd been playing with fire.'

The lady turned quite pale.

'What a frightful place you must live in!' she said.

'What's all the furniture padded for?' Anthea asked, hastily turning the subject.

'Why, you couldn't have little tots of two or three running about in rooms where the things were hard and sharp! They might hurt themselves.'

Robert fingered the scar on his forehead where he had hit it against the nursery fender when he was little.

'But does everyone have rooms like this, poor people and all?' asked Anthea.

'There's a room like this wherever there's a child, of course,' said the lady. 'How refreshingly ignorant you are!—no, I don't mean ignorant, my dear. Of course, you're awfully well up in ancient History. But I see you haven't done your Duties of Citizenship Course yet.'

'But beggars, and people like that?' persisted Anthea; 'and tramps and people who haven't any homes?'

'People who haven't any homes?' repeated the lady. 'I really *don't* understand what you're talking about.'

'It's all different in our country,' said Cyril carefully; 'and I have read it used to be different in London. Usedn't people to have no homes and beg because they were hungry? And wasn't London very black and dirty once upon a time? And the Thames all muddy and filthy? And narrow streets, and—'

'You must have been reading very old-fashioned books,' said the lady. 'Why, all that was in the dark ages! My husband can tell you more about it than I can. He took Ancient History as one of his special subjects.'

'I haven't seen any working people,' said Anthea.

'Why, we're all working people,' said the lady; 'at least my husband's a carpenter.'

'Good gracious!' said Anthea; 'but you're a lady!'

'Ah,' said the lady, 'that quaint old word! Well, my husband *will* enjoy a talk with you. In the dark ages everyone was allowed to have a smoky chimney, and those nasty horses all over the streets, and all sorts of rubbish thrown into the Thames. And, of course, the sufferings of the people will hardly bear thinking of. It's very learned of you to know it all. Did *you* make Ancient History your special subject?'

'Not exactly,' said Cyril, rather uneasily. 'What is the Duties of Citizenship Course about?'

'Don't you *really* know? Aren't you pretending—just for fun? Really not? Well, that course teaches you how to be a good citizen, what you must do and what you mayn't do, so as to do your full share of the work of making your town a beautiful and happy place for people to live in. There's a quite simple little thing they teach the tiny children. How does it go…?

'I must not steal and I must learn,
Nothing is mine that I do not earn.
I must try in work and play
To make things beautiful every day.
I must be kind to everyone,
And never let cruel things be done.
I must be brave, and I must try
When I am hurt never to cry,
And always laugh as much as I can,
And be glad that I'm going to be a man
To work for my living and help the rest
And never do less than my very best.'

'That's very easy,' said Jane. '*I* could remember that.'

'That's only the very beginning, of course,' said the lady; 'there are heaps more rhymes. There's the one beginning–

'I must not litter the beautiful street
With bits of paper or things to eat;

I must not pick the public flowers,
They are not *mine*, but they are *ours*.'

'And "things to eat" reminds me—are you hungry? Wells, run and get a tray of nice things.'

'Why do you call him "Wells"?' asked Robert, as the boy ran off.

'It's after the great reformer—surely you've heard of *him*? He lived in the dark ages, and he saw that what you ought to do is to find out what you want and then try to get it. Up to then people had always tried to tinker up what they'd got. We've got a great many of the things he thought of. Then "Wells" means springs of clear water. It's a nice name, don't you think?'

Here Wells returned with strawberries and cakes and lemonade on a tray, and everybody ate and enjoyed.

'Now, Wells,' said the lady, 'run off or you'll be late and not meet your Daddy.'

Wells kissed her, waved to the others, and went.

'Look here,' said Anthea suddenly, 'would you like to come to *our* country, and see what it's like? It wouldn't take you a minute.'

The lady laughed, But Jane held up the charm and said the word.

'What a splendid conjuring trick!' cried the lady, enchanted with the beautiful, growing arch.

'Go through,' said Anthea.

The lady went, laughing. But she did not laugh when she found herself, suddenly, in the dining-room at Fitzroy Street.

'Oh, what a *horrible* trick!' she cried. 'What a hateful, dark, ugly place!'

She ran to the window and looked out. The sky was grey, the street was foggy, a dismal organ-grinder was standing opposite the door, a beggar and a man who sold matches were quarrelling at the edge of the pavement on whose greasy black surface people hurried along, hastening to get to the shelter of their houses.

'Oh, look at their faces, their horrible faces!' she cried. 'What's the matter with them all?'

'They're poor people, that's all,' said Robert.

'But it's *not* all! They're ill, they're unhappy, they're wicked! Oh, do stop it, there's dear children. It's very, very clever. Some sort of magic-lantern trick, I suppose, like I've read of. But *do* stop it. Oh! their poor, tired, miserable, wicked faces!'

The tears were in her eyes. Anthea signed to Jane. The arch grew, they spoke the words, and pushed the lady through it into her own time and place, where London is clean and beautiful, and the Thames runs clear and bright, and the green trees grow, and no one is afraid, or anxious, or in a hurry.

There was a silence. Then—

'I'm glad we went,' said Anthea, with a deep breath.

'I'll never throw paper about again as long as I live,' said Robert.

'Mother always told us not to,' said Jane.

'I would like to take up the Duties of Citizenship for a special subject,' said Cyril. 'I wonder if Father could put me through it. I shall ask him when he comes home.'

'If we'd found the Amulet, Father could be home *now*,' said Anthea, 'and Mother and The Lamb.'

'Let's go into the future *again*,' suggested Jane brightly. 'Perhaps we could remember if it wasn't such an awful way off.'

So they did. This time they said, 'The future, where the Amulet is, not so far away.'

And they went through the familiar arch into a large, light room with three windows. Facing them was the familiar mummy-case. And at a table by the window sat the learned gentleman. They knew him at once, though his hair was white. He was one of the faces that do not change with age. In his hand was the Amulet—complete and perfect.

He rubbed his other hand across his forehead in the way they were so used to.

'Dreams, dreams!' he said; 'old age is full of them!'

'You've been in dreams with us before now,' said Robert, 'don't you remember?'

'I do, indeed,' said he. The room had many more books than the Fitzroy Street room, and far more curious and wonderful Assyrian and Egyptian objects. 'The most wonderful dreams I ever had had you in them.'

'Where,' asked Cyril, 'did you get that thing in your hand?'

'If you weren't just a dream,' he answered, smiling, 'you'd remember that you gave it to me.'

'But where did we get it?' Cyril asked eagerly.

'Ah, you never would tell me that,' he said, 'you always had your little mysteries. You dear children! What a difference you made to that old Bloomsbury house! I wish I could dream you oftener. Now you're grown up you're not like you used to be.'

'Grown up?' said Anthea.

The learned gentleman pointed to a frame with four photographs in it.

'There you are,' he said.

The children saw four grown-up people's portraits—two ladies, two gentlemen—and looked on them with loathing.

'Shall we grow up like *that*?' whispered Jane. 'How perfectly horrid!'

'If we're ever like that, we sha'n't know it's horrid, I expect,' Anthea with some insight whispered back. 'You see, you get used to yourself while you're changing. It's—it's being so sudden makes it seem so frightful now.'

The learned gentleman was looking at them with wistful kindness. 'Don't let me undream you just yet.' he said. There was a pause.

'Do you remember *when* we gave you that Amulet?' Cyril asked suddenly.

'You know, or you would if you weren't a dream, that it was on the 3rd December, 1905. I shall never forget *that* day.'

'Thank you,' said Cyril, earnestly; 'oh, thank you very much.'

'You've got a new room,' said Anthea, looking out of the window, 'and what a lovely garden!'

'Yes,' said he, 'I'm too old now to care even about being near the Museum. This is a beautiful place. Do you know—I can hardly believe you're just a dream, you do look so exactly real. Do you know...' his voice dropped, 'I can say it to *you*, though, of course, if I said it to anyone that wasn't a dream they'd call me mad; there was something about that Amulet you gave me—something very mysterious.'

'There was that,' said Robert.

'Ah, I don't mean your pretty little childish mysteries about where you got it. But about the thing itself. First, the wonderful dreams I used to have, after you'd shown me the first half of it! Why, my book on Atlantis, that I did, was the beginning of my fame and my fortune, too. And I got it all out of a dream! And then, "Britain at the Time of the Roman Invasion"—that was only a pamphlet, but it explained a lot of things people hadn't understood.'

'Yes,' said Anthea, 'it would.'

'That was the beginning. But after you'd given me the whole of the Amulet—ah, it was generous of you!—then, somehow, I didn't need to theorize, I seemed to *know* about the old Egyptian civilization. And they can't upset my theories'—he rubbed his thin hands and laughed triumphantly—'they can't, though they've tried. Theories, they call them, but they're more like—I don't know—more like memories. I *know* I'm right about the secret rites of the Temple of Amen.'

'I'm so glad you're rich,' said Anthea. 'You weren't, you know, at Fitzroy Street.'

'Indeed I wasn't,' said he, 'but I am now. This beautiful house and this lovely garden—I dig in it sometimes; you remember, you used to tell me to take more exercise? Well, I feel I owe it all to you—and the Amulet.'

'I'm so glad,' said Anthea, and kissed him. He started.

'*That* didn't feel like a dream,' he said, and his voice trembled.

'It isn't exactly a dream,' said Anthea softly, 'it's all part of the Amulet—it's a sort of extra special, real dream, dear Jimmy.'

'Ah,' said he, 'when you call me that, I know I'm dreaming. My little sister—I dream of her sometimes. But it's not real like this. Do you remember the day I dreamed you brought me the Babylonish ring?'

'We remember it all,' said Robert. 'Did you leave Fitzroy Street because you were too rich for it?'

'Oh, no!' he said reproachfully. 'You know I should never have done such a thing as that. Of course, I left when your old Nurse died and—what's the matter!'

'Old Nurse *dead?*' said Anthea. 'Oh, no!'

'Yes, yes, it's the common lot. It's a long time ago now.'

Jane held up the Amulet in a hand that twittered.

'Come!' she cried, 'oh, come home! She may be dead before we get there, and then we can't give it to her. Oh, come!'

'Ah, don't let the dream end now!' pleaded the learned gentleman.

'It must,' said Anthea firmly, and kissed him again.

'When it comes to people dying,' said Robert, 'good-bye! I'm so glad you're rich and famous and happy.'

'*Do* come!' cried Jane, stamping in her agony of impatience.

And they went. Old Nurse brought in tea almost as soon as they were back in Fitzroy Street. As she came in with the tray, the girls rushed at her and nearly upset her and it.

'Don't die!' cried Jane, 'oh, don't!' and Anthea cried, 'Dear, ducky, darling old Nurse, don't die!'

'Lord, love you!' said Nurse, 'I'm not agoin' to die yet a while, please Heaven! Whatever on earth's the matter with the chicks?'

'Nothing. Only don't!'

She put the tray down and hugged the girls in turn. The boys thumped her on the back with heartfelt affection.

'I'm as well as ever I was in my life,' she said. 'What nonsense about dying! You've been a sitting too long in the dusk, that's what it is. Regular blind man's holiday. Leave go of me, while I light the gas.'

The yellow light illuminated four pale faces.

'We do love you so,' Anthea went on, 'and we've made you a picture to show you how we love you. Get it out, Squirrel.'

The glazed testimonial was dragged out from under the sofa and displayed.

'The glue's not dry yet,' said Cyril, 'look out!'

'What a beauty!' cried old Nurse. 'Well, I never! And your pictures and the beautiful writing and all. Well, I always did say your hearts was in the right place, if a bit careless at times. Well! I never did! I don't know as I was ever pleased better in my life.'

She hugged them all, one after the other. And the boys did not mind it, somehow, that day.

*

'How is it we can remember all about the future, *now?*' Anthea woke the Psammead with laborious gentleness to put the question. 'How is it we can remember what we saw in the future, and yet, when we *were* in the future, we could not remember the bit of the future that was past then, the time of finding the Amulet?'

'Why, what a silly question!' said the Psammead, 'of course you cannot remember what hasn't happened yet.'

'But the *future* hasn't happened yet,' Anthea persisted, 'and we remember that all right.'

'Oh, that isn't what's happened, my good child,' said the Psammead, rather crossly, 'that's prophetic vision. And you remember dreams, don't you? So why not visions? You never do seem to understand the simplest thing.'

It went to sand again at once.

Anthea crept down in her nightgown to give one last kiss to old Nurse, and one last look at the beautiful testimonial hanging, by its tapes, its glue now firmly set, in glazed glory on the wall of the kitchen.

'Good-night, bless your loving heart,' said old Nurse, 'if only you don't catch your deather-cold!'

MOSCOW HAS A PLAN: A SOVIET PRIMER

Translated from the Russian by George S. Counts and Nucia P. Lodge (English translation first published by Houghton Mifflin Harcourt, 1931)

Written by M. Ilin. Illustrated by William Kermode

The contribution of Mikhail Ilin, pen name of Il'ya Yakovlevich Marshak (1895–1953), to radical writing for children is discussed in the introduction to his book *Black on White*, in Part Eight. Here we reproduce a section of what is arguably his best-known work in the West. *Rasskaz o velikom plane*, published in the Soviet Union in 1930, was translated into English under different titles by both US and British publishers. Both versions came out in 1931; the British one was given the title *Moscow Has a Plan: A Soviet Primer* and published for children, while the US version was published as *New Russia's Primer: The Story of the Five-Year Plan*, and aimed at teachers and other interested adults. This was a highly political book, which set out to explain the concept of a planned economy and to describe the immense efforts of the Soviet people to make the first Five-Year Plan a success. The translation of this text was valued in the West, where information on the USSR was highly sought after and the appetite for details of the innovations in the social, economic, and education systems was keen. The book was prized, not only for the information it contained, but also for the originality of its style and approach to the education of its readers as it 'communicate[s] to children a breathless, value-laden excitement about the Great Plan' (Henry 1960, 273).

The extract included here contrasts the way people used to live with the future the plan was intended to bring into being. Here and throughout Ilin's text, science in all its forms is regarded as the driver for making life healthier and more enjoyable for all.

XII. NEW PEOPLE

1. A FRAGMENT FROM A BOOK TO BE WRITTEN FIFTY YEARS HENCE

THEY lived in crowded dwellings with little windows, with dark, dirty corridors, with low ceilings. Of every five or six persons, one had to sweep and scrub the floors, cook the food, go marketing, wash clothes, nurse the children. With rare exceptions this work was done by women, the so-called "housekeepers." At that time there were already on the market such inventions as mechanical potato-peelers, meat-choppers, dish-washers, clothes-cleaners, and other devices. But in spite of this, millions of women continued to work with their hands. Small wonder that even by toiling fifteen or sixteen hours a day they were unable to finish their work. Rooms were cleaned thoroughly only twice a year, on the eve of great holidays. Children were always unkempt and ragged. Food was prepared carelessly, was tasteless and deficient in nourishment. Not one house-keeper knew the number of calories contained in two pounds of cabbage or a quart of milk. The cooking of the food was done in a "kitchen," that is, a small crowded room. Steam kettles were altogether lacking and food was cooked over an open fire. An unheard-of amount of wood was consumed in the process—in those days they still used wood for fuel. The food often burned, and a suffocating smoke spread through the rest of the house. Here in the kitchen also was a garbage pail to hold the wastes of production: potato peelings, herring tails, bones, and so on. During the day this refuse poisoned the air: not until evening was it emptied into a kind of half-closed garbage hole in the yard. No one thought of turning the wastes of the kitchen into fertilizers or to some other useful purpose.

As a rule every room in the house was heated separately. Very few homes were equipped with central heating systems. Even as late as 1930 there were open fireplaces and stoves in nearly every house in Great Britain. This wasted enormous quantities of fuel and was dirty.

The furniture in the rooms was heavy, clumsy, and uncomfortable. Light metal furniture was then almost unknown. The most popular chairs and sofas were covered with cloth and filled with hair or sawdust. In order to raise a great cloud of dust all you had to do was to tap lightly the seat of one of these articles of furniture. On the floor they laid pieces of thick carpet. On the walls they hung little shelves and pictures. The windows, besides being small, were screened with curtains which shut out much light. All of these things were done even though the fact had already been established that dust is a source of disease. If you examine dust under a microscope, you will find that it contains the microbes of various maladies, particles of human skin, tiny bits of clothing, and other dangerous things. Yet no one seemed to realize that dust is a social enemy as terrible as flood or fire.

The houses in which people lived were completely unsuited to rest after the work of the day. In one crowded apartment they read, cooked their food, prepared for examinations, washed their clothes, received their guests, nursed their children. When they returned home exhausted from their labours, they were unable to find the rest they needed to renew their energy and vigour for the following day.

In the majority of families, children had no care during the entire day because their mothers were at work outside the home or busy with household duties. Every large building boasted a yard which was somewhat like a well surrounded by four stone walls. In this yard there was usually a hole to receive the refuse from the kitchen. And this dark place, without sunlight, without trees, and without grass, was the children's playground.

Still worse lived the people in the villages. One political leader wrote as follows at the beginning of the twentieth century:

"Most of the peasant huts are eighteen by twenty-one feet. In such a hut are housed on the average about seven people, but there are huts—little cages—no larger than twelve feet square. The stove occupies about one-fifth of the total air space. It plays here a tremendous role in the life and the economy of the family. Not only do the peasants warm themselves by it, but they also sleep on it and use it for drying clothes, shoes, grain, hemp. Not only do they bake and cook with the stove, but they also depend upon it for steam baths. And under the stove chickens, calves, and sheep are often protected from the frosts of winter. Not infrequently the cow is also brought into the hut at the time of calving. Practically the only furniture is a table which serves both cooking and dining purposes. On this table too all kinds of housework are done, harness repaired, clothes are made and mended. A common saying among the peasants is: 'We are so poor that we haven't even anything with which to feed the cockroaches.'"

Thus lived millions of people. And the remarkable thing is not that they existed, but that they did not all die.

2. NEW LIFE AND NEW PEOPLE

All this will be written about us a few decades hence.

We live badly. We change nature, but as yet we have not changed our own selves. And this is the most essential thing. Why have we begun this tremendous task which will take not five, but fifteen, twenty, and perhaps more years? Why do we mine millions of tons of coal and ore? Why do we build millions of machines? Do we do these things merely in order to change nature?

No, we change nature in order that people may live better.

We need machines in order that we may work less and accomplish more. By the end of the Five Year Plan the working day in a factory will be reduced by 50 minutes. If we assume that the working year consists of 273 days (not counting rest days and holidays), the worker will labour 227 hours a year less than he did at the beginning of the plan. And 227 hours is almost 73 seven-hour working days.

He will work less and yet accomplish more. During seven hours in the factory he will do what now requires eleven-and-a-half hours.

And if this is so, his wages will be raised by fifty per cent.

In comparison with conditions before the revolution, every worker will labour three hours less a day and yet will receive twice as much pay.

But this is not all. Work will be made easier. No longer will there be bent backs, strained muscles, swollen veins on the forehead. Loads will travel, not on people's backs, but over conveyers. The heavy crowbar and hoe will give place to the pneumatic hammer and compressed air.

Instead of dark, gloomy shops with dim, yellow lamps there will be light, clean halls with great windows and beautiful tile floors. Not the lungs of men, but powerful ventilators will suck in and swallow the dirt, dust, and shavings of the factories. Workers will be less fatigued after a day's labour. There will be fewer "occupational" diseases. Think of all the people who die now of these illnesses! Every metal-worker has lungs eaten up by metal dust. You can always tell a blacksmith by his pale face, a stoker by his red inflamed eyes.

After we build socialism, all will have equally healthy faces. Men will cease to regard work as a punishment, a heavy obligation. They will labour easily and cheerfully.

But if work will be a joy, rest will be a double joy.

In such houses even cockroaches refuse to live. This picture was taken long ago, before the revolution

Can one rest now in a crowded and noisy home amid the hissing of oil burners, the smoke of the kitchen, the drying of wet cloths, the filth of dim windows, dirty furniture, spittle-spattered floors and with unwashed dishes on the table!

After all, man is not just muscles with which to work. He is not a machine. He has a mind that wants to know, eyes that want to see, ears that want to hear, a voice that wants to sing, feet that want to run, to jump, to dance, hands that want to row, to

swim, to throw, to catch. And we must organize life so that not merely certain lucky ones, but all may be able to feel the joy of living.

After socialism is built there will no longer be dwarfs—people with exhausted, pale faces, people reared in basements without sunshine or air. Healthy, strong giants, red-cheeked and happy—such will be the new people.

But to accomplish this we must have new cities and new houses. Our whole life, even to the last kitchen pot, must be changed.

At every entrance you will be greeted by green giants—oaks, pines, lime trees.

Happy singing of birds and the calm, sustained, refreshing voice of trees, instead of the present clang and rumble and roar, will be heard in the streets of the city.

There will be none of that incessant bustle and scramble which now shatter the nerves of all of us city dwellers.

Institutions will be situated far from dwellings. People must live in quiet and peaceful places.

There will be less traffic in the streets and no such colossal cities as we now have. A city of one hundred thousand inhabitants will be considered too large.

Every future city will be a workers' village near a factory. And factories and unions of factories will not all be brought together in one centre as at present: they will be distributed throughout the entire country according to a rational plan. Our raw materials are found, not in one place either, but in a thousand places.

This is the way a city will be built. But how about the village?

There will be no village. Bread and meat and milk will be secured from factories in govfarms and colfarms. Around each of these agricultural factories other factories will be constructed—food, flour, conserve, meat, refrigeration. All of these will constitute a single union of factories, but agricultural rather than industrial. And around each of these unions a city will rise—an agricultural city. This means that the difference between city and village, between peasant and workman, will disappear. Even the words *peasant* and *labourer* will pass away.

Only the word *worker* will remain.

This will happen after we construct socialism. But already during these five years we shall build about two hundred socialist cities, thousands of house-communes. Already the difference between city and village is being effaced.

Socialism is no longer a myth, a fantasy of the mind. We ourselves are building it.

But the task of building socialism is not easy.

We are surrounded on all sides by enemies.

Like the builders at Dnieprostroy we have raised protecting walls around us. But any minute the water may break through the walls, rush into the enclosure, overturn and destroy everything that we have done.

And that is why the work must go on so rapidly and with such concentration.

More quickly must be erected the stone dams of factories and mills. More quickly, because time does not wait.

If we try hard enough we can fulfil the Five Year Plan, not in five, but in four years, or even sooner.

[...]

5. THE LITTLE FIVE YEAR PLAN AND THE BIG FIVE YEAR PLAN

Do not imagine that the Five Year Plan is wholly the work of grown-ups.

Every child can be a builder of the Five Year Plan.

"The Lysvensky Factory Children's Brigade constructed a water and a wind mill and started a dynamo.

"On the Briansk road ten miles from Moscow in the village Peredelkino, the Khamovnichensky Region Children's Brigade electrified their camp. They dammed a small river, set up a water wheel, attached to it a small dynamo from a cinema apparatus, stretched wires to the camp, and henceforth illuminated their tents with electricity during the darkness of the summer nights.

"The youngsters of Ribinsk, while studying their own region, found deposits of lime which is entirely suited for use as fertilizer. The Novosiberian Comsov-youths' and Children's Brigades discovered resources worth many millions of pounds sterling. They went on a scouting expedition and stumbled upon beds of coal and iron.

"On the outskirts of Moscow a children's city working independently built a macadam road approximately three hundred yards long and planted apple trees on either side.

"The children of the Zherdevsky Colfarm collected apple-cores and planted the seeds. They thus started a fruit orchard. Next year they will supply every household with valuable cuttings."

All these accounts I have taken from the report of the Children's Brigade Rally. There are dozens of such items in the report.

You thus see how children can help achieve the Five Year Plan. Fulfil your own little plan and then the big plan will be fulfilled before the assigned time. Whether it will be a task which requires a few days or a few weeks matters not: it will be your contribution.

Here it is—the Children's Five Year Plan:

(1) To discover beds of lime and phosphorus.

(2) To gather useful junk: rags, ropes, wool, bones, scraps of metal, and so on. All of these things will come in handy in our factories. Every child should collect not less than forty pounds a year.

(3) To build wireless sets and loud-speakers. Within the next few years seventy-five thousand wireless sets should be installed in villages. Not one school should be without a loud-speaker.

(4) To learn to get full marks for sorting grain grown on your parents' farms, for seed.

(5) To gather ashes for fertilizing fields. Each Children's Brigade should gather two tons of ashes a year.

(6) To destroy ten marmots a year in the regions infested by these animals; to clear one-fifth of an acre of land of parasites; to destroy all injurious insects on one fruit tree and on ten vegetables; to catch or destroy five rats and ten mice.

(7) To build one starling house and two feeding houses a year; to raise the number of starling houses to a million and a half and of feeding houses to two millions. Birds are our allies: they will help us destroy parasites.

(8) To organize in five years, five thousand children's bird-preserving clubs, to found five thousand collective bird preserves, and to build five thousand chicken houses.

(9) To add two good laying hens to the possessions of every peasant household.

(10) To plant ten trees each in five years; to create Children's Brigade forests of seventy-five million trees.

(11) To destroy bedbugs, cockroaches, and flies in five hundred thousand houses. Each troop should clean up ten houses.

(12) To teach the illiterate to read and write. Each troop should endeavour to wipe out illiteracy in its region.

These are only some of the chief tasks for children. If you wish to learn the details, read "The Report of the Children's Brigade Rally."

Grown-ups will build large electric stations; children can build small ones. Grown-ups will build large houses; children can build starling houses and bird-feeding houses.

And do not imagine that these are trifles.

If children fulfil their Five Year Plan, they will save from parasites grain worth £400,000.

If children add two good laying hens each to the possessions of each household, they will make a present to the State of five billion eggs, £20,000,000.

From pennies, millions are composed; weak hands, if they be many, can move mountains and plant forests of trees.

Herein lies the power of children.

'PROBLEMS AND SOLUTIONS'

from *An Outline for Boys and Girls and Their Parents*,
ed. Naomi Mitchison
Victor Gollancz, 1932

Written by Olaf Stapledon. Illustrator not identified

Olaf Stapledon (1886–1950) was a philosopher, futurologist, and writer who taught that civilizations are caught in a perpetual series of cycles of advancement and self-destruction, each cycle being more spectacular at both extremes than the last. This view coloured his predictions for the future as set out in *An Outline for Boys and Girls and Their Parents*, an ambitious and contentious reference book edited by Naomi Mitchison (1897–1999) for the publisher, Victor Gollancz.[1]

'Problems and Solutions' sets out a progressive vision of how governments and nations, economists and the military, health services and schools, people, and families of all ages and backgrounds could come together to make life better and more secure for all. Without total reform on a global scale, Stapledon predicted, another world war was inevitable. Such a war, he warned, would be 'far worse than the last' (720), involving bombs, poison gases, and other weapons developed since the last war to damage enemy populations, including children.

As well as identifying the problems that he believed needed to be solved before the hoped-for future could be achieved, the piece provides suggestions and vignettes speculating about what that future might be like. Most are based on Stapledon's understanding of how society was being reorganized in the Soviet Union; from parent–child relationships through systems of managing work, to a fully accountable, Communist government. While many of his predictions came true, he was soon to be disabused of the ideal nature of the Soviet system.

1. Mitchison's volume is discussed in detail in Kimberley Reynolds's *Left Out: The Forgotten Tradition of Radical Publishing for Children* (2016).

PROBLEMS AND SOLUTIONS

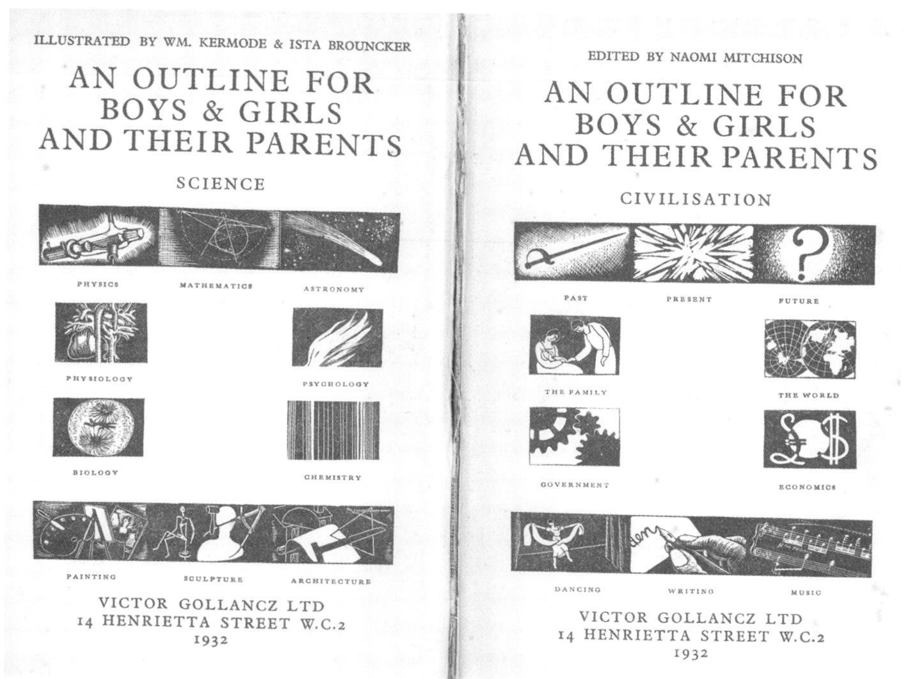

ILLUSTRATED BY WM. KERMODE & ISTA BROUNCKER

AN OUTLINE FOR BOYS & GIRLS AND THEIR PARENTS

SCIENCE

PHYSICS MATHEMATICS ASTRONOMY

PHYSIOLOGY PSYCHOLOGY

BIOLOGY CHEMISTRY

PAINTING SCULPTURE ARCHITECTURE

VICTOR GOLLANCZ LTD
14 HENRIETTA STREET W.C.2
1932

EDITED BY NAOMI MITCHISON

AN OUTLINE FOR BOYS & GIRLS AND THEIR PARENTS

CIVILISATION

PAST PRESENT FUTURE

THE FAMILY THE WORLD

GOVERNMENT ECONOMICS

DANCING WRITING MUSIC

VICTOR GOLLANCZ LTD
14 HENRIETTA STREET W.C.2
1932

A4. THE KIND OF WORLD WE WANT

[...] To-day people have very different ideas about what the world should be like. Most do not care what it is like so long as their own nation or their own social class is prosperous. And so the world as a whole is an ugly muddle, full of unnecessary pain and hate. But the world which we want to make must be of such a pattern that it will seem right to every kind of person.

[...] But we have not only to want it. We must fight for it, in one way or another. If we are to do this, we must care for it very much. And, so as to care for it, we must try to see it with the mind's eye. We must imagine as clearly and fully as we can the world that we want to make. It must come alive in our hearts. We must help everyone to see it and earnestly desire it to be real. To-day, either through laziness or fear or selfishness or blindness, most of us are content with the bad old world. Most want to use modern knowledge merely to prop up that tottering old world, not at all to make a new world on a better plan. All this must change. It can only be changed by those who have the will to change it, to live for changing it.

Let us think now about some of the particular problems that must be faced at once if we are to begin making a better world.

[...]

C3. NATIONALISM AND WORLD-LOYALTY

The love of one's country, or nation, once played a great part in helping men to care for something more than themselves or their own families or villages. But to-day patriotism is doing very great harm to the world. Because people find patriotism so easy and exciting, they cannot learn to feel loyalty to the whole world of men and women. If we want to avoid having very horrible wars, and perhaps wrecking our civilisation, this world-loyalty must somehow be brought to life in the majority of people.

In some ways the world is, all the while, becoming more and more one single pattern, one system. When a stone is thrown into a pond, ripples spread all over the pond. Just so, in the world, now that there is so much communication between different countries, so much travel by land and sea and air, so much letter-writing, telegraphing, wireless, so much trade, so many international arrangements about trade and about money, what happens in one country affects all other countries. If one country refuses to use goods made in another, people in the other will be thrown out of work. To-day we see posters telling us to "Buy British" so as to help British industry and give work to British workers. If we do so, what is to happen to the people in foreign countries who have been making things for us? They are thrown out of work. If they happen to be in Germany, where things are much worse than they are here, the effect will be very serious [...].

But, though the world is quickly becoming one in this sense, it is only very slowly becoming one in another sense; people are only very slowly beginning to feel loyalty toward the world as a whole. This feeling for the world as a whole is a high-grade activity; and few are able to do it at all constantly. But it will come. It must. The young, either the present young or those that will follow after, will very surely feel this loyalty. Meanwhile, what stands in the way is our rather blind and mean loyalty to nations, our too easy and comfortable and cheaply exciting patriotism. Patriotism must be outgrown.

[...]

We must not allow any people to be ruled by the government of another people. If there are peoples that cannot be trusted to manage their own affairs without harming the world, they must be governed, not by one or other of the powerful nations, but by the world-government. At present the parts of the world that are less civilised, or merely less able to defend themselves, are nearly all governed by some great foreign national State or other.

[...]

C4. WAR

In the world that we want to make there must not be any national armies. Long ago, war was perhaps a good thing for the world, but now it is wholly bad. Not only does it destroy many precious lives and much hard-won wealth. It also poisons men's minds, so that their powers of high-grade living gradually fail. In the last great war, millions of the best young men of Europe and America were killed, or maimed for the rest of their lives. Millions more, who came through with no bodily hurt, were really very seriously damaged in other ways. They had spent four of the best years of their lives in a barbarous and filthy occupation, instead of living the kind of life that was suited to them. Deep down in their hearts they were poisoned with disgust and shame, with shame about the war and the world and human nature itself. Some had gone out to fight in the hope of making a better world. They suffered terrible things, and found that the world merely grew worse and worse. Some thought that war was going to be a glorious adventure. It turned out almost entirely boredom, beastliness, mud, and horror. Some people to-day are apt to remember the moments of adventure, and forget the months of weariness.

Those who did not see the war cannot possibly imagine what it was like. Nor can they realise what it has done to men's minds. War rouses very strong feelings of fear and hate. When people are busy fearing and hating very violently, they lose the power of thinking coolly and clearly. They believe any stories that make the enemy seem brutal and their own nation noble. In the last war some people even believed that the Germans were selling dead babies as meat in butchers' shops. If anyone dared to think differently from the rest about the war, or about the rightness of his nation's part in it, he was treated as an "outsider" and cruelly bullied. In the war-mood all the old low-grade ways of feeling and behaving cease to be properly controlled by the finer, high-grade ways.

After the last war the victorious nations disarmed the beaten nations. They promised also to disarm themselves, but twelve years after the war they have still not done so. They also forced the beaten nations to agree to pay for all the damage caused by invasion, and also for the whole cost of the war. This they did because, being still in the war mood, they believed that the enemy alone had caused the war. Since then, feelings have cooled somewhat, and most people realise that the war was caused, not by one nation, but by the whole muddled condition of Europe. Yet even to-day the victors, or the most powerful of them, still insist on the payment which they made the enemy promise at the point of the bayonet.

If there is another war, it will be far worse than the last. Ever since the last war, people have been inventing more terrible bombs and poison gases. Unfortunately, to-day we are much more able to damage an enemy than defend ourselves. We could destroy the cities of the enemy people, but could not prevent the enemy from destroying ours. A few enemy planes over London could smash half the city and poison millions of people. The next war will not be a gallant adventure. It will be more like being run over by a motor or crushed under a falling house, or like dropping into a furnace.

Why are there wars? How can we prevent them? The causes of war are patriotism, fear, greed. Patriotic people want their nation to be strong enough to bully others. Since all nations are patriotic, all are terrified of one another. Therefore they spend an immense amount of money on armies and navies, so as to feel "secure" against one another. But the more "security" they have, the more they fear and hate their neighbours, because they know that they themselves are feared and hated, on account of their armament. Sooner or later they are sure to start fighting. A great armament is like a loaded pistol carried in a man's pocket. Every time he quarrels with anyone he is tempted to use his weapon. He fingers the thing in his pocket. A touch may send it off.

Another cause of war is greed. Some nation, or some powerful group within it, wants to have control of a coal-field or oil-field which is possessed by another nation. Or else it wants to prevent other nations from competing with it in selling things at high prices to the natives of some uncivilised country. Then, again, there is generally some nation which is blamed for all the wrongs of the world. It becomes the "scapegoat" for the sins of all the others. The scapegoat used to be Germany; now it is Russia. Wars with Russia are likely to be caused by the fact that the rich people of Europe are frightened lest Europe should follow Russia's example and do away with rich people altogether.

Clearly all national armaments must be abolished. This is one of the greatest needs of the world to-day. The mere expense of war, and of the preparation for war, is a terrible burden on the world. Ever so much thought and labour and material which might have been used for making a better world is now used merely for destruction. Three-quarters of the money paid in taxes to the British State goes to pay for past wars and prepare for future wars. Only a quarter is spent in ways really useful to the people.

So long as there are armaments, the peoples cannot trust one another. So long as the peoples do not trust one another there will be armaments. What is to be done about it? One plan is to arrange a programme of gradual disarmament, to be agreed on by all the nations. This would be something very good. It would save an immense amount of money, and it would very greatly help to persuade the people to trust one another. But this alone is not enough. Aeroplanes that are used in peace-time for carrying passengers and mails can easily be used for carrying bombs. And bombs can be made fairly quickly. There is really no chance of doing away with war altogether until most men and women in all countries have learned to care more for the world as a whole than for their nation.

[...]

There is one other cause of war. People who live humdrum lives in modern towns, spending nearly all their days in safe but tiresome work, naturally want adventure. They think that war will give them the chance to live a violent and chivalrous life. [...] [T]his need for adventure and courage is wholesome, and should be satisfied, though not by war. Everyone while he is young ought to have the chance of some kind of skilled and dangerous action, for hard games, rock-climbing, exploring, dangerous scientific research, flying, and so on. Rather than preserve war, we had better allow duels again, and tournaments.

C5. RICH AND POOR

Many people nowadays agree that war is bad. But unfortunately not nearly so many agree that there should not be rich people and poor people. Even those who do agree are seldom anxious to do anything much about it, if they happen to be fairly well off themselves. In the world that we are going to make, no one will be allowed to have a big house and three cars while elsewhere a whole family lives in a single room and cannot even share a push-bicycle [...].

At present, owing to the way money works, and the laws about it, some people inherit the power of setting others to work for them. Some gain this power by luck, or clever trading on other people's wants. The result is that, while many lead shockingly cramped lives, others have far more power and pleasure than is good for them. The many do not have the chance to grow up freely and fully in body and mind. They cannot use all the powers of life that they have, and they cannot develop other powers that they might have if they were better treated. They may also be tormented by a sense of injustice. Society treats them so badly that they cannot feel any loyalty toward it. Why should they?

All this is fantastically wrong and harmful to the world. The ideal is that everyone should have all the wealth that he can use for his own and the world's good, but that no one should waste anything in undertakings which are of no real benefit to the whole. The ideal also is that no one should have power over another through the possession of money. A man should never have power over others except when he has to do so in service of the world, as policemen and railway officials and park-keepers have power. The ideal is that wealth should be shared out evenly, that no one should be favoured. Each of us should regard his own possessions as "held on trust" from the world, so that he may live his life well for the world's sake. Surely all this, which some of the old still find so difficult to see, must be quite obvious to every intelligent child who looks at the world with fresh eyes.

'DANGER! HIGH TENSION!'

from *The 35th of May, or Conrad's Ride to the South Seas*
Jonathan Cape, 1933

Written by Erich Kästner

This story refers to Cockaigne, a fourteenth-century peasant land of luxury, or what has come to be known as a utopia. There is a long tradition of utopian writing: Sir Thomas More's book of that name dates from 1516; Pieter Bruegel the Elder depicted *The Land of Cockaigne* (1567); in Shakespeare's *The Tempest* (1610–11), Gonazalo gives a speech about a possible utopia (2.i); and there have been many others since, including the song 'The Big Rock Candy Mountain' featured in Part Six which, like Cockaigne, expresses a yearning for luxury with no work required.

Socialists and Marxists grappled with the idea of utopia, often citing and adapting a key passage from Frederick Engels's *The Principles of Communism* (1847). Engels put it this way:

> [The] development of industry will make available to society a sufficient mass of products to satisfy the needs of everyone .... [E]xisting improvements and scientific procedures will be put into practice, with a resulting leap forward which will assure to society all the products it needs. In this way, such an abundance of goods will be able to satisfy the needs of all its members. (1969, 81–97)

The phrases 'development of industry' and 'scientific procedures' establish Engels's vision of a modern utopia, for it is these that will bring about 'abundance'. It is important to remember that this is an idealized view of the future, and will only be realized if the workers come to own the means of production. On the other hand, in the real world, socialists and Marxists reclaimed the worth of labour and reviled 'bosses' often in terms that equated them to idle 'parasites' (see also 'The Story of the Island of Fish' in Part One).

The article was first published in *Vorwärts* (Forward), the most influential of the German socialist papers of that time. We can assume that Kästner was, at least in part, poking fun at this Marxist utopia, though he leaves the suggestion at the end that maybe it is worth trying!

Erich Kästner's (1899–1974) fun is in the nonsense tradition, but perhaps it is the flipside of the view that humans in the here and now are dominated by machines, as expressed in two films of this period: Fritz Lang's *Metropolis* (1927) and Charlie Chaplin's *Modern Times* (1936). In similar vein, the supposed ability of machines to liberate us from domestic work was mocked by the two short Looney Tunes cartoons, *Dog Gone Modern* (1939) and the remake, *House Hunting Mice* (1947). This is in contrast to mainstream and progressive thought which often welcomed the modernity of anything from electric trains to vacuum cleaners.

In the 1930s, when his book was being read for the first time, Kästner had a worldwide reputation for writing one of the great classics of children's literature, *Emil and the Detectives* (1929; English translation, 1931), which relates to automation in one respect: the customary view in children's literature of the city as dangerous, wicked, and fallen is reversed, since Berlin and its machines (buses, trams, telephones, newspaper printing) is presented as exciting—a place that children could use to do good things.

The 35th of May is a surreal/absurdist story about Conrad, his Uncle Ringel, who takes care of him after school one day a week, and the talking horse they meet on the street named Negro Caballa. The events take place on the 35th of May—an impossible date for impossible events. To help Conrad with some homework on the South Seas, the three companions decide to travel there via Uncle Ringel's wardrobe. They pass through to many lands where Kästner uses a combination of allegory, metaphor, and satire to critique most of the means of social organization and power used over time. In this extract they travel to a future which includes images of many devices, including mobile phones, which had not yet been invented.

DANGER! HIGH TENSION!

WHEN they left the Topsy-Turvy Country they came to an Underground Station. They went down by the escalator and found a train waiting at the platform. So they got in and took their seats.

'This is a funny train,' said Conrad. 'There's no conductor and no driver. I wonder where the thing goes to.'

'We shall find out,' returned his uncle. Just then the train gave a jerk and started moving, and within a second they were rushing between the concrete walls of the tunnel like a flash of greased lightning. Uncle Ringel fell off his seat. 'Perhaps we shan't find out after all,' he said. 'My dear nephew, if I should meet with a fatal accident, don't forget in your grief that I've left you my shop.'

'And if you should survive me, dear uncle,' said the boy, 'my school books and case of compasses are yours.'

'I'm sincerely grateful,' returned his uncle, and they shook hands with each other, deeply touched.

'Don't get sloppy,' said the horse, and looked out of the window. The underground train shot onward like a rocket. The lines groaned, and the train shivered as though it were frightened of its own speed.

Uncle Ringel got up and sat on the seat. 'If anything happens to me now,' he said in a desperate voice, 'there'll be nobody to look after the shop to-night.' But just then he fell off his seat again, for the train stopped as though it had rammed an iceberg.

'Let's get out,' shouted Uncle Ringel. He scrambled up, wrenched open the door and stumbled on to the platform. Conrad and the horse threw themselves after him.

When they had ascended the escalator, and could look about them, they stood for some time rooted to the spot. All round were mighty skyscrapers.

'My withers!' said the horse, at last.

Conrad began to count the floors in the nearest building. He got as far as forty-six, then he had to stop because the floors above that were hidden in the clouds. On these clouds were projected the following notice:

ELECTROPOLIS

THE AUTOMATIC CITY

DANGER! HIGH TENSION!

The horse wanted to turn tail on the spot. 'Let's leave the beastly South Seas to look after themselves,' he said. But Conrad and his uncle had not the slightest intention of doing so, so they crossed the great square that lay in front of them, filled with hundreds of cars, and Negro Caballo had to follow whether he liked it or not.

'Nobody seems to do any work here,' said Uncle Ringel. 'They're all joy-riding in cars. Can you understand it?'

Full of curiosity, Conrad had been running along beside one of the cars. He came back and shook his head. 'What do you think?' he said. 'These cars move of their own accord without either a chauffeur or a steering-wheel. It's a complete mystery to me.' One of the cars braked and stopped alongside them. A nice old lady was sitting at the back. She was crocheting a shawl, and said in a friendly tone, 'I suppose you've come from the country.'

'More or less,' returned Uncle Ringel. 'Can you explain how these vehicles guide themselves?'

The old lady smiled. 'Our cars are all directed from one centre,' she explained. 'The steering apparatus is worked by an ingenious combination of an electro-magnetic field with wireless control. Quite simple, you see!'

'Frightfully simple,' said Uncle Ringel.

'Simply frightful,' growled the horse.

And Conrad said crossly, 'And I've been wanting to be a chauffeur!'

The old lady put down the shawl. 'Why do you want to be a chauffeur?' she asked.

'To earn money,' answered the boy.

'Why do you want to earn money?' asked the old lady.

'What a funny question!' said Conrad. 'Without working you can't earn a living, and if you don't earn a living you have nothing to eat!'

'What old-fashioned ideas!' exclaimed the old lady, 'My dear child, here in Electropolis we only work for fun, or to keep slim, or to make a present for somebody, or to increase our knowledge. All the necessities of life are produced by machinery and given away for nothing.'

Uncle Ringel reflected for a moment. 'But before the food can be prepared in the factories,' he said, 'the seed has to be sown. And your cattle don't grow in the fields like weeds, do they?'

'The farmers outside the city look after that,' replied the old lady. 'But even they don't have to work very hard. Agriculture has been mechanized in every possible way. Machines do most of the work.'

'And do the farmers supply you with cattle and grain for nothing?' asked the horse.

'The farmers get everything else they need in exchange for their products,' explained the old lady. 'Everybody can have all he wants. It is a well-known fact that the soil and machinery produce more than we need. Surely you know that!'

Uncle Ringel felt a little ashamed of himself. 'Of course, we know that,' he said. 'But all the same, most of the people at home are wretchedly poor.'

'Well, that is really the limit!' cried the old lady sternly. But soon she smiled again. 'Now I'm going to drive to the Artificial Park,' she said. 'All the trees and flowers there smell of ozone. That's very healthy. Good-bye.' She pressed a button, leaned forward to a speaking-trumpet, and called into it, 'To the Artificial Park! I want a cup of coffee in the restaurant by the Carbonic Acid Pond!'

The mysterious car set itself obediently in motion and glided away. The old lady leaned back comfortably, and went on with her crochet-work.

The three friends stared after her like stone images, and Uncle Ringel said, 'Well, upon my soul! And some day it'll be like that all over the world! I hope you'll live to see it, my boy.'

'Like the Land of Cockayne,' said the horse.

'With one difference,' put in Uncle Ringel.

'Namely?' asked the horse.

'The people here work. They are not lazy. I admit they only work for fun. But you can't blame them for that. Well, we'd better get a move on!'

They turned into a busy street to inspect the shop-windows of Electropolis. But scarcely had they stepped on the pavement than they all fell flat on their backs, and thus, without the slightest intention of doing so, they went sliding along the street.

'Help!' cried Conrad. 'The beastly pavement's alive!'

Actually the pavement consisted of a moving band, which saved people the trouble of walking. You simply stood on it and rode down the street without so much as having to wiggle your toes. If you wanted to enter a shop, you stepped off the moving band and stood on firm paving-stones.

'That old dame with the crochet-work might have told us about this,' grumbled Negro Caballo. He went riding on his hind-quarters along the main street of Electropolis, and could not get up on account of the roller-skates. Uncle Ringel and Conrad came to his assistance and finally got him on to his feet again. After that the moving pavement seemed quite fun.

Uncle Ringel wanted to look in the window of a confectioner's shop, and stepped off the moving band. But he had not yet got used to it and banged his head against a wall. As he did so, they heard a strange noise, and could not make up their minds where it came from. Then Conrad tapped the wall with his knuckles and the singing noise grew louder. He scratched at the wall with his nail. 'I say!' he cried. 'The sky-scrapers are made of aluminium.'

'This town is most conveniently planned!' said his uncle. 'We must send our mayor here to pick up a few tips.'

What impressed them most was the following: a gentleman was travelling along the pavement in front of them, when suddenly he stepped off, took a telephone receiver from his pocket and called a number. 'Listen Gertrude,' he said, 'I shall be about an hour late for lunch to-day. I have to look in at the laboratory. Good-bye, darling!' Then he put away his pocket-telephone, stepped on to the moving band and rode off, reading a book.

Conrad and the horse felt the hair stand up on the backs of their heads. A few people, travelling past in the contrary direction, said, 'Look, those two with the horse must be provincials.'

Uncle Ringel shrugged his shoulders and tried to appear as much like an Electropolitan as he could. In doing so he fell over again. 'Never mind,' he said, when Conrad tried to help him up, 'I'd rather sit down to it.'

They left one street and entered another. The aluminium skyscrapers began to sing softly under the rising wind.

After a quarter of an hour they came to the end of the moving band and left the skyscrapers behind them.

Now they had to continue their way on foot. They marched on at a smart pace and came presently to a gigantic factory. 'Electropolitan Cattle-Conversion Centre.' Conrad ran on ahead through the gates.

Innumerable herds of cattle were waiting to be converted into useful objects. They crowded, stamping and mooing, in front of a vast funnel that must have been sixty feet in diameter, and jostled each other into the funnel. Oxen, cows, calves—they vanished by the hundred, sucked mysteriously into the shining metal mouth of the funnel.

'Why do men slaughter poor animals?' asked the horse.

'Yes, it's terrible!' agreed Uncle Ringel. 'But if you'd ever enjoyed a nice juicy steak you'd take a more lenient view of the matter!'

Conrad ran along the side of the great building. They heard the noise of motors and pistons. Uncle Ringel and the horse had some difficulty in keeping up with the boy.

At last they reached the rear of the factory, and there they saw a long line of electric goods-trains, and the finished products of the Cattle-Conversion Centre pouring out of shoots in the factory wall into the waiting trucks. From one of the shoots came leather trunks, from another casks of butter, calf-skin shoes tumbled out of a third, tins of corned beef from a fourth, great cheeses from a fifth, and out of the sixth were pouring masses of chilled meat. From the other shoots came horn combs, breakfast sausages, tanned hides, bottles of milk, violin strings, cases of tinned cream and many other articles.

As soon as the trucks were filled a bell rang. Then the trains moved forward, bringing empty trucks under the shoots to be loaded.

'And not a soul in sight! Nothing but cattle!' cried Uncle Ringel. 'Everything electric! Everything automatic!'

Just as he said these words a man came sauntering across the factory yard. He nodded to them. 'I'm on duty to-day,' he said. 'I do a day a month. Twelve days in the year. I look after the machines.'

'One question, neighbour,' said the horse. 'How do you spend your time on the other three hundred and fifty three days of the year?'

'Don't worry about that,' said the man, cheerfully. 'I've got an allotment, and I'm fond of playing football, and I'm learning to paint. And sometimes I read history books. It's very interesting to think of the muddled way people used to do things!'

'I agree!' said Uncle Ringel. 'But where do you get all the vast quantities of electricity you consume in your city?'

'From the Niagara Falls,' said the man. 'Unfortunately, it's been raining very heavily there for some weeks and we are getting rather anxious. The current has got so strong and the voltage so high that we are afraid the fuses may blow at the generating station. Oh, there's the four o'clock paper!'

'Where?' asked Conrad.

The engineer looked up in the air and the others followed his example. The news appeared on the sky in white letters on a blue ground. 'No Danger to Electropolis,' it ran, and then followed a certificate issued by the Security Commission.

Apart from that, there was a report of the economic negotiations with Mars and the latest results of research in various scientific institutes. There were also items from the next day's radio and home-cinema programmes. Finally an instalment of a serial story was thrown on to the vault of heaven.

Conrad was about to begin reading this story when there suddenly broke out a terrific hullabaloo. The products of cattle-conversion poured down the shoots in the factory wall at an ever-increasing pace. It simply rained trunks and corned beef, butter, shoes, cheese and tinned cream. The trucks overflowed. And then bricks, window-frames and parts of machinery began to fly out of the shoots.

'Gracious heavens!' cried the engineer. 'The factory's eating itself up!' And he rushed away.

The disaster began with the floods at Niagara, which drove the city electricity works with a hundred times their normal power. The machines of the Cattle-Conversion Centre were no longer being fed, for all the cattle had been converted. At last they began to run backwards; they sucked the casks of butter, the cheese, the trunks, the shoes, the chilled meat, the breakfast sausages and all the other goods out of the railway trucks and poured the original cattle out of the funnel at the other end by the factory gates. The oxen, calves and cows ran bellowing madly down the street and into the city.

Uncle Ringel and Conrad had mounted Negro Caballo and were driven along by the infuriated herds of cattle. The automatic cars shot past them like flashes of lightning, dashed into each other, or flew into the houses and up the stairs. The electric lamps melted. The Artificial Park kept on rapidly blooming and withering. The newspaper for the day after to-morrow was already appearing in the sky.

All this was too much for the horse. He stopped in the road and his knees began to knock together.

'Excuse me, Caballo!' said Uncle Ringel, and raising his walking-stick he dealt him such a mighty whack across the haunches that the animal forgot his fears and galloped liked mad through the surrounding chaos.

After some minutes they left the town behind and were in safety.

'A ticklish matter this machinery,' said the horse.

They looked back and saw the lifts shooting out of the tops of the houses. The noise of the tottering aluminium skyscrapers was like a war.

Uncle Ringel wiped his forehead and patted the horse's neck. 'That's the last of Utopia!' he said.

Conrad took his uncle by the arm. 'Don't worry about that,' he reassured him. 'When I'm grown up we'll build a new one!' And then they rode forward, keeping straight on, towards the South Seas.

VILLAGE AND TOWN

Puffin, 1942

Written and illustrated by S[tanley] R[oy] Badmin

This book belongs to the Picture Puffin series edited by Noel Carrington, who was instrumental in introducing many aesthetically and politically radical books to British children. Carrington was also editor of the magazine *Design for Today*, and had a keen interest in all aspects of modern architecture and design.

Village and Town appeared at the height of the Blitz, by when debates about rebuilding Britain after the Second World War abounded. It seeks to involve children in discussions and plans for what Britain could—and should—look like in the future. In sixteen double-page spreads, S. R. Badmin (1906–89) provides a history of building, informing young readers about materials, functions, and the relationship between buildings and infrastructure. Badmin's text makes the case that to work effectively in a modern, globalizing, technologically advanced world, Britain needed new kinds of buildings, roads, and communications. The book argues that every previous age created the kinds of buildings it required, but the twentieth century had thus far failed to follow suit. The result, according to *Village and Town*, was an acute housing shortage, inefficient industry, and an unhealthy population, all contributing to diminish the British economy and way of life.

The closing image on the book's back cover shows one of Britain's few modernist buildings: St. John's Wood Underground station. On one side is a multistorey car park, with an impressive block of new flats rising vertically behind it. The book's message is clear: good contemporary design must have a place in a modern Britain.

NEW STYLES AND TRADITION

You will see to-day new buildings with new shapes, houses altogether unlike those of twenty years ago. That is partly because new materials in building lead architects to design in new ways, and partly because they often have to design new types of buildings [. . .]. In course of time we shall find these new shapes quite natural, as we do the 'New Style' buildings you saw on page 23, though those shocked the old-fashioned people at the time. Be sure that if a building is well designed for its purpose, without trying to be new fashioned or old fashioned, it will fit in with its surroundings just as all the houses do in the old villages we love. The English style of building does not mean using bricks or stone or thatched roofs, but buildings which are solid, suitable and not fussy in appearance. The shapes of buildings may soon be different again, for architects are already experimenting with and using still newer materials, such as glass bricks, aluminium, and plastics such as 'Bakelite.'

THE FUTURE

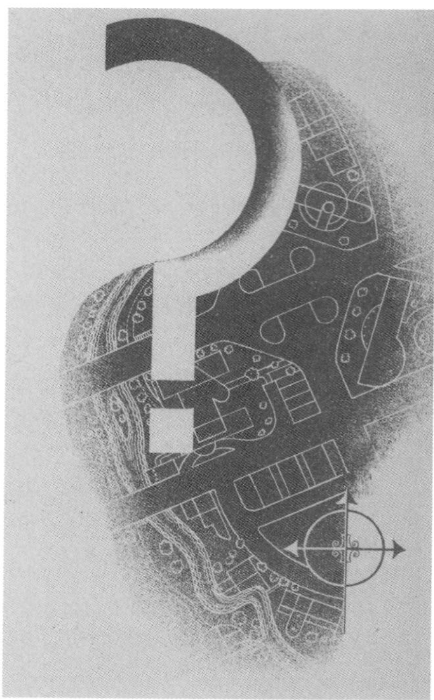

The big question mark is for the future. In rebuilding our houses and replanning our cities how can we use and develop our new, clean, thoughtful ways of building so that everyone will benefit? Do you know we could have much better houses than we have, if they were well designed and better use was made of standardised doors, windows, cupboards and stoves? Do you know we could have towns which were clean and smokeless, which were easy to get about, which had plenty of playing grounds and no slums? And we could keep the country as real country for farming or holidays, instead of eating it up with bungalows. We could do all that and much more if we made plans in advance, instead of muddling along as we do now, allowing people to build more or less where and what they fancy whether it is ugly or not. Is it possible for planning to be carried out when so many people own so many different pieces of land? Look at your own home town. Surely something better must be built next time?

If you would like to read more about building here are two good books for you—"Our Inheritance," by J. A. Richards, and "Living in Towns," by Ralph Tubbs, Penguin Books

Back Cover

THE CHILDREN'S CORNER

MICKY Mongrel has said good-bye. And to-day we were going to start our new children's feature in the adventures of a group of Young Pioneers.

But GLADYS, the creator of Micky, who will also illustrate the new feature, has been bitten by a counter-revolutionary influenza germ.

So to-day we just show you Mr. Moneybags reading angrily our birthday number—see his eyes nearly popping out of his head with rage!

WORKS CITED

Albertine, Viv. *Clothes, Clothes, Clothes. Music, Music, Music. Boys, Boys, Boys.* London: Faber and Faber, 2014.

Anderson, Tom. 'The Revolution'. *The Young Socialist* 8.5 (May 1908), 238; editor's response, 8.6 (June 1908), 248.

Burke, Peter. *Popular Culture in Early Modern Europe*. London: Temple Smith, 1978.

Castle, Kathryn. *Britannia's Children: Reading Colonialism through Children's Books and Magazines*. Manchester: Manchester University Press, 1996.

Dusinberre, Juliet. *Alice to the Lighthouse: Children's Books and Radical Experiments in Art*. Basingstoke: Macmillan, 1987.

Ellis, Havelock. *Studies in the Psychology of Sex*, vol. VI: *Sex in Relation to Society*. 1927. Accessed at http://www.aolib.com/reader_13615_31.htm on 16 August 2014.

Engels, Frederick. 'The Principles of Communism', in *Selected Works*, vol. 1, 81–97. Moscow: Progress Publishers, 1969.

Eve, Matthew. 'A History of Illustrated Children's Books and Book Production in Britain During the Second World War'. Unpublished doctoral thesis, Oxford University, 2003.

Floud, J. E., A. H. Halsey, and F.M. Martin, *Social Class and Educational Opportunity*. Melbourne, London and Toronto: Heinemann, 1956.

Fussell, Paul. *The Great War and Modern Memory*. Oxford: Oxford University Press, 1975.

Gorky, Maxim. 'Soviet Writers' Congress 1934'. Accessed at https://www.marxists.org/archive/gorky-maxim/1934/soviet-literature.htm.

Grant, Gwen. *Private—Keep Out!* Illus. Faith Jacques. London: Heinemann, 1978.

Greenway, Betty (ed.). *Twice-Told Tales: The Influence of Childhood Reading on Writers for Adults*. New York: Routledge, 2005.

Gurney, Peter. *Co-operative Culture and the Politics of Consumption in England, 1870–1930*. Manchester: Manchester University Press, 1996.

Huberman, Leo. *Man's Worldly Goods: The Story of the Wealth of Nations*. London: Victor Gollancz, 1936.

Isaacs, Susan. *Intellectual Growth in Young Children*. London: Routledge, 1929.

Kanwar, Asha S., and Arnold Kettle. 'An Interview with Arnold Kettle'. *Social Scientist*, 15.7 (July 1987), 54–61.

Kelly, Catriona. *Children's World: Growing up in Russia, 1890–1991*. New Haven and London: Yale University Press, 2007.

Kettle, Arnold. *An Introduction to the English Novel*. London: Hutchison University Library, 1951.

Kirschner, Paul. 'The Dual Purpose of *Animal Farm*'. *Review of English Studies*, 55.222 (2004), 759–86.

Kohl, Herbert. *Should we Burn Babar? Essays on Children's Literature and the Power of Stories*. New York and London: New Press, 2006.

Lenin, V. I. *Report on the Work of the Council of People's Commissars* (Polnoe sobranie sochinenii), 5th edn, vol. 36, 15–16. Moscow, 1975–9.

Lindsay, Jack, and Edgell Rickword (eds). *Spokesmen for Liberty. A Record of English Democracy through 12 Centuries*. London: Lawrence and Wishart, 1941.

Linehan, Thomas. *Communism in Britain, 1920–1939: From the Cradle to the Grave*. Manchester: Manchester University Press, 2007.

Mickenberg, Julia L. *Learning from the Left: Children's Literature, the Cold War, and Radical Politics in the United States*. New York and Oxford: Oxford University Press, 2006.

Morton, A. L. *A People's History of England*. London: Victor Gollancz, 1938.

Nicholson, Heather Norris. 'Journeys into Seeing: Amateur Film-Making and Tourist Encounters in Soviet Russia, c. 1932'. *New Readings* 10 (2009), 57–71.

Ognyov, N [Mikhael Grigoryevitch Rozânov]. *The Diary of a Communist Undergraduate*, trans. Alexander Werth. London: Victor Gollancz, 1929.

Oppenheimer, Paul (trans. and ed.). *Till Eulenspiegel, His Adventures*. Oxford and New York: Oxford University Press, 1995.

Overy, Richard. *The Morbid Age: Britain and the Crisis of Civilization, 1919–1939*. London: Penguin, 2010 (first published 2009).

Pearson, Joe. *Drawn Direct to the Plate: Noel Carrington and the Puffin Picture Books*. London: Penguin Collectors' Society, 2010.

Pollitt, Harry. 'Stories We Can Gladly Give Our Children'. *Daily Worker* (16 December 1936).

Reynolds, Kimberley. *Radical Children's Literature: Future Visions and Aesthetic Transformations*. Basingstoke: Palgrave Macmillan, 2007.

Reynolds, Kimberley. *Left Out: The Forgotten Tradition of Radical Publishing for Children in Britain 1910–1949*. Oxford: Oxford University Press, 2016.

Reynolds, Kimberley. 'Firing the Canon! Geoffrey Trease's Campaign for an Alternative Children's Canon in 1930s Britain', in Bettina Kümmerling-Meibauer and Anja Müller (eds), *Canon Constitution and Canon Change in Children's Literature*. London: Routledge, 2017.

Rose, Jonathan. *The Intellectual Life of the British Working Classes*. New Haven and London: Yale University Press, 2001.

Rosen, Harold. *Are You Still Circumcised? East End Memories*. Nottingham: Five Leaves Press, 1999.

Rosenfeld, Alla. 'Does the Proletarian Child Need a Fairy Tale?' *Childhood* 9 (Winter 2009), n.p. Accessed at http://cabinetmagazine.org/issues/9/rosenfeld.php on 5 November, 2012.

Rust, William. *The Inside Story of the Daily Worker: 10 Years of Working-Class Journalism*. London: Daily Worker, 1939.

Samuel, Raphael. *The Lost World of British Communism*. London: Verso, 2006.

Shortt, Edward. 'Socialist and Revolutionary Schools'. Memorandum by the Home Secretary. National Archives CAB/24/136, 25 April 1922.

Spufford, Francis. *The Child that Books Built*. London: Faber and Faber, 2002.

Stephens, John, and Robyn McCallum. *Retelling Stories, Framing Culture: Traditional Stories and Metanarratives in Children's Literature*. London and New York: Garland, 1998.

Tatar, Maria. *Enchanted Hunters: The Power of Stories in Childhood*. London and New York: W. W. Norton, 2009.
Trease, Geoffrey. 'Revolutionary Literature for the Young'. Letters from writers' section of *International Literature: Organ of the International Union of Revolutionary Writers* 7 (1935), 100–2.
Trease, Geoffrey. 'Fifty Years On: A Writer Looks Back'. *Children's Literature in Education* 14.3 (1983), 149–59.
Trease, Geoffrey. *Tales Out of School*, 2nd edn. London: Heinemann Educational, 1964.
Trease, Geoffrey. *A Whiff of Burnt Boats*. Bath: Girls Gone By Publishers, 1971.
Warner, Sylvia Townsend. 'Adventures of the Little Pig'. *Left News* (September 1937), 514.
Wiseacre, Mr. 'Books on Delicate Subjects'. *The Young Socialist* 13 (1913), 220–1.
Zornado, Joseph. *Inventing Childhood: Culture, Ideology and the Story of Childhood*. London: Garland, 2006.

PERSONAL ACKNOWLEDGEMENTS

A great many people have enthusiastically—and generously—supported this project. We would especially like to thank the following: Ruth, Sid, and Deb Bloom; Adrianne Buckley; Dr Rachel Carys Garden; Richard Gombrich; Natalia Grant-Ross; Naomi Korn; Janette Koslover; the staff of the Labour History Archive and Study Centre (LHASC), People's History Museum, Manchester; Olga Maeots; Elizabeth Mann; Jo Manning; Kika and Jehane Markham; the Trustees and Meirian Jump, Librarian and Archvist, Marx Memorial Library; the *Morning Star*; John Cunningham and Ralph Gibson, Society for Co-operation in Russian and Soviet Studies; the Worker's Music Association; the staff of the Working Class Movement Library. Jacqueline Norton, at Oxford University Press, backed this project from the beginning, and Eleanor Collins has been an outstanding co-creator at all stages.

NOTES ON THE TEXT

When reproducing original material we have corrected any obviously inadvertent minor mistakes including typographical errors, inconsistent punctuation, and misspellings of words that are correctly spelled elsewhere.

For presentational reasons, we have not provided facsimile versions of the illustrative material reproduced in this volume. In resetting the material, care has been taken to be faithful to the text–image relationship, rhythm of page breaks and turns, and key elements of design. Inevitably the original design and aesthetic impact of the books have been affected, but the editors and publisher believe it was better to make these adjustments than to leave out this important aspect of the publications discussed.

TEXTUAL ACKNOWLEDGEMENTS

'Anon', 'Blacking His Shirt', from *Martin's Annual* (Martin Lawrence, 1935). Reproduced by kind permission of Lawrence and Wishart.

'Anon', 'A Life with a Purpose—or a Grave in Malaya', from *Challenge* (1949). Reproduced by kind permission of Challenge and the Young Communist League Britain.

'Anon', extracts from *The Red Corner Book*. Courtesy of Lawrence and Wishart Ltd.

S. R. Badmin, extracts from *Village and Town* (Puffin, 1942). Reproduced by kind permission of Penguin Books Ltd.

Korney Chukovsky, *Wash 'Em Clean* (Foreign Languages Publishing House, n.d.). Korney Chukovsky's Russian texts copyright © by Dmitry Chukovsky, 2018. English publishing rights are acquired via FTM Agency, Ltd., Russia, 2017.

F. Le Gros and Ida Clark, from *Adventures of the Little Pig and Other Stories* (Martin Lawrence, 1936). Reproduced by kind permission of Lawrence and Wishart.

Daily Worker, 'The First Labour M.P.'; 'Hunger-Strike Heroine'; 'In Great-Great-Great Grandfather's Day', from *Daily Worker Children's Annual* (1957). Reproduced by kind permission of the *Morning Star*.

Michael Davidson, 'Red Front', from *Martin's Annual* (Martin Lawrence, 1935). Reproduced by kind permission of Lawrence and Wishart.

Olive Dehn, *Come In* (Shakespeare Head Presss, 1946). Reproduced by kind permission of Jehanne and Kika Markham.

Eleanor Farjeon, 'Tom Fool', 'Greed the Guy', from *Tomfooleries* (The Daily Herald, 1920). Reproduced by kind permission of The Daily Herald.

'The First of May' from *Moonshine* (The London Publishing Company and George Allen and Unwin, 1921). Reproduced by kind permission of George Allen and Unwin.

Alan Gifford, selected 'Songs of Struggle', from *If I had a Song: A Song Book for Children Growing Up* (Workers' Music Association, 1954). Reproduced by kind permission of the Workers' Music Association.

L. Gombrich, 'How Till Bought Land in Luneburg', from *The Amazing Pranks of Master Till Eulenspiegel* (The Adprint Studios, London; Max Parrish and Co Limited, New York, 1948). Reproduced by kind permission of Richard Gombrich.

Peggy Hart, extracts from *The Magic of Coal* (Puffin Picture Books, 1945). Reproduced by permission of Penguin Books Ltd.

Fielden Hughes, from *Hue and Cry* (Beaver Books/Chatto Educational, 1956). Reproduced by kind permission of Elizabeth Mann.

M. Ilin, extracts from *New Russia's Primer: Story of the Five-Year Plan*, translated from the Russian by George S. Counts and Nucia P. Lodge. English translation copyright © 1931 renewed 1959 by Houghton Mifflin Harcourt Publishing Company. Used by permission of Houghton Mifflin Harcourt Publishing Company. All rights reserved

Erich Kästner, 'Danger! High Tension!', from *The 35th of May, or Conrad's Ride to the South Seas* (Jonathan Cape, 1933). Reproduced by kind permission of Pushkin Press.

Arnold Kettle, *Karl Marx: Founder of Modern Communism* (Morrison and Gibb, 1963). Reproduced by kind permission of Martin and Nick Kettle.

Jennie Lee, extracts from *Tomorrow is a New Day: A Youth Edition* (Puffin Books, 1945). Reproduced by kind permission of Penguin Books Ltd.

Alan Lomax, from *The Big Rock Candy Mountain* (1955). Reproduced by kind permission of the Association for Cultural Equity.

Ed McCurdy, 'Last Night I had the Strangest Dream' (1950) © Folkways Music Pub. Co. Inc., USA, assigned to Kensington Music Ltd. of Suite 2.07, Plaza 535 King's Road, London SW10 0SZ. International Copyright Secured. All Rights Reserved. Used by Permission.

N. Nosov, 'The Telephone', from *Jolly Family* (Foreign Languages Publishing House, 1950). Reproduced by kind permission of Igor Petrovich Nosov.

Nikolai Ognyov, from *The Diary of a Communist Schoolboy* (Victor Gollancz, 1928). Reproduced by kind permission of Cyrus Gabrysch.

Barbara Niven and Ern Brook, *The Little Tuskers' Own Paper*. With kind permission of the *Morning Star*.

Out of Bounds, 'T.P.', 'Side-light on the Blackshirts'; 'Anon.' 'Fight War and Fascism'; Phyllis Baker, 'Hero-Worship Adrift: Film-Star Hero or Games Mistress?'; and Giles Romilly, 'Morning Glory (Sex in Public Schools)', from *Out of Bounds: Public Schools' Journal against Fascism, Militarism and Reaction* (1934). Courtesy of the Bodleian Library, University of Oxford.

Helen Zenna Smith, from *Not So Quiet: Stepdaughters of War* by Evadne Price (Copyright © Evadne Price, 1930). Reproduced by kind permission of A M Heath & Co. Ltd. Authors' Agents.

Geoffrey Trease, 'The People Speak', from *Bows Against the Barons* (Martin Lawrence, 1934), reproduced by kind permission of Hodder and 'A New Kind of Park', from *Red Comet* (Lawrence and Wishart, 1937) reproduced by kind permission of Lawrence and Wishart.

'Alex Wedding', 'The Story of the Island of Fish', from *Eddie and the Gipsy* (Martin Lawrence, 1935). With kind permission of Akademie der Künste, Berlin, in association with Aufbau Verlag GmbH & Co. KG, Berlin. First published by Malik-Verlag, Berlin 1931.

Amabel Williams-Ellis, extracts from *How You Began* (Gerald Howe Ltd., 1928). Reproduced by kind permission of Dr Rachel Carys Garden.

T. H. Wintringham, 'Steel Spokes', from *Martin's Annual* (Martin Lawrence, 1935). Reproduced by kind permission of Lawrence and Wishart.

The Woodcraft Folk, *Songs for Elfins* (selected songs, *c.*1950). Reproduced by kind permission of the Woodcraft Folk.

Every effort has been made to trace and contact copyright holders prior to publication. If notified, the publishers will be pleased to rectify any errors or omissions at the earliest opportunity.

PICTURE CREDITS

p. xxii — Cover, Alex Wedding's *Eddie and the Gipsy. A Story for Boys and Girls* (Martin Lawrence, 1935). Image supplied courtesy of the Bodleian Library, University of Oxford, Fix. 27842 e.444.

p. xxii — One of John Heartfield's photographic illustrations for *Eddie and the Gipsy. A Story for Boys and Girls* by Alex Wedding (Martin Lawrence, 1935). Image supplied courtesy of the Bodleian Library, University of Oxford.

p. 29 — Front cover, *Adventures of the Little Pig and Other Stories* by F. Le Gros and Ida Clark (Martin Lawrence, 1936). Courtesy of Lawrence and Wishart Ltd and The Bodleian Library, University of Oxford.

p. 43 — With kind permission of the *Morning Star.*

pp. 52–61 — Images from Harry Golding and Albert Friend's *War in Dollyland (A Book and a Game)* (Ward Lock & Co, 1915) courtesy of Princeton University Library.

pp. 94–100 — Courtesy of Lawrence and Wishart Ltd and The Bodleian Library, University of Oxford.

pp. 104–7 — Details from *The Red Corner Book*. Courtesy of Lawrence and Wishart Ltd and the Marx Memorial Library.

p. 111 — Front cover, *Bows Against the Barons* by Geoffrey Trease (Martin Lawrence, 1934). Reproduced by kind permission of Hodder.

p. 113 — Illustration by Michael Boland for Geoffrey Trease's *Bows Against the Barons* (Martin Lawrence, 1934). Reproduced by kind permission of Hodder.

pp. 137–46 — *The Little Tuskers' Own Paper* (Daily Worker League, 1945). Reproduced by kind permission of the *Morning Star*. Images courtesy of the Marx Memorial Library.

p. 147 — With kind permission of the *Morning Star*.

p. 164 — Front cover, *Red Comet: A Tale of Travel in the U.S.S.R.* by Geoffrey Trease (Lawrence and Wishart, 1937). Reproduced by courtesy of Lawrence and Wishart. Image supplied by the Marx Memorial Library.

pp. 173–83 — Images from *Wash 'Em Clean*, courtesy of the Society for Co-operation in Russian and Soviet Studies.

pp. 185–9 — Images from *What is Good and What is Bad*, courtesy of the Society for Co-operation in Russian and Soviet Studies.

pp. 191–7 — Untitled images by Donia Nachsen for *Timur and his Comrades*

pp. 233–41 — Permission to reproduce *Come In* by Olive Dehn (Shakespeare Head Press, 1946) courtesy of Jehanne and Kika Markham

p. 243 — from *Daily Worker Children's Annual* (People's Press Printing Society, 1957). Reproduced by kind permission of the *Morning Star*. Images courtesy of the Marx Memorial Library.

p. 254	With kind permission of the *Morning Star*
pp. 276–83	'Songs of Struggle', from *If I had a Song: A Song Book for Children Growing Up* compiled by Alan Gifford (1954). Reproduced by kind permission of the Worker's Music Association.
p. 304	Image detail from 'Fight War and Fascism', from *Out of Bounds: Public Schools' Journal Against Fascism, Militarism and Reaction* (1934). Image courtesy of The Bodleian Library, University of Oxford.
pp. 314–15	'Blacking his Shirt', from *Martin's Annual* (Martin Lawrence, 1935). Courtesy of Lawrence and Wishart Ltd and the Marx Memorial Library.
p. 322	With kind permission of the *Morning Star*
p. 333	Front cover *PollyCon: A Book for the Young Economist* by E. F. Stucley, Illustrated by Hugh Chesterman (Basil Blackwell, 1933). Image courtesy of The Bodleian Library, University of Oxford.
p. 335	pp. 11–13, 'The Beginning of Trade', from *PollyCon: A Book for the Young Economist* by E. F. Stucley (Basil Blackwell, 1933). Image courtesy of The Bodleian Library, University of Oxford.
pp. 339–41	'The Fate of Books', from *Black on White: The Story of Books* by M. Ilin, illustrated by N. Lapshin (George Routledge, 1932).
pp. 345–53	Front cover and 15 unnumbered pages, from *The Magic of Coal* by Peggy Hart (Penguin, 1945). Reproduced by permission of Penguin Books.
p. 391	With kind permission of the *Morning Star.*
pp. 412–20	From *New Russia's Primer: Story of the Five-Year Plan* by M. Ilin, translated from the Russian by George S. Counts and Nucia P. Lodge. English translation copyright © 1931 renewed 1959 by Houghton Mifflin Harcourt Publishing Company. Used by permission of Houghton Mifflin Harcourt Publishing Company. All rights reserved.
pp. 423–9	Images from 'Problems and Solutions' in Naomi Mitchison (ed.), *An Outline for Boys and Girls and Their Parents* (1932). Courtesy of the Bodleian Library, University of Oxford.
pp. 439–41	pages 31–2 from *Village and Town* by S. R. Badmin (Penguin, 1947). Reproduced by permission of Penguin Books.
p. 442	With kind permission of the *Morning Star.*

INDEX